'[A] scintillating, swash-buckling debut . . . terrifically fun'
Sunday Times

'Sharp, modern and absolutely delicious' **Taylor Jenkins Reid**

'Delicious – frothy, gossipy and glamorous' *Daily Mail*

'Charming, witty and infectiously exuberant . . . absolute perfection. I only wish it hadn't ended!' **Santa Montefiore**

'A thoroughly modern heroine . . . with wit, style and energy. A formidable Austentacious talent – I can't rave enough about it' **Janice Hallett**

'An addictive read' *Sunday Express*

'Divine – an utter delight!' **Nina Stibbe**

'Will fill the *Bridgerton*-shaped hole in your life' *Red*

'This book captivated me. What a sassy, witty, delicious tale' **Sophie Kinsella**

'Plucky, witty and bright . . . fans of *Bridgerton* will swoon' **Nita Prose**

'A diamond of the first water! Shades of Heyer with a dash of modern roguishness . . . Full of heart and swooningly romantic' **Beth Morrey**

A Lady's Guide to Fortune-Hunting

Sophie Irwin grew up in Dorset before moving to south London after university. *A Lady's Guide to Fortune-Hunting* is her debut novel and was an instant *Sunday Times* bestseller. It has sold in nearly thirty countries worldwide.

Sophie spent years immersed in the study of historical fiction, from a dissertation on how Georgette Heyer helped win World War Two, to time spent in dusty stacks and old tomes losing herself in Regency London while researching this book. Her love and passion for historical fiction bring a breath of fresh air and a contemporary energy to the genre and Sophie hopes to transport readers to a time when ballrooms were more like battlegrounds.

@SophieHIrwin
@sophie.irwin
www.ladysguide.co.uk

A Lady's Guide to Fortune-Hunting

SOPHIE IRWIN

HarperCollins*Publishers*

HarperCollins*Publishers*
1 London Bridge Street
London SE1 9GF

www.harpercollins.co.uk

HarperCollins*Publishers*
Macken House, 39/40 Mayor Street Upper,
Dublin 1, D01 C9W8, Ireland

First published by HarperCollins*Publishers* 2022
This edition published 2023
1

A catalogue record for this book
is available from the British Library

ISBN: 978-0-00-851956-8

Printed and bound in the UK using 100% Renewable Electricity
at CPI Group (UK) Ltd

This book is produced from independently certified FSC™ paper
to ensure responsible forest management.

For more information visit: www.harpercollins.co.uk/green

For Fran, who got me started.

And my family, who kept me going.

Without thinking highly either of men or of matrimony, marriage had always been her object; it was the only honourable provision for well-educated young women of small fortune, and however uncertain of giving happiness, must be their pleasantest preservative from want.

Jane Austen, *Pride & Prejudice*

1

Netley Cottage, Biddington, Dorsetshire, 1818

'You're *not* going to marry me?' Miss Talbot repeated, disbelievingly.

'Afraid not,' Mr Charles Linfield replied, his expression set in a kind of bracingly apologetic grimace – the sort one might wear when confessing you could no longer attend a friend's birthday party, rather than ending a two-year engagement.

Kitty stared at him, uncomprehending. Katherine Talbot – Kitty to her family and closest acquaintances – was not much used to incomprehension. In fact, she was well known amongst her family and Biddington at large for her quick mind and talent for practical problem-solving. Yet in this moment, Kitty felt quite at a loss. She and Charles were to be married. She had known it for years – and it was now not to be? What should one say, what should one feel, in the face of such news? Everything was changed. And yet Charles still *looked* the same, dressed in clothes she had seen him in a thousand times before, with that dishevelled style only the wealthy could get away with: an intricately embroidered waistcoat that was badly misbuttoned, a garishly bright cravat that had been mangled rather than tied. He ought at least, Kitty thought, staring at that awful cravat with a rising sense of indignation, to have dressed for the occasion.

Some of this ire must have seeped through to her expression, because all at once Charles swapped his maddening air of apologetic condescension for that of a sulky schoolboy.

'Oh, you needn't look at me like that,' he snapped. 'It isn't as if we were ever *officially* promised to one another.'

'Officially promised to one another?' Kitty's spirit returned to her in full force, and she discovered, in fact, that she felt quite furious. The irredeemable cad. 'We've been speaking of marriage for the past two years. We were only delayed this long because of my mother's death and my father's sickness! You *promised* me – you promised me so many things.'

'Just the talk of children,' he protested, before adding mulishly, 'and besides, it isn't as if I could call things off when your father was on death's door. Wouldn't have been at all the thing.'

'Oh, and I suppose now that he's dead – not a month in the ground – you could finally jilt me?' she said wrathfully. 'Is that really so much more "the thing"?'

He ran a hand through his hair, his eyes flicking to the door.

'Listen, there's no point us discussing it when you're like this.' He affected the tone of a severely tried man holding onto his patience. 'Perhaps I should go.'

'Go? You can't possibly drop news such as this, and not explain yourself. I saw you just last week and we were discussing marrying in May – not three months away.'

'Perhaps I should have just written a letter,' he said to himself, still staring longingly at the door. 'Mary said this was the best way to do it, but I think a letter would have been simpler. I can't think properly with you shrieking at me.'

Kitty cast aside her many irritations and, with the instincts of a true hunter, fixed only on the salient information.

'Mary?' she said sharply. 'Mary Spencer? What, exactly, does Miss Spencer have to do with this? I had not realised she had returned to Biddington.'

'Ah, yes, yes, well, she is, that is,' Mr Linfield stammered, beads of sweat appearing on his brow. 'My mother invited her to stay with us, for a time. It being so good for my sisters to make other female acquaintances.'

'And you spoke to Miss Spencer about bringing our engagement to an end?'

'Ah, yes, well she was so sympathetic to the situation – to *both* our situations – and I must say it was good to be able . . . to speak to someone about it.'

Silence, for a moment. And then, almost casually, 'Mr Linfield, do you mean to propose to Miss Spencer?'

'No! Well, that is to say – we already . . . So, I thought best to – to come here . . .'

'I see,' Kitty said – and she did. 'Well, I suppose I must commend you upon your confidence, Mr Linfield. It is quite the feat to propose to one woman whilst already being engaged to another. Bravo, indeed.'

'This is exactly what you always do!' Mr Linfield complained, mustering some courage at last. 'You twist everything around until one doesn't know which way is up. Have you thought perhaps that I wanted to spare your feelings? That I didn't want

3

to have to tell you the truth – that if I want to make a career for myself in politics, I can hardly do it married to someone like *you*.'

His derisive tone shocked her. 'And what exactly is that supposed to mean?' she demanded.

He spread his arms, as if inviting her to look around. Kitty did not. She knew what she would see, for she had stood in this room every day of her life: the worn chaises huddled by the fireplace for warmth, the once elegant rug on the hearth now moth-eaten and shabby, shelves where there had once been books now standing empty.

'We may live in the same town, but we're from different *worlds*.' He waved his hands about again. 'I'm the son of the squire! And Mama and Miss Spencer helped me to see that I cannot afford to make a *mésalliance* if I am to make a name for myself.'

Kitty had never been so aware of the sound of her heartbeat, pounding a drum loudly in her ears. A *mésalliance*, was she?

'Mr Linfield,' she said, softly but with bite. 'Let there be no lies between us. You had no issue with our engagement until you encountered the pretty Miss Spencer again. A squire's son, you say! This is not the sort of ungentlemanly conduct I would have expected your family to condone. Perhaps I ought to be pleased that you have proven yourself to be so utterly dishonourable before it was too late.'

She landed each blow with the precision and force of Gentleman Jackson, and Charles – Mr Linfield forever, now – staggered backwards from her.

'How could you say such a thing?' he asked, aghast, 'It is not *ungentlemanly*. You're becoming quite hysterical.' Mr Linfield was sweating thickly now, twisting uncomfortably. 'I do want us to remain great friends, you have to understand Kit—'

'*Miss Talbot*,' she corrected with frigid politeness. A shriek of rage was howling through her body, but she contained it, gesturing sharply to the door with a wave of her hand. 'You'll forgive me if I ask you to see yourself out, Mr Linfield.'

After a quick bob of a bow, he fled eagerly from her, without looking back.

Kitty stood motionless for a moment, holding her breath as if to prevent this disaster from unfolding any further. Then she walked to the window, where the morning sun was streaming in, leant her forehead against the glass, and exhaled slowly. From this window, one had an uninterrupted view of the garden: the daffodils just beginning to flower, the vegetable patch, still thick with weeds, and the loose chickens picking their way through, looking for grubs. Life outside continued on, and yet on her side of the glass, everything was utterly ruined.

They were alone. Completely and utterly alone now, with no one to turn to. Mama and Papa were gone, and in this hour of most grievous need, where more than ever she wished to ask for their advice, she could not. There was simply no one left to whom she could turn. Panic was rising within her. What was she to do now?

She might have stayed in this position for several hours, were she not interrupted by her youngest sister, ten-year-old Jane, who barged in only a few minutes later with the self-importance of a royal messenger.

'Kitty, *where* is Cecily's book?' she demanded.

'It was in the kitchen yesterday,' Kitty answered without looking away from the garden. They ought to weed the artichoke bed this afternoon, it would need planting before long. Distantly, she heard Jane call to Cecily to pass on her words.

'She's looked there,' came the reply.

'Well, look again.' Kitty dismissed her impatiently with a flap of a hand.

The door opened and closed with a bang. 'She says it's not there and if you've sold it, she'll be very upset because it was a gift from the vicar.'

'Oh, for goodness' sake,' Kitty snapped, 'you may tell Cecily that I can't look for her silly vicar book, because I have just been jilted and need a few moments' reprieve, if that is not too much to ask!'

No sooner had Jane relayed this unusual message to Cecily, than the full household – all of Kitty's four sisters and Bramble the dog – descended upon the parlour, instantly filling the space with noise.

'Kitty, what is this about Mr Linfield jilting you? Has he really?'

'I never liked him, he used to pat me on the head as if I were a child.'

'My book is *not* in the kitchen.'

Kitty told them as briefly as she could what had happened, with her head still resting on the glass. There was silence after this, as Kitty's sisters stared uncertainly at each other. After a few moments, Jane – having grown bored – wandered over to the creaking pianoforte and broke the silence by bashing out a jolly tune. Jane had never received music lessons, but what she lacked in talent she made up for in both fervour and volume.

'How awful,' Beatrice – at nineteen years, Kitty's closest sister in both age and temperament – said at last, appalled. 'Oh, Kitty dear, I am sorry. You must be heartbroken.'

Kitty turned her head sharply. 'Heartbroken? Beatrice, that is quite beside the point. Without my marrying Mr Linfield, we are all ruined. Papa and Mama may have left us the house, but they also left an astonishing amount of debt. I was depending on the Linfield wealth to save us.'

'You were marrying Mr Linfield for his *fortune*?' Cecily asked, a judgemental note in her voice. The intellectual of the family at eighteen years of age, Cecily was felt by her sisters to have a rather over-developed sense of morality.

'Well, it was certainly not for his integrity or gentlemanly honour,' Kitty said bitterly. 'I just wish I'd had the sense to wrap it up sooner. We should not have pushed back the wedding when Mama died, I knew that a long engagement was asking for trouble. To think that Papa thought it would look unseemly!'

'How bad is it, Kitty?' Beatrice asked. Kitty stared silently at her for a few moments. How could she tell them? How could she explain all that was about to happen?

'It is . . . serious,' Kitty said carefully. 'Papa re-mortgaged the house to some quite disreputable people. The sales I made – our books, the silverware, some of Mama's jewels – were enough to keep them at bay for a while, but on the first of June they will return. Not four months away. And if we do not have enough money, or proof that we can start paying them, then . . .'

'. . . We will have to leave? But this is our home.' Harriet's lip wobbled. As second youngest, she yet remained more sensitive than Jane, who had at least stopped playing to sit quietly on the stool, watching.

Kitty did not have the heart to tell them that it would be worse than just leaving. That the sale of Netley Cottage would barely cover their debts, with nothing left after to support them. With nowhere to go and no obvious means of income, the future would be a dark place. They would have no choice but to split up, of course. She and Beatrice might find some employment in Salisbury, or one of the larger towns nearby, perhaps as housemaids – or lady's maids if they were truly lucky. Cecily – well, Kitty could not imagine Cecily being willing or able to work for anyone – but with her education she might try a school. Harriet – oh, Harriet was so young – would have to do the same. Somewhere that would provide room and board. And Jane . . . Mrs Palmer in the town, singularly mean-spirited though she was, had always had a sort of fondness for Jane. She might be persuaded to take her in until she was old enough to find employment, too.

Kitty imagined them all, her sisters, separated and cast to the wind. Would they ever be together again, as they were now? And what if it was far worse than this already-bleak scenario? Visions of each of them, alone, hungry and despairing, flashed before her eyes. Kitty had not yet wept a tear over Mr Linfield – he was not worth her tears – but now her throat ached painfully. They had already lost so much. It had been Kitty who had had to explain to them that Mama was not going to get better. Kitty who had broken the news of Papa's passing. How was she now to explain that the worst was still to come? She could not find the words. Kitty was not their mother, who could pull reassurances from the air like magic, nor their father, who could always say things would be all right with a confidence that made you believe him. No, Kitty was the family's problem solver – but this was far too great an obstacle for her to overcome with will alone. She wished desperately that there was someone who might carry this burden with her, a heavy load for the tender age of twenty, but there was not. Her sisters' faces stared up at her, so sure even now that she would be able to fix everything. As she always had.

As she always *would*.

The time for despair had passed. She would not – could not – be defeated so easily. She swallowed down her tears and set her shoulders.

'We have more than four months until the first of June,' Kitty said firmly, moving away from the window. 'That is just enough time, I believe, for us to achieve something quite extraordinary. In a town such as Biddington, I was able to ensnare a rich fiancé. Though he turned out to be a weasel, there is no reason to believe the exercise cannot be repeated, simply enough.'

'I do not think any other rich men live nearby,' Beatrice pointed out.

'Just so!' her sister replied cheerfully, eyes unnaturally bright. 'Which is why I must travel to more fruitful ground. Beatrice, consider yourself in charge – for I shall be leaving for London.'

2

It is not uncommon to encounter persons who are in the habit of making outlandish claims. It is rarer to meet persons who are also in the habit of fulfilling them, and it was to this second group that Miss Kitty Talbot belonged.

Not three weeks after that gloomy morning in the parlour of Netley Cottage, she and Cecily were rattling in a stagecoach on their way to London. It was an uncomfortable journey of three days spent jiggling in their seats, accompanied by an assortment of persons and poultry, the Dorsetshire countryside fading slowly from view as they passed through county after county. Kitty spent much of the time staring out of the window – by the end of the first day, she was the furthest she had ever travelled from home.

Kitty had known for a long time that she would have to marry rich, but she had quite counted upon being able to do so whilst remaining close to Biddington, and to her family, with the Linfield match plotted and executed with her mother. In the weeks and months following her mother's death, she had been all the more grateful to have already wrapped up her future so neatly with Mr Linfield, who lived nearby. In the darkest of times, to know that she did not need to leave her family's side for a single moment was a gift indeed, and yet now she had left most of her sisters far behind. With every mile the stagecoach put between them and Biddington, the anxious knot in her chest grew larger. This was the right decision – the only decision – Kitty could make for her family, but it felt so very wrong to be without them.

What a fool she had been, to trust in Mr Linfield's honour – and yet she still could not understand how he had so quickly fallen out of love with her. Miss Spencer was pretty, yes, but dull as a fish; it did not make sense for it to have happened so quickly. Besides, she had thought that the rest of the Linfields had not been overly fond of Miss Spencer. What was Kitty missing?

'What a *fool*,' she said again, out loud this time. Beside Kitty, Cecily shot her an affronted look, and she added, 'Not you, me. Or rather, Mr Linfield.'

Cecily returned to her book with a huff. Once the heavy tome given to her by the vicar had been found, she had insisted on bringing it with her, despite Kitty pointing out that a book of its size and heft might not be the choicest companion on a hundred-mile journey.

'Do you want me to be miserable in every way, Kitty?' Cecily had asked her dramatically. The honest answer at that moment – standing hot-faced over her sister's hulking case – was *yes*, but Kitty had capitulated and was resigned to lugging the absurd cargo all the way to London. She cursed again her father's ridiculous and expensive decision to send Cecily to be educated at the Bath Seminary for Young Ladies for two years. It had been entirely motivated by a desire to keep up with the local gentry – the Linfields in particular – and all Cecily seemed to have gained in her time there was an inflated sense of her own intellectual superiority. Yet despite her passionate defence of the book, Cecily had not been paying it much attention; instead she bothered Kitty with the same questions that had obsessed her the whole trip.

'Are you quite sure that you understood Aunt Dorothy's letter correctly?' she whispered now, finally taking heed of Kitty's repeated rebuke not to share their private business with the entire carriage.

'How else could it be understood?' Kitty hissed back, not a little irately. She sighed, calmed her voice, and explained again with a passable imitation of patience. 'Aunt Dorothy knew Mama when they both worked at the Lyceum Theatre. They were very close – Mama used to read her letters aloud to us, do you remember? I wrote asking for her help, and Aunt Dorothy has offered to introduce us to London society.'

Cecily harrumphed.

'And how can you be sure that Aunt Dorothy is a respectable woman, with good Christian morals? We might be walking into a den of iniquity for all you know!'

'I must say, I do not think the time you have been spending with the vicar has done you any good at all,' Kitty told her severely. Privately, though, she too harboured a few fears about Aunt Dorothy, though Mama had always insisted she was very respectable. But it would do no good to confide in Cecily, when Aunt Dorothy truly was their only option. 'Aunt Dorothy is the only person of our acquaintance with a residence in London.

Papa's family are all on the Continent now – not that they would have helped us anyway – and she was kind enough to pay for our travel, too. We cannot turn up our noses at her aid.'

Cecily still looked unconvinced, and Kitty leant back into the seat with a sigh. Both of them would have preferred Beatrice to accompany Kitty on this mission, but at the end of Aunt Dorothy's letter had been a clear instruction: *Bring your prettiest sister.* And as Beatrice was currently – by her own admission – half girl, half forehead, and Cecily was the possessor of a sweet prettiness very much contrary to her sulky nature, she was the obvious choice. That she was also a complete bore, Kitty hoped would not matter. Kitty comforted herself with the thought that Beatrice was a far better person with whom to leave the management of the house and the younger girls, under the watchful eye of the vicar's wife. If it had been Cecy in her stead, by the time they returned there would be no house left to save.

'I still think our efforts would be better spent finding honest, gainful employment,' Cecily was now saying. 'With my education, I would make a very fine governess.'

There was a pause while Kitty considered the horror of placing the responsibility of the family's finances in Cecily's hands.

'Be that as it may,' Kitty said in a low, careful voice, 'the going rate for a governess is not more than five and thirty pounds a year. Not nearly enough, I'm afraid. My marrying someone rich really is the quickest way out of our mess.'

Cecily opened her mouth – presumably about to utter another judgemental but entirely useless comment – but before she could they were interrupted by a small boy in the forward seat telling his mother loudly, 'Mama, we're here!'

And sure enough, peering out of the window, they could see London's great sprawl on the horizon, long plumes of smoke trailing into the sky above it like beacons. Kitty had heard so many tales of London, which had been spoken of wistfully by her parents like a great friend they had lost. They had told her of its height and breadth, of its beauty and regality, of its bustle and opportunity – the queen of cities, they had called it. Kitty had long desired to see it for herself, this alien country that seemed to be the first love – and real home – of both her parents. And as they began to trundle through the city in earnest, her first impression of it was . . . dirty. With soot everywhere, smoke billowing from chimneys high above, horse droppings left in the street. Dirty and – and *messy*, with streets crashing into each other rudely, before zigzagging off in another direction. Buildings teetering at bizarre angles – buildings that were not always square, or rectangular, but haphazardly drawn, as if by a child. And it was bustling, yes, but loudly – so loudly! With the incessant sound of wheels and hooves clacking over pavements, yells from street peddlers, and a sense of hurry hurry hurry all around them. It was loud, and messy, and dirty, demanding of attention and respect and so very—

'*Magnificent*,' she breathed. 'Cecily, we're here at last.'

At Piccadilly, they swapped the stagecoach for a hackney cab, which took them to Aunt Dorothy's residence on Wimpole Street. Kitty could not yet tell the difference between fashionable and unfashionable boroughs in London, but was pleased that, though Aunt Dorothy's street was not nearly as grand as some of the lofty mansions they had passed, it seemed sufficiently well-to-do to spare her any blushes. The cab halted in front of a narrow town house, squashed in between two others, and after Kitty had parted with a precious coin, they walked up the steep steps, and knocked. The door was answered by a housemaid with bright red hair – how thrilling to see that Aunt Dorothy had actual servants – and they were taken up to a small parlour containing their honorary aunt.

Despite Kitty's careless dismissal of Cecily's doubts on the journey, she had harboured a secret fear that they might be greeted by a heavily made-up female, complete with a comical wig, a bawdy laugh and damp petticoats, which would not at all do for what Kitty had in mind. She was relieved, then, to see a striking woman of fashion within, her generous figure encased neatly in a morning dress of dove grey. Her brown locks were uncovered, but the informal style suited her – there was a cunning glint to her eye which woul ill-suit a sedate bonnet or widow's cap. Aunt Dorothy rose from her chair. She stood still, surveying them for a moment from under dramatically dark brows. Kitty and Cecily held their breath, both quite uncharacteristically nervous. Then – a smile. She held out two bejewelled hands.

'My darlings, you look so much like your mother,' she said. And they fell into her arms.

Aunt Dorothy had squeezed many lives and roles into her one and fifty years. As an actress, she had enjoyed a varied and glittering career onstage, while offstage, she had spent her hours entertaining a selection of London's most generous gentlemen. Having accumulated a not inconsiderable sum of money in this manner, upon her forty-first birthday she had dyed her fiery red hair a dark brown and rechristened herself, in both name and conduct, as affluent widow Mrs Kendall. As Mrs Kendall she began to enjoy a different lifestyle on the fringes of polite society, spending her days in houses that – as a young lady – she had only spent evenings. Though Kitty had worried Aunt Dorothy's storied past could very well be more hindrance than help – after all, actresses were hardly considered respectable – from her deportment it was clear that her transformation to a lady of quality was unerring. Seeing her, Kitty felt surer that Aunt Dorothy would be able to guide them through their next steps in London, to lend wisdom to Kitty's pursuit of a fortune. But though Kitty had a thousand questions to ask her aunt, for their first few hours together, all they spoke of was their mother.

'I should have liked to come to her funeral,' Mrs Kendall told them fervently. 'You must know that I would have come, but your father thought . . . it might not be wise.'

Kitty understood this vague explanation perfectly. In a better world, it would have meant everything to have Aunt Dorothy there with them – to share stories of Mama's life before, so they might still learn new things of her even as she was gone. But Mr Talbot had acted in the family's best interests by keeping Aunt Dorothy away. Her presence might have raised questions . . . and some things were best left in the past.

'It was a beautiful day,' Kitty said instead, clearing her throat. 'Crisp and cool. She would have loved it.'

'You never could keep her inside if the sky was bright,' Aunt Dorothy said, her smile pained but sincere. 'No matter the day.'

'I did a reading,' Cecily piped up. 'From *The Book of the Duchess* – her favourite.' No one had understood a word of it, of course, Kitty reflected privately, but Cecily had read clearly and well.

They spent many more hours exchanging memories, their chairs inching together, their hands clasping at points, growing closer in that sure, inexorable way people do when they have shared in such a loss together. By the time conversation turned at last to Kitty's broken engagement, the sky outside was dark.

'You were quite right to come,' Aunt Dorothy reassured Kitty, pouring three liberal glasses of ratafia. 'London is just the place – what a disastrous thing it would be to commit yourself to Bath or Lyme Regis at such an hour. Consider me your fairy godmother, my darlings. I am quite sure we can sort an excellent match for each of you in just a few short weeks.'

Cecily's attention – which had wandered a little – shot back to the present. She looked at Kitty with wide, accusing eyes.

'Aunt Dorothy, it is only I who shall be making a match,' Kitty said firmly. 'Cecily is too young.'

Aunt Dorothy looked surprised. 'Are you quite sure? Would it not be wise to find husbands for you both?'

'Quite sure,' Kitty affirmed. Cecily breathed a sigh of relief.

Aunt Dorothy looked unconvinced but rallied almost immediately. 'I suppose she can still help us catch the flies, then!' she declared. 'We have much to do first, mind. We must sort your clothes, your hair, your . . .' She gave a waft of her hand that seemed to encompass everything about them. 'And there is not a day to lose – the Season is about to begin.'

3

They awoke the next morning earlier than their host – city hours, Kitty supposed – but any suggestion of laziness was quickly disproved by the brisk manner in which Aunt Dorothy conducted the day.

'There is no time to waste,' she said, ushering them into their cloaks, out of the house and into a hackney. The first stop, upon Kitty's request, was to a discreet building on Bond Street where she sold what remained of her mother's jewels for the total sum of ten pounds to cover their London expenses. It was to be their very last accounting and Kitty tremored to think that ten pounds – which would disappear quickly enough – was all that stood between them and a debtor's prison. She pushed the thought aside with an effort. It might seem foolish to spend their precious coins upon fripperies, but the day of indulgence that lay ahead was as necessary as last year's repairs to Netley's leaking roof.

'Morning dress, evening dress, hats, gloves, shoes, petticoats – we need it all,' Aunt Dorothy explained, as they rattled over the cobbles. 'For the *ton*, it is Mrs Triaud for dresses; Hoby's for boots; Lock's for hats. But for us, Cheapside will do just nicely for it all.'

Despite its name, Cheapside to Kitty seemed resplendent. A sea of drapers, confectioners, silversmiths, booksellers, hosiers, milliners, cobblers, shop after shop for street after street and mile after mile. Steered by Aunt Dorothy as their unflappable guide, they cut a swathe through them all: they were measured for morning, walking, evening and ball dresses, they tried on hats and stroked hands over impossibly soft stockings, they parted with shilling after shilling in the name of investment. It was late into the afternoon by the time they returned to Wimpole Street, much fatigued. But Aunt Dorothy was far from finished.

'Dresses are easy,' she said grimly. 'It is far harder to act as young ladies of quality. Have you spent much time in polite society?'

'We have dined many times at Linfield Manor,' Kitty offered, not sure if this counted. Mr Talbot and the Squire, even before their children's engagement, had been great friends – sharing an interest in expensive brandy and gambling – and so the Talbots had often been invited to dinner parties at the Linfield's grand home.

'Good,' Aunt Dorothy approved. 'To start, I want you to imagine that every time you leave this house, you are at a Linfield dinner party. Stand tall and still, walk slowly – none of this bustling about, every move must be languorous and graceful. You must speak softly and enunciate clearly, strictly no slang or vulgarity, and when in doubt say nothing at all.'

For three days, Aunt Dorothy drilled them in the proper

ways of walking and of dressing their hair in the latest style, of holding a fan, a fork, a purse. Becoming a gentlewoman, Kitty soon began to appreciate, was to contain one's self so tightly that one could not breathe – your whole body had to become a corset, with indelicacies, gracelessness and character kept strictly within. Kitty listened intently to every morsel of information and corralled Cecily into doing the same – it was her sister's usual habit to let her attention drift off as soon as she recognised a conversation did not interest her – and by the time their first dresses arrived, they were reeling from the education.

'Thank goodness,' Aunt Dorothy declared, as the packages were brought in, 'at least now you can leave the house without any blushes.'

Kitty and Cecily took the boxes upstairs, where they unpacked them with more than a little wonder. Fashion, they were discovering, moved much faster in London than Biddington, and so the beautiful items inside bore only passing resemblance to the dresses they were used to. Morning dresses in pretty blues and yellows, muslin gowns, thick cloaks, satin spencers and, most breathtaking of all, two evening dresses that were finer than anything Kitty had ever seen. Into these, the sisters helped each other with careful hands. They dressed their hair as Aunt Dorothy had shown them, carefully arranged with fresh flowers, and when all was done, they looked quite different.

Standing before the full-length mirror in Aunt Dorothy's bedroom, Kitty was taken aback by their reflection. She was used to Cecily always appearing as though she had only just awoken from a deep sleep, but now she looked something of an angel, the floating skirts in shining white making her look as if she were about to disappear, her fair hair, arranged in ringlets on either side of her head, softening her face still further. Kitty, too, was dressed in white, as was usual for a young lady in her first Season. The pallor of the dress contrasted sharply against the darkness of her eyes and hair – naturally straight but cajoled now into matching her sister's curls – and emphasised the dramatic slash of her brows above bright eyes. The girls in the mirror looked impressive, Kitty thought. They looked as if they belonged here, in London.

'Very handsome indeed!' Aunt Dorothy clapped her hands in delight. 'I think you are ready. We will begin tonight.'

They arrived at the Theatre Royal at Covent Garden as dusk was falling, and lit by candlelight, the theatre looked quite beautiful, with its high vaulted ceilings and ornate interior. Though it was not yet as busy as it would be in high Season, there was a still hum of excitement all around.

'Look at all these people,' her aunt said appreciatively. 'Can you sense the opportunity in the air, my darlings?'

'"Marks of weakness, marks of woe,"' Cecily said sombrely, in what Kitty recognised as her quoting voice. Aunt Dorothy eyed her suspiciously. As they moved into the great entrance hall, she hissed into Kitty's ear, quietly, so Cecily could not hear, 'Is she a fool?'

'An intellectual,' Kitty explained softly.

Aunt Dorothy sighed. 'I was afraid of that.'

They made their way slowly to their seats, Aunt Dorothy peering intently around and waving to acquaintances in the crowd.

'We are very lucky,' Aunt Dorothy said in an undertone as they entered the upper gallery. 'I had not thought to see so many eligible men so early in the Season.'

Kitty nodded, settling into her seat, but she was distracted. She had glimpsed the most regal family she had ever laid eyes on, and her attention had been immediately, and totally, transfixed. Seated high above them, in their own private box, the three strangers, even to Kitty's uneducated eyes, seemed to stand out from the crowd. Beautiful and beautifully dressed, the young man, young lady, and dashingly handsome woman must be a family – a family that, as she watched them smile and laugh together, had not a care in the world beyond their own enjoyment. Aunt Dorothy followed the direction of Kitty's gaze and clucked disapprovingly.

'There's no point sending your eyes up there, my dear. I admire your ambition, of course, but let us remember our station.'

'Icarus,' Cecily chipped in vaguely – whether in agreement or simply to lend some intellectual colour to the conversation, it was unclear.

'Who are they?' Kitty asked, still staring upward. The temptation to gossip quickly overcame Dorothy's disapproval.

'The de Lacys,' she said, leaning in. 'The Countess Lady Radcliffe and her two youngest, Mr Archibald de Lacy and the Lady Amelia de Lacy. The whole family is as rich as kings. Of course, it's the eldest son, the Earl of Radcliffe, who has the lion's share, but the two younger ones will receive a handsome fortune each, too – at least eight thousand a year, by my estimation. Expected to make fabulous matches, the lot of them.'

She leant back in her seat as the performance started, but even as the audience began to gasp and laugh, Kitty could not take her eyes from the de Lacys. What must it be like, to know from birth that your future was an assuredly safe and happy one? To tower over the rest of society, in that exclusive box? They looked as though they belonged there, Kitty could admit, high above. Could there ever have been a world in which she herself might have belonged up there with them? Her father had been born a gentleman, after all, and before his marriage would have mixed with lords and ladies such as them without thinking. Had events unravelled a little differently . . . Kitty felt a nonsensical pang of jealousy for this alternate version of herself, who might have shared a set with the golden de Lacy family. It was not until Aunt Dorothy nudged her with her elbow that Kitty finally looked away.

At the interval, Kitty and Cecily were kept busy by their aunt, who introduced them to all manner of men and women, wealthy merchants and their sons, daughters and wives, lawyers, military men dressed in dashing colours and the prettily dressed women on their arms. It was more people in one night than Kitty had met in her life to date, and she could not help but feel a little daunted – as if she were again a girl of fifteen, approaching the Linfield manor for her very first evening soirée and feeling terribly frightened of doing something wrong. She remembered her mother whispering reassurances into her ear that night, the scent of her rosewater perfume tickling her nose. *Eyes and ears, my darling,* she had said. *Watch and listen and do as they do, it is not so hard.*

Kitty took in a breath so deep that she fancied she could almost detect that rosewater scent upon the air, mustered her courage, and set herself out to impress. As one would mould a hat to suit a fashion, she moulded herself to suit her conversational partner: to the men who fancied themselves great wits,

23

she provided a ready laugh, to the vain she was admiring, and to the shy she smiled often and spoke more. Dorothy was in transports on the return home.

'Mr Melbury, now he's one thousand a year,' she relayed to them in the carriage, 'Mr Wilcox looked quite taken with Cecily, and—'

'And we agreed Cecily is not here to make a match,' Kitty interjected. Beside her, Cecily's shoulders relaxed once more.

'Fine, fine.' Aunt Dorothy waved a dismissive hand. 'Mr Pears was a little harder to read, but he has a lovely shipping fortune of two thousand a year coming his way upon his father's death. And Mr Cleaver—'

'Are there any men of your acquaintance who value more than two thousand a year?' Kitty interrupted again.

'More than two thousand a year?' her aunt asked. 'What on earth were you expecting, my child?'

'Mr Linfield had a fortune of four thousand a year,' Kitty said, her brow wrinkling.

'Four?' her aunt repeated incredulously. 'Goodness me, the Squire must have done very well for himself. But you cannot expect such a miracle to be repeated, my dears. One would be hard pressed to have such a fortune without land, my darling, and you won't find many landed gentlemen in my circles.'

Kitty digested this unpleasant news. She had known Mr Linfield was wealthy, wealthy enough that paying off their considerable debts would be no issue – but she had assumed they would be able to find many more of his kind in London.

'I should not expect to encounter men of equivalent fortune?' Kitty clarified, stomach clenching unpleasantly.

'Not in my set,' Aunt Dorothy laughed.

Kitty felt hot and foolish. She yearned to be back at Wimpole Street again, so that she might have ink and paper to sit down with the numbers calmly. Would two thousand a year suit, when she had her sisters to support and eventually dower too? Was it enough?

'How much debt do you have?' Dorothy asked, shrewdly.

Kitty told her. Cecily – who Kitty had not thought to be listening – gasped, and Aunt Dorothy granted herself the indulgence of an unladylike whistle.

'Oh my,' she said, eyes wide. 'Mr Pears it shall have to be then.'

'Yes,' Kitty agreed, though a little dubiously. Two thousand a year was certainly better than nothing, but there was more to it than simply paying the debt. Was two thousand a year enough to clear their not inconsiderable sum, keep Netley, and then after, to secure her sisters' futures, too? For what if one of her sisters should need a dowry, to secure the gentleman of their choice? What if all of them did? What if, instead, one needed funds to marry a poor man? Or Cecily, who would surely be happiest with no husband, but a great number of expensive books in her possession. She would have expected Mr Linfield to do all this, but the kindest man in the world, with only two thousand a year to spend, would not be able to promise her the same.

'Would a place such as . . . Almack's be where gentlemen of more fortune frequented?' she asked thoughtfully.

'Almack's Assembly Rooms? Kitty, you would be reaching for the stars,' Dorothy said, much exasperated. 'There is a vast difference between polite society and high society. High society – the world of lords and ladies, land and fortune – is not a place to which I can give you access. You must be born to that world and there is no other way to secure an invitation. Put these dangerous notions aside and focus your attention instead on the likes of Mr Pears – you would be lucky indeed to have such a husband.'

They had arrived at Wimpole Street. Kitty went up to their bedroom without speaking further. In a state of some melancholy, she ruminated over Dorothy's words all the way through her nightly ablutions and was still not done when Cecily blew out their candle and got into bed beside her. Her sister fell instantly asleep, and Kitty listened to her breathing in the dark, jealous of the ease with which Cecily could cast aside the worries of the day.

Two thousand would not mean the end to their worry and their strife, but it would help, at least. Her mother had settled for far less than two thousand a year, after all – this was a sum, in fact, far greater than what Mr and Mrs Talbot had been given in exchange for their leaving London together so many years ago. It had not been enough for them, of course – especially since Papa had never quite been able to adapt his lifestyle from that of an affluent single gentleman to a father of five with a rapidly decreasing income of five hundred pounds a year. Kitty might not enjoy gambling or hundred-year-old port, but she still had four sisters to support – and unlike her Mama and Papa, would not have the luxury of a loving marriage to ease her mind when the pennies began to pinch.

Kitty wished, for perhaps the hundredth – the thousandth, the millionth – time, to be able to speak to her mother. Kitty was grateful to have Aunt Dorothy as a skilled London guide, but it was not the same. She wanted desperately to speak to someone who knew her intimately, to someone who loved her sisters as much as she did – who would be just as haunted as she was by the visions of Jane, Beatrice, Harriet and Cecily alone and stranded in dark and unkind corners of the country – and someone who would understand that no lengths were too great in the pursuit of their happiness, as Mama would. She would know what Kitty ought to do next, Kitty felt sure, and she would not be bothered by such self-limiting silliness as hierarchy or social tiers – after all, it was she, and not Aunt Dorothy, who had had the gumption to fall in love with a gentleman far above her station.

Kitty rolled onto her side, trying to marshal her rebellious thoughts into order. It was useless to ruminate upon matters she could not possibly change. Her mother was gone, and this was Kitty's task alone to bear, now. Aunt Dorothy was the only advisor she had, and she had laughed when Kitty had asked after men of greater fortune than Mr Pears. The laughter had not been malicious; she had honestly considered it absurd, and perhaps Kitty should heed that.

Sleep came uneasily that night, in fits and starts as exhaustion fought with anxiety for dominance. And even as sleep finally drew ahead, Kitty was still wondering: was it so wrong to wish that, if she had to sell herself for her family's sake, it would at least be to a higher bidder than Mr Pears?

4

Kitty awoke the next morning longing for a break from the clutter of London's streets. After breakfast she persuaded Cecily to walk with her to Hyde Park. Accompanied, at Aunt Dorothy's insistence, by her housemaid Sally – who followed two steps behind – Kitty and Cecily found their way to the park easily enough. They began their turn around the Serpentine, their quick pace – despite Aunt Dorothy's teachings – quite incongruous to the languorous gait of the other ladies, and Kitty breathed in the clean air and bright green of the grass and the trees with relief. Though far more structured than any of the landscape in Biddington, the view was as close to home as any Kitty had seen so far in London.

Kitty wondered if their parents had ever walked here, together. Certainly not on a day so fine as this, of course. Theirs had not been a traditional courtship: being so heartily disapproved of by Mr Talbot's family, it had by necessity taken place outside of the public eye, upon the fringes and margins and quiet places of society. When a day was fine and the *ton*

flocked to London's green fie___
indoors and away from the hordes –
to have visited Hyde Park together in th__
when one could be assured of privacy. Her __
have minded that, Kitty knew. Though born and
city, she loved nothing more than being outside in the
rain or shine, whereas Mr Talbot's passions had lain m__ in
indoor pursuits.

Some of Kitty's fondest memories of her father had been
playing cards together in the parlour, each Sunday afternoon,
for as long as she could remember until the very day before
his death. He taught her the rules of whist, faro, and all
manner of card games, and they had gambled always with
real money – though with only pennies by Kitty's insistence
– as Mr Talbot firmly believed that one played differently
with money on the table. Kitty could still remember playing
piquet for the first time together. After learning the rules,
Kitty had opted to bet with only a single ha'penny at each
juncture.

'Why so few, my dear?' her father had clucked at her. 'You
have a good hand.'

'In case I lose,' she had said, as if it were obvious. He let out
a puff of smoke from his pipe and shook a finger at her,
admonishingly.

'One must never begin a game by conceding,' he warned.
'Play to win, my dear, always.'

'Oh,' Cecily's voice startled her out of her reverie and back
to the present. 'I think I know her.'

Kitty looked up. And there they were, the de Lacys from
the theatre, taking a promenade around the park. Dark-haired

Amelia, wearing a smart pelisse and a scowl, and the yellow-haired Mr de Lacy, looking distinctly bored.

'What do you mean, you "know her"?' Kitty demanded sharply.

'We went to school together,' Cecily replied vaguely – already in danger of losing interest. 'She was only a little younger, and we shared a love of literature. Lady Amelia de . . . something.'

'And you didn't think it was worth mentioning?' Kitty hissed, gripping her arm tightly.

'*Ow*,' Cecily complained. 'How could I have mentioned it any earlier, I've only just seen them?'

They were to cross paths in just a few moments. Kitty might hope that Lady Amelia would look up, recognise Cecily in turn, but her gaze was cast downwards and there were nearly ten yards separating them – a veritable gulf.

It would not do.

They were within ten paces now, and she curled her toes. Then, just as the gap closed to five feet, she flicked her ankle out and affected a stumble. Her shoe went sailing through the air, and she leant heavily into her sister with a gasp. 'Oh no!'

Cecily was startled but bore her weight easily enough. 'Kitty? Do you need to sit down?'

'Miss Talbot?' Sally hurried forward to help, but Kitty waved her off.

'I twisted my ankle,' she gasped. 'But – oh but where is my slipper? It's come off.'

One, two, three—

'I beg your pardon, miss, but is this yours?'

Yes. She looked up to see the young gentleman – Mr de Lacy – proffering the slipper with a blush and eyes that were growing more eager as he glimpsed her face.

30

'Thank you,' she gasped gratefully, taking it from him. Feeling a blush of her own would be fitting, Kitty willed her cheeks to obey, without success – she cursed the fact that she was not the blushing sort.

'Cecily? Miss Cecily Talbot?' Lady Amelia had now approached, recognition in her eyes. If only Cecily were not to let her down now . . .

'Lady Amelia,' a short bob of recognition, a hand outstretched.

'Do you live in London now? Is this your sister?' No such social intricacies were displayed by this young lady – the indulgence of the rich.

'Yes – my sister, Miss Talbot. Kitty, this is Lady Amelia and . . .' Cecily looked at Mr de Lacy questioningly. Really, she was doing very well. The best of sisters.

'Her brother, Mr de Lacy.' He rushed to introduce himself with a ready smile, his eyes flickering admiringly between the sisters.

'Have you hurt yourself very badly?' Lady Amelia demanded. 'Archie, for goodness' sake, offer her your arm, won't you?'

Mr de Lacy – Archie, it seemed – sent a foul look his sister's way.

'You must allow us to escort you home,' he said gallantly. 'You ought not to be walking much further on a sprained ankle, we can drop you off in our carriage. Here, lean on my arm.'

Kitty accepted graciously, taking the proffered arm and leaning on him enough to place her slipper back on under her skirts. Mr de Lacy cleared his throat, looking away. Soon their procession was walking slowly towards a row of carriages in the distance. Cecily and Lady Amelia walking ahead, their heads bent together in a quickly resumed intimacy, Kitty and

Mr de Lacy following behind. It took Kitty a second to realise she was limping from the wrong foot – she corrected this hastily enough that she was sure no one had noticed.

Kitty might be walking slowly, but she was thinking quickly. This was an opportunity she could never have predicted, and she was certainly not going to botch it. They had, she imagined, only twenty minutes with which to make a mark upon the de Lacys – the six or seven minutes it would take them to find the de Lacy carriage, followed by the short ride thereafter to Wimpole Street. Kitty did not know Mr de Lacy, at all – did not know the best avenue for attack to suit his character – but how different could he be to the rest of his gender?

'I quite consider you my hero, Mr de Lacy,' Kitty said, turning wide eyes to stare up at him. 'To rescue us so kindly. I do not know what we might have done without you.'

Mr de Lacy ducked his head bashfully. Yes, quite so – the fishing line grew taut in her hands.

'Just what anyone would do,' Mr de Lacy protested. 'The gentlemanly thing, you know.'

'You give yourself far too little credit!' she insisted warmly, before adding, as breathily as she could: 'Did you serve upon the Peninsula? You have the bearing of a soldier.'

Mr de Lacy went a bright pink.

'No-no,' he hastened to correct her. 'I was too young – I should have liked to go, but I had not yet finished school. My brother fought at Waterloo – wasn't supposed to, of course, being the firstborn – but he's never heeded that sort of thing . . .' He trailed off, conscious that he was straying off topic. 'But I was captain of the cricket team at Eton you know!'

'Oh *marvellous*. You must be a very fine sportsman.'

Mr de Lacy was pleased enough to accept this compliment, however blushingly. In fact, over the next few minutes he was pleased to discover all sorts of new things about himself: that he had a soldier's bearing, a hero's instincts, a strong arm, yes, but also that he was terribly amusing and strikingly clever. His opinion was listened to intently, a story from his school-days that his family had listened to with only polite indulgence was to Miss Talbot quite hilarious – as Archie had always suspected to be the case. Miss Talbot had an excellent sense of humour, Archie thought. He had quite no idea, of course, that during their compliment-filled conversation, Miss Talbot was also skilfully extracting a steady stream of information from him: that he adored his elder brother Lord Radcliffe, the head of the family, but that this man was rarely seen in London, that Mr de Lacy would soon be twenty-one, upon which date he would receive the majority of his fortune. No, all Mr de Lacy knew was that he had never enjoyed a walk quite so much in his life. In fact, he thought Miss Talbot the best conversationalist with whom he had ever spoken.

All too soon, they reached the carriages and Lady Amelia stopped in front of an elegant barouche, its hood lowered in deference to the spring air. The coachman and footman sprang to attention at their approach. After instructing Sally to return to Wimpole Street on foot, and sparing a moment to admire the horses – four perfectly matched greys – Kitty was handed in. Lady Amelia and Cecily arranged themselves next to each other on the forward seat, so Mr de Lacy was forced to sit beside Miss Talbot. He cleared his throat, painfully aware of their proximity, and made sure to leave a polite distance between them. Kitty, for her part, looked sideways up at Mr de Lacy from under her eyelashes – a more difficult feat than she had thought – and was rewarded by another blush when he caught her gaze.

The horses moved smoothly off, and the streets of London began whipping past them. Kitty recalculated rapidly – the traffic of the busy city streets was being navigated far more swiftly than she had anticipated, as if the de Lacy insignia was enough to have horses and carriages leaping out of their way, and so it would take them mere minutes to reach Wimpole Street. She heaved a dramatic sigh, looking up at Mr de Lacy.

'Do you think—' she began to ask, before cutting herself off and looking down in calculated regret.

'Yes?' Mr de Lacy asked eagerly.

'No, it was most wrong of me to even think it,' Kitty insisted. 'You have been too kind already.'

'I beg of you, ask me anything, Miss Talbot,' he said.

She capitulated gracefully. 'My sister and I so depend on our daily walks for fresh air – I cannot bear to be without them. But I fear Cecily is not strong enough to support me, on a sore ankle . . .' She trailed off meaningfully, and Mr de Lacy clucked sympathetically, thinking hard. Then, he was struck with an idea.

'Why, we shall join you again, and you may lean upon me!' he declared gallantly.

'Are you sure it would not be too much trouble?' Kitty asked. 'We would be most grateful.'

'Not at all – don't mention it – not at all,' he gushed.

They had turned onto Wimpole Street.

'Then, shall we meet upon the morning, by the West Gate?' Kitty asked, smiling up at him.

'Marvellous!' Then, stricken with doubt, he asked, 'If you are sure your ankle will be well enough by then?'

'I have no doubt it shall be,' Kitty replied, with perfect truth.

They exchanged warm goodbyes and the sisters watched the gleaming carriage – so much taller and grander than the street around it – turn the corner away from them. Kitty breathed out a rapturous sigh. One made one's own luck, in her belief – and she had a feeling she was about to be very lucky indeed.

My dearest Beatrice,

We have arrived safely in London, and Aunt Dorothy is all that we had hoped she would be. You need not harbour a single worry about us — Aunt Dorothy and I are both confident I shall be engaged before the Season is out. A few more months of courage, and then all will be well, I promise.

How are you faring? Write back as soon as you receive this with all the news of home. Have you replenished the store cupboard, yet? Are you are finding the coins I left sufficient? If they are not, I shall contrive to send you more, so write directly if you are becoming at all uncomfortable. Should you find yourselves in immediate trouble, call at once upon Mrs Swift — I am sure she will help until I can be contacted.

It still pains me that we will miss Jane's birthday. The fair should come to Petherton that week, and I put aside some pennies for the express purpose of your visiting it — you will find these in Papa's desk. Do try to make it as jolly a day as possible, despite our absence.

I do not have the space to write a minute account of our doings, but I will strive to remember each specific detail for you, so that I may relay it all when we return. You three must do the same for Cecily and me, so that once we are together again it will be as if we were never truly apart for a moment.

We miss and love you and shall return as swiftly as we can.

Your loving sister,

Kitty

5

Lady Radcliffe, widowed at the young age of six and forty, had been left with a handsome fortune and a set of freedoms far greater than those she had enjoyed as a wife. She had of course mourned her husband deeply and still felt his loss sharply, but after a period she had begun to appreciate the enjoyments life offered when one was not beholden to a person whose austere nature did not lend itself to frivolity. Several years after his passing, the life of a very wealthy widow was, in fact, suiting Lady Radcliffe quite well. Her chief passions in this new chapter were her children (and worrying over them), high society (and amusing herself within it), and the observation of her own health (or rather, the lack of it).

It was enough to keep anyone busy, and Lady Radcliffe could be forgiven for the rare occasions when her patronage of one passion did lead her, most unfortunately, to overlook another. It was thus not without a little alarm that Lady Radcliffe roused herself from the scrutiny of a trembling left hand – a symptom, no doubt, of her recent bouts of faintness – to find her second son afflicted with a brand-new female obsession.

'Who is Miss Talbot?' Lady Radcliffe did not believe she had heard the name before. Archie rolled his eyes, a little aggrieved.

'You know, Mama,' he said. 'The Talbot sisters – we have been walking with them each day in Hyde Park.'

'You have been meeting the same young ladies each day?' Lady Radcliffe's brow furrowed. It was not unusual for Archie – or any young man of his age – to fixate upon new female acquaintances, but this was quick work indeed.

'Yes,' Archie said dreamily. 'She's the most beautiful creature you ever did see, Mama. I consider myself the luckiest man alive to have met her by such happenstance.'

A little disturbed now, Lady Radcliffe demanded to know how, exactly, they had met these Talbot girls. Archie's reply was quite incoherent – encompassing a slipper, a sprain and a rapt description of the exact colour of the elder Talbot sister's eyes – and did nothing to alleviate his mother's misgivings. When one was as wealthy and well-born as a de Lacy, one simply had to maintain a suspicious mind. In Lady Radcliffe's view, the world was riddled with as many risks to one's good name as it was to one's health, and it was crucial to be equally vigilant against both. Lower-birthed hangers-on would always try to acquaint themselves with titled and honourable persons such as them, as parasites did throughout nature. Their consequence, their wealth, their position in society, were tempting treasures after all – ones that had been cultivated and guarded for centuries. And when one had three children of marriageable age, as she did, the threat was even greater. Lady Radcliffe was all too aware that each of her children, with a bountiful endowment apiece, would be a choice catch for a discerning fortune-hunter.

'I should like to meet these young ladies, if they are to be such friends of yours,' she said firmly, interrupting Archie's description of an amusing ditty he had told the day before – one Miss Talbot had found very droll.

'You would?' Archie said, surprised. 'I had thought you were feeling quite at a . . . *low ebb* this week.'

'If you are referring to my fainting spells,' Lady Radcliffe said sniffily, detecting a note of doubt in her son's voice that she found most ill-mannered, 'then you should know I am feeling much improved. I should like to meet these Talbots. Invite them to call here after your walk.'

Archie agreed brightly to the idea, oblivious to any ulterior motive on his mother's part, and later that morning trotted off happily to Hyde Park. In contrast, Lady Radcliffe spent the time before their return working herself up into a highly nervous state. What a fool she had been to let herself be distracted at such a time – Archie was clearly infatuated by this young lady, who would no doubt prove to be a most unsuitable person, if she was going around losing shoes. Lady Radcliffe wondered if she ought to write to James, now, to warn him – but decided against it, in the end. Her eldest son was sheltering, as he had done ever since his return from Waterloo, at Radcliffe Hall in Devonshire – and while Lady Radcliffe did like to keep him abreast of all family matters, she also tried not to bother him unless it was truly necessary. His involvement in the Hundred Days' War might have been very much against her wishes – and his father's – but Lady Radcliffe could not now begrudge him his isolation. After all, what did she know of war?

Time passed slowly when one was anxious, and it felt like an age before Archie and Amelia returned, Talbot sisters in tow. By this point, Lady Radcliffe's worried anticipation was such that she quite expected to greet two damp-skirted charlatans with red-lipped grins upon their faces. She was relieved, instead, to see that the Misses Talbot certainly *looked* like pretty young ladies of quality: their walking dresses and pelisses were in the latest style – though certainly not, she thought with a critical eye, the work of Mrs Triaud – their hair was dressed becomingly, their movements graceful and understated. Perhaps she had been wrong to think this anything more alarming than another case of Archie's calf love. She rose to greet them.

'How do you do, Miss Talbot, Miss Cecily – it is so wonderful to meet you,' she said softly. There was a pause, as she waited for them to curtsey – as the higher-ranking lady, it was for the Misses Talbot to curtsey first – and after a beat longer than was usual, both ladies sank low. Far lower than was correct – in fact, quite as low as one would curtsey to a duchess. Lady Radcliffe winced. Oh dear.

Archie clapped his hands bracingly. 'Is Pattson bringing in refreshments?' he asked, bounding over to an armchair and collapsing into it. A second later, he shot up in embarrassment.

'Pray forgive me – Miss Talbot, Miss Cecily, would you sit?' he asked with a flourishing gesture of invitation.

They all sat. Lady Radcliffe reviewed the young ladies again, her critical eye renewed and now lingering over the hems of their dresses, which were a little mud-splattered, and the glimpse of their shoes, which had the unmistakable wooden buttons of Cheapside origin. Hmm. Pattson walked briskly in, ushering behind him three maids carrying trays bearing delectable morsels of cake and the finest fruits of the season. Lady Radcliffe fancied that the elder Miss Talbot was eyeing the display a little wondrously, as if she had never seen anything so sumptuous in her life. Oh *dear*.

'Miss Talbot, Archie tells me you are staying with your aunt,' Lady Radcliffe said, endeavouring at least to appear polite. 'Does she live near the park?'

'Not so very far,' Miss Talbot said, taking a small bite of delicious fruit. 'Wimpole Street.'

'Lovely,' Lady Radcliffe said, without an ounce of sincerity. Wimpole Street was certainly not what she would consider a fashionable part of town. She turned next to the younger Miss Talbot.

'And Amelia tells me you attended the Bath Seminary for Young Ladies together,' she said.

'Yes, for two years,' Miss Cecily answered, in a clear high voice.

'Only two?' Lady Radcliffe asked. 'Was your education moved elsewhere?'

'No, we ran out of money, so I was brought home,' Miss Cecily told her, helping herself happily to a mouthful of cake.

Miss Kitty Talbot froze with her glass in mid-air. Lady Radcliffe set down her plate with a decisive clink. Good God, it was worse than she could have thought. How terribly *déclassé* not only to suffer from such a revealing lack of funds, but to speak about it in public – with strangers, too! They must be removed from the house immediately.

'I have just remembered,' she declared disingenuously to the room. 'We are expected to call at the Montagu's today.'

'We are?' Archie said, a slice of cake on the way to his mouth. 'I had not thought them back in London, yet.'

'Yes, terribly forgetful of me.' Lady Radcliffe stood. 'But we should be considered most rude if we did not go. My most sincere apologies, Miss Talbot, Miss Cecily, but I am afraid we must draw this visit to a premature close.'

Lady Radcliffe, with the aid of the indispensable Pattson, ushered the Talbot sisters from the house in a flurry of forceful politeness – the upper-class equivalent of throwing them out by the scruff of their necks. They landed upon the doorstep only a few moments later, Archie rushing after them and apologising profusely.

'It is most unlike Mama to forget such a thing,' Lady Radcliffe heard him say urgently. 'You must excuse us – terribly unfortunate thing to have happened – awfully rude of us to invite you for so short a visit.'

'It is quite all right,' Miss Talbot said warmly. 'Will we see you in Hyde Park upon the morrow?'

Not if Lady Radcliffe had anything to say in the matter.

'Yes, yes of course,' Archie promised, recklessly.

'Archie!' Lady Radcliffe's voice rang out commandingly onto the street and Archie darted back inside with a final apology to his beloved. At Lady Radcliffe's sharp gesture, Pattson shut the door firmly behind the Talbot sisters.

'Of course she got rid of you,' Aunt Dorothy said, exasperation thick in her voice. 'It is a miracle you were even let in the door. What on earth can you have expected? Really, Kitty, I cannot for the life of me understand why you are so surprised!'

In the wake of their disastrous visit to Lady Radcliffe's house,

Kitty had felt it necessary to confess to their aunt exactly what they had been doing on their daily walks – having previously kept quiet for fear of her aunt's disapproval. As predicted, Aunt Dorothy had unabashedly dubbed her a fool.

'I'm not *surprised*,' Kitty said crossly, 'I'm frustrated – if Cecily hadn't let slip that awful thing about us not having any money—'

'Even if she hadn't, Lady Radcliffe would have sniffed you out a second later,' Aunt Dorothy said tartly. 'I know her sort – they spend most of their time worrying about fortune-hunters. Mark my words, my dear, you will not be seeing that boy again.'

Contrary to Aunt Dorothy's predictions, the next day they did indeed see the de Lacys in Hyde Park, Archie looking a little sheepish but pleased to see Kitty nonetheless. As soon as they were in earshot, Lady Amelia burst out gleefully with 'Mama thinks you're after our fortune! Are you?'

'Amelia!' Mr de Lacy said, scandalised. 'What a thing to say!' He gave Kitty an earnest, apologetic look. 'Terribly sorry, of course we know you aren't – it's just that Mama – she is used to thinking—' He stammered around the issue for a few more moments before finishing feebly, 'She's very protective of us.'

This gave Kitty a pretty accurate idea of the kind of accusations that had been levelled at them, after their departure from the Radcliffe house. Kitty repressed a groan of frustration. She was so tired of all these men being utterly hamstrung by other women. It was time for an offensive strike.

'I quite understand,' she said to Archie. 'It is of course natural that she should want to protect you. It is clear to me that she sees you still as a boy.'

'But I am not a boy any longer,' he said, his jaw setting stubbornly.

'No,' she agreed. 'Of course you are not.'

They began to walk.

'I hope – I hope it was not Cecily's words about our financial situation that gave your mother pause,' she said quietly.

Archie stammered meaninglessly in response.

'My papa always taught us,' Kitty said, staring off into the distance as if deep in a memory, 'that it was our characters, who we are on the inside, that matters . . . But I know not all people feel the same way. If it will upset your mother, perhaps it is better that we are not friends.'

This was utter fiction of course, but the bluff played out well.

'Oh, do not say that, Miss Talbot,' Mr de Lacy implored, aghast. 'We mustn't let Mama ruin our friendship – she's terribly old-fashioned, you know, but I myself quite agree with your father. In fact,' he drew himself up to his full height to prepare for a romantic declaration, 'in fact, I-I should not care if you were a pauper or a prince!'

Misgendering aside, Kitty was quite pleased with this statement. It suited very well for Mr de Lacy to consider himself a romantic hero, and Lady Radcliffe the dragon guarding the castle.

'Mr de Lacy, it is such a reassurance to hear you say so,' she praised.

Kitty stopped on the path, forcing him to halt with her.

'I hope you do not consider me too forward,' she said, pushing as much warmth into her voice as she could. 'But I am beginning to think you a most treasured friend.'

'Miss Talbot, as do I,' Archie breathed. 'I am quite determined that we should still see each other. I shall speak to my mother today; I am sure I can make her see sense.'

Very well played, indeed, Kitty congratulated herself. Just so. When they parted an hour later, Kitty felt rather pleased with how the day had gone. But no sooner had they returned to Wimpole Street than Cecily spoke up, apropos of nothing.

'Do you care for Mr de Lacy?' she asked, as Kitty tugged the ribbons of her bonnet loose.

'Why do you ask?' Kitty said, frowning. The knot at the base of her chin was quite troublesome.

'I heard what he said – that it would not matter if you were a prince or a pauper. But that isn't true for you, is it?'

Kitty shrugged her shoulders, forgetting for a moment Dorothy's strict instructions that she was not to do anything so unladylike any more.

'I admire him, certainly,' Kitty said defensively. 'He has many admirable qualities. But if you are asking me if I am pursuing him for his fortune, then of course the answer is yes, Cecily. What else did you think we were here for?'

Cecily looked a little lost. 'I suppose,' she said haltingly, 'I suppose I thought you would try to find someone rich who you also cared for.'

'That would be very nice,' Kitty said tartly, 'if we had all the time in the world to do it – but we now have only eight weeks, before the moneylenders will be at Netley. And this time they will not leave empty-handed.'

6

The next day dawned bright and sunny. Excellent weather, in Kitty's opinion, for a spot of fortune-hunting. This auspicious start, however, proved to be short-lived, for when they met the de Lacys, Mr de Lacy looked as bashful as a lamb.

'I am afraid Mama was not to be persuaded,' he admitted, as soon as they began their turn. 'I tried speaking to her – I promise I did – but she quite nearly went into hysterics when I tried to explain what your papa said about one's insides.'

Kitty had the sinking realisation that the imagery of this speech might have become rather garbled in translation.

'She's written to our brother about you,' Lady Amelia chipped in, gleeful again – she was quite thrilled by the theatrics that the Talbots had introduced into an otherwise very dull month.

'Whatever for?' Kitty asked, alarmed. The last thing she wanted was another protective de Lacy descending upon her.

'Suppose she'll want him to weigh in – forbid me from seeing you or somesuch,' Archie said without concern. 'Nothing to worry over – James always sees through her guff.'

Be that as it may, Kitty was keen that Archie be distanced from his mother's influence before she became any more motivated to separate them. But how to do it?

'Mr de Lacy, may I ask you a question?' she asked, as Cecily and Lady Amelia moved off ahead of them. 'I am still unused to London ways, you see. Is it regular for a man such as yourself, of your age and stature, to still lodge with his mother?'

Mr de Lacy looked taken aback. 'My schoolfriends all do so,' he confessed. 'James, my brother, does still have his own lodgings in town, though the family house is his now – Mama did offer to leave, but he wouldn't hear of it. Though as he is hardly ever in London, he rarely uses either house.'

'I see,' Kitty said thoughtfully. 'Do you think he would grant you leave to use them, should you like to? I own that were I in your shoes, I should very much like the freedom living alone would offer.'

'What do you mean?' Mr de Lacy asked, uncertainly. The idea of having his own lodgings had never occurred to him.

'Well, one could do what one wanted, whenever the fancy struck,' Kitty suggested. 'Come and go as one pleased, and suchlike.'

'I would not have to answer to Mama or Pattson, who always seem to have something to say about everything I do,' Mr de Lacy said, catching on.

'You could breakfast for supper,' Kitty said roguishly. 'And stay up as late as you like.'

'Oh, I say,' he chuckled, finding this idea quite scandalous.

'Just a thought,' she said. 'It could be marvellous, you know.'

Kitty hoped this had been enough to prompt some action from the boy, but upon the next day, perceived at once this tactic to have been a mistake. Lady Amelia greeted them with the news that they had been forbidden from ever seeing the Misses Talbot again – a decree that they seemed all too cheerful to disobey, the attraction of youthful company in an otherwise deserted London proving too powerful to ignore.

'Mama almost fainted when Archie said he wanted to find his own lodgings,' Lady Amelia told them. 'She lays all the blame on you, Miss Talbot.'

'Tosh,' Mr de Lacy dismissed at once. 'A load of dramatics. Do not think on it for a second, Miss Talbot, she'll come around soon enough.'

'Will she not notice you have left to meet us, as normal?' Cecily asked.

'Not a jot,' Mr de Lacy said. 'Got one of these new fainting spells – forget what she's calling them now. Two doctors have been already, and we slipped out amidst all the confusion.'

'Good thing too,' Lady Amelia agreed. 'Can't bear to discuss her health a second longer. Besides,' she linked her arm through Cecily's, 'makes it quite exciting – all very clandestine.'

Kitty's heart sank at this. It would not do at all for theirs to become a clandestine arrangement. Clandestine meant scandal, and Kitty knew very well where scandals ended up. It was not a life she wanted for herself, at all.

'Mr de Lacy, I am dismayed to have caused so much upset,' she said. 'I do not want your mother to dislike me so.'

Archie gave a careless wave of his hand, brushing this concern off entirely. 'She'll come around, don't you worry,' he said dismissively. 'You simply must hear about Gerry's latest letter – my friend from Eton, you know, should be in town in a week or so. Damnedest thing—'

Mr de Lacy barrelled on with a long and uninteresting story about Gerry's latest escapade, and though Kitty laughed along, her attention was firmly elsewhere. While Mr de Lacy might move through life with the cheery self-assurance that everything would work out in his favour in the end, Kitty did not. She highly doubted that Lady Radcliffe would change her opinion without some outside intervention, and so she must think of a way to make Lady Radcliffe like her. But how to do it?

'I am so sorry to hear of your mother's illness,' she said softly, once Mr de Lacy had finished his soliloquy. 'I only wish there was something I could do.'

'Wouldn't worry your head about it,' Mr de Lacy told her. 'The doctors will say there's nothing wrong with her, she won't believe them, and it will be some hocus-pocus medicine from cook or Lady Montagu that will cure her in the end. Before the whole thing starts up again.'

'Is that so,' Kitty said thoughtfully. Then, after a beat, 'Have I ever told you that I have a great interest in medicine?'

'You haven't – at least, not that I can remember,' Archie confessed.

'I do. In Dorsetshire, you know we are most comfortable with the use of herbal remedies,' she lied. 'Your mother's fainting spells sound most familiar to me; I am sure Mrs Palmer from our town was similarly afflicted and I have a recipe of the elixir that cured her. Would you permit me to write her a note recommending it?'

Mr de Lacy looked a little thrown by this, but nodded willingly enough, and when they were deposited onto Wimpole Street Kitty bade the carriage wait as she darted inside to pull out some writing paper. In her best penmanship, she wrote a quick note to Lady Radcliffe, before dashing back out to hand it to Mr de Lacy.

'You are most prodigiously kind, Miss Talbot,' Mr de Lacy told her, admiration shining in his eyes.

Kitty thanked him modestly. She was not, of course, in the least motivated by kindness, and the remedy she had written of was entirely fictional and completely harmless. Kitty's experience of healthy persons who suffered often from sickness, such as Lady Radcliffe, had taught her that they valued sympathy for, and the discussion of, their infirmity very highly. She hoped that the obvious dismissal of Lady Radcliffe's illnesses by both her children and medical professionals might have created in the lady a hunger for a sympathetic ear. It was a shot in the dark, Kitty knew, but the only one she could think of making.

The mood in Wimpole Street the next morning was low. They were all tired, Aunt Dorothy from a late-night game of whist with her old friend Mrs Ebdon, Kitty from the tension of the past few days, and Cecily from . . . Well, whatever sort of thing made Cecily tired. The auspicious spring weather had broken, with a chilly breeze brought in from the east. The three women stared out of the window, a little gloomily – the weather having, as it did for all British persons, an infectious quality upon their mood. Though in Biddington, at least, such a paltry chill in the air would not have kept them indoors all day. Kitty's other sisters were no doubt striding into town, unheeding of the weather – though Kitty could not truthfully know what they were doing, for she had yet to receive a letter from them in return. They had agreed to write only sparingly, the cost of receiving post an extravagance they could barely afford, but Kitty yearned to hear from them, nonetheless.

'Help Sally in with the breakfast, would you, dear?' Aunt Dorothy asked Kitty, but before she could, the door had opened and Sally entered – with a note in hand, instead of her usual tray.

'It's for you, miss,' she said, handing it to Kitty. 'Boy who brought it says it's from Lady Radcliffe.'

Her disbelieving tone made it clear she rather thought this a lie. Kitty broke the seal. The note, written in beautiful cursive upon thick cream paper, was short.

Dear Miss Talbot,

Thank you for your solicitous note. The recipe you sent proved to be most effective – I partook of it yesterday and my symptoms have quite disappeared. If you would be kind enough to call upon me tomorrow, I should like to express my thanks in person. I will be at home between two and four o'clock.

Yours,

Lady Helena Radcliffe

Kitty smiled.

7

The seventh Earl of Radcliffe sat in the breakfast parlour of his country house, calmly availing himself of his morning meal and perusing a parcel of letters. The London Season not yet beginning for two more weeks, he was not alone in spending this time away from the bustling city, much of the *ton* availing themselves of the same opportunity. He was singular, however, in having avoided London for the past two years almost entirely. Since the death of his father and his ascension to the title of Earl, Lord Radcliffe had preferred to remain at the family seat in Devonshire, rather than face London's ravenous hordes. And yet, in his crisp white shirt, impeccably arranged cravat, and shining black Hessian boots, he still looked every inch the sophisticated London gentleman – his only concession to location being the casual disarray of his dark curls.

'Anything of note, Jamie?' his friend, Captain Henry Hinsley, formerly of the 7th Brigadiers, called lazily from his relaxed sprawl on the chaise longue.

'Just business, Hinsley' Radcliffe called back, 'and a note from my mother.'

Hinsley gave a short bark of laughter. 'That's the third letter this week. Is she ill?'

'Always,' Radcliffe murmured absently, his eyes moving down the page. Hinsley propped himself up on his elbows, the better to regard his friend.

'Lumbago? Pox?' he suggested, grinning. 'Or is she just up in arms about the chit Archie's enamoured with?'

'The latter, although the young lady in question has graduated from "chit" to "harpy".'

'Spare my blushes, James.' Hinsley clasped a hand to his heart. 'What has the poor girl done to deserve such defamation?'

Radcliffe began to read aloud. '"My dear James, I must implore you to fly to London at once. Our dear Archie, my precious son, your younger brother" – does she think I've forgotten who Archie is? – "is on the cusp of ruin. He spends every waking moment with the harpy, who has him securely within her grasp. I fear it may soon be too late."'

Radcliffe ended the soliloquy in tones of such portentous doom that Hinsley let out a shout of laughter.

'After his virtue, is she? Lucky boy. And are you to ride to his rescue?'

'That does seem to be what is expected,' Radcliffe said wryly, finishing the letter. 'Although I can only imagine bursting in on my little brother's clandestine tryst might be a trifle awkward.'

'Awful thing to do to a family member,' Hinsley agreed promptly. He then paused, considering the matter. 'You think there's anything to it? Archie stands to inherit a pretty penny 'pon his majority – stands to reason that she might be after it.'

Radcliffe looked up from the page incredulously. '*Et tu*, Harry? Have a little faith, my dear man. Archie is only a boy, and this is nothing more than his usual calf love. I receive these letters each year. If he ever formed a serious attachment, I'd be hearing it from Archie himself, rather than our mother.'

He waved the letter at Hinsley, remonstrative, but his friend just grinned slyly. 'You think the boy still worships you, then? Even though you've been hiding down in the country these past two years? Barely set eyes on him, I would think, the way you've been avoiding them.'

'I haven't been avoiding them,' Radcliffe said coolly. 'My mother is more than capable of running the family. She doesn't need my help.'

It sounded weak, spoken aloud, and he frowned to hear it.

'Asking for it now, though, isn't she?' Hinsley looked at him evenly – uncharacteristically serious. 'You know you're going to have to start being a proper lord someday, James. You can't hide down here for ever.'

Radcliffe pretended he had not heard this. He knew Hinsley meant well – knew that, having fought together on the Continent, Harry might even understand the reason he was so reluctant to don a mantle his father should still be wearing. They had seen the same horrors, after all, though Hinsley, who had served in Wellington's army for far longer than Radcliffe, seemed to find it much easier to brush them off. And though he and the rest of the country might think the wars were over, it didn't feel that way to Radcliffe. Here, at Radcliffe Hall, it was easier – managing the estate, speaking to tenants, learning his duty. He could accept that. But returning to the city as an Earl, taking his father's seat in the Lords, chaperoning his family around London into gaudy ballrooms as if nothing had ever *happened* – no. He couldn't do it. And he didn't need to.

'I thank you for your concern, my dear friend,' he said after a pause, keeping his voice mild and even. 'But as I said, were Archie truly attached, he would have written.'

There was a cough from his butler. 'I believe there is a letter from Mr Archibald in that pile, my lord,' Beaverton said politely.

Hinsley laughed. 'Oh no!' he crowed. 'Written to confess he's in love, has he?'

Radcliffe frowned, flipping through the stack of letters until he found the one with his brother's writing upon it.

'Yes,' he said, eyes moving much faster across the page. 'It appears he is. And that he thinks he should like to marry the girl.'

'By George!' Hinsley stood, moving to peer over Radcliffe's shoulder to read the letter for himself. Radcliffe twitched it away in irritation. Shoving it back into the envelope, he drained his coffee cup and stood from the breakfast table.

'How can that be, in only a few weeks?' Hinsley wondered, helping himself to more coffee.

'How indeed,' James said grimly. 'I'm afraid we're going to have to cut your stay short, Harry. It appears I'm needed in London after all.'

Lord Radcliffe felt a certain degree of trepidation when he walked into the de Lacy family residence upon Grosvenor Square to find it shrouded in near darkness and funereal silence, the curtains at each window drawn against the bright sunshine. He was greeted, as was usual, by Pattson, who had run the house for as long as Radcliffe could remember and had been as much a fixture in his childhood as his parents. Radcliffe gripped his arm in firm welcome. There was an expression of distinct relief on the man's face.

'What is it this time, Pattson?' he asked apprehensively.

'A *migraine*, I believe is what it is called, my lord,' Pattson responded, so quietly he barely moved his lips.

'Oh Lord, French, is it? Where did she hear of it?' An international malady was always worse.

'I gather,' Pattson said carefully, 'that the diagnosis came by way of Lady Jersey, who has suffered similarly.'

'I see. And is it . . . serious?' Radcliffe queried. Past experience told him that it was best to pay heed to such ailments, as an overly jocular view could cause irreparable offence.

'In lower circles, I think it is more commonly known as a *headache*,' was the delicate response. 'It has come on rather quickly – in fact, directly after Lady Jersey's visit.'

Pattson's face was utterly expressionless. Radcliffe repressed a smile and entered the drawing room quietly. It was even darker in this room, so it took a moment before he was able to make out the shape of his mother, lying in dramatic repose across the chaise longue.

'Good morning, Mother,' he called softly into the room, taking his volume cue from Pattson.

The Countess sat bolt upright. 'James?! Is that you? Oh, how wonderful.' She sprang energetically up from her seat.

'I can't see a thing!' she said indignantly, before calling, 'Pattson! Pattson! I can't see a thing, please open the curtains, it's a veritable morgue in here.'

In her aggrieved state, she did not seem to recall that it was her own instruction that had made it so, but Pattson said not a word – pulling the curtains aside in a few quick movements and flooding the room with light. Lady Radcliffe was *en déshabillé,* her hair only loosely dressed and her grey gown simple. She tripped lightly towards her eldest son, arms outstretched, and folded him into a warm embrace.

'James, my darling, it is wonderful to see you.' She stepped back, holding his hands and drinking him in.

'And you,' he smiled, clasping her hands warmly. 'How have you been? I hear from Pattson that you have been quite under the weather.'

'Oh, pish,' she dismissed this swiftly. Pattson, over her shoulder, looked mildly pained. 'You know I am never knocked down for long.'

This was true. It occasionally bordered on the miraculous the way Lady Radcliffe's maladies vanished just in time for the social occasions she was most looking forward to.

'But why are you here, James? I thought you had determined to stay at Radcliffe Hall for the foreseeable.'

He raised his eyebrows. 'I had – but your letters have been quite compelling reading. You must tell me the whole of Miss Talbot and Archie.'

If he had expected a live rendition of her dramatic letter, he was to be disappointed.

'Oh, please, James, you don't need to say a thing,' she exclaimed, putting her hands to her cheeks in good-humoured faux embarrassment. 'I know I've been a goose!'

'A goose . . .' he repeated. It was mildly irritating, he could own, to have travelled so swiftly so far a distance, but it certainly made matters less taxing.

'Yes, I own I thought Miss Talbot to be a fortune-hunter –

and most unsuitable for Archie besides – but we really have nothing to be worried for.'

'That is a relief,' he said, wondering how quickly he could be ready to depart again for Devonshire.

'I know, I know. I can't believe I had misjudged her so utterly. She's the most wonderful creature.'

'Mmm,' he said absently. His greys would need to rest, which might delay him – then his mind caught up with his mother's words.

'Mama – do you mean to tell me that Archie and this Miss Talbot are still acquainted?'

'Of course they are! Why, she and her sister are now quite frequent visitors to the house. Miss Cecily and Amelia both attended the Bath Seminary, you know, and they are closely acquainted with the Dorsetshire Linfields. I own, I had utterly misjudged them – you know how I worry about all my children, that you might be victim to a bad sort due to our wealth.'

Radcliffe did know. In her letters, his mother had used the more damning phrase 'havey-cavey jade'.

'I was most wrong; Miss Talbot is in fact the kindest young lady. Why, she was most solicitous when I had my fainting spells last week and, indeed, quite cured them with a remedy from Dorsetshire.'

'Did she?' he murmured thoughtfully, reclining into his chair.

'Yes, and I really do feel a person's attitude to the health of others is most revealing of their character, don't you agree?'

'I find myself in complete agreement. It is *very* revealing,' he replied.

His tone was even, but there must have been something in it to give his mother pause because she went on, slightly anxious.

'I would prefer Archie to have friends with greater consequence, of course. But I think, in the event that their attachment proves enduring, that he would be happy. And as his mother, that is what I care for above all else.'

His mother's own marriage having been one of convenience, arranged by her parents to one much older than herself, Radcliffe could believe this – and he could not disagree with the sentiment out of hand. But . . .

'I thought we had agreed that both Archie and Amelia are far too young to be considering long-term attachments?' he said mildly.

'We did,' she admitted. 'And they are. But I see no danger in allowing them to pursue their acquaintance. Ten to one they will both grow out of it. Why should they not enjoy each other's company for a little while? Why, they share all the same interests!'

He hummed again.

'James, please don't be disagreeable,' she said reprovingly. 'If you have time to linger, I am expecting them any moment. They are such good influences, inviting Archie and Amelia on their daily walks, I fancy it is the most outdoor air Amelia has had in years. Fresh air is, of course, so good for the constitution. Once you meet Miss Talbot, I'm sure you'll adore her,' Lady Radcliffe said reassuringly. 'We all do – even Dottie.'

'I'm sure I would like very much to meet her,' he said quite affably, though inside, the flames of suspicion had been fanned.

And after all, though Dottie was a discerning judge of character and admittedly difficult to impress, Dottie was also a cat.

8

Miss Kitty Talbot followed Mr de Lacy and Lady Amelia up the stairs to their grand Grosvenor Square house, feeling very pleased with herself. It was a state she had found herself in semi-permanently for the past week, now that the Countess's affections had been won as well as her son's. Kitty's solicitous and hugely sympathetic treatment of the lady's health had charmed her thoroughly and, once Kitty's Dorsetshire remedy (elixir of restoration, Kitty had called it, though it was simply water flavoured with elderflower stems and dried sprigs of thyme) had cured Lady Radcliffe's fainting spells, she quite considered Kitty an angel.

Kitty calculated – from the warmth in Mr de Lacy's voice when he spoke to her, the length of his admiring stares when they were together, the enthusiasm with which he begged to see her – that their impending engagement could not be more than a week away. She was just considering this happy state of affairs as they walked into the drawing room, when she was jolted from it by a shout of 'James!' from her side. Mr de Lacy and Lady Amelia both dashed forward to greet a tall figure unfolding himself from a high-backed chair, and Kitty was left by the door, blinking. She felt not a little perturbed. By the greeting and the name, this could only be Lord Radcliffe, but she had been given to understand that this gentleman was not often seen in London.

The younger de Lacys were swarming their brother like over-eager puppies. From Lord Radcliffe's very irregular contact with his family, she had assumed he held no great love for them, yet she could see his affection quite clearly – in the warmth of his eyes as Archie wrung his hand for far too long, the indulgence of his smile as he tilted his head in Amelia's direction as she tugged on his elbow. The distraction offered her the opportunity to observe him openly, and she was glad of it. Radcliffe was tall, with a lean build that suggested a sporting lifestyle, and admittedly handsome, with thick dark hair, kind grey eyes, and an easy, confident bearing. Though this did not endear him to Kitty. In her experience, the more handsome the man, the less character he possessed, and that was before one added in wealth and a title to the mix. Kitty moved forward slowly, Cecily trailing behind her, to curtsey before Lady Radcliffe.

'I hope we are not intruding, my lady,' Kitty said. 'I had not realised Lord Radcliffe was visiting.'

'No, my dear, of course you are not,' Lady Radcliffe said, beckoning them forward. 'James, James – I would like to introduce you to the Misses Talbot, our dear new friends.'

'Miss Talbot, Miss Cecily,' Radcliffe greeted them, bowing as they curtseyed.

They rose and Kitty caught his eye properly for the first time. Had she really thought them kind? It must have been the light, for they were chilly now, and weighty with cold assessment. Kitty felt, for one awful moment, utterly seen. As if this man knew every single shameful thing she had ever done or thought, and condemned her for each one. Her breath caught, she found she was quite capable of blushing after all. He looked away, the moment passed, and Kitty recovered herself. They seated themselves around the drawing room, and Pattson brought in a tray of refreshments. She accepted a slice of cake with a murmur of thanks.

'Miss Talbot,' Radcliffe addressed her, as she took her first mouthful. 'You must tell me how you came to be acquainted with my family. Archie's letter mentioned something about . . . a slipper, was it?'

'Oh goodness!' Kitty looked down in calculated embarrassment. 'Yes, I am so grateful that Lady Amelia and Mr de Lacy came to our aid on that day, for it was an awkward predicament. Yet how wonderful that it should be the cause of two such great friends reuniting.'

She smiled at her sister, but Cecily did not bestir herself to add any commentary. Difficult thing. Mr de Lacy was gazing adoringly at her, though, a melted pool of butter, and Kitty tried to take reassurance from that.

'Yes, a wonderful – even miraculous – coincidence,' Lord Radcliffe agreed, and though his tone remained polite, Kitty felt a stirring of unease.

'I suppose I must be very lucky,' she said. She turned to Lady Radcliffe, hoping to dismiss this line of questioning. 'I hear the weather is to continue improving, ma'am. I hope we can look forward to a break in humidity, which must surely be a cause for your ghastly *migraines*.'

'As do I, my dear,' Lady Radcliffe said in fatalistic tones, 'though I for one do not expect an improvement.' She turned to her son. 'Was Radcliffe Hall in good shape, when you left?'

'Oh, very,' he said promptly.

'Mr de Lacy tells me that Radcliffe Hall is quite beautiful,' Kitty said, smiling ingratiatingly at Radcliffe. 'I should so love to hear more about it, my lord.'

'I am afraid most of our company would find such a description very dull,' Radcliffe said coolly. 'You must tell us instead of your family seat – Netley, is it?'

Her smile tightened. 'By all means, though I am afraid to call it a family seat is a little generous.'

'Is it?' he asked. 'From what Archie told me, I imagined the lands to be quite extensive.'

It took a great deal of self-restraint on Kitty's part to avoid sending an accusatory glance in Archie's direction. Seeming to sense that he had made a misstep, Mr de Lacy hastened to interject.

'No, no, James. Impressive, I did say, but I meant in beauty rather than scale.' He seemed very pleased with this turn of phrase, beaming to himself and looking towards Kitty for approval. Kitty gave another smile, as it would not serve to appear cross. Still, was it too much to expect him not to actively hinder their endeavours with unhelpful exaggeration? And now it looked as though she was being purposefully misleading. It was most vexatious.

'I'm sure I don't know about that,' she demurred. 'We think so, at any rate.'

She tried again to include Cecily in the conversation by glancing to her for some commentary, but Cecily was staring vaguely off into the distance. Kitty supposed they were lucky that gormlessness was not considered a sin in women.

'I'm sure,' Radcliffe said smoothly. 'In the West Country, yes?'

Something in his tone made her feel a sense of caution, but there was no way of not answering.

'Dorsetshire,' Kitty confirmed. 'Just west of Dorchester.'

'I'd love to see it,' Archie enthused. His genuine enthusiasm softened her towards him a little.

'Whenever you like,' she promised, reckless. He beamed.

From there, Mr de Lacy and Lady Amelia – tiring of their brother's interest in Miss Talbot – took over conversation. Kitty, in turn, was able to redirect her concentration back to ingratiating herself with the family, listening attentively and giving liberally of tinkling laughs and murmurs of interest at each appropriate point. By the time they took their leave, both Lady Amelia and Mr de Lacy were in quite high spirits, from the intoxicating combination of Kitty's ego-stroking and their brother's undivided attention – and Kitty felt that she had handled the day's unexpected challenge favourably, in the end. From here, all she needed to do was to prove to Radcliffe how incandescently happy she made his brother. After all, if his mother had no objection, why should he?

They made their goodbyes, Mr de Lacy fervently promising to see her on the morrow, and she curtseyed to Radcliffe last. Then, for the second time that day, she caught that same expression in his eye – the one that cut her to the quick, and told her, clearly, that she did not belong here. She settled into the de Lacy carriage – which Lady Radcliffe had had ordered around as soon as she learnt they intended to walk home – feeling ill at ease. Why should he look at her so contemptuously, when she had the approval of the rest of his family? What on earth had she done, to provoke such a reaction? She was not at all certain – and she did not like it one bit.

By contrast, Radcliffe, leaving the family home for his own lodgings on St James's Place several hours later, felt very certain of three facts. Firstly, that his younger brother and entire family were dangerously infatuated with Miss Talbot. Secondly, that Miss Talbot harboured no true romantic attachment to Archie whatsoever, beyond a fancy for his wealth. And thirdly, that it would be down to him to scotch the whole affair.

9

Kitty slammed the note down onto the breakfast table, causing her sister and aunt to jump.

'The de Lacys have called off today's walk,' she said crossly in explanation. 'Mr de Lacy is spending the afternoon with Radcliffe, while Lady Radcliffe and Lady Amelia have been invited to view the Elgin Marbles with Lady Montagu's daughters.'

'It is natural for Radcliffe to want to spend time with his brother, is it not?' Cecily said airily. 'And I should like to see the Elgin Marbles myself.' She added this last wistfully. Husband-hunting had not, Cecily had been disappointed to find, left much time thus far for sightseeing.

'Twice this week?' Kitty snapped. 'It isn't natural, it's *intentional*. Radcliffe is trying to end our acquaintance.'

Cecily looked a little confused, not following this leap of logic.

'I did warn you!' Dorothy sang out, her face partially hidden from behind the latest edition of *La Belle Assemblée*. 'You might have been able to fool the mother, but this Lord Radcliffe seems to quite have your measure . . . It's not too late to try for Mr Pears, you know.'

Kitty stood abruptly. 'Get your hat, Cecy, and call for Sally – we're going out.'

'Now?' Cecily called plaintively after Kitty as she dashed across the room. 'Where?'

'Do you want to see these Marbles or not?' she called over her shoulder.

Archie was in high spirits on the walk back to Grosvenor Square, through the soft purple dusk of the evening. Radcliffe had taken him to his club, White's, twice this week, a hallowed threshold Archie had expected to be thirty and almost dead before being able to cross. It was even more thrilling than he could ever have imagined: the dark rooms, the low murmur of male conversation, the haze of cigar smoke. *Smashing*. So tickled pink was he that he could not help giving Radcliffe a blow-by-blow account of their final game of whist, though his brother had also been at the table.

'Did you see his face when I laid out my hand, James?' Archie asked in a gush of boyish excitement.

'I did,' Radcliffe said patiently. 'He was certainly displeased.'

'Absolutely howling, wasn't he,' Archie boasted gleefully. 'What a facer!'

For Radcliffe, the afternoon had held a little less allure. He had in his youth spent much time in White's and its sister venues, but had not felt the need to visit in years. However, it had been time well spent, of that he was certain. Archie may be boring him excessively with a minute account of the afternoon, but he hadn't spoken of Miss Talbot since the morning. The previous day, Archie had extolled upon Miss Talbot for hours, his adoration of her, her various and sundry virtues, and his desire even of perhaps marrying her. Radcliffe was pleased to see the prescription of some light gambling take its intended distracting effect. A few more days of this and the threat of Miss Talbot would be relegated firmly to the past. Still, he was relieved when they arrived back at Grosvenor Square – much looking forward to handing Archie back over to his mother and retreating to the relative quiet of St James's Place.

'Pattson, are my mother and sister at home?' Archie called, bounding into the hall. 'I simply must tell them about the game!'

Perceiving that if he remained, he would be expected to listen to Archie's oration for a second time, Radcliffe opened his mouth to say goodnight – picturing, in his mind's eye, the fire and blessed silence of his study – when Pattson answered.

'They are taking refreshment in the drawing room with the Misses Talbot, my lord.'

'Miss Talbot is here?' Archie lit up like a candle. 'Marvellous! Are you coming, James?'

'Yes, I rather think I am.' Radcliffe followed him calmly to the drawing room.

'My dears!' the Countess greeted them. 'What splendid timing!'

'How fortuitous,' Radcliffe bowed to the assembled ladies, 'that we should find you all here, lying in wait.'

'You make us sound almost wicked!' Miss Talbot said sunnily. Archie gave a shout of mirth at this joke, but Radcliffe did not laugh.

'Do join us,' Lady Radcliffe instructed. 'James, the Marbles were just as magnificent as you said they would be. And we were so pleased to stumble upon the Misses Talbot there too!'

'What a lovely . . . coincidence.' Radcliffe's eyes rested for a moment on the elder Miss Talbot, who raised her chin.

'By George, isn't it just?' Archie said, rather struck by this – entirely forgetting that it was he who had informed Miss Talbot of his mother and sister's plans by letter this morning. The addition of the Misses Talbot to his already top-drawer day had sent him quite giddy with joy. Remembering his manners, he bowed to the ladies so deeply that they might be duchesses, rather than – as Radcliffe was beginning to appreciate – villainous barnacles. They seated themselves, Archie predictably settling himself down next to his beloved, appearing to commit himself to the task of pleasing her.

'Miss Talbot, it has been an age,' he declared. Stricken with the realisation that the fault lay with him, he stammered out an apology for the cancellations. 'You see, I have been at White's,' he explained reverently, with the earnest enthusiasm of the young. 'It's the most wonderful place.'

Radcliffe, ignoring Archie, regarded Miss Talbot directly. She did not look like a villain, he supposed, but then was that not the devil's way? She had dressed herself – much as the wolf does – to blend in, in the latest style of diaphanous skirts and feathered ringlets intended to give young ladies an air of intense fragility. She wore them well, he could admit, though he detected a strong sense of vitality – even sturdiness – about Miss Talbot that did not at all fit in with this fashionable sensibility. One could not say that one expected Miss Talbot to, as was à la mode, faint dead away at any moment, that was for certain.

It was clear, by the undisguised adoration in Archie's eyes – reminding Radcliffe very much of a small dog waiting on a treat – that none of this had been noticed by his brother. It was not only embarrassing but impolite, too, for Archie was patently paying no attention to Miss Cecily's description of the Marbles. Though Radcliffe did not entirely blame him, given how very dull it was. It was the elder Miss Talbot, in the end, who rescued them all from the tedium, though with less than altruistic motivations.

'My lady,' she began, 'I must tell you of a most interesting book I was reading this morning. It spoke at length of the fortifying remedy of exercise upon the brain. Lady Amelia tells me you are an able horsewoman, and I am persuaded that a ride might in fact be the cure to your current malady.'

'Top idea!' Archie said immediately, before his mother could respond. 'Mama, let us all ride out tomorrow!'

'I am not quite sure,' his mother demurred. 'You children ride with such energy; I feel quite overcome with fatigue already.'

'Oh,' sighed Miss Talbot, eyes downcast. 'If only I had a mount in the city, I would be quite happy to accompany you, Lady Radcliffe, at a comfortable pace.'

'Why, you must make use of our stable,' Lady Amelia piped up, horrified that one should not at all times have a horse at one's disposal.

'Yes, quite! In fact, let us all go,' Archie declared. 'Make a party of it, ride out to Wimbledon! Tomorrow! Miss Talbot, you can ride Peregrine.'

Kitty let out a dramatic gasp, hand clutching her heart. 'You should not tease me so,' she pleaded in mock distress. She turned to Lady Radcliffe. 'If it would not be an imposition?'

she said, with pretty deference. But it was Lord Radcliffe who answered.

'Not at all,' he said smoothly. 'In fact, I will play escort.'

'Famous!' said Archie.

'Yes . . . delightful,' Miss Talbot agreed.

Radcliffe wondered if her teeth were gritted and fought the urge to bare his own.

The chatter of Archie and Amelia took over, as they planned the expedition with some excitement, but little awareness that they had been played as easily as if they were common puppets. Radcliffe had been foolish to consider the matter finished, he could see that now. Quite foolish indeed. The Misses Talbot did not linger for long after that – why would they, Radcliffe thought darkly, now that they had entirely achieved their object in visiting. They exchanged jolly farewells, pretty curt-seys and fervent promises to meet early in the morning for their adventure.

It was in a state of introspection that Lord Radcliffe arrived at his London home, only a few streets over – and so it was not an entirely welcome surprise to find his friend, Captain Hinsley, ensconced in his study and availing himself liberally of his most expensive brandy.

'Well, James?' he demanded eagerly. 'Got rid of her yet?'

'No,' Radcliffe said regretfully, pouring himself to a glass. 'She has proven just as stubborn and dangerous as all of my mother's letters warned – not that Mama remembers any of that now. Miss Talbot has got them all quite wrapped around her finger. Lord only knows what she would do to the family's good name if I had not returned in time. Luckily, it is little more than a week before the Season starts, and Archie will be nicely distracted by a horde of young women trying to catch his attention. All I have to do is to keep him from proposing to her in the next seven days, for his own good.'

Hinsley looked at him for a moment, and then grinned broadly. 'Look at you!' he said, almost proudly. 'You're starting to sound like your father, ain't you?'

Radcliffe looked at him with more than a little disgust. 'Such things you say to me,' he said. 'I most certainly am not.'

'You are,' his friend persisted. 'All this talk of Archie's own good, the family name. Who's to say that's not what the old man was saying about you, before he packed you off to the Continent to take notes for Wellington?'

Radcliffe sent him a cutting look. 'You know very well that's not all I did,' he said.

'Yes and thank God old Bonaparte did escape, or else you would have been bored to death in Vienna,' Hinsley said with an irreverent grin.

'And yet I am not going to banish Archie from the country because I believe him to be over-indulging in alcohol and gambling,' Lord Radcliffe said, ignoring Hinsley's comment to return to the original point. 'I am trying to make sure he doesn't fall prey to such a person as Miss Talbot.' He sipped his drink thoughtfully for a moment, then said. 'You are not totally wrong, however. I may not have agreed with my father on most topics – hell, I spent a lot of my life hating him – but he knew, and I know, that being a part of this family means protecting one another from such vipers. Which is what I mean to do.'

'You don't want him marrying a nobody,' Hinsley said, knowingly.

'I don't want him marrying someone that cares not a jot about him,' Radcliffe corrected. 'Mark my words, in a month's time we won't even remember her name.'

10

Kitty and her sister were already saddled up by the time Lord Radcliffe rode up to Grosvenor Square the next morning, Kitty atop the mare usually reserved for Lady Radcliffe, who – when she could be persuaded to bestir herself – was a surprisingly fine horsewoman. The bay was the most beautiful stepper Kitty had ever seen and polite to a fault, which was all for the better as it had been a while since Kitty had ridden – the loss of Mr Linfield having also taken away the Talbots' only access to a stable. Lady Radcliffe would not be joining them after all, having come down with a most egregious attack of exhaustion, but neither Kitty nor Radcliffe were surprised or disappointed by this news. Both of them felt the day's task would be more easily completed without her presence.

Though the dense urban forest of London seemed to Kitty never-ending, they quickly left it behind, cobbled streets giving way to dusty track, busy pavements graduating smoothly to grassy verge. To relax would be dangerous – this day was as essential as any so far at securing her future – but Kitty felt, nonetheless, some of the tension leave her as the land opened up before her. The tension was renewed immediately, of course, when Radcliffe situated his mount to the left of hers early on in the journey. The path only allowing for two horses to ride alongside this left Mr de Lacy jostling along behind them looking a little put out and craning his neck to be able to hear them.

Miss Talbot knew an interrogation of sorts was to be expected after her appearance at Grosvenor Square the day before – but even so, she could not have predicted how direct an approach Lord Radcliffe felt able to take, once finally relieved from the constraints of his mother's presence.

'Devonshire, you said your family hails from?' he asked, apropos of nothing.

'Dorsetshire, my lord,' she corrected. 'Though originally from London. I was born here in the city.'

'Hmm, and you left for?'

'The fresh air,' she said promptly.

'And yet you returned for?'

'The company.'

'Other siblings?'

'Four younger sisters.'

'No brother?'

'None.'

'Parents?'

'Dead.'

'Disease?'

'James, I say!' Mr de Lacy exclaimed in some indignation, only to be roundly ignored both by his brother and his beloved.

'Typhoid,' Kitty answered. 'My mother first, my father following a year later.'

It shocked her a little, to hear this said out loud so baldly. To have it surmised in just one sentence, as if any explanation could encompass what they had been through – but she would not give Radcliffe the satisfaction of seeing this upon her face. He was clearly trying to catch her in a lie. As if she would be so foolish as to keep the truth of her family's financial situation from Mr de Lacy. What on earth would be accomplished by his discovering only on their wedding night that she had a collection of unmarried sisters and her father's encumbered estate as her dowry?

'And do you plan to return to Dorsetshire once you have secured a match?' Kitty was not expecting so direct a hit, and Mr de Lacy gave a squawk of surprise too, the thought not having occurred to him.

'We plan to remain in London for only the Season,' Kitty admitted slowly. 'I wanted to introduce Cecily into London society. She is far too young to be considering marriage, of course, but I felt it prudent to allow her to experience something of the world in preparation. I feel it my duty, with our mother gone.'

Kitty did not have to see Mr de Lacy to know he had melted at this – she could tell by the shape of Radcliffe's frown.

'I must say,' she said, taking control of the conversation, 'you both ride very well! In fact, far better than I would have expected from city persons!'

'Oh, a hit!' Mr de Lacy said gleefully. 'Not going to let that stand are you, James?'

Radcliffe ignored him. 'You are too kind, Miss Talbot, though you forget, perhaps, that I make my home in the country – and so I cannot accept the compliment.'

'Oh, yes, I do forget,' she lied. 'Silly of me – Lady Radcliffe had told me that it has been almost two years since you were last in London. Radcliffe Hall must be beautiful indeed, to have kept you away from your family so long.'

He did not react – he was the more experienced fencer – but Kitty fancied she saw a tightness around his eyes. 'Business keeps me in the country.'

'You must have a lot of business to see to, my lord,' she returned, keeping her voice light and playful. 'It is a wonder that you do not have a man to help manage the estates, if there is such a lot of work to be doing – another pair of safe hands would surely allow you to visit more.'

'Oh, we do!' Mr de Lacy was eager to defend his brother. 'A brilliant chap, Mr Perkins – he's been around ever since our father . . .' He trailed off, realising that this was proof of his brother's neglect, rather than the contrary. Turning her head slightly, she could see that he looked rather uncertain – his idol tarnished for the very first time. Kitty smiled.

'I'm sure you'll forgive me, Miss Talbot,' Radcliffe said sharply, 'if I trust my expertise over yours. It does not behove a lord to leave the running of land to another. It is the duty that comes with the title.'

'You must think very little of your fellow lords, then,' she said, with an ambitious stab at innocence, 'for they spend each spring in London, do they not?'

'And what of your aunt, Mrs Kendall – is she your mother's sister or your father's?' Radcliffe said sharply, quite as if she had not spoken at all.

'My mother's,' was her prompt response. Her third lie of the day, now – but one that had felt necessary from the very beginning, to keep their history as pristine as possible.

'I am sorry not to have met her yet,' Mr de Lacy said with real regret.

Radcliffe looked over at Miss Talbot, his eyes shrewd. She kept her expression even – but it was no use.

'Most remiss of you not to introduce yourself,' Radcliffe told his younger brother reproachfully.

'Is it?' Archie said, at once guilty. 'She must be invited to Grosvenor Square! Why don't you all dine with us, tomorrow evening?'

'You are too kind,' Kitty said quickly, thinking fast. Aunt Dorothy would most certainly *not* be entering Grosvenor Square, not when she was so opposed to Kitty's already precarious plans. 'But my aunt has not even called upon your mother.'

'Then we shall call upon her at once!' Archie said, undeterred.

'Aunt Dorothy tires easily, too,' Kitty added hastily. 'And though it has been many years since my uncle passed away, she still considers herself in full mourning.'

The path widened and at last the five were able to ride together, Archie chivvying his mount up to ride beside Kitty.

'Would a quiet dinner with Mama really be so tiring?' he said to her, doubtfully.

'What is this?' Lady Amelia demanded, now in earshot.

'Archie is attempting to invite Miss Talbot's aunt to dine with us tomorrow evening,' her eldest brother explained. 'He has not yet proved successful.'

'Oh, we cannot,' Cecily piped up. 'We promised to accompany Aunt Dorothy to Vauxhall Pleasure Gardens upon tomorrow evening – don't you remember, Kitty?'

Kitty could have slapped her quite happily.

'Ah yes,' Lord Radcliffe murmured. 'I had heard the Pleasure Gardens were becoming quite popular with mourners.'

'Famous!' Archie expostulated. 'We shall accompany you!'

Kitty could not refuse – could not think what other excuse she could make – so merely changed the subject, hoping the matter would drop. The rest of the morning passed without rancour, and Kitty could almost forget herself enough to find enjoyment in the de Lacys' company, as they cantered along grassy tracks and took daring jumps over hedgerows. There was not much opportunity for further conversation, and Kitty was relieved to have the break. They rested their mounts for a time at Wimbledon, partaking in refreshment at a local inn. Kitty prompted Cecily to relay her opinion of William Cowper's *oeuvre*. Kitty did not understand who this man was – or what *oeuvre* even meant – but knew the associated lecture well, and as predicted it lasted quite almost the whole return journey.

Back at Grosvenor Square, Kitty refused Lady Radcliffe's offer of refreshments, hoping that without further conversation, the dreaded Vauxhall Gardens plan might lapse into obscurity. But Archie, quite stricken with guilt at having neglected his romantic duty so severely, was not to be fobbed off, and he put the suggestion to his mother immediately.

'Oh splendid!' Lady Radcliffe said, clapping her hands merrily. 'Let us all go – we can hire a box!'

'You are not, perhaps, feeling too tired?' Kitty asked desperately.

'No, I am quite well now!' Lady Radcliffe declared brightly – the healthy old boot, Kitty thought mutinously.

Their fate was sealed, and Kitty had no choice but to surrender to it. She painted a smile on her face as she bade farewell to

Lady Radcliffe, Lady Amelia and Mr de Lacy – who pressed her hand with meaningful warmth – but it quite slipped from her face as she turned to Radcliffe.

'Until tomorrow, Miss Talbot,' he said as he bent his head over her hand.

'Yes, until then,' she agreed.

They paused there for a beat, looking at each other with mutual calculation. It occurred to them both, then – though of course they did not know it – that they might equally have agreed to pistols at dawn.

Radcliffe found himself, steering his curricle through London's traffic, yearning for his father's presence. Having now met Miss Talbot, he could appreciate the value of the former Lord Radcliffe's cold fortitude in the face of threats to his family's prestige in a way he never had before. It would be of course only the family's reputation that he would be concerned with – not, as James was, with its happiness – and yet, he would undoubtedly have known what steps were necessary to squash the threat, all without breaking stride. As de Lacys had done for centuries, after all.

Whereas Radcliffe, in this moment, doubted that he himself was equal to this task. To have underestimated his opponent so thoroughly was nothing short of galling, and his father would surely (had he been alive) have lost even more respect for his firstborn (were that possible). Radcliffe could almost hear him as if it were he, and not Lawrence – his tiger, perched on the groom's seat and watching Radcliffe's handling of the reins with an expert eye – seated behind him.

I do find it damning, his father would no doubt say, *that not even the diplomatic career that I arranged for you has given you the slightest degree of competency in your lordship. You always were so terribly wasteful.*

Radcliffe was not sure exactly how his short-lived career as an attaché at the Congress of Vienna should have made him an experienced ridder of fortune-hunters – though it was true that Miss Talbot seemed just as committed to her land-grabbing as any Foreign Secretary there – but no doubt his father would be rolling in his grave nonetheless. Radcliffe's even shorter experience of warfare that had followed – a career progression that had incensed his father beyond measure – was no help to him now, either. Of course, on the battlefield, Radcliffe would have been free to shoot Miss Talbot, a not unappealing prospect. He entertained himself for a moment by imagining this, and then moved on to remembering the war room at Waterloo, to the formidable figure of the Iron Duke puzzling over his foe's mind, his motivations, his psychology.

Radcliffe approached the busy junction at the corner of Regent Street and he smoothly checked his horses. As they paused, a couple of well-dressed bucks halted their promenade to admire his famous greys. But not even such frank admiration of his horses, usually so satisfying, could lift his introspection.

'Cheer up, Radcliffe,' Lawrence called jovially from behind him. The observers gaped to hear a servant address the famous Lord Radcliffe without an honorific, and Radcliffe felt a genuine smile curl his lips for the first time that day.

'Am I to hope,' he asked politely, 'that you shall soon begin to properly address me? We are not, my dear fellow, on the Continent any more.'

'And don't I know it,' Lawrence replied darkly. 'Much more

excitement there. Much more excitement in Devonshire, even. Here we just seem to ride from house to house.'

'How awful for you,' Radcliffe apologised. 'Do let me know if there's anything I can do to make your stay more palatable.'

He was only partially joking. After the danger of their life in Europe, and the freedom at Radcliffe Hall, Radcliffe could well understand that Lawrence's role in London – accompanying Radcliffe around town to hold and exercise his horses – would be dull in comparison.

'You could take me to Tattersall's,' Lawrence suggested promptly, with an unrepentant grin.

'At the earliest convenience,' Radcliffe agreed, a little ironically.

Lawrence was an astute character, and Radcliffe guessed that this over-friendly interjection was in equal parts natural and calculated. Having known each other for so long, it was easy enough to read the other. Familiarity bred knowledge and, as Wellington was so fond of saying, knowledge was power.

'As it happens,' Radcliffe continued after a pause, his voice thoughtful, 'I do have a task for you, that you might perhaps find more diverting.'

'What's that, then?' Lawrence demanded suspiciously.

'How well do you know Dorsetshire, my boy?'

11

In the balmy moonlight of a precipitously warm spring evening, Vauxhall Gardens seemed quite otherworldly. Alighting from the boat that had taken them across the river, they walked upon paths walled by tall trees, gleaming lamps hanging to light their way. Kitty's eyes were wide as they passed singers, jugglers and all manner of spectacle and entertainment, the lamps and half-darkness lending them all such glamour. It felt like a fairy garden from one of the stories Mama would tell them all at bedtime – where one ought not to step off the path for fear of what dangers would lie there.

Watching Lady Radcliffe and Aunt Dorothy gliding ahead of her, Kitty knew that she need never have worried about her aunt's performance. As with any challenge, Mrs Kendall had risen to the occasion splendidly.

'I am not in support of this endeavour, Kitty – I think it unwise and reckless and likely to collapse on top of you,' she had said severely the night before. 'But of course I will help.'

They had disagreed a little over her choice of costume. Aunt

Dorothy, displeased with her casting as a retiring widow, had poured herself into a dress that, whilst made from a stone-coloured crêpe, had a neckline that could not truthfully be described as sober in the slightest.

'Trust me, darling, I shall have far more luck making friends with your Lady Radcliffe dressed like this,' she had said. 'From what I hear, she's quite dashing.'

Her only concession, in the face of Kitty's uncertainty, had been to don a pair of black gloves, though Kitty could not help feeling she was still showing rather too much bosom for a widow – gloves or no gloves.

It was apparent, however, that Dorothy had understood her audience well. Lady Radcliffe had been visibly relieved to find Mrs Kendall a woman of fashion, rather than an austere and disapproving widow – and, dressed in the first style of elegance herself, was displaying quite as much décolletage as Mrs Kendall. And though Aunt Dorothy, true to Kitty's description of her, had faithfully relayed to the whole party her love of her late husband and the loss she still felt at his passing (et cetera), she had then promptly dispensed with the topic altogether, transitioning swiftly onto the latest *on dits* from the *ton*, a subject far more to Lady Radcliffe's liking. The gossip – passed to Aunt Dorothy from Sally, who seemed to know all the housemaids in London – was fresh enough that Lady Radcliffe was quickly enamoured of her new friend.

It was obvious that Radcliffe had also come prepared for battle. He had invited along his friend, Captain Hinsley, and the role of this gentleman was evidently to be her chaperone, for there was not one move that she could make without the man joining her. The aim was plainly to prevent any kind of romantic moonlight tête-à-tête between herself and Mr de Lacy – an astute strategy, given that Kitty was utterly determined to speak to Mr de Lacy alone by the end of the evening. This farce with Radcliffe had gone on far too long, and it was high time a proposal be induced. If only she could rid herself of her irritating guard.

An opportunity presented itself in the rotunda. As they were listening to the orchestra, a group of impeccably dressed men broke away from their own party to hail Radcliffe loudly. Radcliffe stiffened, clearly not at all pleased, but the men were advancing upon the group, arms out and delight upon their faces.

'Radcliffe! And Hinsley! I didn't know you were in town.'

In the ensuing bevvy of greetings exchanged, Kitty slipped back to stand next to Mr de Lacy. She caught his attention by laying a hand upon his arm.

'Would you escort me to the refreshments, Mr de Lacy?' she asked softly. 'I find myself quite parched.'

Tripping over himself with eagerness, Mr de Lacy rushed to agree – and not a moment too soon, for Kitty saw Captain Hinsley make to catch up with them. He was stalled by Aunt Dorothy, who embroiled him into her conversation with Lady Radcliffe, and Kitty took her chance, slipping out of the rotunda with Mr de Lacy in the opposite direction. They should not be gone more than ten minutes, and they would steer quite clear of the dark paths, or the close walks – or any place indeed that could impinge upon her honour or his. And yet, much could be achieved in ten minutes alone, even in a brightly lit, crowded garden. She waited until they were safely out of earshot before speaking.

'I am most glad to have a chance to speak to you alone, Mr de Lacy,' she said.

'By Jove, so am I,' he said, pressing her hand with his. 'Absolutely marvellous evening, is it not?'

'It is,' she agreed. 'But I was desirous of speaking to you as I am in most serious need of an advisor – and it is only you to whom I can turn.'

'Goodness!' He looked flattered and a little alarmed, for he was not much used to giving advice. 'What can be the matter?'

'My aunt tells me I must marry, and quickly,' Kitty said, trying to convey in her voice a sense of barely repressed despair. 'She has found a Mr Pears for me, who is certainly a good man, and a kind one, but I find it difficult to countenance.'

'By George – why not?' Mr de Lacy was agog.

'You must know, Mr de Lacy . . .' She paused and took a deep breath, as if to muster courage, satisfied to find his eyes fixed unblinkingly upon her face. 'You must know – or I feel you must at least suspect – that my affections lie elsewhere . . .'

She let the statement hang in the air for the moment unattended, staring directly at Mr de Lacy so that he had no means of misinterpreting her words, and had the satisfaction of seeing his face flush a deep pink.

'I own, I had – I had thought perhaps that was it,' he breathed.

'And so you see I am in quite the predicament,' she went on. 'Do I have the courage to refuse Mr Pears, when it is true that I do need to marry, in order to support my sisters? I have already confessed to you, Mr de Lacy, that the state of my father's finances do indeed make marriage most essential. And yet to act against my heart . . .'

She would have liked her eyes to glisten with unshed tears, but alas, they remained bone dry.

'Miss Talbot,' Mr de Lacy said fervently. 'Miss Talbot, what if – what if you were to marry *me*?'

She gasped dramatically at this most shocking turn of events.

'Mr de Lacy,' Kitty said. 'Do you truly mean it?'

'I-I think I do,' he stammered. 'In fact – I'm sure of it! You can't be going around marrying people called Pear, it isn't at all the thing. You must . . . you must know, that I feel very deeply for you? Why, I have loved you for years, Miss Talbot!'

Kitty did not feel the need to remind him that they had only known each other for weeks. She pressed her hand upon his, with feeling.

'I am quite overcome,' she breathed. 'Oh, you have made me most happy, Mr de Lacy.'

'Please,' he entreated, 'call me Archie.'

'Archie. You must then do me the honour of calling me Kitty. But—'

'But?' he asked, anxious.

'Oh Archie, I do feel we must be certain of your family's approval. It does not feel right to make such a step without it.'

'Of course, you are right!' Archie hastened to agree. 'Terribly improper of me, in fact – I should have spoken to my brother before – don't know why I haven't yet, I did mean to.'

'Then we are in perfect agreement – as always.'

They smiled at each other – he, breathless with excitement, she with exultation. She had almost done it. She could feel victory within her grasp.

* * *

'I couldn't stop it, James, her aunt had me absolutely trapped,' Captain Hinsley was saying at that moment to Radcliffe, who had a polite smile fixed upon his face. 'But there they are! They can't have been gone more than ten minutes. Nothing to worry about.'

Hinsley, thought Radcliffe darkly, had clearly not spent long enough in Miss Talbot's company.

'My dears, we were just beginning to worry about you,' Lady Radcliffe called in greeting as Mr de Lacy and Miss Talbot approached.

'I'm sorry, Mother, I was just escorting Kit— Miss Talbot, to procure some lemonade.'

A lesser man might have paled, but Radcliffe gave no discernible reaction to Archie's slip of the tongue. His mother, equally well-bred, only widened her eyes a very slight amount, while Mrs Kendall had to look down to hide her smile. In their ten minutes alone, Archie had clearly been invited to use Miss Talbot's first name. Fast work indeed. They must be separated again – at once.

'Shall we dine?' Radcliffe suggested loudly to the group, and Hinsley appeared immediately at Miss Talbot's side to offer her his arm. She took it gamely enough – the offensive ground ceded, for the moment – and the group made off toward the supper-boxes. Radcliffe had just enough time to breathe a sigh of relief before Archie appeared at his left side, jaw jutting out determinedly.

'I need to talk to you, James. About K— Miss Talbot. It's terribly important, we must speak.'

Oh Lord. 'Yes of course, old boy,' Radcliffe said reassuringly. 'But perhaps this is not quite the right location for a proper conversation — and from tomorrow I am away for a few days — can it wait a little?'

Archie rolled this around in his mind. 'I suppose,' he said at last. He fixed his brother with a stern look. 'But I shan't forget.'

Aunt Dorothy held her character through dinner, through the performances, through the carriage ride home — but as soon as they stepped over the threshold of Wimpole Street, she could not hold her tongue a second longer.

'Is it done?' she said. 'Are you engaged?'

'Not quite,' Kitty answered, pulling at the buttons of her cloak. 'But he did propose.'

Aunt Dorothy clapped her hands.

'Did you accept?' Cecily demanded. 'Can we go home now?'

'Almost,' her sister promised. 'I could not accept until he has his family's approval — it would not be safe otherwise. I invited him to propose again once he has it.'

Her aunt nodded approvingly. 'Quite so. I should not think the mother will object, if he's insistent enough.' She paused thoughtfully. 'But you were right to be careful about the brother. Very watchful eyes, he has — and not at all pleased with you.'

'There is not much he can do about it now, anyhow,' Kitty said carelessly. Throwing herself into an armchair, she hoisted one leg over the arm and sank her body into it with most unladylike dishevelment. 'It would take a miracle indeed to force Archie to go back on his word. A few days more and I will have caught our fortune good and proper.'

Cecily let out a small, judgemental sniff. 'I am not sure I like the way you both speak of him. Like he's a — a fox you're hunting.'

Kitty was too pleased to be cross. 'Cecy, we both know very well how much you will enjoy being rich. Think of the books!'

This appeal to Cecily's intellectual self was felt to be less morally repugnant than previous arguments, and Cecily unbent enough to smile at the thought.

'Besides,' Kitty said, 'all men of his sort are destined for loveless marriages of convenience, anyway. And if some woman is going to enjoy his fortune, why shouldn't it be us?'

Kitty's grin was all triumph. She could not suppose anyone in the world had ever felt as relieved as she did now. She had done it. Mr de Lacy – *Archie* – had proposed to her. No one could take that away from her – not even Lord Radcliffe.

12

Over the next two days it was clear. Radcliffe had, indeed, capitulated. Mr de Lacy and Lady Amelia had resumed joining the Talbot sisters for their daily walks without the expected chaperonage of their elder brother – although with enough attendants that any intimacies beyond the exchange of coy glances and secretive smiles were impossible. There had been no retaliation, no attempts to force Archie and Kitty apart again, no word from Radcliffe at all, in fact. Kitty had won – well, almost. Archie had yet to formally speak to either his brother or mother regarding their betrothal – both having reportedly left London for the weekend – but he had vowed, passionately and at length, to secure both their approvals when they returned.

Kitty was in the midst of writing a second letter to Beatrice that Sunday – to reassure them that all was in hand, and that she had received a proposal – when Sally entered and informed her that Lord Radcliffe was waiting below.

'Are you quite sure?' Kitty asked, wrong-footed, but Sally

merely demanded whether he was to be shown in or not. Kitty stammered out her assent and then, chastising herself for her nerves, stood and ran a hand through curls that were in a little less than their usual order.

Radcliffe looked rather out of place in their parlour, which suddenly appeared narrower, the ceiling lower, in the face of his presence. From the way his eyes lingered on the furniture – so expensive to Kitty's eyes when she had first arrived, and yet so dingy compared to that of Grosvenor Square – he knew it too.

'Good afternoon, Miss Talbot. Please do excuse my incivility in appearing without an invitation.'

Miss Talbot was gracious enough to grant the excuse.

'How may I help you, my lord?' she asked, with equal politeness, gesturing for him to be seated. 'Are your family quite well?'

'Yes, very well. A state in which I plan to keep them.' At this he looked at her very directly in the eye and let a silence fall. They both maintained this, each waiting for the other to break it – and Kitty was grimly satisfied when it was he, not she, that spoke first.

'Miss Talbot, I'm afraid I must now draw your acquaintance with my family to a close. Forgive me for speaking plainly, but I will not allow you to bamboozle Archie into marrying you, for no greater reason than your avarice.'

There was something about the way he spoke, with such soft contempt, that was more powerful than had he shouted at her. Kitty felt her neck grow hot. She wondered if she should protest that he had her all wrong, that she loved Archie, but something about his cool gaze told her that this would be quite useless.

Instead, she let the curtain fall, observing him as calmly as he was observing her. Two gazes of assessing calculation meeting honestly at last.

'I see. And may I ask, my lord, if the only reason you protest to such a marriage is that you think me a fortune-hunter?'

He made an eloquent gesture with his hands. 'Forgive me, do I need more of a reason than that?'

'Yes, I rather think you might – I am not sure why my practicality is so abhorrent to you.'

'Practicality?' he repeated. 'You would call it that, rather than calculation – greed – manipulation? I'm afraid it is these far less honourable words that I would use to describe you, Miss Talbot.'

'Only the rich have the luxury of honour,' she said coldly. 'And only men have the privilege of seeking their fortune on their own. I have four sisters who depend on me, and the professions open to women such as I – governess, seamstress perhaps – will not keep even half of them fed and clothed. What else am I to do but seek a rich husband?'

'You are heartless,' he accused.

'And you are naïve,' she returned, her colour high. 'If Archie is not to marry me, he will marry whichever well-connected young woman who is thrown in his way – all of them caring as much for his purse as his heart. Can you deny that?'

'But at least that would be his choice,' he snapped back. 'Rather than marrying a lie.'

'What lie? I have not pretended to be anyone I am not. He knows I am not wealthy; he knows my family situation. I have been honest.'

'Honest?' he drawled, contempt in his voice.

'Yes,' she said.

'So then, am I to believe he knows the whole truth about your family?' he asked pointedly.

'I am not sure what you mean, my lord,' she said slowly, though she was quite frozen in her seat.

'I think you do,' he said. 'You see, I know the reason your parents left London for Dorsetshire so very suddenly.'

Kitty clamped her jaw shut, lest she give anything away. He could be bluffing – he must be bluffing.

'If you are to blackmail me, my lord, then I must ask you to actually say the words,' she bit out.

'Very well then.' He inclined his head in mock courtesy. 'Your parents were . . . acquainted before their marriage, were they not? In fact, your mother made quite a lucrative career out of being . . . acquainted with several gentlemen, I am told. As did your "Mrs Kendall".'

Kitty did not speak. She was not even sure she was breathing, though her heart was beating loudly in her ears.

'And when your father decided to marry his mistress,' Radcliffe went on, in that same soft voice, 'his family would not approve of the match – understandable, I suppose – and banished him from London to avoid the scandal. Quite the fall from grace for him, I should imagine.'

A silence fell in the aftermath of these words.

'May I ask, my lord,' Kitty refused to allow her voice to tremble, 'how you came to develop this delightful little theory?'

His eyes were bright with triumph. 'My tiger, Lawrence – useful chap, does far more for me than just holding the horses – heard the whole from your Mr Linfield's manservant a few days ago. Did you know that was why Mr Linfield broke off your engagement so suddenly? I'm afraid your father confessed the whole to the Squire while deep in his cups one night shortly before his death. After such a revelation, the Linfields could not countenance the marriage.'

Kitty jerked her head in a forceful shake, even as the words rang horribly true. So that was why she had lost Mr Linfield, why his parents had thrown Miss Spencer in his path so hastily – because Papa had revealed the family secret, after all their years of keeping it safely hidden. She felt a hot rush of despairing rage – at her father, at Radcliffe, at the whole world for landing her in this mess.

Radcliffe took a pinch of snuff with a graceful twist of his wrist, and the casualness of this action – when she was suffering from such a shock – so infuriated Kitty that it quite crystallised her thoughts.

'And what exactly,' she asked coolly, marshalling herself once more, 'is the relevance of my mother's background to this discussion?'

Radcliffe raised a single brow. 'I find it hugely relevant,' he said calmly. 'I do not imagine – honest though you may have been about your family's financial destitution – that you have divulged the scandalous details of your parentage to Archie. And Archie, kind-hearted though he is, would not take such a revelation warmly. A love affair is exciting, to be sure, but Archie has been raised with an admirable dislike of scandal. And should the news spread, you will not find this city a welcoming place.'

Kitty clenched trembling fingers into a fist. 'And I suppose in order for the news not to spread, you would have me leave London?' she asked bluntly.

'Oh, I am not so heartless as that.' He shut his snuffbox with a decisive snap, as if readying himself to leave, the deal done. 'You may decide for yourself where you go, and when. You may even attempt to seduce another member of the *ton* – it matters not to me,' he said carelessly. 'But I would ask that you leave Archie, and my family, alone.'

Silence again. Kitty supposed he could have been more ruthless in his victory, more vindictive. Were she in his shoes, she would have seen him off on the morning post personally.

But then again, was it so kind? The London Season was about to begin in earnest, and without any proper connections, Kitty could only exist on its peripheries, where the very wealthy did not frequent. Pointless. And with limited funds, expensive. She would instead have to commit herself to one of Aunt Dorothy's original choices for her. Two thousand pounds a year was not to be sniffed at, after all . . . She thought of the easy way the de Lacys treated their wealth. As if it were barely worth their consideration – simply a fact of life, much like the air they breathed. What she wouldn't give, for her sisters to have the same security . . .

'Do we have an understanding, Miss Talbot?' Radcliffe drew her attention back to him. His tone was not unkind, now. Did some part of him feel a measure of sympathy for the loss he could see in her eyes?

'An understanding,' she said slowly, pausing over each syllable. 'Yes, I think so. I understand that you feel you need to expose me to be rid of me. And I also understand that, in response, I will take Archie to Gretna Green to be married there. I feel it is safe to assume, given the affection you bear him, that upon our marriage you would do your best to hush up the scandal of our elopement.'

Radcliffe, famed for his poise and calm on even the bloodiest of battlefields, felt his jaw drop.

'Gretna Green?' he repeated, foolishly.

'I own the thought of travelling such a long way on a Sunday to be rather daunting – but if it is truly necessary, I imagine I will be up to the task. After all, needs must.'

Radcliffe found himself gaping at her incredulously.

'Needs must,' he echoed faintly. He stared at her, seated so primly upon her seat, a vision of elegance masking an evil soul.

'Miss Talbot,' he began again, over-emphasising the 't's as if resisting the desire to spit it at her. 'I have never in my life encountered a woman so lacking in female delicacy as yourself. I cannot fathom how you have the gall to sit there threatening my brother's virtue like some . . . some two-penny theatre villain!'

'Two-penny?' she repeated, a little hurt. 'I must say that feels awfully unkind.'

He stared at her, helpless, before – all at once – dissolving into laughter. She stared at him warily. Was he having a nervous breakdown, perhaps? His family was inclined to sickliness, after all.

'Would you like some tea?' she offered cautiously, this seeming the only recourse open to her. He let out another bark of laughter.

'That would be simply marvellous, Miss Talbot,' he replied, with a courteous bow of his head. She went out of the room to call for Sally, and in a few moments returned – Sally carrying a tray, and Miss Talbot following behind with cups. He watched her pour, the echo of his laugh still upon his lips.

'I seem to have underestimated you once again,' he commented matter-of-factly, as Sally closed the door behind her. 'And so, we find ourselves at an impasse. I cannot allow you to marry my brother. I am willing to do whatever it takes to keep him from you, but I should like to avoid an unpleasant scene on the road to Scotland.'

'I have no other alternative,' she said simply and without embarrassment. 'I would make him a good wife,' she added cajolingly, looking up at him through her eyelashes. For a beat, he appreciated how easily she must have ensnared Archie.

'Doing it a little too brown,' he said mockingly, and the coy look was replaced with a scowl. 'Surely you must be able to find yourself another rich young man to target?' he pressed, wondering what it said about him that he was willing to sacrifice any other man in London, to rid his family of this cursed woman.

'You say that as if it's easy. The hallowed halls you walk in are impenetrable, my lord. I only met Archie by chance, and I don't suppose another such opportunity will simply fall into my lap. For it to be worth me giving Archie up . . . I would need introductions. Invitations. Patronage, for want of a better word.'

'And you imagine that I might be able to achieve such a thing?' he asked curiously.

'Lord Radcliffe, I am under no illusions about your standing in society,' she kept her voice reasonable. 'Nor what you are able to achieve given the right motivation. I'm sure it would be well within your talents to establish me firmly enough within society that I might do the rest.'

Radcliffe could not believe he was even countenancing this conversation.

'You would have me as your accomplice in fortune-hunting?' he asked, disbelieving.

She gave a sharp nod. 'Yes. Or else your blessing to mine and Archie's engagement.'

'This is madness,' he said, trying to appeal to her sense of reason.

'Think on it by all means, my lord.' She shrugged again, though inside she was holding her breath. 'I can assure you my threat was not an empty one. I will not fail my family.'

Lord Radcliffe sat back in his chair, unsettled. Propriety and good sense dictated, of course, that he should refuse this offer categorically. It was not proper, nor right – nor even truly necessary. If he acted quickly enough, he could prevent her villainous threat from being carried out. He could whisper into his mother's ear all that he had discovered, whisk Archie away to the country and thus inoculate his family against this infectious Miss Talbot. Yet he could not be sure, exactly, what havoc this unscrupulous woman might wreak in retaliation. The de Lacy name and standing would not easily be stained – but was he willing to risk it, when he had so far underestimated her at each and every turn?

Would it be so bad to agree? At least by her method, he might more easily monitor the outcome. And . . . he imagined, for a moment, Miss Talbot rampaging through polite society, and its starched stuffy gatekeepers – except this time, with his family safely out of harm's way. It was not an unappealing vision. What chaos might she cause? How might she disrupt the agendas of all the managing mamas who had so doggedly followed in his footsteps since his twenty-first birthday? It would certainly put them all in their place to have one of their precious sons snatched out from under them by such a viper. And were she to succeed or fail, Archie would regardless have his eyes opened to her true nature.

Kitty let him ponder in silence for a moment, then spoke softly to him – as the snake might have spoken to Eve, he thought.

'Your mother is holding a dinner party next week – to which she has invited the most illustrious lords and ladies of her acquaintance. Persuade her to invite me, and I will most surely secure an invitation to the first balls of the Season.'

'Is that all?' he said sardonically.

She considered. 'No,' she said – he raised his eyes to heaven to ask for strength – 'at my first ball of the Season, you shall dance with me.'

'An invitation and a dance?' he mused. Another silence. 'This is most irregular,' he told her severely. 'And if it in any way poses harm to my family I shall act without remorse to destroy you.'

'But . . .?' she did not seem fazed by this.

'But I believe we have a deal. I will see to it that you are introduced to polite society. And in return we shall be rid of you for ever.'

She smiled.

He wondered if this was how Faust had felt.

13

After her family and her health, Lady Radcliffe's next most consuming passion was her long-standing social rivalry with Lady Montagu. It was the competitive spirit between these two ladies that had first given birth to Lady Radcliffe's annual dinner party to open the Season: Lady Montagu – also a Countess and having the advantage of two daughters, all older than Amelia – had opened previous London Seasons with sumptuous balls. With Amelia not yet out, Lady Radcliffe could not host her own rival event, but the past two years she had instead hosted an intimate dinner party a few days ahead of the Montagu ball, a night that was no less talked about and enjoyed, for it being a small affair. Indeed, its exclusivity made the invitations all the more precious and it was a *coup d'état* that Lady Radcliffe performed with great relish. The guest list was compiled months in advance of the invitations being issued, to a very select group of fourteen or sixteen persons, the family's dearest friends and their offspring – who all belonged, coincidentally, amongst the very cream of high society.

To ask his mother to make such a late addition to the seating plan, then, was not a task Radcliffe expected to be easy. And indeed, the Countess looked at her son as if he had quite gone mad, when he first suggested that she invite the Misses Talbot and Mrs Kendall.

'Why, it would be not more than a day's notice!' she said at first, quite appalled. 'It would quite throw out the table to have so many ladies in attendance. And besides . . .' she hesitated. 'I am very fond of Mrs Kendall and the Talbots, as you know, but this is always a most . . . exclusive event. Mrs Burrell, in particular is such a stickler . . .'

She trailed off, not liking to put into actual words that Mrs Kendall and the Misses Talbot, as prettily behaved as they were, would not meet Mrs Burrell's standards of gentility. They were untitled, unconnected and unknown, after all.

Radcliffe sighed. Time to take a leaf out of Miss Talbot's manipulative little book.

'The truth is, Mama, that I was hoping to attend the dinner this year, and I thought the addition of the Talbots the easiest way to avoid throwing the table out. I cannot imagine any other members of the *ton* being unoffended by the late invitation.'

Lady Radcliffe's eyes lit up. 'James! Do you mean it? I own I had not expected to ever persuade you to attend – you have said such cruel things about the Montagus and the Sinclairs in the past.'

'Which I regret,' Radcliffe lied. 'If we invited Hinsley, as well as Mrs Kendall and the Misses Talbot, that would make for even enough numbers, would it not?'

Lady Radcliffe considered this for a moment. It was not ideal, of course, to invite three persons who would not add to the evening's consequence, but to have James and Captain Hinsley there would most definitely make up for it. Lady Radcliffe was an astute enough member of society to recognise that James had only accrued glamour in his absence from London. His surprise return would no doubt add something special to the evening. Only one point of contention remained.

'And it does not worry you to have Miss Talbot thrown again into Archie's way?' she asked. 'Since I returned from Richmond, Archie has several times hinted that he means to request your approval to address her formally. If you intend to oppose the match, perhaps it would be unwise—'

'I am no longer concerned on that front,' Radcliffe said reassuringly. There was no need to mention that Archie had attempted such a request twice already – though Radcliffe had thankfully been away from home on both occasions. 'I assure you, Mother, neither Archie nor Miss Talbot's affections are truly attached.'

'Then I shall write to the Talbots this moment!' his mother declared, brow clearing. 'Could Hinsley be persuaded to wear his regimental colours, my dear?'

'A dinner party?' Aunt Dorothy's voice was as scandalised as if Kitty had suggested they tie their garters in public.

'Yes, isn't it marvellous?' Kitty beamed, brandishing the letter. 'Some of the highest lords and ladies will be there – if all goes well, we shall be quite launched onto the Season!'

Mrs Kendall lay a hand upon her forehead. 'Exhausting child,' she said wearily. 'Any time I leave you alone for more than five minutes, you are in the midst of another unwise scheme. We have already been unveiled to Lord Radcliffe – I cannot think this is the right course of action, now.'

'It is,' Kitty said firmly. 'Given that Radcliffe was threatening to tell everyone about Mama, I rather think I should be commended for how I turned it around.'

'Tell everyone what about Mama?' Cecily piped up from the corner. Kitty jumped slightly – she had quite forgotten about Cecily.

'Oh,' she said breezily. 'Nothing to worry about.'

'I want to know,' Cecily insisted. 'If it is about Mama, I deserve to know, too.'

Kitty sighed, recognising the mulish look on her sister's face, and went over to sit beside her.

'This might come as a shock,' she said, not having time to spin the news delicately. 'But Mama used to – that is, Mama was a – a courtesan. That is how she and Papa met.'

Cecily's jaw dropped. 'What?' she gasped. 'That cannot be true. She was an actress.'

'Yes,' Kitty agreed. 'And also a—'

Cecily clapped her hands to her ears. 'Don't!'

Kitty felt a rush of impatience at her childishness. This was not a productive use of her time, when she had so much to prepare.

'I-I cannot believe it. We loved to speak of the great play-wrights together,' Cecily was stammering. 'Of Shakespeare – a-and Marlowe.'

'Come now,' Kitty said bracingly. 'She is still the same person, Cecily, still our mother. This doesn't mean she didn't like Shakespeare and – and whosit. You are just learning something new about her – at the very least, is it not interesting?'

From the nasty look Cecily shot her, Cecily did not think it was interesting.

'How could you not tell me this?' she demanded.

'Mama thought it would upset you – and clearly she was right!'

'But she told *you*!' Cecily accused. Kitty bit her lip, unsure whether to answer truthfully. The truth was, Mama would never have dreamed of disturbing Cecily with such a confidence. Cecily was the precious dreamer of the family, the intellectual – Mama spoke to Cecily about books and plays, and it was only with Kitty that she had spoken of the past. There had been no secrets between Kitty and her mother: they had discussed frankly their financial difficulties, and shared in schemes of how they might escape them; whereas Cecily had had quite a different relationship with her.

'Kitty, we cannot attend,' Aunt Dorothy spoke over Cecily's spluttering.

Kitty frowned at her. 'Why are you so against this?' she demanded. 'This is an opportunity, Aunt – I have a real chance, here.'

'So did your mother, and look how that turned out!' Aunt Dorothy retorted, shrilly. Both Kitty and Cecily recoiled a little in shock. Aunt Dorothy pressed a trembling hand to her mouth.

'I did not mean that,' she said. 'I am sorry . . . You are so like her, you know. She was just as confident that she could have it all – love and marriage and money altogether. But when you get involved with the *ton*, nothing is that simple, and everything can be taken out of your hands all at once. She was sent away and I never saw her again.'

The room fell silent. They had never seen Aunt Dorothy lose her composure like this before.

'The difference is,' Kitty said, 'that I won't be falling in love with anyone.'

'I am not sure that helps.' Aunt Dorothy cast her hands up in frustration. 'It is a most unwise plan. None of us has the faintest idea of how to behave at such an event.'

'I thought *you* might,' Kitty admitted. 'You have socialised with gentlemen before.'

'Not in front of their *wives*,' Aunt Dorothy stressed. 'This is as new to me as it would be to you. There are all sorts of rules that govern these events about which we don't have the faintest idea – and have you thought what might happen if a gentleman in attendance recognises me?'

'It has been ten years,' Kitty pointed out dubiously.

'Ten years that I am reliably informed have been very kind to me,' Aunt Dorothy told her severely. 'It is just as well my hair is black now, not red – there is a reason I avoid these sorts of people, Kitty. And as for you, you look the spitting image of your mother! You had best write back to Lady Radcliffe and let her know we cannot attend.'

'And give up?' Kitty raised her chin in defiance. 'No, I shall find out all we need to know – we are going to that dinner party!'

True to her word, Kitty gamely set out that afternoon on an information-gathering expedition. Her destination, Cecily in tow, was the library, for Cecily had often spoken of the conduct books they were given at the Seminary, which taught them of maidenly virtues. Kitty was to be disappointed, however. To her disgust, even the most academic of these volumes held only the barest and most useless of instructions. How was such nonsense as 'have a sacred regard to truth' and 'possess dignity without pride' to help her at a dinner party? They left empty-handed, and Kitty avoided Aunt Dorothy's eye that evening.

By mutual agreement, they did not speak upon the subject again that night, all retiring to bed early, though Kitty did not sleep. She had grown used, in the days since arriving in London, to the semi-constant noise the city made, but she was not yet fully comfortable with how much sound still filtered in through the window even in darkness. At home, at Netley, when either she or Beatrice couldn't sleep, they would whisper confidences to each other under the covers, sharing their secrets and fears until they belonged more to each other than to just one alone. And while there were some secrets Kitty had not told Beatrice – the true extent of their debts and the full story of their parents' courtship had been burdens she alone had carried – she had grown very used to being able to lean on Beatrice in her uncertain moments. Especially in the years since their mother had passed when Kitty had felt so desperately lonely, to have Beatrice there had been the greatest reassurance she could have asked for.

And now she was without it.

'Cecy?' Kitty whispered into the dark. But a soft snore told her that Cecy was already fast asleep.

Kitty wished she had thought to speak to her father about the etiquette of the beau monde while he was alive. There had been so many chances to do so – but how could she have known how important the knowledge would become? One of the worst things about losing one's parents, for Kitty, had not come in the first few, raw and shocking days of grief. It had come later: it sneaked up on her daily in the frequent instances where she thought of a question to ask them – something she might have always vaguely wondered, but never thought to voice, something inane or something important – only to realise a second later that, of course, they were no longer there to ask. And now more than ever, Kitty would have traded almost anything to ask either one of her parents the questions now circling her mind. To ask Papa about high society – yes, that was one – but also to ask whether she was even doing the right thing at all. Should she listen to Aunt Dorothy, or trust her own instincts? Would they be all right? Lord, to be told everything would all right again, to have the comforting press of a parental hand upon her brow just once more.

Cecily let out a hiccough in the darkness, and Kitty shook her head, clearing it. What she actually needed – practically speaking – was to speak to someone who knew this world like the back of their hand, who knew all the little rules and rituals she would not recognise. Someone who would know exactly how the insiders identified outsiders and – crucially – someone she could speak honestly with, without fear of what her ignorance might reveal to them. It was not until the purple sky had faded to ink black that Kitty admitted to herself that there was really only one person she could speak to.

Lord Radcliffe's butler, Beaverton, was surprised to open the front door of Radcliffe's town house upon St James's Place at 10 o'clock the following morning, to find Miss Talbot and a housemaid staring expectantly up at him from the top step. The proper response to this irregular occurrence was, no doubt, to inform the ladies that his lordship was not receiving visitors and send them on their way. Except, without quite knowing how it was brought about, Beaverton found himself instead delivering the ladies into the library and heading upstairs to break the news to Lord Radcliffe.

'Miss Talbot?' Radcliffe asked incredulously from the depths of his darkened bedchamber. 'Here? *Now?* What the devil . . .?'

He extricated himself with difficulty and arrived in the library not fifteen minutes later, somewhat more dishevelled than he would normally like to present himself to visitors. He stood in the doorway, staring blankly at Miss Talbot. Incomprehensible though it seemed, she was indeed here now.

'Miss Talbot,' he said at last, without bowing. When he said nothing else, Miss Talbot perceived that while he had risen, his manners had not.

'Perhaps we could take some refreshment?' she suggested, feeling that he was in need of some guidance. Radcliffe pressed his lips together, but directed his manservant accordingly and invited her to sit down.

'I was not expecting your call, Miss Talbot,' he ventured, recovering some equilibrium. 'It is also rather earlier than I would expect to receive any call, even expected ones.'

She looked at him in surprise. 'But it is past ten already!' she objected. 'Were you not already awake?'

'Never mind,' he said, with great forbearance. 'Why have you come? I am sure I cannot think we have anything further to discuss, given you no doubt received my mother's invitation yesterday. Unless you wish to renege on our deal . . .?'

'Oh, not at all.' She waved a hand dismissively. 'I mean to keep to my end – you need not worry, Archie is in no danger from me any more. But I should like to ask you some questions.'

He cut his eyes to where Sally was perched on a chair by the door, then back to Kitty – a question. She waved him off again. 'Oh, Sally knows the full, don't worry. She won't breathe a word of it.'

'Indeed,' he said. 'You will forgive me if I do not share your confidence. Perhaps she could await us in the hall. Unless you fear I might have designs upon your person?'

He added this with a touch of irony that suggested the idea was ridiculous; she tried not to feel offended. Once the door had closed behind Sally, some of Radcliffe's hauteur left him.

'I had rather thought that I had upheld my side of the bargain,' he said briskly. 'To see to your introduction and then for you to take it from there.'

'Surely you didn't think it as simple as all that?' she said critically, quite forgetting that she, also, had thought it as simple as all that before Aunt Dorothy had informed her otherwise.

'Pray forgive me, but – yes.'

'There is much I need to know about Lady Radcliffe's event, much that could go wrong, you know.'

'There is?' he said, thinking longingly of his bed.

'Yes indeed. Your mother deemed me an outsider within seconds of our meeting. I must ensure that does not happen again.'

'And your first thought was to ask me for help?' he asked, incredulously. 'Yesterday, each of us tried to blackmail the other.'

'My first thought,' she corrected, 'was to try the library – but I might as well have read the Bible for all the good those silly etiquette books did me. Besides, it is not so strange for me to ask you. I should imagine you would like me to be successful. We do have a deal, you know.'

'A deal I regret making more with each passing moment,' Radcliffe said, rubbing his hands over his face and wishing that he had thought to ask for coffee, not tea.

Kitty ignored this. 'Who shall be in attendance this evening?' she asked.

'The Lady Montagu, her son Lord Montagu, her two daughters,' he listed through his hands. 'Lord and Lady Salisbury, Mr and Mrs Burrell, Mr and Mrs Sinclair, their son Gerald, Mr Holbrook and Captain Hinsley, who you have met already.'

She nodded, committing the list to memory to relay to Aunt Dorothy later.

'When I am introduced to Lady Montagu, how deeply should I curtsey?'

He stared silently for a few moments. 'Medium,' he said at last, hoping this would be the end of it. She stood up.

'Will you show me?' she asked.

'Show you?'

'Yes, will you please demonstrate the appropriate level to curtsey in front of a countess? Clearly, when I first greeted your mother, I did not do it correctly.'

'But I am not a woman,' he pointed out.

'Yet you have seen them curtsey often enough, have you not?' She waved an impatient hand at him.

Had it perhaps been later in the day, had he been prepared for her visit in the slightest, he might have refused. But he was unprepared, and it was very early, so in the face of such insistent instruction, it seemed altogether easier to obey. He stood and did a passable imitation of a curtsey before a countess. Miss Talbot eyed him critically – it was far shallower than she would have thought – then copied before him.

'Does it change, for Lord and Lady Salisbury?'

'Yes, for he is a marquess and she a marchioness – just so.'

He demonstrated again, and then once more, for the Sinclairs and the Burrells, mere misters.

When she was satisfied that she had committed it perfectly to memory, Miss Talbot seated herself once more.

'And what will happen?' she enquired next. 'Are we seated immediately? What sort of things will we eat? Should I sit somewhere in particular? What do you talk about, and what does one wear?'

Miss Talbot was able to extract a veritable treasure trove of information from Lord Radcliffe before his mind awoke fully and he began to object to her presence in his home, so that by the time he commanded her to 'leave now and never return', she was quite happy to do so.

He delivered her personally to the doorstep – grimly suspicious that she might otherwise never go – and bade her a curt good day that she returned with far too much good cheer.

'And little though you may care,' he added severely before he shut the door, 'in polite society, it is considered highly inappropriate for an unmarried woman to be seen visiting an unmarried man's house, maid or no maid.'

She gave an extravagant roll of her eyes. 'Dear lord, city dwellers are so easily scandalised. Do you think it's the lack of fresh air?'

Radcliffe slammed the door after her violently, but Kitty skipped down the steps with Sally quite happily. She had discovered, she felt, all she needed to make a famous splash upon society. She felt prepared enough for anything.

14

'One is never quite sure what to wear at evenings such as this. I do hope Lady Montagu isn't overdressed,' Lady Radcliffe said gleefully, as they stood in the drawing room awaiting their guests. Radcliffe suppressed a smile. It was quite clear that his mother should like nothing better than for Lady Montagu to commit such a faux pas.

As the clock struck seven, the first of the guests began to arrive, and as Radcliffe bowed and murmured greetings to each of them, he was aware of feeling apprehensive waiting for the Talbots to arrive.

'Mrs Kendall, Miss Talbot, Miss Cecily Talbot!' Pattson announced, and the three ladies entered. They were dressed quite charmingly in the latest style: Mrs Kendall in soft mauve, and Miss Talbot and Miss Cecily in the same white gowns they had worn to Vauxhall Gardens – though with shawls of silver gauze added to make the outfits appear new.

'Good evening, Miss Talbot,' Radcliffe said courteously, as Mrs Kendall was greeted by his mother, and Miss Cecily by Amelia.

She inclined her head, saying in an undertone. 'Any more regrets?'

'Oh, many,' he assured her.

She smiled. 'And do you have any eligible suitors for me this evening?' she asked, roguishly.

'Alas, very few, but as you were the one who deemed this event so essential to you, I am afraid this is your error, rather than mine.'

'You must say if you feel yourself unequal to the task,' she said, unable to resist needling him.

'Perhaps I ought to compile a suitable list,' he said thoughtfully, 'of gentlemen rich enough to satisfy you and yet so lacking in moral character that I feel no guilt about unleashing you upon them.'

She cut him a withering look. 'How kind,' she said, moving past him towards Lady Radcliffe.

'Miss Talbot, you look wonderful! That brooch – divine! You must tell me its maker.' This last was a rhetorical question, it appeared, as she immediately said in confidential undertone, 'Lady Montagu is almost late now, I am beside myself with anger. It is very rude – she has no respect for me, it is quite clear.'

'The Right Honourable the Earl of Montagu, the Most Honourable Countess of Montagu, the Lady Margaret Cavendish and the Lady Jane Cavendish,' Pattson announced impressively from the doorway.

'My dears!' Lady Radcliffe called joyfully, arms outstretched in welcome. The ladies greeted each other with almost ludicrous warmth.

'Come, you simply must meet Mrs Kendall and her nieces, the

Misses Talbot, new friends of the family. Lady Montagu is a close friend of mine, and this is her son Lord Montagu – he and Archie are practically brothers. Lady Montagu, it is Miss Talbot who has been so wonderfully helpful with my most recent *malaise*.'

Kitty and Cecily curtseyed before her. 'I have heard much about you all,' Lady Montagu said, with a smiling mouth but assessing eyes.

Kitty took a deep breath in, willing herself to keep calm. It was essential that they leave this evening having ingratiated themselves with each lady present. London might be a man's world, but it was these women who held its keys – it was they who would issue the invitations, spread the gossip and deliver the setdowns that could make or break her.

'Talbot?' Lady Montagu asked now. 'Any relation of the Paris Talbots?'

Yes, thought Kitty, though that was not an association she would like broadcast, in case anyone made the connection to the scandal of her parents.

'No,' she lied calmly. 'We hail from Dorsetshire.'

'Oh, then you must already know the Salisburys?'

'We have not yet been introduced,' Kitty admitted.

'Oh,' Lady Montagu's eyes flickered over her shoulder, as if immediately losing a little interest. 'The Digbys then? Glorious estate, isn't it? My daughters summered there last year.'

'We have not been,' Kitty said, shaking her head. 'Though I do hear it is lovely.'

Lady Montagu looked disappointed, again, and turned instead to Aunt Dorothy.

'And . . . Mrs Kendall, wasn't it?'

Even to Kitty's ears, 'Kendall' sounded a little common. She wished they could have changed it, but it was far too late now. Aunt Dorothy behaved splendidly, telling an amusing anecdote about how she had met her deceased – and fictional – husband, but Lady Montagu was plainly not listening. Having revealed how damningly unconnected they were, Lady Montagu had clearly deemed them as useless to her and was desperate to move on to more fruitful ground.

To Kitty's dismay, this was to be the blueprint for all their introductions: the whole company shared a need, it seemed, to place the Talbots and Mrs Kendall within their social geography, and they were quite baffled when they could not. The Talbots looked and acted like well-born young ladies of quality, and yet they did not know a single person that they should. As they continued to deny their acquaintance of a single high-society family in the whole of the West Country, the hauteur of the assembled guests began to rise. This was a smaller world than Kitty had realised, and one must be categorised within it to be accepted. The saving grace of their situation was that the other guests were all too distracted by Lord Radcliffe's presence to interrogate her properly. Radcliffe was clearly a glamorous figure to them – titled, wealthy and unmarried, yes, but also rarely seen in polite society since his time on the Continent. Serving as attaché to Wellington and then fighting at Waterloo, though his role was only intended to be diplomatic in nature – it was the kind of story that rarely involved first sons, and the relentlessly hierarchical *ton* found it all the more scintillating for it.

Whenever Radcliffe spoke, the whole room quietened a little, as if hoping he might be about to tell a tale of derring-do about the war. He never did, and Kitty was relieved when Lady

Radcliffe announced dinner would be served. Lady Radcliffe had not seated Kitty beside Mr de Lacy, for which Kitty was thankful – given her recent promise to leave Mr de Lacy alone, she had been avoiding his eye all evening – and instead she had Mr Sinclair on her left, and Captain Hinsley on her right.

As they arranged themselves, Hinsley sent her a wink, which she returned with a frosty stare, not having forgiven him for his part in obstructing her pursuit of Mr de Lacy. The first course was served, and despite her nerves, Kitty took a moment to marvel at the dishes as they were offered to her by Mr Hinsley and Sinclair. The quantity alone was impressive: four tureens of artichoke soup sat at the corners of the table, and between them were plates of butter-soaked turbot, a loin of veal, and upwards of twenty side dishes beside – all dressed in sauces Kitty could not name. It was a far cry from the vegetable pudding and larded sweetbreads they had eaten on their last night at Netley.

Radcliffe had said that ladies must first speak to the gentleman on their left, and so she turned to Mr Sinclair, sending him a tremulous smile and hoping he would be an easier conversational partner than his wife – who could not for the life of her understand why Kitty did not know the Beaufort family, and would not let the matter drop. But alas, though Mr Sinclair was good-humoured, he was not so good-humoured as to spare Kitty the usual interrogation.

'Biddington? Ah, I know the area well!' he said. 'You must know Ducky, of course.'

'Ducky'? Had she heard correctly? It had certainly sounded like Ducky. She stared at him blankly. Was Ducky a place? A literal duck that was for some reason famous in these circles?

Her palms grew a little moist as she wondered what the safest response might be, and Mr Sinclair's face became increasingly confused at her silence.

'Lord Mallard,' he clarified at last, when it became clear Kitty was going to say nothing.

'Oh,' she said faintly. A nickname, then. 'No, I am afraid I do not.'

Mr Sinclair's brow furrowed. 'You must,' he insisted. 'He has a hunting lodge in the area, I am sure.'

Kitty could not bear it. She decided to take a calculated risk. It was not enough simply to evade these questions without an explanation, she needed to supply a reason for their obscurity if they had a chance of making it through the evening.

'The truth is, sir,' she said, throwing caution to the wind. 'I do not know a single person in London, other than my aunt and the de Lacy family. You see, my father kept us entirely secluded from society – he was quite terrified that we might be led astray, so we never left our town.'

'Is that so?' Mr Sinclair appeared intrigued by this. 'Eccentric fellow, was he?'

'Very. I must confess my sister and I know very little about the world, so you must forgive my missishness – I am quite terrified of saying the wrong thing!'

'Why, you must be the greenest girls in all of London,' Mr Sinclair declared. He observed Miss Talbot for a moment under his heavy brows, before deciding to find this charming.

'There is no need to be the slightest bit nervous,' he reassured her, gesturing to the room. 'Why, this is the friendliest collection of people in the whole city! You can trust us to look after you.'

Mr Sinclair's self-appointed trustworthiness did not prevent him – once the first course was cleared away and they both turned to their other seating partner – from passing the news of the Talbot sisters' unusual upbringing straight on to Lady Salisbury, who at the earliest convenience passed it on, too. Murmurs of interest greeted the news and by the time the second course (larger still than the first, with a goose, lobster and guinea fowl amongst the plates) had concluded, the Talbots were looked upon as something of a novelty. The hauteur began to lessen. The assembled lords, ladies and the *ton* began to wonder if Lady Radcliffe was not a most discerning host for having discovered such charming oddities as these young ladies. Glancing across the table, Kitty caught Aunt Dorothy's eye and they shared a small smile of relief. Glancing down, she was pleasantly surprised to see Cecily on lively form. She seemed to be giving the young Lord Montagu a long education in Sapphic philosophy, greatly enjoying herself – as people so often do, when allowed to speak at length about their own intellect. Kitty inwardly thanked the manners of the young man in continuing his attention when he must surely be terribly bored.

The *ton* were not so different from normal people, and Kitty was able to observe now that she did not feel quite so under siege. Yes, they spoke in voices like cut glass, and yes, they took politeness to ritualistic levels, and the jargon was, admittedly, utterly incomprehensible – all about Eton and governesses and London, nicknames for lords and ladies you should know, but that you must not use unless you knew them too. But they ate, like everyone else, and gossiped like fiends – though it was dressed up in ribbons and bows of concern and sympathy to make it more polite.

'Ghastly news about the Egerton boy, isn't it?' Mrs Burrell

was saying in an undertone that nevertheless carried around the whole table.

'What happened?' Mrs Sinclair asked, her face concerned, her eyes bright.

'Lost an absolute fortune at cards, the wretched creature, the whole family is up in arms,' Lady Montagu said, shaking her head sadly. 'They've had to sell a hundred acres of land to pay for it.'

'And it couldn't have happened to a better family.' Lady Radcliffe looked a little ill at the news. 'He was at Waterloo, wasn't he, Radcliffe?'

As soon as the words escaped her lips, Lady Radcliffe appeared to regret them. The whole party quieted immediately, staring at Lord Radcliffe, who gave only a vague murmur in response. When it was clear he was not going to indulge them with a story, Lady Salisbury made the plunge.

'My Lord Radcliffe,' she called across to him. 'You must tell us of Waterloo. We are dying to hear your account of it.'

'Radcliffe is rather bored by talking about the war now,' his mother interjected quickly.

'Oh, I'm sure he can indulge us, this once,' Lady Salisbury insisted. 'Can't you, Radcliffe? If we ask nicely?'

'What would you like to know, my lady?' Radcliffe said coolly.

'What was it like?' She leant forward eagerly.

'Awful,' he said, swilling his glass of wine in one hand. His voice was casual, but Miss Talbot fancied she could hear a warning within it – and by the tense look on both Lady Radcliffe and Captain Hinsley's faces, they could too – but Lady Salisbury continued on, quite undaunted.

'It must have been quite the sight,' she said rapturously. 'All the regiments lining up together, the horses, the red coats, the—'

'Death?' Radcliffe supplied, smiling grimly. 'For I confess it is the death I remember most from that day, not the red coats.'

Lady Radcliffe stood abruptly from her chair. 'Shall we retire for tea, ladies?' she sang cheerily, and Kitty abandoned her blancmange with some sadness.

The warm regard with which the Misses Talbot and Mrs Kendall were treated over tea was at utter odds with the earlier chilly reserve of these same ladies. Only Mrs Burrell seemed unmoved by the explanation of their very protective father, while Lady Montagu and Mrs Sinclair – never to be behind on a trend – had decided the Talbot sisters were 'the prettiest behaved creatures' they had ever met. Kitty, for her part, leant more deeply into her character, begging for the ladies' advice on navigating London's social waters. Accustomed as these ladies were to young women desiring to appear accomplished and worldly in their presence, they were refreshed and flattered by so frank an acknowledgement of their lofty societal position. By the time the gentlemen joined them, Kitty had been promised invitations to three balls, all in the next month.

'I think we can count that as a success, can't we?' Kitty whispered to Aunt Dorothy on the carriage ride home.

'Yes.' Aunt Dorothy was looking thoughtful. 'Yes, against all the odds, I think we can.'

She turned to look at her niece, and Kitty wondered if she was going to deliver yet another lecture about the unsuitability, the riskiness, of Kitty's strategy. But her aunt surprised her once again.

'I still think you are quite mad,' she warned her. 'And I still find your relentless perseverance fatiguing. But I must admit, tonight was rather . . . thrilling.' She paused. 'All this to say: I'm *in*, my dear. I shall help you, however I can.'

'Who do you want to marry now?' Cecily interrupted, quite confused. 'It isn't Lord Montagu, is it? The interesting young man I was seated next to at dinner.'

Kitty raised her eyes to the heavens.

'Cecily, I am not so ridiculous to aim at a titled gentleman, especially not one from such a powerful family – do give me some credit.'

'Oh, good,' Cecily said vaguely, her attention fading once more. Content to let the rest of the journey pass in silence, Kitty closed her eyes and let her head fall back upon the seat.

Across town, Radcliffe was walking home – St James's Place being only a short stroll from Grosvenor Square – feeling similarly relieved. Miss Talbot had admittedly played her part very well – he was almost embarrassed on behalf of his set for how easily they had fallen for her wiles in the end.

Almost embarrassed, but not quite. After the grilling Lady Salisbury had given him on Waterloo, he was now very willing to leave them to their fate. And soon, he would be able to wash his hands of the entire affair. He would need to stay in town long enough to give Miss Talbot the dance he owed her, but aside from that there was no need for his further involvement, nor his presence in London. After tonight, he was quite sure that his days spent worrying about Miss Talbot would be over.

15

Miss Talbot's visit to Radcliffe's house the following morning was not exactly spontaneous. That night, Kitty once again found sleep elusive, spending the hours instead in doubt and deliberation. There were a thousand things she did not know about high society – did she really think one night of success meant she could feel at ease? She fell into a troubled doze just before dawn, and by the time the sun had fully risen, it was clear to Kitty that further reconnaissance was absolutely necessary in order to avoid disaster.

Beaverton observed Miss Talbot and Sally upon the front step with dismay, but his reaction was far eclipsed by his master's, who was appalled to learn that this horror was to be visited upon him a second time.

'What now?' he demanded, having slunk reluctantly downstairs to confront the fiend.

'Just a few more questions,' Kitty said, extracting her notebook from her reticule. 'May I begin?'

'Good lord . . .' she heard him murmur faintly.

'At Lady Montagu's ball, which dances are there likely to be?' she asked, head stooped over the book and pen at the ready.

'The cotillion and the quadrille, I imagine, as well as all the usual country dances,' he said, succumbing to the inevitable. 'And the waltz, though I would avoid that until you are established. The sticklers still consider it a little fast.'

Kitty nodded, taking quick notes.

'Is supper provided at private balls, or ought we to eat before?' she asked next.

'It is provided.'

'And is it acceptable to eat – or does high society prefer to think young ladies need not?'

He blinked. 'You can eat,' he said. 'Though most people dine at home first.'

'What time is it appropriate to arrive? The invitation says eight, but does that mean we should arrive at the hour or for the hour?'

The questions went on in much the same vein – enquiries about particulars he had never thought to pay attention to before, and very much wished never to have to think of again. He wondered vaguely where his sense of fight had disappeared to. It was as if all his energy had been sapped from him in the face of that notebook, and all he could do was watch with muted despair as his previously peaceful morning faded away. It was a relief when she snapped her notebook closed, but the ordeal was not quite over. She pulled from her bag a copy of *La Belle Assemblée* and presented him with a picture of a dress within it. 'We were planning to wear something like this – does that suit?'

'I believe so,' he said helplessly.

'Any faux pas that I should avoid?'

'Many.' His answer was now slightly muffled as his head was buried in his hands.

'Care to mention one?' she said tartly.

'No,' he said crossly. Kitty stood to make her leave, perceiving Radcliffe to have run out of patience, and wished him a sunny good morning that he did not return.

'For God's sake, go out the back door!' he called at her back. But it was too late – she had already gone.

It took some time for Radcliffe to regain his equilibrium that day. He received no further visitors, thankfully, but the damage had been done. Rather than spending the day, as he had planned, seeing to his letters and penning instructions back to Radcliffe Hall regarding his imminent return, he instead spent several ill-at-ease hours ruminating over Miss Talbot's effrontery, her impudence – her *audacity*. He almost wished she would return to the house so he could throw her out properly. Even by the time he retired to bed he was still vaguely fearful that he might wake again to the news of Miss Talbot's presence in his home. Fortunately, he did not. Less fortunately, he woke to the news that his brother Archie was downstairs instead.

Archie was a little frustrated by how long it had taken to speak to Radcliffe on the matter of his betrothal. His last two attempts to call upon St James's Place had been unsuccessful, and so he was now addressing himself to his brother days after he had originally planned. Of course, he did not technically need Radcliffe's permission, certainly not once he had reached his majority in a few weeks, but that did not matter to Archie. Radcliffe was the head of the family now, and just as he would have asked his father's blessing to propose, so now must he ask James's. It was only right.

'Archie, to what do I owe the pleasure?' Radcliffe asked, suspecting very well what Archie was here to do.

Archie took a deep breath. 'I wish to speak to you on a matter most important, my lord.'

Radcliffe suppressed a sigh.

'Yes, Archie?'

'If you will remember, I wrote to you – before you returned to London, that is – asking for your permission, your blessing rather, to speak to Miss Talbot seriously about my feelings for her.' He took another breath. 'My mind has not changed. And I should like to discuss—'

Radcliffe raised a hand, feeling the conversation would not benefit from Archie talking himself into a corner.

'Archie, before you go any further, I must say – I do not think Miss Talbot is the right girl for you.'

This brought Archie up short. 'Why?' he demanded. 'You can't believe that tripe Mama once spouted about her being a fortune-hunter, can you?'

'It has nothing to do with that,' Radcliffe lied. He changed tack, perceiving that any slur to Miss Talbot's blasted name would only inspire a courageous and infatuated defence.

'It is just that I am not sure I understand the rush, Archie. It has only been weeks since you met Miss Talbot – is there anything so wrong about pursuing your friendship, for now?'

Archie felt that there was. Miss Talbot had certainly said there was, though he could not quite remember why, exactly. Something about a pear?

'Well – I feel – that is to say, once one is in love, there is no need for delay.' He was rather pleased by this statement – awfully good work on the hop.

Radcliffe hummed, unconvinced. 'Be that as it may, you are still very young. Barely a man. There is time enough for marriage. You ought to be falling in and out of love a dozen more times before you fix a particular attention on one lady.'

His voice was affable, his words kind, but Archie bristled immediately.

'I'm not a boy,' he said hotly. As Radcliffe's face did not shift from its expression of jovial elder, Archie's temper built further. 'Which you might know, if you'd spent any time with the family in the past few years!'

As soon as the words had left his mouth, Radcliffe's eyebrows shot up and Archie regretted speaking so hastily. 'S-sorry, didn't mean it,' he stammered out.

'I was in the country for business, Archie,' Radcliffe reminded him coolly.

Archie kicked at the edge of the rug with his toe. 'Must have been a lot of business,' he muttered, a little bitterly.

Radcliffe, for perhaps the twelfth time that week, cursed Miss Talbot to hell and damnation. His family had had none of these problems until she had started putting her waspish thoughts into their heads.

He raised up his hands in supplication. 'I am not against the marriage out of hand, my boy. My only stipulation is that you see what the Season has to offer. If your attentions are still fixed upon Miss Talbot, and hers upon you, in a few weeks, then by all means let us discuss it again.'

He then pressed a hand on Archie's shoulder, turned him neatly, and propelled him gently towards the door.

'You say that as though we've discussed it *at all*,' Archie complained, dragging his feet a little.

Radcliffe affected not to hear. 'With Montagu and Sinclair back in town, why not ride out somewhere – get out of London – have some fun?' he suggested, nudging Archie gently onto the doorstep and waving him off. 'I'll see you at the Montagu ball on the morrow!' Radcliffe called cheerily, and while the door didn't quite slam behind him, Archie felt it was a near thing. He stared at the burnished doorknob, utterly befogged. What had got into James? He had been distant since he returned from Waterloo, to be sure – but at least when he was in Devonshire, he seemed by his letters to take an interest in Archie's life. And yet now he could not be more slippery. Having his brother back in London had felt like the start of a new chapter for their family, all together again, but it seemed that even while in the same city, James didn't want to have much to do with them.

Archie sloped off down the road, trying to shake off these gloomy thoughts. He would have to speak to Radcliffe again, soon, to convince him that this was a long-standing attachment – he could only hope that Miss Talbot would not mind the delay. Although, he thought bitterly, she had not exactly been that keen to speak to him in recent days, either – cancelling their walks, and not seeming at all concerned about not seeing each other for days and days. There was clearly something he was doing wrong – something he was missing about the proper way to conduct these sorts of things – and in the absence of being able to speak to his elder brother about it, he instead sought the company and advice of his nearest friends, who were finally back in London.

* * *

Gerry Sinclair, having attended the dinner party at Grosvenor Square, was complaining that the younger Talbot sister was a 'dead bore' when Archie joined them at Cribb's Parlour later that day.

'Damn near talked my ear off about Italian opera,' he said indignantly, clutching his glass. 'Who *asked* her, is what I want to know? But they were both devilishly pretty, Archie.'

'But did she look in love with me?' Archie demanded.

'Fact of the matter, is, Archie, that she didn't seem to be paying you much attention at all,' Gerry told him apologetically. 'Sure you heard her right?'

'Yes,' Archie said, though uncertainly. 'I could have sworn that she said I ought to speak to my family before I could offer for her. And she wouldn't have said that, if she wasn't wanting to be engaged to me, would she?'

Gerry agreed that she most surely would not. Rupert, the other member of the group, did not appear to be listening. The young Lord Montagu considered himself a great poet and spent his days penning depressing verses and ruminating on his own artistry. When Archie insisted on hearing his opinion, he said darkly that the conversation threatened to pollute the artistic sensibility of his mind.

'Furthermore,' he added, 'it does not surprise me that you thought Miss Cecily a bore, Gerry, given that her intellect far exceeds that of your own.'

The conversation was thus distracted, and by the evening they were so full of vim that they ventured into Soho, finding themselves in an infamous faro club. Yet here, having availed himself of the refreshments, Archie felt a melancholy set in. He stared morosely around the room at the doubtlessly superior specimens of manhood and, eye landing on a gentleman he recognised as the dashing Lord Selbourne, said darkly to Gerry, 'I bet Miss Talbot would pay attention to *him*.'

'Oh, I'd steer clear of Selby,' Gerry said, turning to peer over Archie's shoulder. 'Looks like a gentleman, still has the title, but heard he's a bounder of the worst sort.'

'Bounder,' Rupert affirmed, with dark significance.

'All I'm saying is,' Archie said crossly, 'he looks the sort that knows how to make a proper offer to a woman – one everyone would take notice of.'

They all stared at Lord Selbourne, who, sensing their gaze, looked up and waved a laconic finger of acknowledgement their way – they looked quickly away, blushing.

'I want to be just like him,' Archie asserted boldly.

'Not a penny to his name, old boy, and riddled with debt – best be yourself,' Gerry told him heartily.

After losing spectacularly to the house, they began a meandering walk back across London. Despite the hour, the streets were still spotted with similarly inebriated persons, and so it was not until a group of men followed them down a narrowing side street that they registered something might be a little off. Moments later, another group appeared in front of them, blocking off the street. Rearing back in confusion, Archie felt the clarity of danger rush through him sickeningly.

'I-I say,' he heard Gerry stammer uncertainly.

Even Rupert's usually phlegmatic disposition had given way to alarm. Feeling, somehow, that the situation could be resolved with a little old-fashioned politeness, Archie swept a bow and asked, courteously, 'How may we help you, gentlemen?'

'Hand over your money,' his adversary said calmly. 'And we won't hurt you.'

'The devil of the thing is, we don't have any,' Gerry piped up. 'Lost all our coins at cards.'

'And the rest of it is all rather tied up,' Archie agreed, quite troubled.

'How very disappointing,' the man said, taking a step forward. Archie saw the flash of a drawn blade.

'I say!' a voice shouted from the street.

A shot rang in the air. The men scattered. Archie let out a gust of air, turning thankfully to their saviour. As he stepped towards them, Archie made out the deep red of his embroidered waistcoat and recognised Lord Selbourne.

'Thank you, my lord!' he gasped gratefully. 'Thanks awfully.'

'No trouble.' Lord Selbourne pocketed his pistol nonchalantly. 'This part of town can be devilishly dangerous. Radcliffe's brother, aren't you?' he asked rhetorically, reaching out a hand to Archie, who grasped it like a lifeline. 'Best we all be off, boys. You never know who you might run into on a night such as this.'

They followed Lord Selbourne obediently all the way to the well-tended streets of Grosvenor Square, where he left them with a smile and a bow. The young gentlemen parted ways dreamily, each one mentally rewriting the events to reconfigure themselves as taking a more heroic role. Even the hysterical confrontation with his mother that followed his entry into the house could not ruin Archie's mood, and he settled into bed with a smile upon his face. Miss Talbot, he felt sure, would have to sit up and listen now.

Dearest Kitty,

We were most pleased to receive your last letter, though it arrived only yesterday – the postal service seems in no hurry to deliver correspondence to our county. You must regale us with a detailed account of each ball – as full as you can fit in one sheet – for we would so enjoy picturing both you and Cecily in such grand places, amongst such lofty persons.

We have been enjoying weeks of temperate weather, though just yesterday a strong wind rose, knocking loose a considerable number of roof tiles in the night. Should the good weather endure, we ought to be fine, though if we suffer a rainy spell it is likely to leak again – what would you advise I do? The funds you left are enough for our weekly expenses, but they will not cover the cost of repair, and I do not think we can manage both.

Jane and I encountered Mr Linfield in Biddington yesterday. He is married now and was odiously patronising. Still, this in no way excuses Jane's behaviour – it was obvious to everyone she fully intended for the turnips to fall upon him. Needless to say, I scolded her thoroughly for the incivility – but I cannot deny it was pleasing to see Linfield covered in vegetables.

We miss you greatly and look forward to your return with extreme impatience.

Your loving sister,
Beatrice

16

The night of their first ball had come, and all was in place. Kitty, Cecily and Aunt Dorothy had been quite rushed off their feet the past few days, busied with modistes, milliners, and dancing lessons, and they were as prepared as they could ever be. Wrapped up in cloaks and piled into a hackney cab, they trundled through London's streets to Montagu House on Berkeley Square.

Having now spent almost six weeks in the capital, Kitty should have been used to the splendour of the houses in London's richest streets, inured to the wealth splashed across the city's most fashionable districts. But she could not have prepared herself for the sight of London in high Season, of how this great city looked, when the world's richest people were all gathered together and trying their very best to show off. The Montagu town house was shining brighter than the moon, windows glowing like lanterns and streaming out golden light onto the square. Their cab paused at the end of the street, unable to proceed with all the vehicles crowding in, and Kitty leant as far out of the carriage as she could to see the spectacle with her own eyes. She watched a stream of glittering ladies descend carefully from carriages – all carrying intricate insignias of grand houses – and glide their way inside. They looked like peacocks, or rare birds from some exotic location arriving for a grand exhibition. What a world this is, Kitty thought, breathless, and what a chance for us. She looked over at her sister, who was peeking over her shoulder, for once totally united in their awe, their eyes as wide as saucers.

'Are we ready, ladies?' Aunt Dorothy asked, gathering her skirts in readiness as the cabs ahead of them began to move once more. When it was their turn to exit, Kitty made sure that her own descent, though unassisted by sprightly footmen, was no less graceful than the other ladies present. From this moment onward, the world would be watching. Kitty caught the skirts of her ballgown in her hand – a satin slip of ivory overlaid with delicate white sarsnet – and walked with her sister and aunt slowly up the drive and into the lion's den.

There must have been a thousand candles lit for the occasion, Kitty marvelled, gazing around. As they made their way further in and she upturned her head to stare at the looming chandeliers above, she guessed it was a thousand candles at the very *least*. Their light cast a flattering glow across the room, making each person seem even more beautiful – glinting off the jewels at their ears, wrists and necks like an intimate caress. Kitty fought hard to keep her mouth shut, but could not stop her eyes from roving helplessly across the room, not knowing where to look. Everywhere in front of her was proof of more wealth than she had ever seen in her life: the jewels, the dresses, the candles, the food, the impeccably dressed footmen revolving like dancers, carrying trays of champagne with effortless grace.

They were greeted kindly by Lady Montagu, who remembered their names and complimented them on their dresses – Kitty examined her face closely for insincerity but saw none – before they were finally able to enter the ballroom properly. Dancing had not yet begun, and groups of people were gathered around, all talking and laughing together. Kitty was satisfied that their dresses – while not so ornate as some of those around her – were very much in the right style. Yet this moment of relief was short-lived, as she soon realised that no one in the ballroom was willing to converse with them until they were formally acknowledged by someone else first. No one had warned her to prepare for this. Kitty searched the room frantically for any familiar face, but she could hardly see past the coldly judging expressions aimed at them, swimming before her dizzyingly.

'Lady Radcliffe is waving at us,' Aunt Dorothy said soothingly into her ear. 'Look, over there.'

Kitty followed her eyes and Lady Radcliffe was indeed smiling and beckoning to her. Breathing properly again, she led her sister and aunt over as though they had all the time in the world. Eyes and ears, and just do as they do, Kitty reminded herself.

'You look marvellous!' Lady Radcliffe greeted them merrily. They tried to return the compliment, but she would not hear it. 'I am a total wreck,' she insisted. 'I have hardly slept – you would not believe the night we've had— Oh Mrs Cheriton, how wonderful it is to see you. Have you met Mrs Kendall?'

In Lady Radcliffe's company, everything all at once became far easier. The de Lacys knew so many people, and Lady Radcliffe was generous with her introductions. Within moments, Kitty felt quite as if she had smiled, curtseyed and complimented her way through half of the beau monde. After a few minutes, Mr de Lacy appeared – having been sent to procure refreshments by his mother – very pleased to see Miss Talbot, and most eager to update her on the night's excitement. Not liking to interrupt her conversation, he instead had to turn first, reluctantly, to Miss Cecily.

'Warm tonight, isn't it?' he said with polite cheer. 'Can you believe it's already April?'

'"With swift and silent pace, Impatient time rolls on the year",' said Cecily sombrely.

'. . . Right you are,' Mr de Lacy agreed, a little warily. He never much liked it when people quoted poetry at him. Always made one feel terribly foolish, as you never knew quite what people *meant* by it, especially if you couldn't remember which stuffy old boot had said the thing in the first place – which Archie never could. He abandoned Cecily to Lord Montagu as soon as he could, to hover at Kitty's shoulder.

Kitty had thought that allowing the flames of Mr de Lacy's passion to die gently would be the kindest and easiest resolution to their short-lived romance. Doing so, she hoped, would avoid any kind of nasty conversation that might necessitate a distance from his family, on whom she very much still depended. But she had not expected Mr de Lacy to be so quivering with excitement to get her alone, even now. As soon as she allowed him to silo her into conversation, he at once began to spill forth a rambling tale of his adventures the previous night, appearing quite confident that she would be agog to hear its conclusion. To be fair to him, Mr de Lacy had no way of knowing, of course, that her affection was a far more flighty creature now that she had no financial incentive to stroke his ego. Kitty nodded along, smiling politely, while scanning the room behind him for more interesting persons.

'And then we were set upon! By highwaymen!' he said in delight. 'They had muskets a-a-and knives, and had very much committed themselves to murdering us or at the very least robbing us blind. And all looked to be lost, but then – BAM! A shot fired!'

'Is that Beau Brummell?' Miss Talbot interrupted, unable to help herself.

Mr de Lacy was quite shocked at this appalling lack of feeling. After a beat of silence, he answered in chilly tones, 'I'm sure I couldn't say, ma'am, though I feel sure that Mr Brummell is still on the Continent.'

Ma'am? Kitty looked back at him in surprise to see a rigidly cross expression upon his face.

'Oh, Mr de Lacy, pray forgive me,' she said, forcing herself to focus only on him. 'It was a moment of distraction, do go on – I must hear the end.'

'Well, you displayed so little anxiety about my being *murdered*,' he said to her hotly, pride very much injured, 'that I have a great mind not to tell you whether I was or not.'

Despite this strong stance, Kitty coaxed out of him the end of the tale, and at its conclusion was able to say, with complete truth, 'That sounds altogether alarming, Mr de Lacy. Have you told your brother?'

'Told me what?'

Radcliffe had appeared behind her, looking – she could admit – rather debonair. For all that he claimed to hate modern society, he played the role of fashionable young lord well.

'James, you would not believe it,' Mr de Lacy said, regaining some of his breathless excitement. But he was to be disappointed in this audience, too, for his brother merely took a laconic pinch of snuff.

'I have already heard the whole from our mother,' he said. 'Twice – both an epistolary and in-person rendition – so I have no need to hear it a third time.' Archie wilted visibly, so he added, more warmly, 'I must say it is a relief to find there is no reason to believe you murdered after all.'

'Oh, you know Mama, always getting into a snit. It wasn't at all like that,' Archie assured him.

'I'm glad to hear it. She was all for finding you a nearby turret to spend your days in.'

'Really?' Archie said, agog. 'Damned strange thing to do.'

'Do not worry yourself,' his brother reassured him, 'I explained to her that you don't have the hair for it.'

Taking a moment to mull this over, Archie realised that he was being made fun of and gave out a shout of laughter.

'Perhaps I might suggest calling for a carriage on your next evening in Soho?' his brother suggested gently.

'No fun in that,' Archie said, horrified. 'Wouldn't be at all the thing.'

Kitty was once again paying little attention to their conversation – gazing over at a group of young men standing with her sister and wondering at their wealth – so she did not heed her next words as much as she would usually.

'You ought to take with you a pistol, then,' she said vaguely. The tall gentleman, at least, must be rich – one simply had to look at his fob watch!

Archie spluttered. Radcliffe inhaled his snuff rather more sharply than he had intended.

'I don't have one,' Archie admitted, turning to his brother and asking, 'should I?'

'No,' he replied calmly, at the same time as Miss Talbot continued, 'It would help you scare such fellows off, in future. Shooting is not so hard, with a little practice. Forgive me, I believe my aunt requires my attention.'

She bustled off, glad to be free of them both, and they stared after her – for once, quite united in their speechlessness.

17

Miss Talbot did not expect to be able to find a husband in just one night – she might be green, but she was not so naive as *that* – but she was pleased to have attracted a good deal of attention so far, aided immeasurably by her association with the de Lacys.

While many of the men she spoke to would of course be motivated more by curiosity than anything serious, she fancied that at least some of them might call upon her the next day – and she made it very clear that she would be amenable to this attention. Favourable first impressions established, all that was left was the dancing.

As per their arrangement, she had held the first spot in her dance card free for Radcliffe, but even as other couples were seizing the hands of their partners, she could not spot him in the crowd. If she had saved the first one for him in vain – well, he would *not* like the consequences. She scanned the crowd for his tall figure. The crowd parted a little, and she spotted him walking towards her – rather as one might approach the gallows – and he proffered his hand in invitation with a faintly ironic bow.

'I believe I am promised to you for this dance?' he said, voice courteous but words a wicked twist on the usual declaration. She took his hand graciously, wishing she were able to give him her best scowl.

'You took your time,' she said to him sweetly, with a tight grip upon his arm.

'I'm being blackmailed, you see,' he explained politely, as he escorted her towards the dance floor. 'The anxiety of which does not lend itself to punctual timekeeping.'

'You would have been more anxious had you not upheld our deal,' she said serenely.

'A gentleman's honour can always be trusted. I only wish they might say the same of a lady's,' he rejoined.

Kitty forbore from returning a riposte, aware, as they took their places – they were to start with a country dance – of hundreds of eyes upon them. She smiled, for the first time this evening with genuine feeling. Yes, this would do quite nicely. The elusive Lord Radcliffe, nary glimpsed in polite society for two years, now dancing with the unknown – and very dashing – Miss Talbot? This would put her firmly upon the map.

'You are looking very pleased with yourself,' Radcliffe told her, without pleasure. 'I cannot believe that dancing with me will do so much for you.'

The violins struck up. He bowed, she curtseyed.

'You are a man and know very little besides,' she said dismissively. 'This is *everything*.'

They moved silently for a few beats, as the steps of the dance brought them together and then apart.

'Have you a shortlist yet?' he enquired, when they were next within intimate speaking distance. 'Of possible victims?'

'If you mean *suitors*,' she answered, 'then not as such. I have conversed with so many men this evening it is difficult to keep track.'

Coming from another, this would be the most shameless boast – but Kitty delivered it in tones of mild aggrievement that made clear to Radcliffe she truly was distressed by the challenge of keeping so many names straight in her head.

'Mr Pemberton and Mr Gray seemed most particular, however,' she went on. 'And Mr Stanfield of course is very charming.'

'Lord Hanbury didn't make an impression, then? Or Lord Arden?' he said, with a smirk upon his lips. 'I saw you conversing with them both at length.'

'I am a realist,' she told him primly. Lord Arden, it was already clear to Kitty, was quite the biggest lech in the whole of London. 'Besides, I would never set my sights upon a lord.'

He looked a little surprised at this.

'A titled man has far less freedom to choose his own path,' she explained. 'It would not be a sensible move.'

'For once we are in agreement,' he said. 'Any man with a title would consider it his duty to find out everything about his future wife – and not a single one of my acquaintance would countenance such a background as yours.'

Though she was used by now to such insults from Radcliffe, this still rankled. Her background, indeed – as if she were not, like so many of the women here, the daughter of a gentleman.

'What of you, then, my lord?' she asked frostily, as their hands rejoined. 'I'm sure your mama has grand ambitions for your marriage.'

'Hmm,' was all he said.

'Has she not?' she pushed.

'Whether she has or has not,' he answered coolly, 'bears little relevance to my actions, and even less to this conversation.'

'Was that a set down?' Kitty asked, intrigued and pleased at the discovery. 'If it was, it was very good.'

'Regardless,' he seemed committed to ignoring her, 'you are right at least to avoid Hanbury. His family estate is quite encumbered – I should not be surprised if he declares bankruptcy within the year – and he most certainly intends to marry an heiress.'

'That is most useful to know,' Kitty said, surprised. 'Are there any other almost-bankrupt lords I should be aware of?'

'Planning to make more use of me, are you?' he enquired. 'I am very much afraid that is where my advice dries up.'

'I should think you might try to be a little helpful,' she complained, aggrieved.

'Miss Talbot, having now more than dispensed with my side of our little deal, I do not at all desire to be helpful.'

The dance was drawing to a close now. And so it seemed – by the finality of Radcliffe's words and his tone – was their acquaintance.

'I do hope,' he said as the music stopped, bowing over her hand, 'that you can take it from here?'

'Yes,' she said. 'Yes, I believe I can.'

Archie wandered aimlessly through the rooms, moodily tasting of the buffet in the supper room and ignoring all attempts to draw him into conversation. He wasn't at all sure why his fighting off a set of bandits had not garnered more excitement or respect from the object of his affections, or why she seemed so keen *not* to speak with him. It went beyond the pale. What was the point of exciting things happening to one, if it did not seem to matter to the people one most wanted to impress? And then his own brother to have treated him so much like a child, right in front of her!

Archie squashed another slice of plum cake in his mouth, to assuage his distress, before skulking off once more. Still preoccupied by his dark thoughts, just as he was on the point of damning the whole party to hell, Archie quite collided with a gentleman exiting the card room.

'Good God, terribly sorry!' he cried, even as his arm was caught securely in the other's to stop his fall.

'My dear boy, don't be,' the gentleman drawled. 'It's not every day someone swoons into my arms.'

Detecting a joke at play, Archie looked up, grinning, into the face of the amused Lord Selbourne. 'My lord!' he said in delighted greeting.

'Ah yes, Mr de Lacy,' he said, smiling. 'Good to see you again.'

Thrilled to be recognised by someone he now considered a god, Archie beamed.

'Care to join me for a game?' Selbourne asked, though he had appeared to be about to leave the room altogether.

Archie hesitated. The music was starting up and he did feel his mother would expect him to be involved in the dancing. He looked back towards the dance floor to see the set was already beginning to form. Damnation – if he hadn't spent so long sulking, he could have plucked up the courage to ask Miss Talbot to dance, which might've solved everything. He searched the room for her, wondering if he might still be able to bring

it about. There was her sister, being led to the floor by Montagu
– he had taken a shine to her, hadn't he? – and there was Miss
Talbot ... dancing with Radcliffe. How odd. He had not
thought James even liked her all that much.

'Mr de Lacy?' Lord Selbourne's voice brought him back to
the present. 'A game?'

'Yes indeed,' Archie agreed, happy to be distracted from this
latest puzzle. He followed Selbourne into the dimly-lit antechamber, where they joined a table of men Archie did not
recognise, who were just forming a new game of whist.

'Insipid game,' Selbourne muttered to Archie, 'but it's the
best they'll do here.'

Archie murmured his agreement, though he was far from
considering this turn of events insipid. He could not wait to
tell Gerry – the boy would be beside himself with jealousy.

'Aren't you devilishly rich, my boy?' Selbourne asked
provocatively, peering at Archie over his cards.

Archie was not used to people saying this so overtly. 'Yes, I
think so,' he said, before admitting, 'Or, at least, I will in a few
weeks – upon my majority.' His mother had always impressed
upon him the importance of honesty, and though it might
lower him in the man's estimation to know he was not yet one
and twenty, he thought it best to speak the truth.

'If I were you, I'd be having an awful lot more fun,' Selbourne
said carelessly. 'Is this really your idea of a good time?' He
waved to the room in such a way as to intimate his total disgust
for the entire ball and its contents.

'Well, I suppose not,' Archie said. 'Of course not. Damned
squeeze.'

'I'm only here out of duty, of course,' Selbourne said languidly.

'Only way it seems to get a wife, and my mother does nag so. Family name and all that. But when I'm *not* here,' he leant in confidentially, and Archie leant in too, hanging upon his every word. 'You can be sure that I know how to have fun . . .'

Kitty's dance card was full the whole night. Once her dance with Radcliffe was concluded, she had a bevy of other requests for her hand within mere minutes. Twirling across the room amongst London's elite, she felt weightless, and truly powerful – the world was within her grasp, and she the only one brave enough to take it. They stayed at the ball into the early hours of the morning, dancing all night in their shimmering slippers, before Aunt Dorothy indicated, with a simple flick of her fingers, that it was time for them to leave. Collecting Cecily on their way – extracting her from where she had trapped Lord Montagu once more into conversation – they bade goodnight to their hostess and headed out into the night.

Kitty leant back into the carriage seat with a sigh.

'Did you enjoy yourself, Cecy?' she asked, an obvious after-thought.

'No,' her sister lied.

18

What a difference a single night could make. After the Montagu ball, the Talbots' social calendar became, if not jam-packed, then certainly pleasantly busy, with a stream of invitations and calling cards landing on their doorstep within hours of their returning home at dawn. Now there were two further balls just this very week to prepare for, as well as countless invitations to dine – from mothers, Kitty assumed, on their sons' requests – and stacks of calling cards from young men bent on affixing their attention with the sisters. She informed Cecy of this exultantly over the breakfast table, but the poor creature was uninterested, picking drippily at her toast.

'I should be reading Plato,' she moaned disconsolately in response. 'Or observing the work of great artists – meanwhile all you have me do is escort you to silly parties.'

'My greatest sympathies, Cecily,' Kitty said. 'But how, pray, do you plan to feed yourself after a day spent reading philosophy? I don't believe it generates money, but then I cannot pretend to understand it wholly.'

No sooner had Sally packed away the breakfast table than she was returning to inform them that a young gentleman was at the door, requesting entrance.

'Send him in,' Miss Talbot said at once, seating herself primly upon the settee. She breathed in, vowing to keep her mind open, her eye discerning, and her mouth set into a smile. First came the unfortunate Mr Tavistock (three thousand a year, as Aunt Dorothy had gleaned from a delightfully indiscreet Lady Montagu) who began by complimenting Kitty upon her sapphire blue eyes. This precipitated an awkward moment where they were both reminded that Kitty's eyes were, in fact, brown, an awkwardness from which they did not recover. Then came Mr Simmons (four thousand a year) who, with his chin held uncomfortably close to his neck, endeavoured to disagree with everything Kitty said, even down to her (very accurate) description of the day's weather. Worst was Mr Leonard, who called for Cecily, and opened the conversation with a compliment so oily Kitty was surprised grease did not drip from his lips.

'Does it get tiring, being the most beautiful woman in every room?' he whispered to her unctuously, causing a quite visible shiver of revulsion to run down Cecily's back.

Kitty felt no qualms about dispatching this man very promptly – Cecily was not to be bothered by men such as that, and all the gentlemen who called for her younger sister in Mr Leonard's wake were watched very closely. Among the callers, Kitty's favourite was undoubtedly Mr Stanfield. It would be a mistake of the gravest degree, she knew, to develop genuine romantic feelings for any suitor, and yet she could see even now how very easy it would be to fall into such a trap with this gentleman. Having spoken with Mr Stanfield at length the night before and been impressed by the deft way he handled a conversation, she was pleased to see him enter Aunt Dorothy's parlour.

Dispensing with the overly complimentary behaviour so preferred by his contemporaries, he merely bowed his head silently over her hand, giving her a leisurely grin, and holding her eyes for what felt like hours. He looked every inch the classic London gentleman – complete with a pristinely starched white shirt, elegantly tied neckcloth, and fine beaver hat clasped in hand – but when he smiled he revealed a rascally handsome face, like a charming pickpocket.

'You must tell me of Dorsetshire,' he was saying now as he seated himself gracefully beside her, holding her gaze – he did this, a lot, it seemed – 'for I hear it is quite beautiful.'

'It is,' she was pleased enough to confirm, describing her home to him happily. He listened and asked questions (which should not, she knew, be such an outstanding proof of character, and yet it was, for there was not one other man amongst her admirers who had done so).

'And are you accepting, in Dorsetshire, of city persons like myself?' he asked, eyes snagging hers yet again. 'Or do you cast us all out for being terribly useless?'

She was being flirted with, she perceived. It was most enjoyable. 'I rather think that would depend upon the person,' she said archly. 'Do you have any skills other than cravat-tying and gambling?'

He laughed. Mr Pemberton was announced by a scowling Sally – who was quite sick already of the extra work these gentlemen were causing – and Mr Stanfield relinquished his post reluctantly.

'Will I see you at Almack's this week?' he asked her. Kitty hesitated. Almack's Assembly Rooms was the most exclusive venue in the whole of London. Her father had even attended on occasion, she knew, and he had dubbed it – as it seemed every member of the *ton* also did – the marriage mart. Kitty knew its hallowed halls opened every Wednesday night, and that one could only attend with a voucher of invitation – but she had not yet got to the bottom of how exactly one *was* invited. Yet another thing that might have been different, had Mr Talbot's family not seen fit to banish her parents so thoroughly.

'Not this week,' she answered evasively.

He nodded, but there was a slight hesitation in his eyes and Kitty cursed inwardly. It was a mark against her, she knew. As an unknown in society, an invitation to Almack's would have assured Kitty's suitors of her quality – the absence of a voucher would be noted.

'But I shall be at the Sinclair ball,' she added. He bowed his head over her hand.

'Then I shall make sure to be there,' he promised, smiling.

Kitty bade him farewell, and he left. She allowed herself, just this once, the indulgence of looking forward to seeing him again.

Miss Talbot had not expected to see Lord Radcliffe for the rest of the Season. In fact, Kitty hadn't thought she would ever set eyes on the man again in her life. She was surprised then, to spot his tall figure loitering by the back of the Sinclairs ballroom later that week. How fortuitous – she made a beeline for him at once. After two further gentleman callers had enquired whether she could be found at Almack's the next

Wednesday, Kitty knew she must find out more about how one secured a voucher. Radcliffe would surely know.

She greeted him brightly, and he returned her greeting without enthusiasm. Still, Kitty persevered.

'Who is it that issues the vouchers for Almack's?' she asked directly. He raised his eyes to the heavens, as if searching for patience.

'Princess Esterházy, the Countess Lieven, Mrs Burrell, Lady Castlereagh, Lady Jersey, Lady Sefton and Lady Cowper,' he listed, ticking them off on his fingers. 'They meet each week to decide who shall be on the list – though I do not think much of your chances.'

'Why is that?' she demanded. 'Is there something I ought to be doing differently?'

'I believe,' he said slowly, taking out his snuffbox at a glacial pace, 'I very much believe . . . that my patience has run out, Miss Talbot. I will no longer permit you to treat me as a lending library – take yourself away, now.'

Kitty felt a spike of frustration. 'Just this one last question!' she insisted.

'No,' he said, calmly availing himself of some snuff. 'Go away before I start shouting to the room that you are a blasted fortune-hunter.'

She scowled at him. 'I must say,' she said hotly. 'If you had even an ounce of kindness, you would try a bit harder to be useful to me. Why, it would cost you nothing to help – to explain about Almack's and just tell me who is who and such-like. I do not think you very charitable, my lord.'

His eyebrows had risen higher through this tirade, and once she had finished, he shut his snuffbox with a decisive snap.

'By George, you are right,' he said, with a maniacal gleam to his eye. 'Most remiss of me – going forward, I shall *dedicate* myself to your cause, Miss Talbot.'

'You will?' she asked, a little wary at this change of heart.

'Oh, I shall be your most loyal servant,' he assured her.

Kitty had been right to be wary, as it quickly became apparent that Radcliffe's offer was motivated by an extremely evil spirit of mischief. For the rest of the evening, he affixed himself to her side like an irritating shadow, whispering 'helpful' commentary in her ear regarding every gentleman she spoke to or looked at.

'Now to your left you will see Mr Thornbury,' he was now saying, *sotto voce*. 'Four thousand pounds a year, not bad at all, but quite mad, you know. Runs in the family – he'd shoot you within the week, thinking you were a fox or somesuch. *That* gentleman, on the other hand – not mad at all, so a point in his favour. But quite riddled with pox, I hear. How does that weigh with you?'

She tried to ignore him, but it was like having a particularly loud and irksome fly buzzing around her, sufficiently distracting that she could not help tuning in despite her best efforts. When strapped for inspiration on damning tidbits about a passing young man, he would just whisper 'rich' or 'poor' into her ear.

'Would you stop that!' she hissed, after it became apparent that her policy of ignoring him was not working.

'I am merely trying to be of use to you, my dear Miss Talbot,' he replied, all faux-contrition, 'I am endeavouring to be charitable, and I do not think that involves allowing you to speak to a loose fish without fair warning.'

'Someone will hear you,' she whispered threateningly.

'Well then, I hope they may also take the warning,' he said, generously.

She cast about for a saviour and grinned widely at an approaching gentleman – who unfortunately appeared to find the expression alarming rather than inviting and swerved away. After she had seen this same action repeated several times, she realised with horror that, 'People think we're courting, now! For goodness' sake.'

Luckily this seemed to shock Radcliffe out of his amusement, and she used the distraction to throw herself into the crowd. Really, was it not enough for him to have ruined her efforts once – was he to be a constant curse upon her? Kitty found herself next to the refreshments table and stood for a moment, pretending to admire the feast but in truth spying for a new dance partner. She spotted Lord Arden oiling his way across the floor towards her, and turned quickly around. She caught the eye of a glamorous dowager – her ample bosom heaving with jewels – and as the lady was smiling at her in obvious invitation, Kitty was forced to approach, though reluctantly.

Kitty had developed a respectful distrust of these sorts of ladies during her time in London. As far as she could tell, the negotiations around the construction – or destruction – of potential marital alliances were performed entirely by these highly motivated women on behalf of their charges. The work might be subtler than a siege – introductions arranged, conversations manipulated, and adversaries degenerated all with a light hand – but it was as cut-throat and as planned as any military campaign.

'Ma'am,' she said politely as she rose from her curtsey, not yet knowing how to address her.

'Miss Talbot, isn't it?' she said, warmly. 'Lady Kingsbury, how do you do? Quick, let us pretend we are having the most serious tête-à-tête, or else Lord Arden will be over here asking for a dance.'

Her eyes were bright with confidential mischief and Kitty warmed to her instantly.

'Tell me,' Lady Kingsbury leant in with exaggerated intimacy. Out of the corner of her eye, Kitty saw Lord Arden turn around. 'Are you indeed about to make quite the finest catch of the Season?' She inclined her head to where Radcliffe was speaking to his mother.

It was so very cleverly done – so inviting, with such an air of friendly gossip – that Kitty was quite breathless with admiration. Were Kitty an ounce less discerning, or at all interested in Radcliffe besides, she might easily give in to the temptation to discuss the matter with the lady.

'I'm sure I do not know what you mean, my lady,' she said. 'If you are speaking of Lord Radcliffe, I only know him through my acquaintance with the family.'

Then, inspired perhaps by the same spirit of evil that had caused Radcliffe to be a thorn in her side all evening, she continued innocently. 'Though I know he *has* returned to London to find a wife, I am sure he has far loftier ambitions than I.'

Lady Kingsbury clucked sympathetically, but it was clear her mind was elsewhere – Kitty could almost hear her mind churning with this delicious little tidbit, and when she bade her farewell, Lady Kingsbury was very quick to turn to her compatriots. Yes, that news would be common knowledge by the end of the evening, and Radcliffe would soon be quite too busy to bother her any longer.

'Miss Talbot, I believe I have this dance?' She turned to see a visibly sweating Mr Pemberton standing in front of her. Pushing aside the echo of Radcliffe's voice – *rich but awful* – she accepted with a smile. Kitty's feelings toward Pemberton were mixed. Tall, large-moustached and intensely patronising, Kitty would have found the man a vicious bore if this opinion were a luxury she could afford. As it was, with eight thousand pounds a year to his name, he had to be considered as a very fine candidate. They spun into an energetic country dance and Kitty was thankful that the steps did not allow for a great deal of conversation, Mr Pemberton apparently being of the belief that she would like an education on the topic of Regent Street's western expansion.

'What few people know—' he began to explain, before they were parted again by the movement of the dance '—the brick is— terribly uneducated— wouldn't *believe*—'

He made no effort to pause his lecture when she was not near to him and so she was unable to follow the tirade; from the looks on the women's faces around her, it was clear that each was receiving out of context pieces of the address as they swapped partners. Thankfully, he did not need much from her except her attention, which she made sure to give in smiling spades. The dance finished, and Mr Pemberton eagerly approached, thrilled with his success, and committed to continuing their conversation.

'Excuse me, Pemberton, but I believe the next dance is mine,' came a deep voice at her side. She turned to see Mr Stanfield at her elbow, a wicked smile upon his face. He offered his hand to Kitty and whisked her away towards the next set – Mr Pemberton left disgruntled in her wake.

'How terribly remiss of me, sir, but I do not believe I have your name in my dance card,' Kitty said, as they took their places.

He grinned at her. 'Would you permit me my rudeness if I admitted it arose from motives of chivalry?' he asked impishly. 'I could no longer consider myself a gentleman were I to leave a lady in the presence of such a dragon.'

She laughed, and then was swept away by the cotillion. Conversation was just as difficult in this dance as it had been with Mr Pemberton, but Mr Stanfield did not attempt it – simply laughing along with her as they managed the quick series of figures and changes. His feet were as quick as his tongue, and together they did not miss a step. The dance ended, too soon, and they drew to a laughing stop, panting and grinning at each other.

'I shall be out of town for a few days,' he told her, bowing. 'But I shall return most eagerly for another dance such as that, Miss Talbot.'

'I can't promise to save you one,' she warned him archly.

'And I should not ask it of you,' he said, grinning. 'For the fear of being called out by one of my thousand rivals.'

Mr Gray – who she had originally promised this dance to – had arrived at her shoulder, looking mightily put out. Mr Stanfield relinquished her laughingly to him and she watched as he wandered across the room to approach another young lady. Kitty eyed her critically. She was fair, with very pale skin and hair and, Kitty could admit, that air of pleasing fragility that men so seemed to like in this city.

'Mr Gray,' she asked, not taking her eyes off the pair – he was asking her to dance now – 'who is that young lady over there – the one that looks like a glass of milk?'

Mr Gray coughed, a little uncomfortably. 'Ah, that is Miss Fleming, I believe, Miss Talbot.'

'I do not know the name,' Kitty said, frowning. She had learnt as much as she could about all the young ladies in her competitive set, but Miss Fleming had not been spoken of by anyone she knew.

'The family is new to town,' Mr Gray said. 'Miss Fleming made her debut at Almack's this week, where I believe she and Mr Stanfield became acquainted.'

Kitty's frown deepened. Almack's appellation of 'marriage mart' was clearly no exaggeration, for Mr Stanfield and Miss Fleming looked to be closely acquainted indeed. Kitty felt a pang of unease. She had felt so smug after the first ball, so confident that she would be able to wrap things up very easily – she had even written home to tell her sisters as much. False hope, she could see now, with a sting of regret at her hubris – if she were not vigilant enough, there was still a great chance that she might fail them. Clearly, whatever lead she might win at the private balls would be negated every Wednesday, when she was left on the fringes, and young ladies of better quality could mount unchallenged attacks on the finest catches of the Season. It could not be borne. Kitty would be extracting Almack's vouchers from one of its patronesses if her life depended upon it.

19

Radcliffe had spent far longer in London than he had ever meant to, and yet, though he could not exactly explain why, he had still not set a date for his return to Devonshire. And this despite the fact that life in the city was becoming increasingly uncomfortable. Since the Sinclair ball, Radcliffe had somehow managed to become entangled in the grips of a queue of persistent young women and their even more persistent mothers.

He had been beset by invitations to balls, routs, card parties, picnics and outings, and by calling card after calling card – he was even plagued by unwelcome visitors to his home, when a young lady and her mother sought his house for a respite from the heat of a mild spring morning, having reportedly come over faint. From this fate, at least, he managed to escape by hurriedly exiting out of the back door. Radcliffe knew that he must always expect a certain dedication of pursuit from the matrimonial market – possessing a title, significant wealth and, unlike many of his fellow lords, all of his teeth – and yet he felt the current siege was reaching near unprecedented levels of fervour. He could not think what had given them all such gumption, and if the trend continued, he would have no choice but to make a cowardly retreat.

It was not until he dined at Grosvenor Square with his mother and sister, that he was offered elucidation upon the situation. No sooner had he entered the dining room than Lady Radcliffe had flung herself into her son's arms, in transports of mingled delight and remonstration. Radcliffe caught the eye of his sister over her shoulder, but Amelia merely smirked at him.

'Is everything all right, Mother? Are you feeling quite well?' he asked cautiously. She released him.

'Don't think I am not most pleased,' she said, quite incomprehensibly. 'But how could you not tell me first?'

It took until the first course was served for Radcliffe to grasp the full meaning of this nonsensical speech – to understand that his mother believed his reason for remaining in London was to find a wife. He felt himself come out in a thick sweat.

'That is simply not the case,' he told her firmly.

'I told you!' Amelia sang.

'Where did you hear such fudge?' he demanded.

'Lady Montagu,' his mother said sulkily. 'And you might know what a blow it was to receive such news from her!'

'There is no such news,' he said through gritted teeth. 'Where did she hear it?'

'Oh, you know,' his mother waved her hand in a vague motion that he supposed was meant to refer to the rumour-mill, 'Lady Kingsbury heard it from someone.'

'Lady Kingsbury always has been an egregious snake,' he said bitterly. 'But where on earth could she have got such fustian nonsense—' He broke off, a sudden memory swimming to the forefront of his mind, of Miss Talbot speaking confidentially to a heavily bejewelled Lady Kingsbury, both women looking his way.

'That little devil,' he said softly.

'I beg your pardon?' his mother was quite affronted, and he apologised profusely.

'May I ask then, James, what is your purpose in remaining with us in London?' Lady Radcliffe said, convinced at last that he was telling the truth. She looked at him, hope and concern warring in her eyes. 'I had thought you could not bear to be among us, after Waterloo.' She reached out to grasp his hand. 'Have you returned to us?'

He squeezed her palm, knowing she did not just mean London.

'I don't know,' he admitted.

She was right that he had stayed away from the crowds, the pomp, the spectacle of the London *ton* ever since he set foot back on British soil, thinner and a little haunted from all he had seen. Barring his father's funeral, he had found every reason he could to avoid . . . the whole world, really. It had felt simpler that way, to keep away from all the heavy expectation of London society, as he tried to understand who he was. Yet now he was finding every reason he could to tarry longer in the city. He could not adequately explain it even to himself.

'I don't know,' he said again. 'But I think I shall stay for a little longer.'

His mother's smile was joyful. 'I am glad,' she said simply. 'Will you escort me to the Salisbury ball tonight? Archie is quite simply not to be depended upon – I do not know where that boy is getting to these days.'

Radcliffe felt confident Miss Talbot was to blame for his current romantic predicament. After his stint in His Majesty's army, he had a certain instinct for skulduggery, which was leading him straight to that irredeemable pest. Thus, when Miss Talbot arrived at the Salisbury ball that evening, she was approached almost immediately by a stormy-faced Radcliffe, who bowed perfunctorily before informing her, quite politely, that she was a harpy.

'Is that so?' she asked, as if he had just told her the weather was a little cold. 'I must confess I am not sure what you are referencing.'

'Though it pains me to contradict you, I am sure that you in fact do know. Is it not down to your doing that I have been invited to make no less than three marriage proposals since we last spoke?'

She could not restrain her smile. 'My lord, I can only apologise,' she said with all the earnestness she could muster. 'Any thoughtless words on my part were only made to protect your reputation from any besmirching association with me.'

'Oh, so you were in fact protecting my honour by inviting a free-for-all upon my person, by every mother and daughter in the city?'

She bit back a bigger smile; she was rather beginning to enjoy these little exchanges with Radcliffe – it wasn't just that to be seen in his company couldn't help but aid her standing in society, but also the pleasure of knowing that while the rest of society had to make do with Radcliffe's polite mask, it was with her alone that he let loose his sarcastic wit.

'Yes, I was,' she replied solemnly.

He looked at her levelly. 'You will live to regret this,' he promised her. 'I will repay you for the discomfort you have caused me.'

'If we are going to exchange threats,' she said. 'It would be better that we do it whilst dancing, so that we are not over-heard.' She looked at him expectantly. 'Aren't you going to ask me?'

'I rather thought it was you who just asked me,' he said. 'If we can call it asking.'

'No, I asked whether you were going to ask me,' she corrected firmly. 'But as you're clearly going to be difficult, I would now rather you didn't.'

'That suits perfectly, for my answer was going to be no. I make it a general rule only to dance with persons I like – and certainly not shameless jades.'

She bristled in offence. 'Are you in the habit of being this rude to everyone you encounter?'

'On the contrary,' he said coolly. 'I am considered rather charming by the entirety of the *ton*.'

'Well, I'm sure we cannot blame them for *that* foolishness,' she snapped. 'So many of the *ton* being in the habit of marrying their first cousins.'

He inhaled sharply, choked on his mouthful of champagne, and then let out a coughing bark of mirth.

'Oh, very well done, Miss Talbot,' he told her, never one to begrudge a good hit.

'*Now* will you dance with me?' she asked.

'Never!' he declared, with a theatricality that belonged on the stage. Kitty turned from him with an equally dramatic flourish, suppressing a shiver of something – pique, no doubt, that he wouldn't dance with her this evening. It was, of course, merely frustration that she wouldn't get the accompanying boost of visibility to the eligible gentlemen present. No more than that.

She had work to do tonight, after all, and for once, it wasn't just to do with charming the gentlemen. The Lady Patronesses of Almack's were the highest ranking and most esteemed members of Regency society, and they each wielded extraordinary social power. An Almack's voucher from one of these ladies would be the ultimate seal of approval – it was far more than a card of invitation, and no less than the difference between society and Society, Mr Talbot had once said. He, Kitty knew, had rather considered these parts of high society a little dull – preferring to spend his time with their mother than with the fusty *ton*. There was an irony in this, Kitty thought – that she was reduced to scheming to access the same places that Mr Talbot had avoided – but she was far too preoccupied to appreciate it.

To secure an Almack's voucher, then, Kitty had several possible avenues of attack. The Princess Esterházy and the Countess Lieven she discounted straight away. Not even Kitty had the courage to speak to such high-ranking ladies. She had met Mrs Burrell, of course, at Lady Radcliffe's dinner party, though she could not see her anywhere. She identified Lady Cowper by way of Lady Kingsbury, and spent the better part of an hour hovering on the periphery of their group, trying to be included, but it was a fruitless endeavour. Frustrated, she abandoned this and cast about again. As luck would have it, Kitty spotted the Countesses Lady Radcliffe and Lady Montagu deep in conversation with Lady Jersey across the room. *Famous.* She made her way across to them.

'Miss Talbot!' Lady Radcliffe cried. 'How are you, my dear?'

But then, to Kitty's horror, instead of bringing her into the conversation, Lady Radcliffe began to guide her away with a hand upon her elbow. 'Lady Montagu, Lady Jersey, do excuse us.'

Kitty looked longingly over her shoulder towards Lady Jersey, as Lady Radcliffe took her to a quiet corner of the room.

'I have been wanting to speak with Mrs Kendall, my dear,' she said confidentially. 'But you will do just as well. Do you think it wise to let Miss Cecily set her cap at Lord Montagu so obviously?'

Kitty blinked at her.

'Set her cap?' she repeated, a little incredulous. 'My lady, you must be mistaken. Cecily has no notion of setting her cap at anyone.'

Lady Radcliffe squeezed her arm, gently. 'Perhaps you have not noticed that she has danced twice with Lord Montagu, just this evening alone, then? And twice too at the Sinclair ball. It does look a little fast, my dear.'

Kitty blinked again. Dear lord, was two dances in one evening really such a claxon symbol of marital intent to these people? She wished Radcliffe had felt the need to share that detail with her. She thanked Lady Radcliffe profusely, and looked wildly about for Cecily. Ah. There she was. Speaking to Lord Montagu, Kitty noted with exasperation, which did not help her case and . . . and looking quite about to dance with him a *third* time. Kitty did not run across the room, but she most certainly hastened.

'Cecily!' she said brightly. 'And Lord Montagu, how do you do? Lord Montagu, I am afraid your mother is looking for you – she quite wants to speak with you most urgently. Perhaps you should find her?'

Lord Montagu looked perplexed and a little cross at the interruption, but slouched off, nonetheless.

'Cecily,' Kitty hissed. 'You weren't to know, but you must only dance with a man once an evening. More than that is to be considered awfully fast by these people.'

It was Cecily's turn to look perplexed. 'How terribly prudish,' she said, only mildly interested. 'It sounds most foolish to me – why, in Ancient Greece—'

'But we are not in Ancient Greece!' Kitty interrupted, a little shrill. 'We are in *London*, and these are – these are the rules.'

'But I like dancing,' Cecily complained. 'It is the only bit of all this that I like.'

Kitty did not have time for this. She cast about for Lady Jersey again, but the lady was nowhere to be seen. The grandfather clock in the corner struck eleven, and the sound of its twangs audible even over the hubbub of the evening made Kitty feel quite distressed. Time was running out – tonight – this week – in general. She had to get the vouchers.

Just then she spotted Mrs Burrell across the room. Thank goodness. She did not know a single woman with whom she was conversing, but that surely did not matter – she had met Mrs Burrell before, and after all, she was the lowest ranking lady amongst all the patronesses.

'Come, Cecy,' she commanded, marching off towards her.

'Mrs Burrell,' she greeted the woman with a deep curtsey. Mrs Burrell looked at her without any discernible sign of recognition.

'We met at Lady Radcliffe's soirée last week,' Kitty reminded her.

'Oh . . . yes,' Mrs Burrell said at last, in a glacial drawl. 'Miss Tallant, wasn't it?'

'Talbot,' Kitty corrected, but from the little glint in the lady's eye, she felt suddenly sure she knew that. 'I just wanted to tell you,' she persevered, 'how magnificent I think your dress.'

Compliments were always safe, surely?

'Thank you . . .' Mrs Burrell said, with the same disconcerting slowness. She made a show of looking Kitty up and down. 'I also like . . . the embroidery upon your fan.'

It was praise so specific that it felt as damning as an insult, and from the smirks around her – and one audible titter – this had been noted by all the ladies present. Kitty felt her face grow hot. She opened her mouth – to say what she didn't know – but was interrupted again.

'I believe that woman is trying to catch your attention,' Mrs Burrell pointed out coolly. 'You should go to her before she . . . overexerts herself.'

Kitty glanced over to see Aunt Dorothy gesturing to her vigorously. She glared discouragingly, but her aunt continued the insistent summons.

'Do not let us keep you,' Mrs Burrell said sweetly, and there were titters again. Curtseying a farewell, they retreated, Kitty's face aflame.

'For goodness' sake, put your hand down,' Kitty hissed at Aunt Dorothy. 'You're embarrassing me.'

'You were embarrassing yourself,' her aunt hissed back, seizing her arm and leading her away from the dance floor. 'One cannot simply walk up to persons such as Mrs Burrell, even I could have told you that. She is the highest stickler imaginable and everyone is quite terrified of her, even Lady Radcliffe finds her daunting. You were about to receive the most humiliating of set downs.'

'But we have met before,' Kitty complained. 'How else am I meant to secure Almack's vouchers if I cannot speak to these ladies?'

'Rid the notion from your mind, I beg of you,' Aunt Dorothy said sharply. 'It is never going to happen, and you cannot bring it about by these methods.'

'And you said this wouldn't happen, either, and look where we are!' Kitty couldn't help saying hotly, gesturing to the ballroom around them. 'When will you start believing in me, Aunt?'

Aunt Dorothy appeared to keep her cool with considerable effort.

'It is not a matter of belief,' she said with forced patience. 'There is a reason Almack's is considered exclusive, even amongst polite society, and there is no point wasting energy chasing the impossible. You already have several wealthy gentlemen dangling after you – is that not enough?'

Kitty swallowed another hot-headed retort. How to explain, without sounding as if she had lost her head? Being in this room was of itself such an achievement, Aunt Dorothy was right about that, but it was not the fait accompli that Kitty had imagined. There were places she was still not allowed to enter, places that persons like Miss Fleming were invited to while she was not. The advantage Almack's gave them . . . It was not something she could easily overcome; and as Mr Stanfield was growing ever more conspicuous in his attentions to Miss Fleming, Kitty knew she might never stand a chance at his level without it.

'Why do you want it so much?' Aunt Dorothy asked imploringly, when Kitty did not answer.

'I–I just,' Kitty faltered. 'It could have been mine. If things – if things had gone differently for Mama and Papa, I would have had all this without thinking about it for a second. I am not so different to these other ladies, Aunt. They are not better than me. It feels so close – I cannot help but want to reach for it.'

She searched Aunt Dorothy's face for some understanding, and did see her eyes soften, a little.

'I understand why it might feel unfair,' Aunt Dorothy said quietly. 'But you cannot try to right all the wrongs of the past – remember why we are here. We cannot be distracted from that. You are reaching for the unattainable, you must believe me this time. Can I trust you will let it rest, now?'

Kitty looked down at her feet, chastised. Aunt Dorothy was right and she knew it – they had only six weeks, now. She must keep on track – keep thinking with her head and not her heart. 'Yes, all right,' she agreed. 'I'll let it rest.'

'Good.' Aunt Dorothy nodded briskly. 'Now, I must find that charming gentleman I was speaking to the other night – I think he will very much like my new gown.'

Aunt Dorothy bustled off in pursuit of compliments. Kitty looked over at Cecily, still feeling at odds and wanting badly to discuss the unfairness of it all with someone.

'My necklace is feeling a little loose,' Cecily told her, holding a hand up to the jewels at her collarbone – paste, of course. Kitty motioned for her to turn around so she could examine it.

'Ah,' she said, seeing the problem immediately. 'You did not tie it correctly. Stand still for a moment.'

She frowned over the delicate work, glad for the distraction. 'Your poets ought to write more about this sort of thing,' she told Cecily absently, fiddling with the necklace's lever, being careful not to pinch the delicate skin of Cecily's neck as she did so. 'Social rules and politics and the like – it could fill books, I'm sure.'

'Er – they do, actually,' Cecily told her. 'Quite a few of them, in fact.'

'Oh.' Kitty felt, for the third time that evening, rather foolish. She took a deep breath before rejoining the fray. They hadn't long left, and Aunt Dorothy was right – Kitty must keep on track. Now was not the time to lose her head to sentiment.

20

It was April 20th. Kitty had six weeks left to secure a fortune. At least, however, she had the comfort of a number of suitors to choose from. Of these, Mr Pemberton was certainly the most persistent. With a fortune as large as his moustache, he was the richest, too.

And yet, though she had to remind herself that this did not matter, he was also the most irritating. If she were to describe Pemberton favourably, she would focus upon his kindness. A kindness so potent that it manifested as intense condescension in all their conversations, as Pemberton explained all the things in the world that she – as a frail, innocent woman – must know little of. He was kind enough, even, to not require from Kitty any of her own thoughts or opinions, and would never dream of distressing her by asking after either. Indeed, any time she did make an overture towards joining his soliloquy, he simply raised his voice enough to drown her out.

Her favourite suitor, if she permitted herself one, was Mr Stanfield. Kitty had long been resigned to the fact that she should not expect to like her husband. His outstanding quality would have to be, she knew, his wealth, and she could expect little else. And yet . . . it might be pleasant, if she could like him. To enjoy spending time with him, even. And with Mr Stanfield, it seemed like this could very well be possible. The future looked a little brighter, with him in the role. With six thousand a year to his name he had more than enough funds to satisfy her, but indeed it was not this fact that made his company so enjoyable. Their conversation was diverting, Kitty was conscious of his presence in a room even when they were not talking and, moreover, she could admit to thinking of him when they were not together. This last was always the most potent, naturally, upon each Wednesday evening when they were separated – he to Almack's, to flirt with other women out of her sight, and she to whatever alternative entertainment she could find.

But Kitty must put Mr Stanfield from her mind that day, for she had an appointment that afternoon to accompany Mr Pemberton to Tattersall's, London horse auction house – and most unusually, she was quite genuinely looking forward to it. Kitty had always thought, had the Talbots been richer, that she would have been a most committed horsewoman. As it was, with her only prior access to a stable being through the Linfields, her appreciation of fine horseflesh had been in the main theoretical. Thus, when Mr Pemberton had gallantly offered to purchase and keep a mare in his stable for her, that she might ride whenever she liked, she knew she must seize upon the opportunity. It was usually a gentleman's space, but, intrigued to see it for herself, she had induced him to invite her along too – it had taken a little persuading, but the desire to flaunt his knowledge did, in the end, prevail.

The noisy enclosure was filled to the brim with horses of all kinds – beautiful greys built for prancing ahead of a highly sprung phaeton; speckled piebalds of stunning proportions she could imagine herself riding across Hyde Park; staggeringly tall thoroughbreds with muscles coiled and gleaming. Kitty breathed in the air, relishing that specific scent of mingled straw, horsehair, and manure – a smell that should be repellent and yet was utterly wonderful – before forcing her attention back to her companion and the task at hand.

'Gosh, I don't know where we should begin,' she said in the tremulous tones of the overwhelmed, laying a hand over her heart in affected dismay.

'Do not worry yourself, Miss Talbot, I am here to help you,' Pemberton assured her. 'It is not nearly so confusing as it looks.'

He was clearly greatly enjoying playing the role of kind benefactor. Miss Talbot gave herself a pat on the back. This afternoon was to be something of a turning point in her capture of Mr Pemberton's affections. Nothing pleased the man more than displaying his own wisdom, especially in contradiction to her own. However, after only several minutes, she perceived her grave mistake. Mr Pemberton's horses being so fine, she had assumed that she could trust in his choice, but after spending a few moments in his company as he perused the horseflesh on offer with a commentary that lacked a single jot of common sense, Kitty began to suspect that Mr Pemberton's groom did not allow the man within a mile of this establishment. Goodness, would she have to praise whatever poor creature he chose, to avoid tarnishing the man's ego? She began to fear that they would be leaving with a most rash purchase.

'Gracious, you know such an awful lot,' she gushed with

inner foreboding, watching Mr Pemberton handle a pretty bay's mouth roughly.

'Watch it,' a stableboy muttered, disentangling the two. Mr Pemberton did not appear to hear.

'I have spent many years cultivating a knowledge of horse-flesh,' he explained with loud importance. 'Once you know what you are looking for, I assure you, it's really quite simple.'

His actions consistently proving quite the opposite, Miss Talbot felt her smile become somewhat fixed as Mr Pemberton began to extol the virtues of a mare that anyone with two eyes could see was not only short in the back but quite viciously tempered. Why, it would throw her within the week; she was quite appalled. It would not do – she could not risk dying before she had got married, not even to hasten the marriage itself. She was about to declare herself quite faint, feeling this was the only possible escape, when she noticed with horror that Radcliffe was walking nearby, scanning the horses with a discerning eye, a young man walking beside him – Radcliffe's tiger, from the look of his livery.

Miss Talbot turned her head away and down. While their last encounter had not ended with too much hostility, she had not forgotten Radcliffe's promise to repay her for the discomfort she had caused him. And she doubted he had either. She prayed they would walk on past without noticing her . . . but it was too late. She had been spotted, and Radcliffe was walking towards them now, eyes alight with mischief, clearly bent on causing her an upset. He drew closer. Glancing from Miss Talbot, to the horse and on to Mr Pemberton – who had yet to notice his arrival, still lecturing to himself – Radcliffe seemed at once to reach a perfect understanding of the situation. His lip curled. Miss Talbot shot him a warning glance, which he ignored. Would a shooing hand gesture be too rude?

'Good lord, Pemberton,' Radcliffe drawled, 'you are not seriously thinking of purchasing this creature, are you?' His tiger chuckled from beside him, shaking his head.

Mr Pemberton turned, bristling. 'This is the horse Miss Talbot desires, yes,' he blustered, quite untruthfully, 'I am purchasing it on her behalf.'

'Even worse,' Radcliffe retorted, 'I thought you wiser than this, Miss Talbot. Pemberton, you'd be better off looking at the pretty piebald by the west gate. This one will be throwing a leg within the first month.'

He left, with a mocking bow towards Kitty that told her he knew exactly what kind of mess he had left in his wake. Pemberton did not want to tarry a moment longer – especially when he saw with outrage Kitty's longing glance towards the piebald Radcliffe had pointed out. This was quite the cherry upon the top of his rage, and he stormed out towards his curricle, Kitty hurrying quickly behind for fear he might actually leave her there. Despite its promising start, the event could no longer be called a success, she thought gloomily, listening to Pemberton's splutterings and ruminations on the drive home. The fact that Pemberton had been humiliated was bad enough, but for the humiliation to have taken place in public and in front of the object of his affections was simply too much for a man who invested so much worth in his public image.

Kitty had been tarred by the brush of this encounter – and though it was of course within her talents to regain her former position, it would take a great deal of effort. She sighed, ignoring Pemberton's diatribe against Lord Radcliffe except to offer agreement at intervals, though inside, her own insults against the man's person were far more imaginative. Indeed, by the time Kitty was returned home – Mr Pemberton bidding her a cold good afternoon – she had become quite cross with Radcliffe.

Later that evening, Kitty, dressed in a gown of pale blue crêpe, Cecily, in faintest pink satin, and Aunt Dorothy, in dashing violet, arrived at the grand town house that was to host that night's ball. Spotting Lord Radcliffe, Kitty promptly left Cecily and Dorothy to their own devices and approached in high dudgeon.

'Dance with me,' she demanded, walking straight up to him. He eyed her warily.

'Thank you, but no,' he said. 'I should have mentioned that I also do not dance with persons who appear to want to murder me.'

'Dance with me,' she repeated. 'I have some things I should like to say to you.'

'Dear God,' he groaned. 'What now?'

'I shall tell you *what now*,' she hissed at him. 'What on earth did you think you were doing at Tattersall's today? What was that?'

'I rather thought,' he said, 'that I was helping Pemberton to avoid making a very unwise purchase. Surely you could see that it wasn't a good choice?'

'Of course I could,' she snapped. 'But I never would have let him buy the creature – and my method of ensuring this would not have caused Mr Pemberton so much distress. You have set me back in his estimation something awfully – you must never do such a thing again!'

Radcliffe's only response was a small smirk, and Kitty's anger quite boiled over.

'Is this a joke to you?' she demanded. 'Because this is my family at stake, my lord. My ten-year-old sister, Jane, will have nowhere to live if I do not have something to show to the moneylenders who will be banging on our door in less than six weeks.'

He looked taken aback, but she continued mercilessly. 'My sister, Harriet, is fourteen, and the most romantic creature you ever did meet. I don't know how I would tell her that she will never be able to marry for love, because I could not secure her future for her. And Beatrice—'

He raised a hand. 'You have quite made your point,' he said. She glared at him, chest heaving with the force of her emotion.

'I apologise,' he said simply. 'It will not happen again.'

Kitty blinked, glare dissipating. She had not expected an apology. 'Thank you,' she said at last.

They looked at each other for a few moments. 'I think that is the first time you have actually done what I asked of you, without argument,' she said, a little uncertainly. She was not sure how to speak to him now that the air was not weighed down by animosity.

'Am I the only person you have met that does not immediately do your bidding?' he asked curiously.

'I suppose I am used to having my way,' she allowed. 'I'm the oldest in my family, so perhaps it is force of habit.'

'Oh, that will be it,' he agreed at once. 'Nothing at all to do with the militant planning or iron will, of course.'

Kitty looked at him with a touch of surprise, an ember of warmth lighting in her chest.

'Why, that almost sounded like a compliment, my lord.'

'I'm losing my touch, it seems,' he said. 'You are, of course, also lacking anything resembling moral integrity, and I imagine that goes a long way towards contributing, too.'

'Oh, of course,' she said, smiling. There was no sting in his words, and only humour in his grey eyes, so she found herself quite happy to accept the teasing. She had not been teased in a while, and it felt – not unpleasant.

'May I procure for you a refreshment, as proof of my apology?' he asked, proffering an arm. She moved to take it – instinctively, without hesitation, as if this were the hundredth time this had happened, and not the first – before catching herself. She had matters to attend to, and the only men she ought to be spending time on were her suitors.

'I find I am not thirsty,' she refused the offer and the arm. 'You shall owe me a favour instead.'

'Oh, shall I?' he asked, lip twitching at her lofty tone. 'That sounds dangerously vague to me. Are you sure a glass of wine would not do?'

'I am,' she said grandly. 'It shall be a favour of my choosing, at a time of my appointment.'

He eyed her suspiciously. 'Am I to expect another early morning call? I warn you, Beaverton is now under strict instructions to shoot on sight before ten o'clock.'

She smiled mysteriously. 'I suppose you shall have to see.'

21

'And so, I told him . . .' Aunt Dorothy gave a dramatic pause, her smile coquettish and intriguing '. . . why would I play whist with a lord, when I could play faro with a prince?'

Lady Radcliffe let out a peal of laughter at the punchline, joined by Mr Fletcher, Mr Sinclair and Lord Derby. Kitty looked on with an indulgent smile. Were Kitty a pettier character, she might find some enjoyment in reminding her aunt that not so many weeks ago it was she who was warning Kitty against the *ton* with all the doom and gloom she could muster. As it was, Kitty felt no reason to ruin Aunt Dorothy's fun – so long as it remained firmly within the bounds of propriety, that was. Kitty resolved to keep an eye on her aunt and Lady Radcliffe's developing friendship. The two ladies had, in recent evenings, taken to flirting with every gentleman that crossed their path with increasing fervour.

They had relaxed a little now, Kitty, Cecily and Aunt Dorothy. The greatest challenges of the Season were behind them; they knew the rules now, they were *in* and safely so, with nary a whisper of suspicion about them. Aunt Dorothy had even stopped worrying about being recognised, her chief fear of those first few balls, as she walked around eyeing all the men with suspicion. By contrast, just now Mr Fletcher – the newest admirer in Mrs Kendall's coterie, a silver-haired gentleman with a very distinguished set of side-whiskers – was roguishly challenging her aunt to a duel of whist in the card room, which she accepted without a question. Kitty declined to observe with a smile. She was sure the sight would be impressive – especially since she knew for a fact that Aunt Dorothy was the most accomplished cheat – but Kitty had business to attend to.

She and Mr Stanfield had already danced once this evening, a quadrille, but Kitty's eyes had been drawn to him over and over through the night. Often, she would look over to find him already looking back, their gazes dragging against each other's for long moments again and again, making her heart beat faster inside her chest. It was a flirtation that was no less thrilling for it taking place from across a ballroom and Kitty did not want to miss a second of it.

Not being able to see Mr Stanfield at that moment, Kitty cast idly about for Cecily, instead. For someone who claimed to have no interest in balls, Cecily disappeared confidently enough into the crowds these days. Was that her? Kitty frowned. She had seen a glimpse of a pink-dressed figure partially hidden by the bulk of that detestable lech Lord Arden, and craned her neck to get a better view. There were so many people squashed in the room, it was hard to see. Yes, there was Cecily . . . shrinking back from Lord Arden, who was quite towering over her. Kitty moved purposefully forward, cutting through the crowd like a hot knife through butter.

'Cecily!' she called, as soon as she was within hearing distance.

'Ah – Miss Talbot,' Lord Arden sent Kitty an oily smile, quite unperturbed by her sudden appearance. 'I was just asking for your sister's hand for the next set.'

His eyes roved avariciously over Cecily's form and Cecily took an involuntary step back. Kitty stepped forward.

'I'm afraid my sister's dance card is full,' she said firmly. Lord Arden's eyebrows rose haughtily.

'And yet she is not dancing now,' he said softly, upper lip beginning to sneer.

'Why, every lady needs a rest, my lord,' Kitty said, baring her teeth in a smile. 'I'm sure you understand.'

Lord Arden was not to be deterred. 'There are many dances this evening,' he cajoled. 'I am sure, Miss Cecily, that you will be well rested enough for one of them.'

'Her dance card is full,' Kitty insisted. Weaker characters might consider the attentions of this loathsome man to be a necessary tax, but Kitty did not. 'And I would suggest, my lord, that you consider it *permanently* full.'

There was an audible gasp and Kitty looked over to see an eavesdropping Lady Kingsbury clap her hand over her mouth in theatrical shock. Lord Arden turned purple with mortification.

'Never,' he said, voice shaking with anger, 'never have I been so insulted in my life.'

He stalked away. Lady Kingsbury was still staring at them. Kitty looked at her, expecting to find sympathy in the lady's face – after all, they all knew very well what Arden was – but Lady Kingsbury merely shook her head with a little smile, before quite obviously turning her back upon them. The cut direct.

'Do you think he was very cross?' Cecily whispered.

'I do not think he will bother you again,' Kitty said, not much caring if he was or not. 'Come, let's find some champagne.'

Yet even as she spoke, the fissures of gossip from this confrontation were spidering their way through the ball like cracks in a flagstone. Even as they picked their way through the masses in search of the supper room, a slight chill began to emanate from the crowd. She noticed that there were more eyes looking in her direction than was usual – judgemental eyes, too. She smiled at Mrs Sinclair as they passed each other, but the lady avoided her gaze. Strange – what could she have done to offend her? By the third time this had happened, Kitty began to realise something had gone very wrong.

'What is this I hear about you being terribly rude?' Mr Stanfield's voice spoke quietly in her ear. Kitty turned quickly.

'What do you mean?' she asked, her heart beating a little fast.

Mr Stanfield chuckled. 'Rumour is you gave Arden the most egregious and vulgar set down. Well done, I say.'

He seemed to find the whole thing amusing, but Kitty could not bring herself to laugh with him.

'Do people really care?' she asked. 'I did not think he was much liked.'

'Oh, you know them,' he said with a careless wave of the hand. 'Best not to pay attention. Anyway, I came to say farewell – I must escort my mother home.'

He left her, and Kitty stared around the ballroom. *You know them*, he had said. But Kitty did not. She had not expected this reaction in the slightest. After all, she had heard most of the women here complain of Lord Arden's wandering hands at least once. And yet it seemed that the unwritten rule was that one could only condemn him behind his back and never to his face. And while the likes of Lady Jersey could be considered rude without it having consequences for her reputation, it was becoming very clear that Kitty could not.

Lady Kingsbury – a hateful woman, Kitty now saw – was spreading the gossip like a fast-acting poison. Never had a tide changed so quickly and when Kitty and Cecily had been given the shoulder by two further ladies they had quite considered as friends, Kitty began quietly to panic. Surely this could not ruin them?

'I think we had best find Aunt Dorothy and Lady Radcliffe,' she told Cecily, who nodded, lips pressed together. Safe in the protective circle of Lady Radcliffe's approval, Kitty felt sure this would all cease to matter. Except that they could not find either of these two ladies, anywhere. As they searched the card room, then the ballroom, Kitty could feel the figurative temperature of the crowd dropping even further. She searched instead for a friendly face – *any* friendly face – where they could find refuge, the empty space around them feeling like a quarantine. She tried to make eye contact with Mr Pemberton as she passed, but he eluded her, affecting to appear deeply in conversation with Miss Fleming.

'Ought we to leave, Kitty?' Cecily whispered. Her dreamy and distracted nature usually protected her from noticing such slights, but even she was now looking anxious.

'No,' Kitty insisted. 'No, we cannot retreat.'

Yet what other options did they have? Do as they do, her mother would have said – and the *ton* were about to dance. But with Mr Stanfield gone, Kitty could not be sure that any one of her other suitors would now come to her rescue. Who else, amongst all these sheep, would not care about her sudden fall from grace?

Across the dance floor, her eyes fell on Radcliffe. Well . . . it was not exactly a *friendly* face. She led Cecy forward, ignoring all the figures that were shrinking away from them.

'Lord Radcliffe, Captain Hinsley, good evening,' she said, in businesslike tones.

'Miss Talbot,' Captain Hinsley greeted her with a bow and a smile as if they were old friends.

'Watch yourself, Hinsley, she might be armed,' Radcliffe warned.

'Are neither of you dancing?' Kitty asked pointedly, ignoring this remark. 'I think they are making up the set now.'

It was a blatant move, totally lacking in subtlety – and both men's eyebrows shot up.

Captain Hinsley recovered first, bowing gallantly. 'Is it too much to hope your hand is not already promised, Miss Talbot?'

'It is not,' she said, placing her hand in his. She held onto Radcliffe's gaze, challengingly. She was thinking of the favour he owed her and knew he was too. He raised his eyebrows further. She jutted her chin, challengingly, and cut her eyes to Cecily, with strong meaning. He sighed.

'Miss Cecily, would you do me the honour?' Radcliffe asked.

Cecily had quite missed the silent interchange between her elder sister and Radcliffe – though Captain Hinsley had watched it, much intrigued – but smiled gratefully, nonetheless. They made their way to the floor.

'Do you know which dance it is?' Cecily asked.

'The quadrille, I believe,' Radcliffe answered.

'It is properly pronounced *quadree*,' Cecily corrected him, with an ostentatious French flourish of the word. Radcliffe paused – but what else, really, was there to say, except, 'Thank you, Miss Talbot.'

Radcliffe had danced only twice that Season, once with the elder Miss Talbot and once with his mother. He was widely known to be as stubborn as a mule about it, and so the *ton* watched with surprise and interest as he led Miss Cecily Talbot onto the floor for only his third dance of the whole year. Kitty watched them watching and hoped this would constitute enough of a reminder as to why they had accepted the Talbots in the first place.

Kitty felt so agitated that she could not think of a single thing to say to Captain Hinsley as they took their places, but he fortunately seemed perfectly able to run the conversation by himself.

'Miss Talbot, I feel I should thank you,' he said. 'This has already been the most interesting Season I've seen in years.'

'Is that so?' she said, trying to scan the crowd without appearing to do so.

'And to get Radcliffe dancing too . . . He's awfully good at it, once you get him out here – wouldn't think it to look at him, though, would you?' At this he sent a roguish grin Kitty's way, as if to invite her to join him in disparaging Radcliffe.

'Wouldn't you?' she said, still distracted. 'One only has to see him ride to know he's graceful.'

The music began before Hinsley could answer – though his eyebrows were now sitting a little higher upon his forehead – and soon they were too busy with their *chassés* and *jettés* to speak. The quadrille lasted only six minutes, but by the time it was over, Kitty could tell their position upon the social ladder was far less precarious. Radcliffe relinquished Cecily to a glaring Lord Montagu – who had just made a late arrival – and Kitty accepted Hinsley's escort to the refreshment table. There he left her, with a knowing smile which Kitty failed to interpret, beckoned back to the dance floor by Lady Derby, and Kitty had the relief of accepting a lemonade from a new gentleman, able to breathe more easily.

'I do not believe we have met,' she said to the stranger, smiling – she was willing to look kindly on any gentleman, right now.

'We have not, though I have long wished to be acquainted, Miss Talbot. I am Selbourne,' he said in a slow drawl. 'I must say, I do admire your work.'

'My work?' she repeated, frowning.

'Come now,' he said chidingly. 'There is no harm in speaking openly. I am a friend of Mr de Lacy's, you know, and he has told me all about you. Though he doesn't realise, of course, how the story sounds to one such as I.'

'I am sure I do not know what you mean, my lord,' she said slowly.

'I quite recognise you for a kindred spirit, you know,' he said smoothly – too smoothly. 'Both of us, on the outskirts of all this' – he gestured to the room – 'both doing our best to win, despite it all.'

'Is that so?' she asked politely, though her hackles were beginning to rise. 'I'll have to take your word for it, my lord, though I for one fail to see the similarity.'

He smiled, approvingly. 'A fine hitter, too. Miss Talbot, I feel I have known you for all my life.'

She did not answer, not in the least wanting to encourage such a troubling conversation, but Selbourne persevered.

'I should like to speak to you properly, you know. I believe we could be . . . most helpful to one another.'

'Would that I could say the same,' Kitty said coolly, 'but I think you have me confused for someone else.'

He smiled, still unperturbed. 'I see you are determined not to speak to me.' He bowed with a little flourish as the music drew the dancers on the floor to a close. 'But do think on it, Miss Talbot. There is more than one way to make a fortune in this town – and you need not do it alone.'

Kitty extracted herself from his company as soon as she could and was relieved to lay eyes on Aunt Dorothy at last.

'Where were you?' she demanded.

'Shall we go, darling?' Aunt Dorothy said, appearing too preoccupied by a loose thread on her cuff to answer. Kitty agreed, gathering Cecily up too – it would not do to test the waters too thoroughly. As they waited to be handed their cloaks, Radcliffe appeared again at her shoulder.

'Have you thought about what you are going to do once I have returned to Devonshire, and you cannot extract from me dances whenever it suits you?' he asked in a low voice.

'I suppose I shall have to find some other means,' she said wryly. 'Or learn to curb my tongue a little better.'

'Ah, your slight of the reprehensible Arden?' he guessed. He looked at her sidelong. 'Was it a very good set down?'

Her lips twitched. 'My finest so far,' she admitted. 'But it caused such a fuss – I feared for a moment we might be quite undone.'

He shrugged – an informal gesture that did not suit the

ballroom, and not one she had ever seen him do before. She had a sudden vision of what he might look like, striding around his Devonshire lands. He would be more at ease, there, surely, than he was here – though no less striking.

'They are a capricious and unprincipled lot, where titles and wealth are concerned,' he said, with casual condemnation, before adding, '*I* should not like to dance with him.'

He said this as though it was enough of a reason, all on its own. The simplicity of the words helped to calm some of the anxiety within her.

'Yes, exactly,' she agreed, a little surprised to find them so aligned.

He left her with a smile and Kitty climbed into the carriage behind her sister. As they made for home, she tried to explain the whole ordeal to Aunt Dorothy, but Kitty was aggrieved to find that her aunt did not understand in the least.

'Hasn't every lady had to dance with someone she would not like to, at least once?' she was asking, a little nonplussed by all the fuss.

'That doesn't make it right,' Kitty muttered obstinately.

'Perhaps I should have just danced with him,' Cecily whispered from the corner. 'It mightn't have been so bad.'

Kitty reached out in the dark and took her sister's hand.

'No,' she said simply, squeezing the small palm.

22

Lord Radcliffe arrived at Grosvenor Square as dusk was falling. It was Archie's birthday, and the family had gathered for supper to celebrate the occasion. As Radcliffe entered, he could already hear the echo of voices travelling up from the dining room and smiled at the raucous noise. The de Lacys had always made an occasion of birthdays – Lady Radcliffe feeling it was especially important to mark such moments properly – but Radcliffe had not been in London for Archie's these past two years. And so it still seemed peculiar to Radcliffe that he would not find his father in the dining room, too.

Radcliffe stood in the hallway for a minute longer than necessary, struck anew by this strangeness. One did not get used to it, he thought wryly. He had entered this door a thousand times – a hundred thousand times, perhaps – knowing both his parents could be found inside. And now he was to accept that it was no longer true? It felt impossible. Of course, had his father been alive, he would no doubt already be berating Radcliffe for something – reminding him of a task that should have been done, but hadn't, or a misdeed he shouldn't have performed, but had. Or would he? Radcliffe supposed he could not be sure. His father had been incensed by his son's refusal to return to England when war broke out again – more furious even than when he had first sent his son away for the uncertain crime of his frivolous living. Radcliffe had hoped this stance would eventually soften. What to his father had been another grievous failure of family duty had to Radcliffe been the only honourable action he could take, and he had thought his father might one day see that, too. But they had never had the chance to speak further after Waterloo. His father had died before Radcliffe had returned home. And so, Radcliffe would never know if fighting in a war had redeemed him in his father's eyes – finally proving him a worthy son.

'My lord?' Pattson's voice interrupted his reverie, and Radcliffe came back to the present with a start. The direction of Radcliffe's thoughts must have been plain in his face, because Pattson's expression of cool professionalism softened infinitesimally. It was a change not many people would register – but then, Radcliffe had known Pattson quite as long, and quite as well, as any member of his family.

'The rest of the family are in the dining room,' Pattson said quietly, watching him with kind, knowing eyes.

'Yes of course, I'll head that way.'

As he passed, Pattson pressed a hand briefly upon his shoulder – a very rare trespass of propriety that he would not normally allow himself. Radcliffe placed a hand over his without looking up and they stood there silently for a beat, before he moved on without speaking a single word.

'Happy birthday, Archie,' Radcliffe clasped his younger

brother's arm warmly. Archie squeezed his hand back, grinning – though a little weakly. He did look, Radcliffe thought,
rather pale.

'Are you all right?' he could not help asking in a quiet aside.

'Yes, yes,' Archie said, with a wan smile that quickly slipped
off his face. There was a pause and then, he went on abruptly.
'You were right about Miss Talbot, you know.'

'Ah.' Radcliffe felt a pang of guilt. He had quite forgotten
that Archie might be smarting from the Miss Talbot affair –
though at least, he thought with relief, it was nothing serious
bothering him.

'Yes, she's quite forgotten me now,' Archie said with unchar-
acteristic bitterness. 'Setting her cap at everyone but me, it
seems. Thank goodness for Selbourne, he's—'

'Are you sure you do not want a party, Archie?' Lady Radcliffe
interrupted, gesturing impatiently for her sons to take their
seats. 'It is not too late, you know. After all, coming of age is
an important moment – we all want to celebrate!'

'I don't,' Lady Amelia said sourly. 'Why should I celebrate
Archie coming into his inheritance?'

'No, Mama,' Archie said firmly, ignoring his sister. 'I am
quite sick of – I mean to say, I am quite tired. This has been
a . . . busy Season already.'

Radcliffe eyed him a little suspiciously. This seemed unlike
Archie, who had historically always loved his birthday, the Season,
and really, any excuse at all for a celebration. But perhaps that
was no longer true. Radcliffe shrugged it off and before long the
usual hubbub of the family overtook matters. As dinner was
served, Archie seemed to regain his colour, looking and sounding
more like his usual self, and Radcliffe was pleased to see it.

By the second course, Lady Radcliffe and Amelia had resumed their old argument as to when Amelia should be allowed to attend her first ball this Season.

'Next year,' Lady Radcliffe was insisting. 'You are still very young.'

'All of my friends are attending at least one this Season,' Amelia complained loudly. 'Not coming out – but just dipping their toe. Really, I shall be considered quite frightfully green if I'm the only one who hasn't. Just one, Mama, surely there is no harm? After all, I'm only a year younger than Cecily and she's been to heaps of them.'

Lady Radcliffe looked torn. She was not unsympathetic to the plea, but she could not help feeling daunted by the prospect of all her children out in society – and no doubt getting up to no good – at once. She hesitated, undecided. Life seemed full of these sorts of weighty decisions this year, and since her husband's death, she had no one to discuss them with. Except that now, Radcliffe was right there. She turned hopefully to her eldest son.

'James, what do you think?' she demanded.

Radcliffe paused with a spear of asparagus halfway to his mouth. 'What do I think of . . .?' he asked, warily.

'Of whether I should let Amelia be allowed to one ball this Season. Perhaps it would not do any harm – but then, if it will not, what is the problem with waiting?' She looked at him, expectantly. Across the table, Amelia gazed at him, pleadingly. He stared from one to the other.

'I would like your view, James,' Lady Radcliffe insisted when he did not speak.

Radcliffe felt himself begin to sweat. He did not know what his view was and would not feel at all qualified to give it even if he did know. Was there any harm to it? Amelia was still just seventeen, which seemed young – and yet was that the terribly dour sort of opinion his father would have had? Was a terribly dour opinion the right one, anyhow? His cravat was beginning to feel awfully tight.

'It's your decision, Mama,' he said at last, tugging on his collar. 'I would not presume to know better.'

Lady Radcliffe looked a little crestfallen to have the responsibility batted back so easily.

'I shall think on it, Amelia,' she said to her daughter.

Radcliffe knew he had failed to pass her test. But really, why on earth should she call upon him for these matters, when he was barely ten years older than Amelia? Just because he had the title, now, did not mean he had any more experience or wisdom than he had when his father was alive. The late Lord Radcliffe would have had an opinion, of course – and they all would have heard about it, as loud as the church bell's ringing at St Paul's, he thought bitterly. He would have cared: cared for what was proper or improper, cared what other families were doing, and what they would think. Whereas Radcliffe could not muster any sense of that thought or effort within himself, though it was so clearly going to be required of him more and more the longer he stayed in London. Not for the first time, a desire to leave – to escape – warred within him with the desire to remain. Life was simpler at Radcliffe Hall; there he was free from family pressures, and yet . . . the London Season was captivating him more this year than it had before. Some of the responsibility for this lay, he could admit, at the door of Miss Talbot – and the unpredictability she was bringing to matters – and now he had begun the Season he could not help but want to see where it – and she – ended up.

The rest of the evening passed pleasantly enough, with presents exchanged and well wishes given – the food was divine, as always, and the evening ended with a towering cake that Archie dove into with gusto. Radcliffe smiled and laughed along, but he could not help but keep ruminating on his mother's question – the one she had actually asked, and the one that was subtext – though he was no closer to reaching an answer for either when it was time to leave. He and Archie walked to the door together, Archie thanking him again for his gift.

'You will come to me, if you need to, won't you, Archie?' Radcliffe said abruptly, just as Archie was about to turn for the stairs. His brother looked taken aback and Radcliffe swung his hat awkwardly in his hands. 'You may not need to, of course, but . . . If you do. I know we have not spent much time together, in recent years. Perhaps we could ride out, soon, to Wimbledon again – or further afield, if you want.'

Archie nodded, his jaw working furiously.

'I should like that,' he said finally. 'I should like that very much.'

He stared at his brother for a few seconds – and Radcliffe looked back, a little thrown by the strange emotional weight of the moment.

'James—' Archie began, stepping forward, but before he could say anything, Amelia crashed into the hallway, interrupting them.

'Are you still here?' she said rudely to her eldest brother.

'I was just leaving, you unconscionable toad,' he told her imperiously.

But the moment between him and Archie had passed, so quickly that Radcliffe wondered if he had imagined the vulnerability in Archie's face – for it was now quite casual. Radcliffe chastised himself a little, for forcing such a serious moment on what should be a carefree day. This clumsy kind of interference was exactly, he thought, why such things were best left to his mother.

23

A lesser woman would consider Kitty's social calendar to be a trifle stressful, over the next few weeks. But Kitty, ever-mindful of her deadline, was determined to jam as many balls, dinner parties, theatre trips, promenades, exhibitions and recitals into her days as possible. Besides, even if it was a little daunting – gazing at her calendar of events that morning – nothing could dampen her mood *that* day, for she and her family had been invited to call at Mrs Stanfield's town house. This was, Kitty felt, a very good sign.

'Of course,' she said airily to Cecily as they walked, Sally following two steps behind, 'if he wants to marry me, that does not mean I should automatically accept. It would have to be the best offer, naturally.'

Cecily only hummed in response. Their aunt was not with them, having begged off due to a headache. Aunt Dorothy had been getting rather a lot of these recently, though their origins – given the vast amount of champagne she was consuming nightly – seemed far from mysterious.

They arrived to find several visitors already arranged in the lofty drawing room, though Kitty was gratified to receive the assiduous attentions of Mrs Stanfield as soon as they entered. This was surely a good sign, too, and Kitty suppressed a pleased smile. Across the room, Mr Stanfield sent her a wink. As she spoke to the lady, whose bearing was warm and welcoming, Kitty could not help imagining a life where she might be allowed to have both – to win happiness for herself as well as a fortune for her sisters. It would be . . . marvellous. And Kitty could not quite believe how close it seemed actually to be happening.

That is, until Mrs Stanfield's conversation began to beat a very familiar path. She asked first about Kitty's family – from where they hailed, the whereabouts of their family home – and though Mrs Stanfield's bearing remained sunny, Kitty's smile faded a little.

'The air!' Mrs Stanfield sang gaily of Dorsetshire. 'The *hills*. Just beautiful!'

Commenting upon the air and the hills was, Kitty supposed, a safe bet given that most counties could be depended upon to have both.

'You must tell me where your family home is, my dear, for I might even have been there – I know it to be close to the Radcliffe's family estate, is it not?' Mrs Stanfield asked with supreme, and false, casualness. Mrs Stanfield was desirous of discovering her financial situation – as if it even mattered to her, when their family was already so very rich. And yet still she had asked.

'Our cottage is certainly not so far from Devonshire,' Kitty said slowly, 'a day's ride at the very most.'

'Cottage?' Mrs Stanfield repeated, helping herself to a nibble of cake, but keeping her eyes upon Kitty's face, the question quite clear.

It was tempting to lie. So very tempting.

'Cottage,' Kitty repeated firmly. 'Where I live with my four sisters.'

'Four! *Lovely*,' Mrs Stanfield gushed with over-the-top enthusiasm. 'Just lovely. In a cottage, too. What a *blessing*, indeed. I must see to my other guests, my dear, but I do hope you will partake of the apple cake – it is quite delicious.'

She bustled off before Kitty could utter another word. Kitty stared after her, still not quite sure exactly what had happened. She watched as Mrs Stanfield moved through the clusters of guests, passing her son for a brief moment. They did not speak to one another, but Mrs Stanfield must have made some kind of gesture to her son – a meaningful look, a minute hand gesture – for Mr Stanfield looked immediately over to where Kitty was sitting and smiled at her. But it was not the smile of rascally mischief that Kitty privately thought of as hers. Rather, it was a smile of apology. She knew then that he would be calling on her no longer. Kitty took in a deep breath – trying to control the shock of the blow which she felt deep in her stomach – and engaged herself busily back in social niceties. By the time she and Cecily took their leave, he was deep in conversation with Miss Fleming, and they looked to be having quite the time of it.

The superb spring weather they had been enjoying for weeks broke that evening. Low clouds smothered the London skyline, extinguishing the last of the light and casting hazy grey mist over the city. It was a fitting weather for how Kitty herself was feeling. She placed Aunt Dorothy's paste diamonds in her ears and around her wrists, preparing for another outing and resolutely ignoring the sharp pain that had settled beneath her breastbone ever since she had returned from the Stanfield house. She could not give in to a self-indulgent attack of low spirits now, not when she had only herself to blame for having them in the first place. After all, it had been foolish to possess any sort of romantic pretension, and here was the proof of what she had always feared. All she could do now was move onward. There was much still to be done – Kitty still had no proposals to her name, and she could not be happy with a state of affairs where her principal hopes rested upon Mr Pemberton.

She was ruminating upon this at the ball that night, at the edge of the dance floor, when Radcliffe appeared at her side. He offered her a flute of champagne, which she took with a subdued thanks, saying to him flatly, 'I'm not in the mood to argue tonight.'

Radcliffe's innocent eyebrow raise communicated his disbelief, and even hurt, that she should suspect him of so foul a motive. But, reading the lack of amusement in her face, he appeared to relent.

'Noted,' he said instead, turning so that he too faced the sea of dancers, his eyes following their turns and twirls. 'How goes the hunt?'

She investigated his tone for any suggestion of mockery but, finding none, answered honestly.

'I imagine it is easy to guess. Mr Pemberton is rich enough to satisfy.'

'You are no longer considering Mr Stanfield as among the principals?' he asked. 'I imagined him to be your favourite.'

She examined her fan for imperfections – was that a tear in

its lace? 'He was,' she said quietly. 'But I am afraid he is committed to finding a wealthy wife.'

'Ah,' he said gravely. 'I suppose that is not so surprising. The Stanfields are affluent spendthrifts – their expenditures are such as they must depend upon an influx of fresh wealth with every new alliance.'

'It matters not,' she said with a hint of bitterness. 'Pemberton has enough wealth to support my family and allow us to keep our home – though I do need another option, for safety.'

He mulled this over for a moment. 'Your commitment to retaining your family home is, I admit, a little surprising.'

'How so?' she asked, deciding to await his answer before becoming offended.

'Well, you are so obviously at home here, in town. Why not stay in London?'

'My my, Lord Radcliffe,' she said archly, 'and here I thought you couldn't wait to get rid of me.'

He ignored this. 'Why not let Netley go, sell, and make your home elsewhere?'

'I have enjoyed London a great deal more than I thought I would, it's true,' she allowed. 'It is infinitely entertaining, but Netley has been home to me and mine for all of my life. I'm not in a hurry to give that up – and nor would its sale cover the full breadth of our need.'

'So, it's sentiment,' he said, smiling slightly. 'And I thought you above such feeling.'

She flushed but raised her chin. 'And so, what if it is? We have lost much, my lord. Would you sell Radcliffe Hall, if your need were great enough?'

'Point,' he acknowledged wryly. 'I would not, it's true, however tempting it might be. But Radcliffe Hall has been in my family for generations. It's who I am.'

Kitty shrugged. 'Then we are not so different.'

'Perhaps not,' he said slowly.

'Is that surprising to you?' she asked with a wicked glint in her eye that told him she would be very pleased if it was.

'This conversation is surprising,' he said instead. 'I suppose I am not used to discussing property with women.'

She scoffed. 'You are so used to women owning no property that you imagine they have no taste for it?'

He inclined his head in acknowledgement. 'Though when you marry,' he persisted, 'you will hardly continue to live there.'

'And why not?' she asked him.

'I cannot imagine Mr Pemberton willing to give up residence in his family seat to reside in yours.'

She tilted her head. 'Perhaps not. But one of my sisters might like to make her home there, when she is of age. A home is an expensive thing, Lord Radcliffe, and I should like my sisters to not be obliged to marry to find one.' She let that sentence linger for a moment, before lightening her voice and saying flippantly. 'Besides, who is to say that I could not make Pemberton want to live there, were I so inclined?'

He snorted, his sympathetic feeling squashed by this fresh reminder of her manipulative nature. 'I'm sure you are more than equal to it. After all, what does the will of your husband matter in the slightest? He might as well be a life-sized purse, for all the agency you would allow him.'

She narrowed her eyes at him, rankled by his tone.

'And where, my lord,' she said, 'do you imagine *your* future wife residing? At a home of hers . . . or Radcliffe Hall?'

He frowned at her. 'It is not the same and you know it,' he rebutted. 'If I marry, it would be without manipulation.'

Kitty hummed noncommittally.

'It is not the same,' he insisted again.

'Oh, there is no need to be defensive, my lord,' Kitty said loftily. 'It does not make you a bad person, after all – just a hypocrite.'

Kitty placed her glass down upon a passing tray, curtseyed a farewell, and left him. She had tarried long enough. She did not look back, though if she had, she would have seen that Lord Radcliffe was still watching her – his expression quite unreadable.

Kitty stalked through the hall, eyes casting about hawklike for fresh gentlemen. Her eyes were caught, however, not by a prospective suitor, but by a young lady standing alone and looking a little lost. Perhaps it was speaking to Radcliffe about her sisters, but there was something about her – perhaps her slightly luminous forehead – that reminded Kitty suddenly of Beatrice with a sharp pang, and once the resemblance had been noticed she could not stop herself from approaching.

'I do not believe we have met,' Kitty said softly, when she was close enough to be heard over the music. The girl looked up, startled. 'I am Miss Talbot.'

They curtseyed to one another. 'Miss Bloom,' the girl said in a high, girlish voice. 'Pleased to make your acquaintance.'

The young lady made no move to continue the conversation, lapsing back into quiet, and staring longingly across the room. Kitty followed the direction of her gaze to a young gentleman standing rigidly watching the dancers. He was very angular – with elbows, shoulders and kneecaps that were somehow prominent even through his fashionable dark waistcoat and pantaloons – and quite unknown to Kitty.

'Are you an acquaintance of the young man, Miss Bloom?' Kitty asked, and the young lady blushed rosily. Ah.

'Not an acquaintance now, though we used to know each other well,' Miss Bloom said haltingly. 'But I should like to know him better, if only it were possible.'

'Why would it not be possible?' Kitty asked, confused. 'You are both here, are you not?'

The girl shook her head sadly, as if the problem were too large even to speak aloud.

'You are both here,' Kitty repeated again briskly. 'Is the man not wealthy enough for you?'

The young lady looked a little shocked. 'N-no,' she stammered. 'Mr Crawton is, I believe, quite wealthy – he's said to have seven thousand pounds a year at least.'

'Then what is the issue?' Kitty asked impatiently.

'My mama and papa are quite set on my marrying a man with a title,' she explained quietly. 'And so, Mama will not make an introduction between myself and Mr Crawton. She says I might just as well fall in love with a titled man as an untitled one.' She looked over at him longingly. 'We used to know each other as children,' she explained. 'He was so kind – we share so many of the same interests. We are both shy, too, but together it did not seem to matter. I just wish he'd notice me now.'

'But apparently not enough to bring the thing about,' Kitty said tartly. 'How can he notice you, when you're in the corner speaking to me?'

'What else am I supposed to do?' Miss Bloom said indignantly. 'Just walk up to him and start talking?'

'Would that be so bad?'

'Yes! It's just not done – what would I even say? How forward I would seem . . .' she said wretchedly, wringing her hands.

'Well, think of an excuse,' Kitty said crossly. 'Does he know where the refreshments are? Has he seen your mother, for you have quite lost her? Drop your fan and ask him to locate it for you. Dear God, girl, there are a thousand options. Just pick one!'

Miss Bloom shot her a look of growing alarm. 'I cannot,' she said faintly.

Kitty sighed. Could Miss Bloom honestly not overcome the simple obstacle of the length of this room? Still, seven thousand pounds a year was quite a healthy fortune indeed. She looked at Miss Bloom for another moment – should she cajole her into taking her future into her own hands? Try harder to make her see sense, to see that she must grasp the opportunity? It did feel a little too ruthless, even for Kitty, to take Mr Crawton for herself after being taken so far into the young lady's confidence.

Except that this was a ruthless world – and blinding oneself to that served no one. Kitty turned to the room with a decisive swish of her skirts, bidding Miss Bloom farewell over her shoulder. She had a fan to drop.

Netley Cottage, Wednesday April 22nd

Dearest Kitty,

We read your last letter at least thrice this week, and it greatly lifted our spirits. Harriet has not been feeling well and isn't at all satisfied by my attempts to soothe her – it seems I am not nearly so accomplished a nursemaid as you.

We were all heartened by the glittering tales of London. It may already seem commonplace to you, but to us it is as if you have travelled to another world. It sounds very much as if you are beset by admirers, and I am sure will have secured a proposal in no time at all. I hope, however, that amongst your suitors you are able to find one who is sufficient in character, as well as wealth.

This may be our last correspondence. Repairs to the roof have begun, as you instructed, but I'm afraid the money you sent will not quite cover the expense. We have enough to keep us going, but we shall no longer be able to pay the cost of a letter's delivery. Do not fret, we shall be perfectly well!

We are sending all of our love to you and Cecily. We were most pleased by the poem Cecily enclosed in your last letter – though sadly, none of us fully understood the meaning.

Until we can speak again, I remain your loving sister,
Beatrice

24

The engagement of Mr Stanfield and Miss Fleming was announced the following week. And it was fine, it was utterly fine, because whatever Mr Stanfield was doing changed nothing for Kitty, of course. She still had Pemberton as a suitor – he was a veritable fixture at her side these days – and now Mr Crawton, too, who Kitty had been pursuing persistently and successfully ever since their first meeting. In fact, all that mattered from the Mr Stanfield episode was that she had learnt something useful – that a man's annual income was not so revealing a statistic as she had always believed. That she might have engaged herself to Mr Stanfield without knowing his financial unsuitability, despite his six thousand a year, was cause for considerable disquiet – and a valuable lesson. She must be sure of each suitor's financial situation beyond their jointure. The rub was also that one could not simply come out and *ask*, for such a conversation did not lend itself well to a romantic tête-à-tête. So how was she to investigate Mr Pemberton – and now Mr Crawton's – finances to ascertain if she could safely back either one of those horses? The solution seemed too inevitable to deny even to herself. Kitty looked over to the grandfather clock in the corner. Quarter to nine in the morning. She ought really to wait until later . . . but Kitty found she did not want to. By the time she arrived it would be past nine, at least.

'As you know,' Kitty began, speaking to Radcliffe in her most calming tones, for she had arrived at St James's Place to find him in a most disagreeable mood, before she was interrupted by Beaverton bringing in a tray. He served them both hot coffee – his face fixed into an expression of quiet sympathy, such as one might wear at a funeral. Radcliffe accepted his cup like a starving man and regarded Miss Talbot suspiciously through the steam. She began again. 'As you know, I am on the point of choosing between my suitors.'

'Oh, do accept my congratulations,' Radcliffe said sarcastically.

'But it has occurred to me the foolishness of committing myself when all I have to prove their wealth is the assurances of other members of the *ton*.'

He looked at her. 'And that does not satisfy you?' he asked.

'Not at all. What if it transpires that despite his income, he has significant debt?'

A slight cough from Radcliffe was meant, she felt, to draw attention to the irony of this objection.

'Yes, I am quite aware that I have lots of debt,' she said crossly. 'But there's no point in neither of us being rich. I need proof before I go any further with either of my suitors. The stakes are simply too high.'

'Proof?' He glanced once more despairingly at the clock. 'How, exactly, does that involve me?'

'I was hoping you could find out for me,' she said. 'You must see that it would be impossible for me to make enquiries myself,' she added, when he continued to look appalled.

'I do see that,' he agreed. 'However, I do *not* see why I should be doing it, or how you think it will be any easier for me to do so.'

'You are so much better connected than I!' she said at once. 'After all, you found out my secret quite easily enough. Would it take so much to ask a few questions in the right ears? How would you achieve the thing if it were Amelia asking?'

'I'd tell her she surely knows better than to bother me before twelve on a Saturday,' he muttered.

'Be serious.'

'Oh, believe me, Miss Talbot, I am being very serious.'

'Is there nothing I could give you in return to make it worth your while?' she cajoled. 'If you will not do it out of charity, then what is it that you do want? You know I have little money, but I am not entirely without value.'

Radcliffe closed his eyes and took an audibly deep breath. For a moment, his theatrical distress reminded her irrepressibly of his mother and she fought to keep her face still.

'Perhaps I could cure the next of your mother's illnesses,' she suggested.

He scowled at her. 'You know as well as I that my mother will be in quite top health until the last ball of the Season,' he snapped.

She opened her mouth to make another suggestion.

'Very well,' he said, before she could. 'Very well! I'll ask around. And in return, you can owe me a favour.'

'A favour.' She looked at him dubiously. 'Of what sort?'

'It shall be a "favour of my choosing at a time of my appointment",' he said, beginning to enjoy himself. She opened her mouth to argue—

'Please,' he held up an imploring hand to forestall her. 'Let us just leave it there. I shall think of something when I am a little less fatigued, I promise you.'

'All right,' she said reluctantly. 'But you can't ask me to leave town before I have a marriage organised.'

'I won't,' he promised faintly.

'And it cannot be something that would in any way affect my standing in society.'

'All right.'

Another pause. 'Perhaps we ought just to decide upon the favour now, for ease.'

'No.'

'Then we have a deal,' Kitty said promptly. 'How soon can I expect you to have the information for me?'

'Please leave,' he said plaintively. 'You are far too exhausting. The sooner you leave, the sooner I'll have it.'

'Wonderful.' Kitty beamed seraphically. She stood to leave, then hesitated, remembering her other task. She pulled an envelope from her pocket.

'I wonder,' she said tentatively. 'If I might ask one more thing of you . . . I should like to write to my sisters, but the cost to receive post is such that they – well, every penny is already accounted for. Could I ask you to frank my letter?'

Her face was hot – this request, though less audacious than her previous, felt far more difficult to make. Members of the peerage were entitled to have their post delivered free of charge, by the simple means of signing the envelope – though Kitty imagined only Radcliffe's family and close friends would feel confident asking it of him. She braced herself for a denial. But she need not have worried. Wordlessly, Radcliffe held her eyes and held out his hand – he was not wearing gloves – and Kitty pressed the letter gratefully into it. As his fingers curled carefully around the edges, she felt the whisper of his touch against her own gloved hand.

'I'll send it today,' he promised, and she believed him.

Archie hesitated on the edge of St James's Place. He was unsure – even now – whether this was totally necessary. After all, it was not as if Selbourne had behaved ill towards him – on the contrary! At the beginning of their friendship, Archie had of course borne in mind Gerry's warning. He had dubbed Selbourne – Selby, as Archie had been begged to call him – a bounder of the worst sort. And yet as Selby had confidently asserted to Archie that he was emphatically *not* a bounder of the worst sort, it was this that Archie was inclined to believe. And thus far, he could not have been kinder to Archie, inviting him along to house parties and faro clubs, guiding him through the most exciting and decadent nights Archie had ever experienced.

It was just that . . . It was just that now, Archie wondered if the life of a man-about-town was for him. He was so tired, feeling always ill at ease in mind and body. And until his recent birthday, he hadn't a sixpence to scratch with, having spent all of his allowance for the whole quarter in the company of Selby. He could only be thankful that he now had full access to his inheritance.

In the midst of all this uncertainty, Archie felt sure his brother would know what to do. Resolute again, Archie took a bracing step forward, eyes fixed upon the door to number seven. The door opened, and Archie hastened forward. It was unlike Radcliffe to be up and out so early, but Archie could not miss him. He had to speak to his brother today. But no . . . the figure was unmistakably feminine. Archie slowed once more, his eyebrows shooting up. How terribly improper, he couldn't help thinking. A second later, another feminine figure emerged from the house – a maid, it seemed, from the cap. Thank goodness. That did make the thing more appropriate – an official visit, then, rather than a clandestine arrangement. The first lady turned her head in Archie's direction, and he realised – with a sickening jolt in his stomach – that it was Miss Talbot. Miss Talbot who was leaving his brother's lodgings. The same Miss Talbot that he had thought, not so many weeks ago, he himself would be marrying. Archie stood stock still, watching her walk away. It was like *that* between them, then.

No wonder, he thought, with a bleak amusement that felt very alien to him, no wonder Radcliffe hadn't wanted him to marry her. How they must have laughed together, his brother and Miss Talbot. At the silly boy in hopeless love, who had no idea how very foolish he was. Archie turned around, walking slowly away from St James's Place. Life in Selbourne's set might be strange, might make him feel less like himself with every passing moment – but at least it had never made him feel like this.

25

As the year fell properly into May, the first taste of summer became quite palpable. Though the change was not as dramatic as it would have been at Netley Cottage – where the fields and woods around them would burst quite suddenly into life like a match struck in a dark room – the oncoming Season could still be felt in the city. The flowers had made their grand entrances from tightly furled buds, one could still smell the unmistakable scent of warm soil drying from the night's rain.

The mood here was the same as it was in Biddington in May. The British, it seemed – whether in Dorsetshire, in London, north, south, east or west – would always be cheered by warmth and sunshine, even if only for the novelty of complaining about something new. And yet though the similarity should have pleased Kitty, she was instead beginning to feel quite wretchedly homesick. A hundred miles away, Beatrice, Harriet and Jane might be busy in the garden, or walking to the market – that Kitty wouldn't know until she received another letter felt like a constant ache.

Kitty had taken advantage of the fine weather to arrange intimate walks with both Pemberton and Crawton, one after the other, hoping that the illusion of privacy – though Aunt Dorothy and Cecily walked only a few paces behind – might prompt a confession of love from either of them. She was to be disappointed. Pemberton had spent an hour giving her a beat for beat revival of not only his vicar's latest sermon – an entirely uninteresting oration upon the equally dull topics of patience and humility – but also the full conversation he and his mother had shared, following it. Pemberton's mother was a retiring woman, Kitty was told, who preferred not to mix in society unless it was to attend church. Mrs Pemberton, Kitty felt sure, must also be very dull.

Kitty let Pemberton rattle on, while in her mind she was planning the picnic she would take her sisters on as soon as she and Cecy returned home.

'Pride is important, too, however, as my mother and I also agreed,' Pemberton was saying now. 'Pride in one's family and one's family name, you know. It is why she is so set on my marrying a proper Christian woman, with all the right breeding to help launch my political career.'

The term 'breeding' should – in Kitty's opinion – only be used for livestock, and certainly not women.

'I understand,' she said sweetly. 'I should very much like to meet her.'

This was true, in fact, for how else was Kitty to prove to this woman that she had sufficient 'breeding' to suit her? She clearly had high expectations, which would have to be met, even if only on the surface. If this was the reason for his delay in proposal, Kitty was sure she could dazzle Mrs Pemberton with . . . oh, biblical quotes, or something like that.

'Perhaps,' Kitty said with serene virtuosity, 'we might attend a church service together.'

Pemberton beamed. 'She should like that very much, I'm sure. Which is your church?'

Oh, bother.

'Oh, near to my aunt's house,' Kitty said vaguely. 'Very small, you know, though quite beautiful.'

She distracted him by asking him to identify a flower for her, and the resulting lecture of the Latin etymology of all the flora and fauna they passed encompassed the rest of their walk. Kitty had only a few moments' respite before Mr Crawton was due to arrive. Though a more recent suitor than Pemberton, Kitty felt sure she could nudge Crawton, at least, towards a declaration – he seemed always so shocked whenever they spoke, so flattered each time she accepted a dance.

'Another one?' Cecily said in faint distress. 'Now?'

'Hush, dear, Kitty is negotiating,' her aunt chided soothingly. 'Why not tell me that wonderful little story about Shakespeare. I should like to hear it again.'

If Pemberton's greatest challenge was his talkativeness, Crawton's was his shyness. He walked beside Kitty quietly – with permanently wide eyes that made him look always as if he had just this moment tasted something very sharp – and was more than happy to let Kitty manage their conversation. This was certainly an improvement upon Mr Pemberton, but it also did not make the likelihood of Crawton plucking up the courage to state his intentions any greater. Kitty sighed.

'You must tell me of your home,' Kitty instructed him, warmly, wanting to draw him out a little. 'You told me it was in Bedfordshire? I confess I have never been.'

Crawton did not respond. Kitty looked over at him, to find his attention had quite wandered. Their paths were about to cross with a group of chattering young ladies, and Mr Crawton's gaze was quite fixed upon them. This was a rudeness that she would not have expected from him . . . until she saw that the young Miss Bloom was amongst their number. She was looking directly forward, studiously ignoring both Kitty and Crawton, but with a high colour in her cheeks that told Kitty she had in fact very much noticed them. Crawton could not take his eyes off her, even turning his head to follow the sight of her disappearing back. Kitty cleared her throat and he visibly jumped.

'My apologies, Miss Talbot,' he said in a rush. 'My profuse apologies – what were we speaking of?'

'Bedfordshire,' she reminded him gently.

A tight furl of guilt began to gnarl in her chest – an entirely useless emotion, of course, but knowing it was useless did not seem to make it go away. Kitty reminded herself that Miss Bloom had wealth, and good birth, and – for all Kitty knew – a thousand other men she would be just as happy marrying as she would Mr Crawton. The fact that Crawton seemed to share the same affection was utterly irrelevant, and nothing to do with Kitty in the slightest.

And yet the guilt remained.

'Nothing to report,' she told her aunt and sister with a sigh upon their walk home. 'Neither will say they love me yet.'

'You cannot tarry much longer, my dear,' Aunt Dorothy instructed. 'Time is slipping away from us.'

'I know that,' Kitty said tensely. 'It is not I who is tarrying.'

Aunt Dorothy made an unconvinced hum in the back of her throat, but before Kitty could question it, Cecily was piping up.

'And do you love either of them?' she asked.

'Not this again,' Kitty said irritably. 'I think them both very fine gentlemen, with very fine wealth – does that satisfy?'

Cecily gave a moue of distaste.

'That's not love at all,' she said, a little distressed. 'At least I don't believe so – what do you think, Aunt Dorothy? Have you ever been in love?'

Their aunt looked startled by the conversation's turn.

'Ah, just the once,' she said. 'Though it was a long time ago, now.'

'What happened?' Cecily asked soulfully.

'We were happy for a while,' Aunt Dorothy said slowly. 'But then he married a young lady from his own class, and she quite naturally objected to our friendship – so that was the end of it.'

Cecily's eyes began to shine ominously.

'See, Cecily,' Kitty could not help pointing out childishly. 'Love does not always equate to happiness, you know.'

'If they loved you when you did not love them, Kitty, then you would be denying them something beautiful,' Cecily said, voice full. 'I would just find it a little sad.'

This statement fed the guilty feeling within Kitty's chest, making it all the more uncomfortable – and Kitty the more irritable.

'It isn't – we don't have time to feel sad for them,' she snapped. 'Feel sad for us, if you need to be sad for someone. They are men and rich ones at that. They can have any future they want and at least they get to choose it – *we* don't. We don't get to have who – *what* – we want!'

Cecily looked shocked at her vehemence – and even Kitty herself was a little disturbed by it.

'I was just *saying*,' Cecily said.

'Let us walk home,' Aunt Dorothy interrupted. 'There is no use arguing.'

They did not speak further on the way back, but Kitty felt put out, nonetheless. She occupied herself by rehearsing arguments and defences of herself in the privacy of her mind, which she imagined delivering to Cecily and – for some reason – Radcliffe, alternately. They did not understand, either of them. They did not have to worry about what would happen to Jane and Harriet and Beatrice, about how dark a young woman's life could so easily become without money, about the myriad fears and futures that could befall any of them if Kitty lost control for a single moment. But Kitty did – Kitty was always worrying about it. And she had too much to do without wasting time on guilt.

Kitty dressed herself in sharp, jerky movements that evening. They could not afford to purchase any more ball gowns, and so were instead creating the illusion of new outfits through means of clever alterations, the liberal use of feathers, and by the sisters swapping dresses when the occasion demanded it. This was a piece of economy that Kitty stood by, but she could not help feeling like an over-ruffled goose in the pink frothy gown that Aunt Dorothy had purchased with Cecily in mind (the skirts let down, and embroidered with a pattern of silken rosebuds) while Cecily wore her favourite blue crêpe (the skirts taken up and now resplendent with elaborate lace trimming added at the hem and sleeve).

By the time Kitty had finished dressing her hair, however, her agitation had devolved into melancholy, and she took herself into her aunt's boudoir. This had become something of a ritual the past few weeks, as Kitty found something indescribably soothing in sitting upon her aunt's bed, curling her feet up beneath her, and watching Dorothy expertly apply lip stain.

'Do you think I am a good person?' she asked her aunt now.

Aunt Dorothy made a humming sound. 'Do you want me to tell you you're a good person?'

'Only if you believe it.'

Aunt Dorothy sent Kitty a noncommittal sort of expression through the mirror.

'Very reassuring,' Kitty said wryly.

'Good is subjective, darling,' Aunt Dorothy told her, taking out her rouge. 'Many people would consider me a bad person, simply for my previous profession. Does that weigh with you?'

'Of course not,' Kitty said indignantly. 'You were not hurting anyone.'

'Certainly never purposefully,' Aunt Dorothy agreed with a little smile Kitty did not understand. 'But for you, I think, it is more important what you think about yourself, than what the world does.'

There was a pause. 'But do you think – that is, what do you feel Mama would think of me?' Kitty asked, voice small.

Aunt Dorothy eyed her through the mirror.

'Of what you are trying to do, here in London, do you mean?'

Kitty nodded.

'Well, you know her background. She was a very practical woman,' Aunt Dorothy pointed out. 'I'm sure she would understand completely.'

Kitty considered this statement, wanting badly for it to reassure her . . . But it did not quite ring true. Mrs Talbot had been practical, yes, with cunning in spades, too – Kitty had always liked to think they shared that quality. The ruthless bent of Kitty's recent behaviour, however – that her mother had not shared. Kitty could not imagine her mama ever acting to the detriment of another person's happiness. Rather the opposite, in fact, she could unfailingly see the good in people and was forever getting herself embroiled in schemes designed to help one neighbour or another – like when she arranged for poor Mr Swift, so beleaguered after the war, to meet Miss Glover on the merest hunch they would suit well. They had married last summer, though Mrs Talbot had not lived to see it.

'I think,' Kitty said slowly. 'I think she might be a little disappointed that I have not been kinder.'

Dorothy let the statement sit unattended for a while, neither agreeing nor disagreeing but rather considering it – and Kitty – frankly.

'You have made such a mess of your hair, Kitty,' she said finally – a response Kitty had not expected.

'I have?' Agitation did not perhaps lend itself to elegant hair arrangements.

'Come here,' Aunt Dorothy tutted. She rose, seating Kitty before her on the chair and beginning to unravel the curls gently. She dropped the pins one by one onto a silver dish with a clink, and Kitty closed her eyes, letting herself be soothed by the warmth of her aunt's hands, the smell of her vanilla perfume.

'Perhaps,' Aunt Dorothy said softly, pulling a comb slowly through the tangles, 'we ought all to try to be a little kinder. Perhaps that is what being "good" is – trying to pass on kindness, even when it is not convenient. I'm sure you could begin now, if you so wished.'

Kitty absorbed this silently – at last, a little reassured. 'There.'

Aunt Dorothy's hands had stilled and Kitty opened her eyes to see an elaborate knot on the top of her head secured with a jewelled comb, and ringlets – created with curl paper the night before – falling elegantly on either side of her face. Aunt Dorothy had a way with such things that bordered on alchemy. Kitty reached up and clasped the hand that was resting upon her shoulder.

'Thank you,' she said simply, meaning for everything. Her aunt squeezed back.

'Are you ready, my darling?' she asked.

26

There was a palpable sense of urgency amongst the *ton*, that night, as if they were all – just as Kitty was – intensely aware that time was running out. Perhaps she was not the only one conscious of the rising expense and diminishing opportunity of the remaining London Season. The dances were quicker, the champagne drunk faster, the laughter louder – the whole room infused with a frantic sort of energy.

Kitty wandered through the rooms, pretending to herself that she was looking for Pemberton, though it was the ladies' figures her eyes were searching. She found Miss Bloom, as before, standing alone and looking forlorn. Kitty sighed sharply through her nose, gathered her skirts up, and approached the girl at a brisk walk.

'Miss Bloom!' she called in greeting, perhaps a little too loudly, for the girl jumped. Dear lord, the sensibility of these young London women was really far too much.

'Miss Talbot,' Miss Bloom responded, eyeing Kitty coldly. 'Have you come to gloat?'

Ah. Kitty supposed having comforted Miss Bloom upon her

doomed love, and then quickly afterwards pursued the object of her affections quite persistently, Miss Bloom was right to be a little off with her.

'How are you finding the Season?' Kitty asked, ignoring Miss Bloom's words. 'I saw you dancing with Mr Gray – he is a fine man.'

'Oh, *very* fine,' Miss Bloom said, with tremulous sarcasm. 'Except that since you have situated yourself so firmly within Mr Crawton's affections, I have no reason to resist my parents' plans for my marriage to Lord Arden.'

Kitty's shock betrayed her into impropriety.

'Lord Arden?' Kitty said, horrified. 'But he's awful – and quite twice your age!'

'Yes, we all know you have made your opinion of Lord Arden quite clear,' Miss Bloom snapped. She sighed, her face and voice softening into hopeless melancholy. 'But it is no use protesting. It is not as if I have anyone else to turn to.'

When her eyes left Kitty's to stare into the ballroom, Kitty knew who she was looking for. It was not her problem, the fate of this girl – this girl who enjoyed the best start in life and yet who was still, despite it all, losing in a fight that did not seem designed for many women to win, at all.

Kitty sighed again. It would not do. She reached down and seized the girl's elbow, tugging her along.

'What are you doing?' Miss Bloom said in alarm.

'You are feeling unwell,' Kitty told her firmly.

'I am not!' she protested, trying to dig her heels in without otherwise drawing more attention to them.

'Yes, you are,' Kitty corrected. 'You are feeling unwell – and dizzy – and are in need of fresh air. Please do try to keep up.'

'I don't understand, where are you taking me?' Miss Bloom moaned.

'Mr Crawton!' Kitty called imperiously, and the man in question looked up from where he was examining a piece of artwork hung high upon the wall. He looked startled – which was quite normal for him – but upon seeing Kitty and Miss Bloom together his eyes widened even further than usual.

'Miss Talbot?' he said, quite uncertainly. His eyes darted to Miss Bloom again, as if unable to believe she was right in front of him.

'Mr Crawton, you must help us,' Kitty said urgently. 'My dear friend Miss Bloom is feeling quite faint. Could you escort her to some fresh air while I fetch some smelling salts and her mother? Quick, may she have your arm?'

Mr Crawton sprang forward – Kitty was pleased to see that underneath that shy exterior clearly lay a strong sense of chivalry. 'Of course!' he said, looking at Miss Bloom with protective concern. 'Miss Bloom, are you all right?'

'Y-yes,' said the lady, quite faintly. Her translucent visage lent itself quite well to their fiction, Kitty was pleased to see.

'I will be back as quickly as I can,' she promised, before leaning towards Miss Bloom and saying, in confidential but quite audible tones, 'You must not worry yourself, Miss Bloom. I know you do not wish to marry Lord Arden, but there will be a way out, I am sure of it!'

She stepped back, satisfied to note that Mr Crawton had drawn himself up in outrage at her words. It was worth remembering how much men really did enjoy playing the hero, especially to ladies as pretty as Miss Bloom. She watched as Mr Crawton carefully escorted the lady onto the terrace, remaining within sight of the door, of course, for propriety's sake, but perhaps beyond earshot of those who were within. The perfect situation – entirely proper and yet wonderfully intimate. Kitty was satisfied with her work, and glided back over to the refreshment table – unconcerned with fulfilling her promise of smelling salts. Kitty was sure Mr Crawton could take it from there. And though it had rid her of her best remaining suitor . . . she could not bring herself to regret it. She might still be as ruthless as a stoat, but she hoped to be a little kinder now, too.

Kitty was just deciding whether to nibble on a sweetmeat – to gather some much-needed strength before seeking out Mr Pemberton – when a low voice spoke in her ear.

'I would have thought you too busy orchestrating your own engagement to make other matches,' Radcliffe murmured.

'I'm sure I don't know what you mean,' Kitty said guilelessly, choosing a delectable cake, and moving over to stand beneath a portrait of King George II. Radcliffe followed, looking down at her curiously.

'You did not have to do that,' he said, in a strange voice. 'For Mr Crawton – I had quite thought him one of your suitors.'

She nodded. 'His heart lay elsewhere. It didn't feel right, to take advantage of two persons' shyness – not when I could do something about it.'

'You surprise me, Miss Talbot,' Radcliffe said honestly. 'I had thought you too heartless for such kindness.'

It was as much an insult as a compliment, but she was not offended. His words were so close to where her own thoughts had been tonight that she felt sure, suddenly, that he had understood what tonight's actions had cost her, how far she'd had to lean against her natural instincts. She felt very seen, all of a sudden – and it was not an unpleasant sensation.

'So did I,' she said simply.

Before they could continue, they were interrupted. A tall young woman, with an intricately braided tower of hair balanced atop her head, knocked into Miss Talbot roughly as she passed. Kitty hoped she would soon move on, but alas, she recognised Radcliffe with a start and as the memory of his worth and title washed over her face quite transparently, swept into a wobbly curtsey. She was beautiful but, as she rose upwards with a slight stagger, also a little foxed. Kitty looked at Radcliffe out of the corner of her eye. Was this the sort of woman he was destined for? She was obviously wealthy, and terribly fashionable, her hair and dress the sort of outlandish get-up only the truly high-born could get away with, but if Radcliffe was pleased to see the lady, he hid the fact remarkably well.

'My lord, it has been too long!' she declared, offering a bejewelled hand to him and ignoring Miss Talbot.

Radcliffe gave a shallow bow over her fingers, with a polite murmur of greeting, but his eyes were cold. Remembering her first encounter with Radcliffe with a shiver, Miss Talbot was glad that – though they had shared a fair few squabbles – she had not been exposed to such a look in quite some time now. The woman tried in vain to begin a conversation, but Radcliffe was obstinate in his refusal to engage, returning her questions with answers of such brevity that he was only one syllable away from being unconscionably rude.

'It has been an age, since we last met,' the lady was saying now. 'I hear you outfitted yourself quite admirably on the Continent. You *must* tell me about the Waterloo.' Radcliffe, it seemed, did not feel he must, giving no answer and instead settling a serpentine smile upon his face. But the lady was not to be put off, continuing in the same flattering gush. 'My sister was there, you know. At the Duchess of Richmond's ball. She said the sight of you all riding off to battle was magnificent.'

'The sight of us returning decidedly less so, I'm sure,' he said, coldly. 'Given that so very many died that day.'

This at last seemed to convince the stranger of her lack of welcome, and she left with a hurried curtsey, shooting Kitty a nasty look as if it were Kitty's fault she was so painfully tone-deaf. They watched her leave in silence, and as the chilly expression had not left Radcliffe's face, Kitty turned back to examine the portrait above them.

'It must be strange,' she said, quietly, 'to have been there, and now back here.'

Neither of them looked at each other, their eyes still fixed on the painting. She did not turn her head to voice this thought. The moment felt too fragile for that, as if they were under a spell that, for a brief moment, allowed them to be still and truthful with one another – rather than snarling like street cats.

'Very,' he agreed, also quietly. 'It has taken me some time to recollect my peace, after . . . after everything.'

'Did you have nightmares?' Kitty asked.

At this, Radcliffe looked sharply over, his eyes searching her face as if checking for mockery.

'Yes,' he said at last. 'How did you know?'

'Mr Swift in Biddington served in the navy,' she said. 'He was most afflicted, after.'

Radcliffe nodded, and silence fell again, but it was not tense, and Kitty felt no nervousness in breaking it.

'Has London changed, since you were away?'

'. . . Yes and no,' he said, appearing to consider this. 'In many ways, London feels untouched by everything that went on. As though it never happened. And there are moments, here, when I almost believe that too.'

He said this without guard, only honesty in his voice. It was as if, somewhere in the last few minutes, they had crossed a sort of border with one another – one that allowed them, now, to lay bare such vulnerabilities while the ball and its inconsequential guests faded away to the periphery.

'Is that . . . a comfort?' she asked, and the question was followed by a pause so long it did not seem he would ever answer.

'For the longest time, I have hated it,' he said. 'It is why I have kept away. I used to love all the frivolity – loved gambling, and drinking, and flirting. But after, I found myself quite done with all the silliness, all the ridiculous rules we have to live by. As if that matters, after – after the things that happened out there. The people we lost.' He gestured to the other side of the ballroom, where Captain Hinsley was spinning with the dancers. 'Hinsley is the bravest man I know; I only fought in the hundred days, while he spent years on the Continent – and yet it was he who kept me sane when we got back to England. And yet, in a ballroom, none of that seems to matter – his life is dictated only by his wealth or lack of it, not his merit.'

'It is unfair,' she agreed – and though she could easily have pointed out his hypocrisy again, this time for sympathising with Hinsley's plight when he had not done so with hers, she left it unsaid. She found she no longer cared about scoring points against Radcliffe.

'You said you have hated it – do you hate it now?' she asked instead.

'Less than I thought,' he admitted. 'I had not realised how much I missed my family, how much I was neglecting them by staying away. And it has been . . . entertaining, I can admit, watching you cut a swathe through them all. A wolf in sheep's clothing.'

Their heads had turned towards each other as he spoke, their gazes no longer fixed upon the portraits, and as his mouth quirked upwards, she felt her own mirroring it. She was struck, as she had been upon their first meeting, by how much his face changed when he smiled.

'Oh, so that's why you agreed to help me, is it?' she said. 'For the *entertainment*.'

'I'm not sure I can be said to have "agreed" to help you,' he refuted at once, grinning now. 'I was coerced, I was *blackmailed*. I didn't have any choice in the matter.'

She gave a soft laugh. The memory was all at once rewritten to be a humorous part of their shared story, as if it had never been shameful, or fraught – as if they had never even been truly at odds, even for a moment.

'You had a choice,' she argued, rapping him lightly upon the arm with her closed fan.

'Oh, I'm not so sure about that.' The words – though meant lightly, she was certain – sounded quite serious when spoken aloud, and by the surprise in Radcliffe's eyes it had caught him off guard, too. They considered each other for a long, thoughtful moment – grey eyes staring into brown, brown staring back – before he cleared his throat, breaking the tension. She took a hasty sip of lemonade.

'Mr Pemberton, you'll be pleased to hear, is quite as rich as they say,' he said after a beat.

'Oh yes?' she said, forcing her voice into brightness. 'May I ask after your sources?'

'His financial manager, his manservant and his tailor. His bills are always paid on time, his servants report no issues with wages, and his financial manager – once two or three cups into his beer – boasts of a very favourable return on investment. Your Pemberton is as clean as they come: eight thousand a year, quite simply. My tiger, Lawrence, found out the whole – he is a very accomplished spy.'

'That is good news,' Kitty said slowly. And it was, though she did not feel as pleased as she would have expected.

'Does it make your path clear?' he asked.

'Almost. I still need to overcome Mrs Pemberton's final qualms about my quality. But I hope that soon there will only be the where and the how of the proposal to consider.'

'Oh, only that?' Radcliffe said. 'I suppose you will allow Pemberton the privilege of deciding for himself what he is to say to you?'

She scowled at him. 'Yes, of course I will.'

She turned her shoulder dismissively, but Radcliffe was immune to such slights by now.

'I wonder what sort of proposal you should most like, were it up to you,' he imagined. '"Dearest Miss Talbot,"' he did a passable imitation of Mr Pemberton's self-satisfied drone, '"being of sound mind though irritating personality, I promise to you that I am filthy rich and will pay off all of your family's debts." Can you imagine it, Miss Talbot? The romance! The passion!'

'If you are done amusing yourself,' she said, not quite able to take the laugh out of her own voice. 'I shall take my leave – I have much still to do, you know.'

He offered a gloved hand.

'May I escort you to your aunt, then?' he suggested gallantly. And this time, she accepted – the faintest of blushes staining her cheeks.

27

'It is most worrisome, James, no matter what you say,' Lady Radcliffe insisted. 'And try as I might, I cannot get him to speak to me about it!'

'I can't imagine why,' Radcliffe muttered. Lady Radcliffe eyed him a little frostily. Radcliffe avoided her gaze, turning his head out of the barouche to stare onto The Strand in the hope it might discourage her from pursuing the conversation. Had he known, when his mother had requested his escort to the opening of the Royal Academy's annual art exhibition, that she would use it as an opportunity to lecture him on Archie's behaviour, he would have avoided the whole thing entirely. Though he should perhaps have suspected an ulterior motive earlier – when had his mother ever expressed an interest in art before?

'It is all very well being so cavalier,' the Countess said crossly, ignoring all of Radcliffe's attempts to shut the conversation down, 'but I do believe Archie to be getting a real taste for cards!'

'Just like last year he developed a real taste for boxing,' Radcliffe said, 'and the year before a real taste for horse racing.'

'They are not at all the same thing,' Lady Radcliffe dismissed. 'More and more frequently I hear of boys being quite ruined by gambling. You know Lady Cowper's younger brother fled to Paris for just that reason – they hushed it up of course, but it is widely known. And I have never met a young man less interested in cards before this year!'

'Even Archie couldn't become *that* bad at gambling,' Radcliffe said under his breath. He wondered if this was the sort of conversation his parents had shared about him, once, before his father had decided to pack him off to the Continent.

'I thought you might have a proper talk to him,' Lady Radcliffe said, ignoring this. 'Set him straight, you know, put a little fear into him.'

The carriage turned into the courtyard of Somerset House, not a moment too soon for Radcliffe.

'I'm not going to do that, Mother,' he said shortly, not looking at his mother. 'Archie is fine as he is.'

They did not speak to one another as they dismounted and crossed the threshold. Taking a copy of the exhibition catalogue without enthusiasm, Radcliffe's mood was lowered further when he realised the rooms were already thick with members of the *ton*, all of whom were more interested in being seen admiring the paintings on opening day, than the actual admiration itself. What insipid fools they were; Radcliffe had almost been in danger of forgetting it, these past few weeks. Miss Talbot – with her schemes, her favours, and early morning visits to his home – had kept him busy enough that he'd not had time to think of much else. Realising he was absent-mindedly searching the crowd for her figure, he jerked his head away and began instead to flick through the exhibition catalogue.

'What would you like to see, first, Mama?' Radcliffe asked. 'Mr Ward's *Portrait of Mrs Gulliver, in her 104th year*? Or do you think Mr Hodgson's *Interior of a church* might be livelier?'

From the chilly silence that greeted his question, it was clear that Lady Radcliffe was not pleased with him at all – and most likely, doubly irritated to have to endure such a boring afternoon now that her primary objective in acquiring Radcliffe's company had failed. It was a relief, then, to have their names hailed in only the second room. They turned to see Mrs Kendall waving a welcoming arm in her direction, from where she was gathered with Miss Talbot, Lady Montagu and Mr Fletcher – all of whom, save Miss Cecily he assumed, had given up on the paintings entirely.

'I cannot believe the heat, for only May!' Lady Montagu said in greeting, fanning herself vigorously. 'I should not have come if I had known it was to be so stuffy in here. Though of course,' she added hastily, 'one simply *must* see Turner's *Dordrecht*.'

Pemberton appeared, just then, clutching glasses in his hand which he presented to Miss Talbot and her aunt with pride. Though, when he spotted that Radcliffe had joined their company, his pleasure lessened. Radcliffe recollected that he was almost certainly still in Pemberton's bad books, after their conversation at Tattersall's. It felt so long ago to him, though it obviously did not to Pemberton from the mutinous look upon his face – dear Lord, was Miss Talbot really going to marry such a buffoon?

'I have heard,' Pemberton proclaimed, overcoming his annoyance with Radcliffe, 'that the Duke of Wellington has returned to London. Do you think we shall see him at Almack's this week?'

'Wellington always did like a dance,' Radcliffe said without thinking, and had the immediate punishment of having all eyes in the circle turn upon him. Pemberton scowled to have his moment so overshadowed.

'You know him well?' Pemberton asked sulkily.

'A little,' was all the response he gave, hoping this would be the end of it.

Pemberton eyed him for a moment, his dislike of Radcliffe warring with his love of discussing the Napoleonic wars – a subject upon which he considered himself quite the expert. Predictably, it was the latter that won out.

'I, myself,' he proclaimed modestly, 'have studied Wellington's campaigns at length. Indeed, Waterloo is rather my specialist subject.'

'Oh?' Radcliffe's smile grew faintly derisive – and was that a flicker of a cringe on the face of Miss Talbot?

'The battle was not without its flaws, you know,' Pemberton told them all confidentially. 'I'm sure Wellington would be the first to admit that mistakes were made. Why, one only has to look at the use of the cavalry . . .'

It appeared – it very much appeared – that Pemberton truly intended to deliver a lecture to Radcliffe upon Waterloo. It was so ridiculous as to be almost amusing. Almost. But as Pemberton began to enumerate in excruciating detail all the ways in which he thought Waterloo could have been fought better, Radcliffe felt his humour dissipate, and his temper begin to rise instead.

'Of course had I been in Wellington's shoes, *I* would have—'

'I wonder if—' Miss Talbot tried to interrupt, but it was no use. Pemberton simply raised his voice over hers to drown her out, in full swing now.

'—But really, that is what happens when one recruits from the lower classes, not an ounce of discipline between them—'

The arrogance, the ignorance, the sheer pomposity of this man was breathtaking. How dare he speak of discipline, how dare he disparage those who Radcliffe had fought alongside – as if class had anything to do with courage on such a bloody battlefield as Waterloo had been. Radcliffe felt the fingers of his left hand begin to tremble.

'Why, what a shame it is that a man of your wisdom could not be there to save us,' he said coldly as Pemberton paused to draw breath.

The derision in his voice was now quite audible – to all but Pemberton, it seemed, who puffed up in pleasure while the rest of the group flinched a little.

'I don't know about that,' Pemberton demurred, 'though I own I should have liked to see the battle with my own eyes.'

'Let me assure you that the view did not improve with proximity,' Radcliffe said. Pemberton did not appear to hear him.

'One cannot help thinking that it might have made the world of difference,' he told the assembled company, shaking his head a little in sadness. 'My housemaster did always say I had missed my calling as a general.'

'Oh, *undoubtedly* so,' Radcliffe said.

'Radcliffe, perhaps—' Lady Radcliffe lay a hand upon his arm, which he shook off. The polite veneer Radcliffe had managed to hold onto for the Season so far – always precarious whenever the war was brought up – was well and truly cracking.

'Though of course it is much easier to develop a taste for war once the fighting has concluded, is it not?' he bit out.

At last, the antagonistic tone seemed to filter through to Pemberton. He flushed angrily, his earlier distaste for Radcliffe's company recollected in force.

'What, my lord, are you implying?' Pemberton demanded.

Around them, drawn in by the well-honed instinct of the *haut ton* for drama and spectacle, people were beginning to stare. Lady Kingsbury – standing in front of Mr Carse's portrait *The Gossips* – had a hand over her mouth in faux distress, but was making no effort to hide her avaricious regard. Radcliffe hated them all – but none so much as this trumped-up turkey.

'My apologies, Mr Pemberton, for only implying what I intended to make *very* clear,' he said.

In his periphery, Radcliffe could see his mother's face, pale with distress, and Miss Talbot's – mouth set in a firm line, eyes flickering around the room – but the sight was distant in the face of his rage.

'You sir,' he continued with a savage smile, 'are nothing more than a—'

'Oh, my goodness,' Miss Talbot said loudly. 'I'm going to faint from the heat.'

Warning thusly issued, she dove gracefully straight into the arms of a very shocked Mr Fletcher, to the accompanying gasps of all onlookers.

'I say – Miss Talbot?' Mr Fletcher caught her readily enough, but was clearly much shocked, silver whiskers quivering in concern. 'Miss Talbot, are you all right? Pemberton – fetch her a drink at once! She must get some air.'

The conversation was forgotten as all in the company rushed to help. Pemberton disappeared towards the refreshment table,

Miss Talbot was encouraged to lean upon Mr Fletcher's solicitous arm, while Mrs Kendall fanned her gently, and Lady Montagu began to usher them out towards the doors. Radcliffe was left on the sidelines, deflating slowly – and watching the proceedings through narrowed eyes. His experience of Miss Talbot's character and behaviour thus far had not given him much reason to believe she was the fainting type, and though she was accepting the attentions with a wan smile and weak expressions of thanks, her colour was as healthy as ever.

As she was led away, she glanced back over her shoulder at Radcliffe. He caught her eye and raised a single brow, while she sent him the ghost of a wink in return.

It was some time before they found themselves in conversation again, by which point Radcliffe had recollected his calm. His mother having gone in search, with Lady Montagu, of Turner's latest masterpiece and Pemberton being nowhere to be seen, Radcliffe wandered over to sit beside Miss Talbot where she was 'resting' upon a plush red couch.

'I suppose I am to infer from your wink,' he asked quietly, 'that that little performance was for my benefit?'

'For yours, and for your mother's,' she agreed.

'I'm not sure it was necessary,' he told her.

'I'm quite sure that it was,' she disagreed. 'You looked about to land Pemberton a facer, which would have cast a pall over the evening – for everyone but the gossips. Besides, I did owe you a favour.'

'Forgive me,' he said apologetically. 'I had thought the favour was to be of my choosing, not yours – though perhaps that was rather an audacious assumption?'

'I believe,' she said loftily, 'the correct response is to say thank you.'

'I will own that the intervention was fortuitous,' he admitted, smiling a little. 'My mother was already disappointed with me when I arrived, so I would have been quite in the doghouse if I'd started a brawl. Though,' he added, looking at her sidelong, 'I would have perhaps chosen something a little less dramatic.'

'Ah, that is because you lack vision,' she explained, her expression perfectly straight but humour clear in her dark eyes – which were singular for their expressiveness.

'Why is your mother disappointed in you?' Miss Talbot asked.

With hackles still a little raised from his altercation, Radcliffe was tempted to give her a set down, but – seeing that her face was free of judgement – instead let out a gust of air. 'She thinks I am taking a too cavalier an attitude to Archie – or, rather, I suppose she should like me to take a more active role in managing the entire family.'

'And you don't want to?' Miss Talbot asked, head cocking in interest.

He gave a vague shake of the head. 'I suppose . . .' he said slowly. 'I suppose it is more that I don't know how. My father was— He would have taken a very hard line with Archie – I know, because he took a hard line with me. And if that is what being the head of the family looks like, I'm not sure I can do it.'

Miss Talbot absorbed this for a few moments. 'He was a strict parent?' she asked carefully.

He gave a snort of laughter. 'You could say that. He was not fond of . . . too much enjoyment, of excess, my father. He thought one's duty was to uphold the family's reputation, every minute of the day – and he guarded ours fiercely.'

'So when he sent you to Vienna with Wellington,' Miss Talbot said quietly. 'That was because . . .'

'Because he thought me a damage to the family name? Yes. As a younger man I wanted to enjoy everything the world had to offer – the gambling, the drinking, the excess of it all. My father thought it dangerous. He thought having employment would force me to learn some humility, and since Wellington owed him a favour . . . I became his attaché.'

Miss Talbot sucked a slow breath in through her teeth.

'Of course, he was not expecting war to resume,' Radcliffe said heavily. 'No one was. When it did, he demanded I return – but I could not leave *then*. It would have been the height of cowardice. I thought he might understand that, one day. That he might be . . . proud, in the end. But by the time I got home, after the war was over, he was already dead.'

This was the most he had spoken about his father – about their relationship – to anyone before, and it was a relief to say it all aloud – and still more so as Miss Talbot did not feel the need to fill the air with platitudes or false reassurances, instead allowing his confession to rest untouched in the air between them. Perhaps it ought to shock him more that he had chosen Miss Talbot – not Hinsley, not his mother – to unburden himself to, but Radcliffe found that he was not at all surprised by the turn the conversation had taken. In the past few weeks, it seemed that at every occasion they attended, he and Miss Talbot would end up like this, at the edges, sharing strange intimacies. He thought she could probably ask him almost anything and he would answer her.

Radcliffe took a gulp of lemonade, winced to find it singularly tasteless, and lowered his glass. 'This sort of conversation is much better done over brandy,' he said, lightening his voice.

'I'll take your word for it,' Miss Talbot said, more gently than he would have thought her capable. 'It was certainly my father's favourite.'

'He drank?'

'Gambling was his chief vice,' she corrected. 'It was not a problem when he was a bachelor – gambling seems to be an accepted part of a gentleman's life – but when he was disowned, he never could properly adjust to his change in circumstances. The debt grew quite rapidly from there.'

'He started drinking then?' Radcliffe asked.

'No,' Miss Talbot said. 'He drank before. But after Mama died, he couldn't stop. I'm sure it would have killed him if the typhoid had not.'

Radcliffe nodded. 'And then everything was down to you?'

'I suppose one could say that,' said Miss Talbot thoughtfully. 'But I had Beatrice, who is only a little younger, so it is not so bad. And, for all that they left us in quite a mess, I am grateful to my mother and father for such a happy childhood as we had. There was much laughter, in our house – and music, and love.'

'You must think me very weak,' he said conversationally. 'For trying to escape a responsibility you have been shouldering for years.'

'Not so,' she said. 'Though I do think you would benefit from thinking about it more simply.'

'What do you mean?' he asked, frowning.

'You have the title, the wealth, the influence,' she said. 'You have a family that adores you, and though it might have pained me in the past, you are quite clever at protecting them when you try. I feel you are more than capable of choosing what kind of lord you would like to be.'

'How does one choose, though?' he could not help asking.

She shrugged. 'You just do.'

He looked at her. She looked at him. For a moment, it felt as though they were the only two real people in the whole world, sitting there looking at each other, while the rest of London carried on. And then it broke.

'I should go,' Miss Talbot said, her voice sounding a little breathless all of a sudden. 'I can see Pemberton looking for me.'

'Ah yes, the general himself,' Radcliffe said with an ironic twist to his lips. 'Do, by all means, keep him away from me.'

'Behave yourself,' she said mischievously. 'Remember, if all goes well, you are speaking of my future husband.'

'As if I could forget it,' he said.

Dearest Kitty,

What a shock it was, to receive your letter, with Lord Radcliffe's frank upon the envelope. The post boy was quite agog to deliver it, and so unfortunately it was commonplace knowledge to the whole town by the end of the morning. Naturally, all manner of persons have found reasons to call upon us this afternoon. Rest assured we haven't breathed a word, though this is more due to confusion than discretion – I knew you were on friendly terms with Radcliffe, but how are you closely enough acquainted with him to request he frank your letter?

Rest assured we are all well. Harriet is back to full strength (and nothing could ever bother Jane, of course). The weather, while poor at present, is not so inclement to keep us inside – which is all to the well, for the number of card games suited for three players is limited!

Funds are a little low, though I'm sure we shall manage until you are back. I have also enclosed a letter we received from Mr Anstey and Mr Ainsley. I trust you shall forgive my reading it. They write to confirm their intention to visit upon us no later than the first of June. They repeat that if we do not have the assurance of funds by then . . . Well, it is as their last correspondence.

Your loving sister,

Beatrice

28

It was the eleventh of May. Kitty had three weeks, and two pounds remaining. Her courtship of Mr Pemberton was becoming ever more determined, but she still had not extracted a proposal from the man, the burden of which she felt as a physical presence, pressing persistently upon the tender spot between neck and shoulder. What she wouldn't give to shuck it off for one blessed moment . . . but she could not, until it was done.

Mr Pemberton's mother – a strict matriarch who seemed to be the only person Mr Pemberton listened to – was not yet convinced by the Talbots' quality. Having been upfront, as Kitty always was, about the state of the Talbot finances to her suitor, his austere mother was nurturing some doubts about the woman her son was courting, and the anticipated meeting had not yet occurred. Kitty was not quite sure – yet – what her next step was. She had been accepted, unfeasible though it had first seemed, into high society, and was spoken to by lords and ladies very much as if she was one of them – what else was to be done?

Over breakfast that morning, she was listening with half an ear to Dorothy's chatter, while simultaneously also skimming through the morning post and ruminating on the Mrs Pemberton issue, when a word on the card before her shocked her into a loud gasp: Almack's.

'What is it, Kitty?' Aunt Dorothy asked, curious.

'We have been sent Almack's vouchers for tomorrow night,' Kitty said, holding the card up with shaking hands. 'Almack's! From Mrs Burrell. I can't believe it.'

'Oh,' Cecily said vaguely, not looking up from her book. 'Yes, she said she would send them.'

'What?!' Kitty squawked. 'Who said – what are you talking about?'

Cecily looked up reluctantly. 'Mrs Bussell, or Biddell – her name escapes me. I was speaking to her about Sappho at the ball last night – it transpired that we share a common interest in literature. She said she would send us vouchers, for she should like to speak to me again.' She went back to reading, explanation complete.

'Cecily,' Kitty breathed. 'You magnificent creature!' She got up and smacked a kiss upon Cecy's forehead.

'Kitty!' Cecily squirmed away.

'Well, look at that,' Aunt Dorothy said, coming around the table to look at the vouchers herself. 'What a turn-up, indeed.'

'Is it really so important?' Cecily asked, dubiously.

'Cecy, it would be easier for us to be presented at Court,' Kitty said exultantly. 'This should squash all of Mrs Pemberton's doubts about our birth – if we have the Almack's seal of approval, she can have no further qualms. You have done very well, Cecy, very well indeed.'

The next night, they dressed themselves with more than their usual care, Kitty's fingers trembling over buttons. For the occasion they were to wear their very best dresses, long-sleeved evening gowns of white gauze – Cecily's dress decorated with embroidered pink satin roses, Kitty's worn over a striped satin petticoat that she felt was the perfect mingling of demure but dashing. Her face already being quite flushed, there was no need for Kitty to pinch her cheeks, and she instead held her cold hands against her skin to try to cool down.

They left for King Street with more than enough time to spare, but Kitty did not want to leave anything to chance this evening. Almack's was renowned for their strict rules upon dress, behaviour – and timings. The doors closed to new arrivals at eleven p.m. on the dot, and it was even said that Wellington himself had once been turned away for tardiness. Though by hackney cab the journey would not take more than thirty minutes even on the busiest of evenings, Kitty could not bear the thought of the doors shutting on them before they had even entered. But that fate did not occur, and the three women glided into the assembly rooms without issue, their names on the list, their vouchers accepted. They were greeted by the Countess Lieven, who was most gracious, and joined the throngs inside as smoothly as if they did so each week.

Many of the faces within were already familiar to the Talbots, but it felt wonderful nonetheless to be amongst them here – the place Kitty had oft heard spoken of as the beating heart of Society. There were three spacious rooms within, the first elegantly arranged with chandeliers hanging above and chairs lining the walls for those who did not dance – although after the splendour of the private balls she had attended so far in the Season, the rooms did not appear so wondrous. But it was not Almack's appearance that characterised its power, and she was pleased to see its effects at work immediately. When Mr Pemberton spotted her from across the room, his mouth opened in surprise. He bustled towards them.

'Miss Talbot,' he said in delighted greeting. 'I had not thought to see you here, tonight.'

She smiled mysteriously. 'Mrs Burrell was kind enough to send us vouchers,' she said carelessly, and watched as his eyes widened – as Kitty now knew, this woman, of all the formidable patronesses, was most known for her snobbery and hauteur.

'Indeed! I must tell Mother – you know she is a great friend of Mrs Burrell, she will be so glad to hear the acquaintance is shared. In fact, Mother was saying she should like to meet you. Will you be attending the Jersey ball tomorrow evening?'

Just so, thought Kitty smugly.

'I will,' she replied.

'Very good,' he said approvingly. 'I hope you will save me the first dance tonight, Miss Talbot? I should very much like to have the waltz, if the lady patronesses permit it.'

He looked at her with unmistakable ardour in his eyes.

'As would I,' she said faintly. A young lady could only waltz at Almack's once specifically invited to do so by one of the patronesses, and an invitation was not guaranteed – but while Kitty should, she knew, be eager for the honour, she could not help shiver at the thought. Try as she might to bully herself into overcoming this weakness, Kitty still found herself quite averse to the idea of being held so closely by Pemberton. She could see the appeal of the dance, of course, but could not escape the fact that when she imagined dancing it, it was not Pemberton she was partnered with.

As they walked towards the supper room, Mr Pemberton began to enumerate all the ways in which his family was connected – however loosely – to the rest of the Almack's patronesses, an oration that lasted all the way through supper. Kitty was somewhat disappointed to find that, instead of the sumptuous feasts at the private balls she was by now used to attending, refreshments at Almack's consisted only of thinly sliced bread and pound cake. But by the lack of surprise on the faces around her, she supposed that this must be quite normal – the habits of wealthy people were still so mysterious to her – and she smiled to think that she was becoming quite spoiled.

Kitty managed to escape Mr Pemberton once supper was concluded, foisting him upon Miss Bloom – really, the girl owed her some recompense for her recently announced engagement – and circling the edge of the dance floor with Aunt Dorothy, until they were hailed by Lady Radcliffe, who stood with Lord Radcliffe.

'Mrs Kendall!' the Countess trilled in excitement, quite ignoring Kitty, who took the inadvertent snub without offence, as Lady Radcliffe pulled Aunt Dorothy into a low-voiced tête-à-tête.

'Miss Talbot.' Radcliffe bowed in greeting. 'I would express my shock at seeing you here, and yet I find I am not all that surprised. Is there anything you are not able to do?'

She took the compliment with a smile. 'Would you believe it was all Cecily's doing?' She explained the story to him.

He raised his eyebrows. 'Poetry came in useful, after all this time? By Jove, who would have thought.'

'And to think I begrudged her education,' Kitty said contritely. 'Terribly short-sighted of me. I had no idea Mrs Burrell was such an academic.'

'And what do you think of these grand halls, then?' He widened his arms to encompass the room. 'Do they live up to your lofty expectations?'

'They do,' she replied. 'I cannot believe I am here.'

'The food is somewhat disappointing, I know,' he said apologetically.

'*Isn't* it,' she said with great feeling, and they shared a laugh.

'What is on the agenda tonight, then?' Radcliffe asked. 'Any further faux faints?'

'So long as you hold your temper, that should not be necessary.'

'Do not worry, I have already promised my mother to speak only of the weather and my health,' he reassured her. 'Though if your Pemberton approaches, I shall find myself tested, I imagine.'

'You could apologise to him,' Kitty suggested. 'You were very rude.'

'I could never apologise to someone with such a villainous moustache,' Radcliffe informed her primly. 'It would be quite beyond the pale. Besides, it was he who behaved like a dolt, not I.'

Kitty sighed. 'I hope to improve his conversational skills if we marry,' she confessed. 'He would be far more palatable if he were less . . .'

'Narcissistic?' Radcliffe suggested impishly. 'Dangerously deluded?'

'If he listened more,' she corrected.

'Ah, reaching for the stars, I'm afraid,' he said, in commiserating accents.

'Oh, so you believe me unequal to the task?' she said. 'Do you realise that I would have been prepared to marry much, much worse than Pemberton?'

His smile faded a little. 'I believe it,' he said at last. 'And I do not think you unequal. Though I confess to wishing the whole endeavour were . . . unnecessary.'

Kitty faltered, a little perturbed that he should have ruined their fun with such a weighty statement.

'That would have been quite a different world indeed,' she said at last, clearing her throat a little and looking down for fear that the moment would otherwise become quite unbearably intimate.

'Do you expect to be invited to waltz, tonight?' he asked after a pause, and she was grateful for the change in subject.

'I suppose we shall have to see, though I think it unlikely this evening,' she said, trying for levity. 'Are you fearful a lady patroness might suggest yourself as a partner? I have not forgotten the strength of your refusal when last I asked – no doubt Lady Jersey would be shocked by your sudden dash from the room . . .'

Her tone was playful, but Radcliffe's gaze, when it met hers, was intense.

'I rather think,' he said slowly, 'that my answer should be quite different, if you asked me to dance now, Miss Talbot.'

Kitty was silent. She stared at him, for once not able to think of a thing to say. Instead, she allowed herself to imagine it for one stolen moment – what it might be like to waltz with Radcliffe, and not with Pemberton. It would be quite different, she knew. Quite different indeed.

She was not sure how long they would have stood there, in

the wake of these words, but she did not get to find out, as the sound of someone clearing their throat interrupted them. Pemberton was standing before them, scowling at Radcliffe.

'Miss Talbot, I believe you promised me this dance?' he said imperiously. 'It's the cotillion.'

Kitty swallowed. She forced herself not to look over at Radcliffe.

'Yes . . . thank you,' Kitty said, numbly. Mr Pemberton took her arm and walked her away to make up the set.

Radcliffe turned abruptly, too – he'd be damned if he was going to watch. As he headed away from the dance floor, he found himself face to face with Hinsley.

'Harry,' he gripped his friend's arm in welcome. 'It is good to see you. Are you well?'

'Not really,' Hinsley's expression was sour. 'Dashed awful thing to do, only serving lemonade and tea. How am I supposed to get through a conversation with Pemberton on such stuff? Barely escaped with my life.'

'Well, he shall be quite preoccupied with Miss Talbot for some time, I believe,' Radcliffe said. 'So you should be safe now.'

Radcliffe was sure his voice had been calm, his expression even, that he had conveyed nothing out of the ordinary in any part of his bearing – and yet Hinsley was looking at him with dawning realisation.

'Oh, so *that's* how it is,' he said, beginning to smile.

'That's how what is?' Radcliffe asked with a snap in his voice. Hinsley held up his hands, laughing.

'Don't bite my arm off! What's stopping you, then? Worried how Archie would take it?'

'Harry, I do not have the faintest idea what you are talking about,' Radcliffe lied. 'If you are going to continue talking nonsense, I beg you take yourself elsewhere.'

He pretended to catch the eye of someone in the distance. 'Excuse me, I believe Lady Jersey has need of me.'

'I'll expect to see you in Hyde Park tomorrow!' Hinsley called after him, grinning. 'Don't forget!'

Spotting the Lady Sefton approaching with a beady look in her eye, Captain Hinsley beat an early retreat and fled the assembly rooms forthwith. Deciding to walk home, for the night was brightly lit by the moon, he turned right for Mayfair – and ran into Archie, who was hurrying in the opposite direction.

'Slow down, old thing,' he said jovially. 'What has you in such a hurry?'

'Promised my mother I'd escort her,' Archie gasped. 'Quite lost track of time.'

Hinsley grimaced at him. 'It's past eleven, Archie, they'll not let you in now.'

Archie deflated. 'Blast,' he cursed.

Hinsley looked more closely at him. Had the boy always been that pale? He was clammy-faced and sweating, though that could be down to his hasty journey.

'Are you quite well?' he asked.

Archie waved him off. 'Yes, yes, I'm perfectly well. Busy Season, you know how it is.'

Hinsley did, yet now he thought of it, he had not seen Archie at a ball for weeks.

'Perhaps you ought to sleep it off,' he suggested. 'I'll walk you back – fresh air'll do you good.'

For a moment, Archie looked tempted. But then he shook his head.

'I had an appointment to make afterwards, anyhow,' he said, turning left towards the city. 'Good evening, Hinsley.'

Hinsley stared after him for a moment, wondering if he should follow the boy – see where he was going to – but after a few moments of deliberation, he shrugged and turned again for home. He was being a paranoid old fool.

Had Hinsley known, of course, exactly what kind of establishment Archie was heading towards, he would have dragged him back to Grosvenor Square by the ear. But he did not, and so Archie proceeded unchallenged onto Soho and into the gaming hell where he knew he would find Selbourne.

29

If Mrs Pemberton was to be at the Jersey ball, Kitty needed to be prepared. This was the final hurdle, after all, and not a moment too soon. They were getting dangerously close to June – it was already getting far too tight for Kitty's liking.

The de Lacys had invited Mrs Kendall and the Talbots to join them in their box at the Theatre Royal, to catch a matinee performance of *The Libertine* before that evening's ball, but when the de Lacy carriage arrived at Wimpole Street the next afternoon, Kitty only stepped out to send her apologies to Lady Radcliffe.

'I am most fatigued, my lady, and my aunt has bid me rest,' she told her. Radcliffe had stepped out of the vehicle to assist Cecily and Aunt Dorothy up into it – the theatre was one social event her sister was quite happy to attend – and, hearing Kitty's apology, looked at her, concerned. He hoisted Aunt Dorothy up in one easy movement, and as she settled herself within the carriage, Kitty leant in to explain in a low voice.

'Mrs Pemberton is attending the Jersey ball tonight.

A strongly Christian woman, I am told, so I mean to spend the afternoon studying scripture for the occasion.'

'Ah,' he said. 'I wish you the best of luck. Do let me know if you discover any passages in the Bible about marrying for money. I wonder if the Lord Christ was in favour or opposed?'

She shot him an eloquent look – meant to convey how exceedingly tiresome she found him – and he grinned.

'You would leave me alone to protect Mr Kemble's virtue from the lascivious eyes of my mother and your aunt?'

She laughed. Last night they had both overheard the roguish discussion between Lady Radcliffe and Mrs Kendall about the 'strapping' reputation of the leading actor.

'I am sure you are well up to the task,' she told him, smiling.

'You flatter me.' He handed Cecily up into the carriage next, then paused a moment.

'Are you sure I cannot tempt you away?' he asked, with a cajoling tilt of the head.

'I'm sure,' Kitty said, a little faintly.

He bade her good day and the carriage disappeared around the corner. Kitty watched it pass out of sight, wishing for a moment to have gone, anyway. It was not that she was so desirous of seeing the performance, but the company . . . The company she would have no doubt enjoyed. No, Kitty told herself sternly, beating her thoughts back into submission. Absolutely not.

She returned to her room and dedicated herself – for quite the first time in her life – to the study of the Bible. It was, she quickly discovered, very long. And, as she soon realised, quite boring. She wondered bleakly if the Old Testament even mattered – could one just skip to the New and go from there?

Surely to the devoutly puritan Mrs Pemberton, it was the Lord Jesus who was the more important? She flicked through the pages, wishing desperately that there was an index she could consult to save her some time – she could simply look for the pages on virtuous women and marriage, and be done with the whole thing.

Kitty granted herself the luxury of an afternoon doze – biblical study proving quite beneficial to one's slumber – and dressed herself that evening in the most chaste evening dress she had – the ivory white, from her very first ball, except this time she wore no jewellery save for earrings, and plucked the feathers (surely the most devilish of accessories) from her headdress. The first challenge of the evening was that the Pembertons were late arriving, leaving Kitty's nerves mounting higher the longer she was held in anticipation. The second challenge came at nine o'clock when Lady Radcliffe appeared out of nowhere to deliver most unwelcome news.

'What did I tell you about dancing twice with the same man?' she hissed in Kitty's ear. Kitty was confused, until she saw Cecily and Montagu locked into what could only be their second dance of the evening. Oh Lord – why tonight? Was Cecily trying to kill her?

Thanking Lady Radcliffe, Kitty pounced upon them as soon as the dance had finished.

'Lord Montagu, how do you do?' she said briskly. 'Your mother is looking for you again, I'm afraid. Can you spot her? Goodness I can't see for people in this wretched squeeze.'

'"Grant me, kind Heaven, to find some happier place—"' Lord Montagu began portentously.

'Yes, yes,' Kitty interrupted before it could go any further.

'Shakespeare, is it? Very clever. I should find Lady Montagu, if I were you.'

He sloped off obediently and Kitty turned on her sister.

'Cecily, you do remember what I told you about dancing too often with the same man, don't you?' she implored.

The vague look upon Cecily's face told her that this conversation had been quite forgotten.

'Cecily, you are in danger of seeming very fast. I know you do not mean it, but people will start to say you have set your cap at Lord Montagu – and you do not want to look a fool, do you?'

'Why shouldn't I look a fool, when that is clearly what you think of me?' Cecily fired at her, with an unusual flash of temper. 'Do you think I don't know that's how you see me?'

She stormed off, leaving Kitty staring after her. Well. That was unexpected. But Kitty did not have time to think on it for long, because Aunt Dorothy was at her elbow.

'They're here,' she whispered.

Kitty took a deep breath and walked over to meet her future mother-in-law. Her first thought was that Aunt Dorothy must be mistaken, for she had guided her over to the most heavily bejewelled woman Kitty had ever seen in her life. She looked rather as if she had fallen into a well of gold, for every inch of her was dripping with precious stones, from the tips of her fingers to the heights of her impressively lifted bosoms. And yet there was Mr Pemberton at her side – so it must be she.

'Miss Talbot!' Mr Pemberton said brightly. 'May I introduce you to my mother?'

Kitty found herself the recipient of a gimlet-eyed stare.

'It is an honour to meet you at last,' she said, curtseying.

'Hmm.' Mrs Pemberton looked her overtly over. 'Yes, she is pretty enough, Colin. Though a little dour.'

Her son nodded in agreement. Lady Radcliffe, who was standing beside Aunt Dorothy, coughed politely to cover up the awkwardness of the moment.

'Colin tells me you should like to attend church with me,' Mrs Pemberton said next, with the same bald unconcern.

'I should like it above all things,' Kitty lied.

'Hmm. Well, good. Piety is the greatest quality a woman can possess. One must love God above all else, you know.'

Kitty nodded, though surely this lady ranked her jeweller even higher.

'Did you hear that the Duke of Leicester is here, tonight?' Pemberton said, craning his neck to peer into the crowd.

'Did you say Leicester?' Aunt Dorothy asked sharply.

'Oh, Leicester is here, is he?' Lady Radcliffe said happily. 'I have known him for years – oh, yes, there he is. Leicester, over here!'

She waved over a tall, greying gentleman, who bounded over and kissed her hand with smacking enthusiasm.

'Miss Linwood, how marvellous you look,' he said jubilantly.

'Your grace, please, it's been thirty years – you must start calling me Lady Radcliffe!' she said in playful remonstration.

'You'll always be Miss Linwood to me. Though I did hear that boy of yours is back in London, is it true? Could do with him taking his seat in the Lords, you know.'

'You mustn't talk politics tonight, your grace, or everyone will think you a dead bore! Here, I must introduce you to my dear friends, Mrs Kendall and Miss Talbot. And this is Mr and Mrs Pemberton, of course.'

'How do you do?'

The Pembertons were looking very impressed. Kitty curtseyed in greeting to the Duke of Leicester.

'Forgive me, have we met before?' he said curiously.

'I do not believe so, your grace,' she said, with a polite smile.

Beside her, Aunt Dorothy was fanning herself rather vigorously, and Kitty wished she would stop. Draught aside, she was holding her fan rather too close to her face, obscuring half of it, and it looked most unusual.

'I am quite sure we have,' Leicester insisted, eyes fixed on Miss Talbot's face. 'You look so very familiar to me. Is your family from London – perhaps I have met a relative?'

Kitty looked over to Aunt Dorothy, hoping she might chip in, only to find her aunt's face almost totally obscured by her fan now. A horrible thought occurred to Kitty. She had a feeling she might know which of her relatives this man had met, and under what circumstances.

'I am often told I have one of those faces,' Kitty said, inwardly cursing that her father's blood was not strong enough to prevent her striking resemblance to her mother. She cast about for a new topic, but to her horror, the duke's words had inspired more than a little curiosity in the assembled group. Even Lady Radcliffe was eyeing her with interest now.

'Perhaps she reminds you of the youngest Clavering girl?' Lady Radcliffe suggested.

'No dash it, I am quite sure that is not it,' Leicester persisted. Oh goodness. 'Remind me of your name, miss?'

Kitty's mind was an anxious whirl. She could not, of course, deny this man her name – it would look too unusual. But were she to reveal it, did she risk this gentleman making a leap of logic? Might he, had he known her mother once upon a time, also remember why their acquaintance had drawn to a close?

'Miss Talbot, your grace,' she said, unable to deny him.

'Talbot . . .' he pondered for a few moments. 'And – forgive me – you are Mrs Talbot, ma'am?'

His head began to turn towards Mrs Kendall's fan-covered face. Aunt Dorothy would have to respond, to lower the fan – it would look too odd, it would be unforgivably rude, to do anything else. Would he recognise her, as she so clearly feared he might? Kitty's mind was quite blank of ideas. She could not think of a single thing to do to save them. There was no scheme that presented itself to her, no way out of this mess. She could only watch with morbid fascination as their whole world was about to come crashing down on them, right in front of the Pembertons. Kitty opened her mouth to say something – anything that could possibly help – but she didn't have to.

'You will no doubt have met the Harrogate Talbots during your time in Yorkshire, your grace,' came the voice of Radcliffe as he materialised quite out of thin air. 'The resemblance is uncanny, I noticed it myself.'

'The Harrogate Talbots?' Leicester's face cleared of suspicion. He snapped his fingers together. 'That'll be it, no doubt. Dashed but I can't help but be bothered by that sort of thing. My thanks, Radcliffe – and welcome back, sir! I was just telling your mother that I hope we can count upon your presence in the Lords one of these days!'

Radcliffe took a pinch of snuff. 'I'm happy to oblige, your grace, but I do not think you will like how I vote.'

Leicester let out a roar of laughter. In the ensuing melee, Kitty and Aunt Dorothy excused themselves quietly. Kitty sent a look of thanks in Radcliffe's direction, which he returned with a barely perceptible wink.

'That was far too close,' Aunt Dorothy moaned as they scurried away to a safe corner.

'I take it the Duke of Leicester knew Mama – and yourself – in your younger years?' Kitty asked.

'Yes, most intimately,' Aunt Dorothy sighed gustily. 'Thank goodness for your Radcliffe – Leicester is one of those worst sorts of devils who is terribly immoral in his private life, but an absolute stickler in public. If he had recognised me, we should have been in deepest trouble.'

Kitty felt a pang of guilt for ever having disbelieved her aunt in the first place when she spoke of such a risk. She pressed a hand to her heart, willing its pace to ease.

'Of all the people,' she said faintly. 'Of all the moments. Though I suppose we are lucky this is the only time you have been recognised.'

Aunt Dorothy did not reply, appearing quite distracted.

'It is, isn't it?' Kitty asked, frowning.

'I need a drink to settle my nerves,' Aunt Dorothy said fervently. 'I shall be hiding my face for the rest of the evening. Come find me when we can leave.'

She disappeared. Kitty was sorely tempted to do the same, but knew she must return to the Pembertons as soon as it was safe to do so. She kept an eye on them, waiting for them to leave Leicester's side, though it seemed to be taking a long time. She supposed Pemberton would be quite too excited to tell the man his political views to leave any time soon. She sighed.

'What a very melancholy sound – are things with Pemberton not going to plan?'

Kitty turned quickly, not recognising the voice.

'Oh. Lord Selbourne, good evening.' She gave him the tiniest curtsey she could muster. He acknowledged the slight with an unperturbed flick of the fingers.

'Have you thought at all about my offer?' he asked.

'No,' she said, truthfully. 'But then, I'm not sure you ever actually made one.'

'How remiss of me,' he said, with his shark's smile. 'Very well, Miss Talbot. I believe we could be of great use to one another. It would be a shame for you to waste your talents on Pemberton, when there are so many finer catches to be had. I could help you, you know.'

'And in return?' Kitty asked, eyebrows rising; while she could make neither head nor tail of what precisely this gentleman wanted, he was, without doubt, an unscrupulous weasel.

Selbourne held out his hands in affected innocence. 'Would you begrudge a friend a slice of the pie?'

'But then we are not friends,' Kitty said coldly, turning a dismissive shoulder in his direction. But before she could leave, he had caught her lightly by the arm.

'Perhaps you would be more comfortable discussing it in private. I am in Wimbledon this weekend – I have guests on Saturday, but otherwise I am free. Let us discuss the matter further. I'm renting Hill Place, off Worple Road. You can't miss it. '

Kitty was quite bored by this fellow now, and the Pembertons had finally left Leicester's side. She bobbed another insignificant curtsey to him.

'Very well, I must be going now.'

'Happy hunting,' he said, smiling with all his teeth.

Kitty marshalled all of her charm and mental acuity and, for the remainder of the evening, set out to impress Mrs Pemberton with every ounce in her body. The lady was inscrutable – a strange mix of virtuous, snooty and vain that meant charming her was a little like trying to catch a very prickly cat. But when she said her goodbyes that night, Pemberton pressed his hand onto hers with great meaning.

'I have business to attend to tomorrow, but will I see you on Saturday at the Hastings ball? I have something quite important to ask of you.'

30

The last time she had felt so sure of a proposal, Kitty had been jubilant, but try as she might she could not capture that feeling of celebration now. She sat up with Aunt Dorothy that night, sharing a pot of tea despite the lateness of the hour. Kitty tried to plan what she would write to Beatrice to tell her of the good news in the morning, but could not imagine what she would say. How she could spin this into joy, when in truth she was suffering from a most severe attack of the blue devils.

'Tonight was a success, then?' Dorothy prodded her, after they had spent a long few minutes in silence. Kitty nodded.

'Very well done. Though I must ask: are you sure you are prepared for what follows the engagement?'

'In what sense?' Kitty asked.

'Well, I know you have reconciled yourself to being engaged to a man you do not love . . . But are you ready to be married to him? With all that entails?'

Kitty felt a little lost by all the connotations of the question. 'I suppose I shall have to be,' she said finally.

Aunt Dorothy nodded again, though a little sadly. Kitty tried, for a moment, to imagine her wedding day. Her mother had spoken of her own often, declaring it – despite its secrecy, despite all the unpleasantness that followed with Mr Talbot's family – one of the best days of her life. *We were so happy*, she often said, misty-eyed and nostalgic. Kitty had always known hers would be quite different – but the prospect felt worse than it ever had before. Ever since she had . . . well, ever since she had gained a sense of what she would be missing.

'What was my mother like, when you first knew her?' Kitty asked suddenly, into the quiet.

'Before she had met your father, do you mean?' Aunt Dorothy asked.

'Yes.'

Aunt Dorothy paused to consider this. 'She was brave,' she said after a moment. 'She would do absolutely anything for those she cared for.'

Kitty was not sure of her expression, but something in it made her aunt raise her eyebrows.

'You don't agree?' Aunt Dorothy asked.

'I do agree,' Kitty said, hastily. 'It is certainly true, but I suppose I have been . . . a little cross, that she and Papa were always able to do what they wanted – whereas I—' she broke off.

'You cannot,' Aunt Dorothy finished for her.

'Mama did not have sisters,' Kitty pointed out. 'Perhaps it would have been different if she had.'

'Perhaps it would,' Aunt Dorothy agreed. 'Not all of us can follow our hearts.'

Kitty took a large gulp of tea. That was certainly true.

'Their lives were not without sacrifice, though,' Aunt Dorothy reminded her, gently. 'We of course might wish they had been a little more circumspect financially' – at this Kitty gave a dry chuckle – 'but to marry, they had to leave everything behind. Following their hearts did come at a cost.'

'That is true,' Kitty said, with a bitter little shrug of her shoulders.

'I spoke to Mrs Ebdon earlier today,' Aunt Dorothy said, hoping a change in subject would lighten Kitty's dark mood. 'I have mentioned her to you before – Rita runs the faro house on Morwell Street. I was meaning to tell you.'

'Oh yes?' Kitty feigned interest.

'She let slip that the young Mr de Lacy has been getting into an awfully bad crowd. Just gossiping you know – of course I have not told her of the connection between our families – but apparently, he's been seen parading around Soho in the company of that Selbourne boy. Terrible sort, the kind Rita doesn't let into her establishment. Cheat on the card table – and partial to opium, too, I'm told.'

'Mr de Lacy, gambling?' Kitty was quite taken aback – she had not thought it part of the young man's character. And while Selbourne had said they were friends, she had originally supposed this to be merely part of his manipulations.

'And this isn't something you felt the need to tell your dear friend Lady Radcliffe?' Kitty asked, pointedly.

Her aunt looked at her as though she was the most foolish creature ever to have existed. 'And how would I explain my acquaintance with Mrs Ebdon to Lady Radcliffe, hmm? I just thought, given your . . . friendship with Radcliffe, that you might like to give them a warning.'

'Yes, thank you,' Kitty said absently. When was the last time she had properly spoken to Mr de Lacy? Several weeks at least. He was, now she considered the matter, making only the most fleeting of appearances at social occasions, if he attended at all. While Kitty might not want to marry the boy any longer, she still did not want him falling prey to a gambling addiction or getting caught up with a disreputable crowd. He had a good heart and wore it quite on his sleeve – and she of all people should know how easy this made him to manipulate.

Kitty vowed to warn Radcliffe of the danger at the earliest moment, which – fortuitously – turned out to be the very next night. Kitty did not look for him – there never seemed to be a need – but no sooner had the clock struck eleven, than he appeared at her side.

'For you,' he announced, offering her a flute that glittered even in the muted light.

'Is it poisoned?' she asked, with faux suspicion.

'No, no. If I wanted to murder you, I can think of far better means than that,' Lord Radcliffe said, tilting his head in consideration.

'Yes, I suppose you could just bludgeon me,' Kitty suggested. 'Less elegant, but possibly simpler, and there's no lack of convenient places to dispose of an unwanted body around London.'

He looked at her sideways. 'I am alarmed to hear you have given the matter so much thought. Perhaps it is I who should be worried?'

She shook her head, smiling, and took a sip of the champagne for courage. 'Actually, I did have something I wanted to speak to you about.'

'Oh yes? And how went the clash of the Titans?' Radcliffe

asked. At her questioning look, he clarified, 'Did you manage to charm Mrs Pemberton into submission?'

'Oh, it went quite well,' Kitty said as brightly as she could. 'She's a very strange woman, certainly, but by the end of our time together she quite approved. Pemberton tells me that she is a romantic at heart and is pleased that he has secured a love match.'

Radcliffe choked. 'A love match?' he said, incredulously. 'Miss Talbot, doing it far too brown, indeed.'

'It will be! At least on his part, and that comes to much the same thing,' Kitty insisted, a slight blush on her cheeks. Radcliffe enjoyed her discomfiture for a few moments – for it was seldom won and should thus be properly relished as a rare delicacy.

'He will propose tomorrow,' she said, holding her chin high, and he felt some of his good humour dissipate.

'Indeed?' he murmured, trying for disinterested. Which, of course, he was.

'Yes, at the Hastings ball.'

Radcliffe absorbed this for a moment.

'I should then perhaps congratulate you,' he said at last.

She shook her head, looking at him archly from under her brows. 'A touch premature. You never know, perhaps Mr Pemberton's brother will arrive at the eleventh hour to blackmail me. I should not like to celebrate yet, just in case.'

'Of course,' Radcliffe agreed smoothly. 'Most sensible. Though I should not expect there are many men in the world brave enough to stand up to you.'

She laughed. 'Just one, in fact.' Kitty paused. 'I have not yet thanked you, for helping us yesterday with Lord Leicester. It was very kind of you – had you not intervened, I cannot imagine Pemberton would want to marry me.'

Kitty had meant the thanks sincerely, but Radcliffe did not look at all pleased to receive them, giving a short bark of bitter laughter. She frowned, unsure of how she had offended him.

'Can you really mean to marry someone you do not love?' he asked her, quite abruptly.

Kitty's hand faltered as she lifted her glass to her mouth.

'People marry without love all the time,' she reminded him, her voice hardening. 'It is not so rare. You think my *déclassé* background makes me more mercenary, but marriages of convenience are the creation of your class, not mine.'

'It has never been your background that has given me most pause, Miss Talbot,' Radcliffe said, affronted. 'Merely your willingness to sacrifice Archie's happiness for your own ends.'

She looked at him, assessing.

'And if I had truly been in love with him. What then?'

'I don't follow.'

'Would you have accepted our relationship, our engagement, had my background been the same, but my feelings for de Lacy been true?'

'Had I been sure your affection was real, and his also, I don't see why not,' Radcliffe said slowly, sensing there was a trap but unable to detect where.

'Liar,' she said, almost affectionately. 'You would never have countenanced it. You protest that your issue was my deceit, but the gap in our social standing would always have prevented your approval. You would never have given it – even if you believed my sentiment to be true.'

'And how could I ever have believed your feelings to be true?' he said roughly, 'When you are so clearly willing to marry anyone who is rich enough, sentiment be damned?'

'Tell me this, then,' she said. 'Could you ever have looked past my birth? Past my circumstances? Could it ever have truly not mattered?'

Her voice was infused with more emotion than the argument warranted, but she did not care. She had to know. He did not answer, staring at her with eyes full of some unnamed emotion.

'I—' he began, but he could not finish.

'You could not,' she finished for him. They were talking about more than just Archie, now, and they both knew it.

'You would never have wanted Archie more than you needed his money,' he said hoarsely.

'And is that so important?' she asked. 'Is want so much more important than need?'

'It's everything,' he told her, voice raw.

'I understand,' she said.

And she did.

She looked down, then cleared her throat loudly, twice. 'I actually had something quite different upon my mind, to say to you,' she said, brushing past the emotion of their exchange with sheer force of will.

There was a long pause while he appeared to master himself. 'Yes?' he asked at last.

'I thought it best to warn you that it appears Archie *is* in a spot of trouble. He has been seen in the company of Lord Selbourne, haunting all the worst gambling spots in London.'

Radcliffe blinked – he had not expected that. 'Thank you for your concern,' he said dismissively, 'but Archie is quite all right. It is the duty of any young gentleman to walk a little on the wild side, at some point in his life.'

It was Kitty's turn to blink now – for she had not expected

that. 'You think it is his duty to develop a gambling addiction? For that is what my aunt has warned me of – he spends his nights in the company of men who are not even allowed in the faro houses.'

His lip curled. 'You'll forgive me if I trust my understanding of the situation over Mrs Kendall's.'

'Because yours is so superior?' she flashed at him. 'I'm afraid your prejudice is showing, my lord.'

'Do be calm, Miss Talbot,' he said. 'Consider your warning heeded – but I assure you, Archie is in no danger. Do you not think, perhaps, that your experience with your father is colouring your judgement?'

She reared back as if she had been struck. She had told him of her father in assumed confidence, in one of their quiet conversations together – the ones where she felt she might say anything, and it would be held safely. Apparently not.

'Perhaps your experience with your father is blinding *you*,' she flung back at him. 'Perhaps he had good reason for sending you away all along, if you were going the same way as Archie.'

'As if you care about my brother,' he snarled. 'I'd ask you to call him Mr de Lacy – you have long given up the right to use his first name. And since we are exchanging advice, perhaps your attention is better spent on your own family, rather than mine.'

'And what is that supposed to mean?' she demanded.

'Do you not think it unwise to let Miss Cecily and Montagu pursue their romance so boldly?'

'Cecily and Lord Montagu?' She was startled out of her anger for the moment, turning to look for her sister. The pair were standing, heads bent next to the refreshment table. Alone once more – which was not, admittedly, very wise. She ought to say something again to her, the poor girl had no idea what it looked like. She turned back to Radcliffe. 'They are friends, no more – they share an interest in intellectual pursuits.'

He scoffed. 'You are blinded to the truth – they consider themselves very much in love, any fool could see it.'

'You are angry with me, and just trying to cause a nuisance,' she dismissed. 'Do you think I would not notice if my sister were in love?'

'Do you think I would not notice if my brother were in danger?' he returned, pointedly.

They glared at one another, eyes as cold as they had ever been in each other's presence.

'Do you know,' she said, words hot on her tongue, 'when we first met I thought you proud, stubborn, rude and with a sense of superiority the size of England. I had almost begun to think I had misjudged you – but I see now I should have trusted my first instinct.'

'The feeling,' he said coldly, 'is quite mutual.'

They turned as one and walked away. Neither looked back.

31

Lord Radcliffe left the ball in a rage, not bothering to bid goodnight to the host or his mother. He flung himself down the front steps so fast that he ran into Captain Hinsley, who was only just arriving.

'James, slow down – what on earth is the matter?' Hinsley asked, looking concerned.

'Nothing,' Radcliffe bit out. He tried to walk on, but Hinsley gripped his arm.

'Nothing? You're quite shaking with rage, let me accompany you home,' he commanded, turning to walk his friend down the path. Radcliffe attempted to shake him off, but Hinsley had his arm caught fast.

'I'm quite capable of reaching home without a chaperone, Harry,' Radcliffe said, voice dark with warning.

'Of course you are,' Hinsley said soothingly – and clearly with no intention of listening to him. He hurried into the carriage after Radcliffe, seating himself opposite his friend with watchful eyes.

'What has you all at odds then?' he asked again.

'I-I got into an argument with Miss Talbot,' Radcliffe admitted at last. 'It started off about – about one thing, but then it led on to discussing Archie. She made a ridiculous accusation that Archie has fallen into a bad crowd – that I am so blinded by how my father treated my dalliances as a boy, that I cannot see what is right in front of me. She's *wrong*.'

But Hinsley's brow was furrowed. 'Who's the boy become friendly with, that's worried her so?'

'Lord Selbourne and his set,' Radcliffe said impatiently. 'But you're quite missing the point, Harry—'

'Selbourne? I do not like that much at all, James. You haven't been in London for a while, dear boy – old Selby has quite the reputation now.'

'Selbourne? He's harmless. Why, I used to be very closely acquainted with the man – certainly fond of gambling and drinking, but not dangerous.'

Hinsley looked unconvinced. 'From what I've heard, it's a bit more than that. I'll look into it – see if I can find anything out.'

'I beg you – do not,' Radcliffe snapped. 'There is nothing to find out. Archie is not in trouble, and I would thank everyone to stop giving me unasked for advice.'

'What if he is, though?' Hinsley asked, not seeming to take offence at his friend's tone. 'Both she and I think something smoky is afoot – worth looking into, I say.'

'My father dealt in "what ifs",' Radcliffe said. 'I will not do the same kind of interfering for Archie. It does not make you a bad person to want to have a little fun, for God's sake. Archie should be able to live and make mistakes and grow up unfettered by worries of duty and gossip.'

Hinsley held up his hands in surrender. 'All right, all right,' he said, looking at his friend closely. 'What else did you and Miss Talbot argue about?' he asked shrewdly.

'It matters nought,' Radcliffe said shortly. 'I have tarried in London too long. Far too long – I shall leave for Radcliffe Hall tomorrow.' They drew up upon St James's Place and Radcliffe opened the carriage door immediately, without waiting for a footman. 'This is goodbye, Hinsley. I shall write.'

And with that he walked into his house, slamming the door shut behind him.

Kitty held her emotions in all the way through the ball, through dancing a quadrille, three country dances and a cotillion; through two glasses of champagne; through the carriage ride home; through getting into bed. It was only when Cecily had begun softly snoring beside her that she let the sob that had been lodged in her throat for several hours spill quietly out into the night, like a secret.

It was so unfair, so very unfair. What an awful man. What a prejudiced, privileged, awful man. She hated him – she wished never to set eyes upon him or another de Lacy in her life.

She tossed and turned through the night, unable to cool her temper enough to sleep, but by morning, the dawn had brought her a little calm. She rose before Cecily, and busied herself about their room, opening the trunk that had lain unused underneath the window since their arrival, and folding some of their belongings inside it. There was a groan and rustle behind her as Cecily began to wake.

'What are you doing?' she said blearily, as Kitty packed up

her least favourite evening dress – there would surely be no need for it after tonight.

'Just a little packing,' she murmured absently. 'I hate leaving things to the last minute.'

'Packing?' Cecily sat up straight. 'Where are we going?'

'Home, of course,' Kitty said. 'After tonight, it should not be more than a week or so before we can leave. It is my intention to persuade Mr Pemberton to wed quickly – it should not be so hard, he has so little family, and will likely think it romantic. We can honeymoon in Biddington.'

'Next week?' Cecily repeated faintly.

'I'm shocked this should surprise you, Cecily,' Kitty said, exasperated. 'Surely you knew this. I do keep telling you to pay more attention when other people are speaking – then you would not be so surprised all the time.'

Cecy looked distressed. 'I did *not* know,' she said. 'I wish you would have told me sooner. Can we not stay longer?'

'Why should you want to stay? I thought you hated London – you have certainly spent enough time complaining about it.'

There was silence behind her for a few beats, and then all at once: 'I am in love!' Cecily said, so loudly that Kitty jumped half out of her skin.

'Gracious, Cecy, no need to shout – what do you mean, you're in love? You can't be.'

'I am!' Cecy insisted. 'With Lord Montagu – and he is in love with me, too.'

Kitty put a hand to her forehead.

'Oh Lord,' she groaned. 'Cecy – I'm sorry – but we don't have time for this.'

'No time – Kitty, I have told you I am in love!'

'And I heard you.' Kitty tried desperately to hold onto her patience. 'But the fact of the matter is, we simply cannot afford to remain any longer – we have quite run out of money.'

'There are some things more important than money!' Cecy said passionately. 'Look at Mama and Papa.'

'And where did that leave us?' Kitty demanded. 'Papa chose love over money, and it had *consequences*, Cecy! It left me— it left *us*, in a very difficult position.'

'But—' Cecily tried to interject, but Kitty overruled her with a flash of temper.

'We don't get to have who we want, Cecy! How can I get you to understand that?' she burst out. She took a deep breath, trying to calm herself. 'I know it is hard, but we really have got to think of the bigger picture. You must listen to me on this.'

'*You* never listen!' Cecy shrieked at Kitty. 'You say I don't listen, but you never listen to me, and I'm sick of it. You're always overlooking me and dismissing me, and you never listen. But Rupert does. He listens, and he's interested in what I have to say, and – and he values my opinion. You don't! You don't care what I think.'

Kitty was utterly thrown. This was the longest Cecily had spoken, without mentioning Wordsworth, for several years. 'Well . . . what *do* you think?' Kitty asked.

Cecy gaped at her for a second. 'That's not the point!' she wailed. 'I can't think of anything right now.'

'In which case,' Kitty snapped, her temper flaring again, 'I don't have time for these tantrums. Grow up, Cecy – if you don't want to help, the least you could do is to let me get on with saving our family from financial ruin rather than throwing a spanner into things at the eleventh hour.'

Cecy stormed from the room, slamming the door shut behind her.

The sisters did not speak until much later that evening. Cecily left the house soon after breakfast for a walk with Lady Amelia; she told Aunt Dorothy, though Kitty was in the room at the time. Aunt Dorothy, who was about to leave London for the weekend, to visit a friend of hers in Kent, clucked at her nieces' antics.

'You ought to mend those fences sooner rather than later,' she instructed Kitty once Cecily had left. 'And you certainly mustn't be cross with each other in front of Mrs Sinclair tonight.'

In Aunt Dorothy's absence, Mrs Sinclair was to act as their chaperone.

'I suppose you think I was too harsh,' Kitty grumbled, not quite yet ready to see Cecily's side.

'I think you were foolish,' Aunt Dorothy corrected. 'She is a young lady in the first blush of love. And she's your sister. Talk to her properly.'

She kissed Kitty's cheek in farewell.

'Good luck tonight,' she said softly, pressing Kitty's hand. 'I shall be thinking of you. And . . . wish me luck. For the journey,' she added hastily, seeing Kitty's brow furrow. 'It's further than I have travelled in a while.'

'Of course,' Kitty murmured, brushing her aunt's cheek with her own. 'Have a wonderful time with your friend.'

Aunt Dorothy nodded, picked up her suitcase and left. Kitty curled up in her aunt's armchair, sulking. She supposed she had been quite frightfully unsympathetic, but she had been caught entirely off guard. Cecily had never before expressed any interest in romantic feeling, and as Kitty had deemed her far too young to consider marriage anyway, she had quite discounted it as a possibility. And by God, could she have chosen a more inappropriate person to do it with! Throwing her cap at any titled man was dangerous – with all the questions the family would feel honour-bound to ask about Cecily's background – but the Montagus were notoriously protective about their noble line.

But that should not matter. Kitty had clearly been neglecting her for Cecily to keep such a frightfully large secret from her – too wrapped up in her own dramas to pay more than a second's attention to her. By the time Cecily came home from her walk, Kitty was quite convinced that she was, perhaps, the worst and most unkind sister ever to have lived – so much so that, when Cecily declared herself simply too tired to attend the Hastings ball that evening, she capitulated quite easily. After all, it was a longer carriage ride than usual to the Hastings' manor in Kensington, and while Kitty would prefer to have Cecily with her on such an important night, the Sinclairs would be company enough. Besides, it was the least she could do after being so beastly to Cecily that morning. Cecily should be allowed her rest.

Of course, had she known what Cecily had really spent her afternoon doing, she would not have been quite so kind.

32

The problem with these fancy dresses, Kitty thought with some indignation as she jolted towards Kensington in the Sinclair carriage, is that they make one utterly beholden to the weather. Back in Biddington, wearing her usual cotton gowns, she used to charge through life, come hailstone, fire, or brimstone. But here, one had to be more careful – especially when a storm was brewing, as it clearly was tonight.

Despite feeling less than celebratory, Kitty had felt it important to dress for the occasion of her proposal nonetheless, and was wearing her best blue crêpe gown and her favourite gloves. They were ridiculously impractical: cream-coloured, made of soft buttery fabric, with a row of tiny buttons running from elbow to wrist, and she loved them all the more for their high society decadence.

Taking courage from them now, she tottered out of the carriage after Mrs Sinclair, one hand pressed to her head to keep her curls from being upset by the wind, and one hand holding tightly to her cloak. The evening was going to be a *trial*.

Pemberton found her almost immediately.

'Miss Talbot,' he called out to her. Then, a little critically, he added, 'Why do you look so bedraggled?'

'It is very windy outside,' she pointed out, not sure how she was meant to avoid looking bedraggled after walking through a gale-force wind.

He frowned – in disapproval, or disbelief, or both.

'Well,' he said reluctantly. 'I suppose it can't be helped. May I escort you to the gardens? They are quite beautiful.'

He was going to do it straight away, then.

'Yes,' Kitty heard herself say as if from a great distance. She took his arm, and they walked together into the gardens, which were brightly lit and still busy, though the night air was quite as windy as it had been just a few moments before. Ignoring this – as if he could prevent it being so by not acknowledging it – Pemberton led Kitty to a bench in a secluded corner where they sat next to each other. He reached over and took her hand in his. She fought the urge to shake it off. She did not want him to touch her, she thought hysterically. How could she marry someone she did not want to touch her?

'Miss Talbot,' he said with great gravitas.

This was it.

'Miss Talbot,' he repeated. Strangely, despite the wind, there seemed to be an echo within the garden, for though Pemberton's mouth was not moving, she could hear his calls of 'Miss Talbot' repeating faintly.

'Miss Talbot!'

Not an echo. Kitty looked up to see Captain Hinsley hastening towards them. What on earth . . . Drawing closer, Hinsley looked from Kitty to Pemberton and back again.

'Oh hell,' he said despairingly. 'Devilishly sorry to interrupt – may I speak with you for a moment, Miss Talbot?'

'Now?' Pemberton blustered, but Kitty was already getting up.

'An emergency, is it?' she asked eagerly, as he pulled her a few steps away.

'Have you seen Lady Radcliffe?' he demanded as soon as Pemberton was out of earshot.

'Lady Radcliffe?' she said, confused. 'No, not since last night.'

'Blast. Pattson said she'd be here, but she must not have yet arrived—' He broke off and cursed, looking most agitated.

'What on earth is going on, Captain?'

'It's Archie. It's just as you said – or worse – he's fallen into a bad crowd. I've been asking around, and I believe Selbourne has duped him into joining a high stakes game. The devil did the same thing to the Egerton boy, and young Mr Cowper. Word is he gets young men of fortune quite doped on spirits, and then fleeces them of all their fortune with a rigged deck. It's how he plans to regain his fortune – man is up to his ears in debt, you know.'

'Dear God,' Kitty breathed, going quite pale. 'Radcliffe must be told at once!'

'He left for Devonshire today!' Hinsley said miserably. 'Told me so last night – and Pattson said he made his goodbyes to the family this morning. I don't know what is to be done. I don't know where Archie has even gone. I don't know where to *start*.'

A recollected scrap of memory was swimming to the forefront of Kitty's mind.

'But I do . . .' she said slowly, trying to capture the thought.

'I think I know where they have gone, for the toad tried to invite me.'

'Did he? The scoundrel. What did he say?' Hinsley said urgently.

'I can't quite remember – I wasn't properly listening,' Kitty groaned, racking her brains. 'In Wimbledon, certainly . . .'

She turned to look at Pemberton, who waved an impatient hand at her. She should surely go back to him. Let him propose. Accept. That was the right thing to do, she knew. It was simply one of those terrible moments where the right thing was also the selfish thing. And though it pained her to leave Mr de Lacy to such a fate, she could not risk her family for his sake, she just couldn't.

Yet, unbidden, her mind strayed to Radcliffe: halfway to Devonshire by now no doubt, cursing her name, most likely – and entirely unaware of the danger his brother was in. He'd never forgive himself if something happened to Mr de Lacy, that was certain. Kitty bit her lip.

'I'm sorry,' she called, her voice barely audible over the wind. 'I must go.' Pemberton gaped at her, but she turned resolutely back to Hinsley. Her heart was beating fast – so fast – and she was almost certain this was a mistake, but she had to do it.

'I'll remember on the way,' she said. 'I'm sure of it – let's go now.'

They dashed through the hall, Kitty retrieving her cloak as they did so, and fled down the front steps towards the carriages, where a groom was watching Hinsley's hastily abandoned curricle. She spared a moment to glance around, to make sure no one of their acquaintance was watching, but the driveway was blessedly empty and she leapt in after him.

'Are you quite sure?' Hinsley asked Kitty, even as he was directing his bays out onto the road. 'I'm not sure Radcliffe would approve of this—'

'Oh, who cares what he thinks,' Kitty snapped. 'You just drive – I'm trying to remember.'

Gusts of wind whipped through her hair relentlessly, tugging her curls free from their pins. She supposed they were lucky it was not raining, for they would surely be quite soaked through already – but the gale alone made managing the horses difficult enough.

'Give them their heads,' she told Captain Hinsley, as they rattled down Worple Road, watching his hands critically.

'Don't tell me what to do,' he said through gritted teeth, though he loosened the reins anyhow.

'I wouldn't if you didn't seem in such desperate need of instruction,' she snapped back. It had not been long before the two had dropped all pretence at manners.

'Are you sure this is the right way?' he demanded.

'Yes,' she said, more certainly than she felt. 'He definitely said Hill-something, off Worple Road.'

'We can't be far, then.' Hinsley's eyes squinted into the darkness.

'What kind of evils are we to expect there?' Kitty asked – repeating herself, louder, when he couldn't hear over the wind.

'I don't know,' he said grimly. 'I have heard stories – crooked tables – opium – women – private prizefights. We just need to get Archie out before he commits himself too fully. Selbourne always plays this the same way, I'm told – he tempts away young bucks, lets them win their first ten games with him, so they're addicted to the feeling, then turns the tables. Archie is in full possession of his fortune now – and Selbourne will have his eyes upon it, you mark my words.'

'Gracious,' Kitty breathed out.

As if summoned by Hinsley's description, a set of iron bars suddenly rose ahead of them – tall, steel, and imposing. The main gates were shut, but a smaller, person-sized opening stood ajar to their left.

'Right,' Hinsley said, pulling up sharply. He handed her the reins.

'Stay here,' he instructed. 'Walk the horses. I shall return in fifteen minutes.'

'I'm coming in with you,' she said indignantly.

'You are not,' he said firmly. 'I absolutely forbid it; it is far too dangerous.'

'It could be dangerous out here,' she protested. 'What if there are highwaymen – or bandits!'

'They would be brave bandits indeed on a night like this,' he said, but he appeared torn. After a second, he leant under the seat, groping around for a few moments, before sitting up and pulling out a pistol.

'Be careful with that,' he said. 'I'll leave it on the seat next to you. Do not touch it unless you are in danger. Can't imagine anyone else coming this way, but – if they do, shoot it into the air. I shall only be gone fifteen minutes.'

With that, he jumped down from the carriage and, within a few steps, was swallowed up by the darkness.

33

Radcliffe stared out of his window onto the deserted street below. A strong wind had swept through London as dusk fell, flinging rain and red leaves from the nearby trees at the glass. It was the wildest storm he had seen in years. Behind him, his bedroom was packed up. In the morning, he would be leaving for Radcliffe Hall – he had meant to go today, but the weather had made travel quite perilous. He tried to envision Radcliffe Hall in his mind – usually a source of such comfort to him, the place where he felt most at ease in the whole world – but the exercise left him feeling entirely lacking. Isolation did not hold the same appeal it once had.

A polite knock on the door. He looked up to see Beaverton hovering on the threshold.

'A young woman to see you, my lord.' Radcliffe looked to the clock. His first thought was to wonder if he should be pleased that Miss Talbot was choosing to call at nine in the evening, rather than the morning – until he remembered that she no longer had reason to call upon him. By tomorrow she would be engaged, perhaps even was so already. Unless . . .

'Show Miss Talbot in,' he instructed, his curiosity piqued, his heart beating ever so slightly faster. He rose and walked to the fireplace to lean on the mantle, affecting nonchalance – before straightening almost immediately, feeling foolish.

'Ahem,' Beaverton pretended not to notice the moment – protective, as ever, of his lord's dignity. 'On this occasion, it is the young lady who always accompanies Miss Talbot.'

'Her maid?' Radcliffe drew up short.

Beaverton had shown the young lady into the library, and Radcliffe hastened down to meet her. It was indeed the house-maid who had accompanied Miss Talbot on her various visits – Radcliffe recognised the red hair, as well as the disconcertingly direct stare.

'May I help you?' he asked. 'Is everything all right?'

'I hope so,' she said, biting her lip. She was holding herself up straight, but there was the suggestion of nerves about her.

'I know this is mighty strange me calling here alone, my lord, but I'm not sure what to do. Mrs Kendall is in Brighton, and Miss Kitty in Kensington and – I didn't know where else to turn.'

'What's wrong?' he said sharply.

'It's Miss Cecy, my lord. She's only gone and eloped,' she said despairingly, brandishing a letter at him. He took it, noticing that it was already open.

'This is addressed to Miss Talbot,' he said neutrally.

'If you think I wouldn't open a letter like that, when it's clearly got trouble inside, you are dead wrong,' she retorted, suddenly fierce. He scanned its contents, expression darkening.

'Does Miss Talbot know of this?' he demanded.

'No, my lord. As I said, she's at the Hastings ball – and by the time I got there they'd have been halfway to Scotland. I came straight to you.'

Radcliffe nodded distractedly, drumming his fingers upon the table. He could have asked the young woman why, exactly, she felt the need to come to him – could remonstrate her for involving him in a mess that was not his and had nothing to do with him, given Miss Cecily was neither a member of his family, nor even a close acquaintance. Why should he care? But what would have been the point. He was not going to let such a disastrous thing happen to Miss Talbot, not when it would ruin everything the brave creature had done so far for her family. There was no point discussing the whys, not when he had known from the first second that he would be doing something about it.

He strode to the door, opened it imperiously and called out to his manservant. 'Beaverton, send a man to the west and northern gates. Ask them there if they've seen the Montagu carriage pass – and to return as soon as they hear. And send Lawrence in.'

With a few short sentences, there was an army at his command. Lawrence arrived hurriedly, pulling on a jacket as he came into the room.

'Have the carriage brought round, Lawrence, and saddle up my bay, we're leaving for Scotland on a most urgent mission.' Radcliffe turned to Sally. 'Will you join me?' he asked, bowing courteously.

'What do you plan on doing?' she said suspiciously.

'Fetching them back,' he said grimly.

* * *

They rode north as fast as they were able, the wind howling painfully through Radcliffe's ears. Lawrence was driving the carriage, Sally jostling within, but Radcliffe had outpaced them almost immediately on his bay. There was no chance of losing each other on the Great Northern Road, and while the carriage – and Sally's chaperonage – would be essential for the return journey with Miss Cecily, Radcliffe knew his only chance of catching the couple would be on horseback.

The Montagu carriage had been seen leaving for the Great Northern Road not two hours before – the foolish couple had not even the sense to hire an unmarked vehicle, but in this instance their thoughtlessness was quite useful to their pursuers. Radcliffe did not think much of the Montagu carriage against his own horses, and it was not impossible that they should catch up. He gritted his teeth, wanting to wring the Montagu fool's neck. What a scheme indeed. The Montagu family would not countenance this match in a thousand years. And especially not once Miss Cecily and Montagu had spent several nights of the journey together, unmarried. Had they imagined they would make it to Scotland in one night? At best, they might quietly seek an annulment to hush up the scandal – but even this would surely besmirch the Talbot name quite thoroughly, while the Montagus would be able to sail on, unmarred. Mr Pemberton would surely end his engagement to Miss Talbot, out of shame, and though he could not think of anything less he wanted than to see this man married to Miss Talbot, he could not bear to imagine her suffering such a fate.

He turned a corner, and slowed his horse, seeing a dark shape ahead of him. Radcliffe squinted into the black night, barely able to see more than a few feet ahead, but as he rode closer, he was able to make out what looked like a carriage.

'Anyone there?' he called into the darkness, but his shout was carried off by the wind as easily as if it had been a whisper.

He trotted up to it, and as he approached, saw that the vehicle was damaged, one wheel lying several feet away from its body, another still attached but quite askew – its spikes crushed. And worse – much worse – as Radcliffe got close enough to see the whole vehicle properly beneath the pitch-black sky, he could see the trunk of a tree splitting the carriage clean in half. It was crushed beneath the weight. Upon the carriage door, the Montagu crest glinted.

Radcliffe cursed. They can't be far now, he told himself. Someone must have taken the horses from the spokes – they would be at the next inn, he was sure of it. He spared a moment to hope Lawrence would have sense enough not to let Sally see what remained of the carriage when they caught up, and moved his horse on. He did not allow himself to wonder what state Miss Cecily Talbot might be in when he found her.

Kitty waited the full fifteen minutes before following Hinsley up the drive. Well, surely ten minutes had passed, which amounted to the same thing. Hinsley would not thank her for interfering, she knew . . . But what if he really did need her help? She would not hear a shout over the wind – she might not even hear a shot, if it came to that. She stared through the gate into the dark, torn. Kitty knew she could not wait upon the sidelines any longer. She left the safety of the carriage and dashed after him.

The drive was shorter than she would have expected, and Kitty navigated it as best she could in the darkness, soon coming upon the house, a once grand manor that was now slightly faded. The door was standing ajar, with a sliver of light spilling out onto the darkness. She took a deep breath and slipped inside.

She saw Hinsley first. He was in the hallway, standing chest to chest with Selbourne, a snarl upon his face.

'This is all very well, Hinsley,' Selbourne was saying in an infuriating drawl, 'but I am afraid Archie is . . . ah, indisposed and does not want to see you.'

'Let me pass,' Hinsley said with dark emphasis. 'Or I shall make you.'

In Kitty's view, this was just the sort of nonsense men started issuing whenever they were left alone too long. No subtlety whatsoever – and no efficiency, either. Why, if Hinsley could not go up to Archie, Archie could just as well come down to them.

Kitty let out a high-pitched wail of despair. Both men jumped, twisting around to stare at her in shock.

'What the devil!' Selbourne expostulated.

'Miss *Talbot!*' Hinsley did not look pleased at all.

'Oh, I am quite beside myself!' Kitty cried, producing enough noise to wake the dead – or at least, the dead drunk. 'Help! Help! I must have help!'

She stomped clumsily into the room, crashing into a suit of armour standing guard in the doorway, which let out a great clang of displeasure in response and fell heavily to the ground with an almighty racket. She heard footsteps above her, and a door crashed open at the top of the stairs, plumes of smoke escaping ahead of a group of very dishevelled men, who hurried down to the source of the noise. Their waistcoats were unbuttoned, their cravats were untied, and one of them had an unmistakable smudge of rouge on his cheek. Amongst them, like a cherub that had wandered into a devil's tea party, was Archie, blinking into the gloom.

'Miss Talbot?' Archie said disbelievingly, looking utterly floored. 'Hinsley? What on earth are you doing here?'

'It appears,' Selbourne was looking a little harried, 'that both Captain Hinsley and Miss Talbot have seen fit to trespass upon my property and our evening both. They seem to deem you in need of rescuing, my boy.'

'Rescuing?' Archie looked from Kitty to Hinsley. 'Is that true? Do you really think me s-so pathetic as needing to be rescued from a party?'

'Not pathetic,' Hinsley said calmly. 'Just misled. Let us go now, Archie.'

'No, I shan't,' Archie insisted. 'I'm having a nice time, and I'm not some sort of – some sort of child that needs bringing home. I'm not going anywhere.'

'Just so,' Selbourne said, recollecting his usual smug demeanour. 'Let us go back upstairs. Hinsley – Miss Talbot – leave my property before I have you thrown out.'

'Archie, he's trying to cheat you out of your money,' Kitty said urgently. 'He's not your friend.'

'And you are?' Archie let out a derisive bark of laughter.

'We are not going anywhere until you come with us,' Hinsley affirmed, reaching for Archie again.

'Very well.' Selbourne had had enough. 'Lionel?' he called loudly. Another door opened, this time from a ground-floor antechamber, and three hulking figures trooped out. Archie stared at them uncertainly – as did the other guests, backing away in befuddlement. Captain Hinsley stepped in front of Kitty.

'I should very much not like to force you out,' Selbourne said conciliatorily. 'Don't make me, Hinsley.'

'Selby, I say,' Archie said, a little shocked. 'Not sure that sort of thing is needed – how terribly rude. In fact, do you know, I think I'll be off. Yes, I think I ought to go – this is not the thing, *at all*.'

'Archie, I'm afraid I cannot allow you to leave in the middle of a game. It would be very impolite,' Selbourne said it quite mildly, but Kitty felt a chill run down her spine.

Archie stared at his friend, aghast. 'Selby, why did you bring me here?' he asked at last. 'Was it really to cheat me?'

'Go back to the table, Archie,' Selbourne snapped. 'You stupid boy, you don't understand – I need you to go back to the table. Don't make me ask again.'

Lord Selbourne no longer looked urbane, his eyes darting restlessly from Archie to Hinsley to Kitty and back again. In fact, Archie thought he was looking downright squirrelly.

'Lionel,' Selbourne called again, and one of the hulking men began to move forward. 'Take Archie back to his seat, would you?'

'I say – get your hands off me!' Archie squawked, as they began to tug at his arms.

'That is enough,' Kitty said firmly. She sidestepped Hinsley, pulled the pistol out from under her cloak and pointed it directly at Selbourne. The men stilled.

'Oh, blast it,' Hinsley groaned. 'She brought the pistol. Miss Talbot, give it to me.'

'Let's calm down now, shall we?' Kitty suggested politely, ignoring Hinsley. 'There's no need for such rudeness. We're going to leave now, Lord Selbourne, all of us – with our apologies for interrupting the evening.'

The appearance of the pistol had shocked everyone into silence, and it quickly became clear that not one of the men assembled knew quite what to do about it. There was an awkward pause. Archie gaped at Kitty, quite stupefied that such a shockingly vulgar thing was happening in front of him; Hinsley glared at Kitty and held his hand out entreatingly; and Selbourne was staring with wild flickering eyes from Archie to Kitty to Hinsley, quite consternated that his evening should have gone so awry.

'Miss Talbot,' Selbourne was the first to speak, in a passable imitation of his own calm. 'I'm not sure you can expect me to believe that a gentlewoman such as yourself is really going to shoot me.'

Kitty held her hands steady. 'You're a gambling man, Selbourne – are you willing to bet on it?'

He ran a sweating hand through his hair.

'Just let him come upstairs for a bit,' he implored. 'You don't understand the trouble I'm in – I need the money – and he'd barely notice the difference.'

'I say,' Archie murmured again, in quiet shock. Selby did not seem quite so glamorous when he was begging.

Kitty just shook her head. They stared at each other for a beat – then two. Then, on the third count, Selbourne jerked his hand, and his men fell back. Taking this for the signal it was, Archie backed away towards Hinsley and Kitty.

'Er – terribly sorry, Selby, for the inconvenience and – and everything,' he said, with admirable politeness. 'But think I ought to get Miss Talbot home, you know, given the weather. You have a very good evening, my lord.'

34

The inn appeared out of the darkness quite suddenly. Radcliffe cantered ahead, dismounting in the courtyard swiftly and throwing the reins of his horse at the stablehand.

'Hold him!' he commanded, stalking inside.

Ahead of him, leaning against the innkeeper's desk, was Lord Montagu, arguing fiercely with the innkeeper.

'If you would just listen to me – it's important – we just need—' He broke off with a yelp, as Radcliffe caught him by the ear and wheeled him around.

'How dare you!' Montagu yelled in outrage, brandishing a fist. Radcliffe evaded the appendage easily and pulled on the ear again to get the boy's attention.

'Where is Miss Cecily?' he asked grimly. 'Is she hurt?'

'I must say I do not think it any of your business, my lord' – another twist of the ear – '*ow*, stop, let me go. She's in there, she's perfectly well.'

Radcliffe dropped him immediately. 'We'll be having words in just a moment,' he said grimly.

The innkeeper was watching proceedings with a supercilious air of satisfaction. 'I told you, boy,' he said to Montagu. 'Told you people'd be after you.'

'Send one of your men to wait on the road,' Radcliffe instructed the man. 'Look out for my carriage and flag it down – it shouldn't be too far behind now.'

He passed a coin over, and then strode into the antechamber to find a red-nosed and thoroughly miserable-looking Miss Cecily sitting close by the fire. She looked up, shocked.

'Radcliffe? What are you doing here?' she asked in surprise.

'I might ask you the same question. Are you hurt? I saw the carriage.' He scanned her person for injuries.

'I am unhurt,' she said faintly. 'It had already thrown the wheel before the tree fell, so we were all fine – even the horses.'

'Good. Well, up you get – we're going back to London, now,' he said briskly.

'No, I'm not,' she said mulishly. 'I don't have to do what you tell me.'

'I am here,' he said – gathering some last vestiges of his patience from the very bottom of his soul – 'on your sister's behalf. Had you thought how this would worry her?'

'As if she would care!' Cecy said, standing, her whole body trembling. She was taking to dramatics beautifully. 'All she cares about is parties and flirting and a-and—'

'And solving your family's financial troubles so that you have somewhere to live?' he suggested.

She deflated, looking suddenly more like the lost child she was.

'I could not think what else there was to do,' she said miserably. 'She can be so hard to talk to sometimes – I did try.'

'Come,' he said gently, softening in the face of her distress. 'I think it best you try speaking to her again. You can return to London in my carriage, with your maid by your side. Montagu will remain here, to attach no whisper of impropriety to your name. No one need ever know.'

Cecily nodded, tremulously. This agreed, Radcliffe left to procure her some hot tea while they waited for the carriage. He walked almost immediately into Montagu, who was hovering by the door and looked to have gathered back some of his gumption.

'I say!' he said loudly. 'You can't just take her – you might be a kidnapper for all I know! An abductor! I won't stand for it, you hear!'

'Keep your voice down,' Radcliffe said softly, but with a sharp bite. 'You have already almost caused irreparable harm to that young lady's reputation; do not make things worse now. Now, listen to me. Listen. You are to stay here tonight – get yourself a room – and you are not to breathe a word of Miss Talbot's presence here. You will tell people you were on your way to see a family member, when your carriage was damaged. I do not want a whisper of scandal to be attached to her name, do you hear me?'

Montagu swallowed, gulped back a retort, then nodded too. His dramatically tall pomade drooped upon his head.

'I love her,' he said, simply. 'I don't want anything bad to happen to her, ever.'

'Then be glad I got here when I did,' Radcliffe told him. 'Now off you go.'

Lawrence was less than an hour behind, in the end. He must have been driving like the devil to manage it, but he supervised the changing of the horses with no sign of fatigue. They would have to leave Radcliffe's horses here, at the inn, to rest, which Radcliffe knew did not sit well with Lawrence – and indeed, his eyes and tongue were equally critical as he lectured the stablehand on the horses' care.

'I'll be back tomorrow,' Lawrence stressed. 'Once they've had a chance to rest. So don't be lending ours out – they cost more than your life,' he threatened.

'That's enough, Lawrence,' Radcliffe said gently. 'Remember it is they who are doing us a favour.'

'*Hmph*,' was all Lawrence said.

Radcliffe handed Miss Cecily into the carriage, followed by Sally.

'I'd get in yourself too, my lord,' Lawrence directed. 'No point us both getting cold,' he said cheerfully.

His own bay would also be left to rest with his carriage horses – and the inn did not have another to spare. And truth be told, Radcliffe was quite glad to have the chance to rid the chill from his bones. 'I owe you a thousand favours,' he told Lawrence.

'I'll accept a raise,' Lawrence retorted cheerfully.

Inside the carriage, Miss Cecily fell into an uneasy slumber, while Sally looked out of the window into the dark, wide awake.

'We're lucky she didn't get hurt,' she said into the quiet. 'I'll be glad to get her home in one piece.'

'You've gone above and beyond today, Sally,' Radcliffe said, fighting an urge to yawn. 'You have my thanks – and I'm sure Miss Talbot's too.'

Sally nodded.

'Why did you come to me?' he asked, curiously. 'I think you did the right thing, but why was I your first option?'

'Well, I couldn't get to Miss Kitty in time – although she would have solved everything in a trice you know,' she said in a confessional aside. Radcliffe thought with some acerbity that he was not sure how Miss Kitty would have solved it any better than he had, but controlled the impulse to vocalise this.

'And she trusts you,' Sally finished. She looked at him narrowly. 'Reckon she trusts you a lot, in truth.'

As soon as they left the house, as if by prearranged signal, Archie, Hinsley and Kitty began to run. There was no sound of pursuit, but they raced down the path nonetheless, feet flying over rock and stone. They raced through the gate, squeezed themselves three abreast into the curricle, and Hinsley drove the horses off at once. By the time they turned the first corner they were riding at quite ten miles an hour.

'What was that?' Hinsley demanded. 'I told you to stay in the carriage!'

'And I did, until it seemed you weren't coming back out again,' Kitty protested.

'That is a barefaced lie!'

'She was going to shoot him,' Archie said, dazed.

'I was not,' Kitty insisted.

'Give me that pistol,' Hinsley instructed angrily, making a grab for it. 'By George, do you have the faintest idea how to use it?'

'Well, not really,' Kitty admitted. 'But as it turns out, neither do you – it wasn't loaded, you dolt. I checked as soon as you left. Are you honestly a soldier?'

'Dear God,' Hinsley cursed. 'Dear *God*.'

'We were about to be quite trapped there,' Kitty said – now

that she was in the safety of the vehicle, she was quite regaining her usual self-possession – 'there wasn't much else to be done but threaten him most soundly.'

Hinsley let out a peal of wild laughter.

'Hinsley – Hinsley, what on earth is going on?' Archie asked weakly.

'We came to rescue you,' Hinsley said cheerily. 'From certain ruin. Must say it's the first time I've done a rescue with a woman onside, but credit where credit's due – you performed most excellently, Miss Talbot.'

He gave a courteous little flourish of his hand in her direction, and she returned the gesture with even more pomp. 'May I say that you did very well yourself, my dear sir.'

Archie began to think they had both gone quite mad. 'Perhaps I ought to drive,' he said cautiously, as they began to laugh again.

'Best not, dear boy, I can smell the drink on you – and the smoke,' Hinsley said. 'Are you all right?'

'I think so,' Archie said uncertainly. 'But I feel a fool. I do not think Selby is my friend after all.'

'I am sorry, Archie,' Kitty said, real regret in her voice. Archie looked at her.

'But why did you come, Kitty?' Archie asked. 'I must say I do not think it at all proper.'

'I had to come,' she said simply. 'Proper or not. Besides, with your brother left for Devonshire – who else was there to come after you?'

She smiled at him, warmly, and he felt a sense of foreboding in his chest. Blast, the girl was still in love with him. Awfully strange way to behave if that was the case, but the signs were clear as day. No other reason she would come haring after him, Archie could see that.

A few months ago, this revelation would have tickled Archie pink, but he was now coming to the uncomfortable realisation that he was not at all pleased. He didn't really think they were all that suited, after all – why, she had held a gun at his friend! Yes, it was a friend who he now knew to be quite villainous, but still.

Not the thing, he thought darkly. Not at all what you'd want your wife to be doing, either – shooting at people, willy-nilly, or threatening to, which was not much better. But how, he thought with horror, was one to turn down such a lady – she'd probably try to shoot *him*! He lay back into the curricle, quite exhausted.

35

The return journey seemed shorter to Radcliffe, now that he was not plagued with anxiety, and it was not long before London's lights were starting to shine through the little window of the carriage. He banged on the roof, waking Cecily with a start.

'Take us to Wimpole Street first!' he called out to Lawrence.

Not ten minutes later, though, there was a returning bang on the ceiling from the outside, and Lawrence's voice calling back in.

'My lord? I think you ought to come out.'

Opening the door onto the street, the cause for Lawrence's words was immediately quite clear, for their path was blocked by a mud-stained curricle coming the other way, upon which sat Captain Hinsley, Archie, and Miss Talbot – all of whom looked very windswept.

'Radcliffe!' Hinsley called out in relief. 'There you are!'

Sally and Cecily got out from the carriage behind Radcliffe as Kitty stared.

'What's going on?' Radcliffe and Kitty said together, each glaring at the other.

'Perhaps we ought to go inside,' Hinsley said hastily. 'Rather than hash it all out on the street.'

'Hash all *what* out?' Radcliffe said sharply.

'Cecily, Sally, what is going on?' Kitty had caught her sister's arm and was tugging her into the house. 'Come in, all of you.'

They fell into the house eagerly, all of them relieved to get out of the gusty air. The two stories were told quite haphazardly, over the top of one another, interspersed with exclamations of shock, as well as Radcliffe and Miss Talbot's loud demands for explanations that there was no space to give. But little by little, much as one assembles a jigsaw, all present gathered a clear enough picture of how the other party had spent their evening.

'Cecily!' Kitty gasped, quite stricken. 'How could you do such a thing?'

Her sister burst into tears and ran out of the room. Meanwhile Radcliffe had turned on Hinsley furiously.

'By God, how could you let her do such a thing?' There was real, fierce anger in his voice. 'She could have been hurt.'

'Let her?' his friend expostulated, bridling in indignation. 'Good God man, have *you* ever tried telling her what to do?'

'It's my fault,' Archie confessed miserably. 'I got quite caught up in it all, a-and Gerry and Ernie and Hinsley all tried to tell me, but I wouldn't listen. It all got terribly out of hand.' He looked very young, and very miserable. Radcliffe's heart went out to him.

'The fault is mine,' he said roughly, reaching out to clasp Archie's shoulder. 'I should have noticed – I should have been there. And I don't just mean this year.'

Archie's face melted, and they embraced.

'I'm sorry, Archie,' Radcliffe said, slapping him on the back.

'I suppose I ought to go home before Mama has a fit,' Archie said gloomily as he stepped back.

'Shall I drop him off?' Hinsley offered, watching them with a smile.

'No, I will,' Radcliffe said. He clasped Hinsley's arm next, gripping it tightly. 'Thank you, Hinsley. I'll call on you tomorrow.'

Theirs was a friendship of too long a standing to need more than these simple words. Hinsley squeezed his hand back.

'Wait for me in the carriage, won't you?' Radcliffe said to Archie. 'I'll be just a moment.'

Archie and Hinsley left, Hinsley shooting Radcliffe a saucy wink that he studiously ignored. And then it was just Miss Talbot and Radcliffe – Kitty and James – left standing in the dimly lit parlour.

'What you did tonight, for Archie – you didn't have to do that,' he said, as soon as they were alone.

'Nor did you, for Cecily,' she retorted hotly. 'But now we have both embarrassed ourselves by doing things we ought not to have done, perhaps we can get on with the rest of our evenings.'

She was not quite sure what it was she was cross about, and why she was targeting her ire at him of all people – only that she was aware once again of feeling uncomfortably seen by him, aware of that heavy gaze upon her. This gentleman notices, she reminded herself: he doesn't just see, and she wasn't sure she could bear it any more.

'Are you all right?' he asked.

'Well, let me think!' she said brightly, beginning to take off her cloak with quick ungraceful movements. 'I am *not*, as I had planned

310

to be by the end of the evening, engaged to Mr Pemberton. I am *not*, as I thought I was, a sister kind enough not to disregard Cecily to such a degree that she felt elopement a natural way of getting my attention.' She tossed the cloak to the side, uncaring of where it fell. 'I *am*, however, still in possession of a large quantity of debt and – oh yes – absolutely no closer to solving any of it.' She was fumbling now with the buttons on her gloves, but her hands were too cold to gain much traction on the silk, and in a fit of rage began to flap them ineffectually in the air. 'So yes, I'm *very well*,' she said.

She continued to struggle with the gloves until her left hand was caught in mid-air by one larger than her own. Motioning for her to hold it still, Radcliffe bent and began calmly to undo the tiny buttons along the inside of her arm. She watched him, wrong-footed. He made quick but careful work of the left glove and pulled gently at the fingertips to loosen it off her hand. It suddenly felt very intimate, though he had not touched her skin once, and despite the chilliness of the room, she felt a rush of warmth. Kitty proffered the other arm automatically when he gestured for her to do so, and stared at his bent head, the furious wind quite taken out of her sails.

It was so like him to startle her like this.

'I hope you know – I am very grateful for your actions tonight. For what you did for Cecy,' she said at last, as he was nearing her wrist. The last button was proving tricky, and he frowned over it. She wondered if he might be able to feel the pulse of her heartbeat through the fabric.

'And I you,' he said, not looking up. 'For fetching Archie from that place. It was very brave – braver than any one person has a right to be.'

She blushed, fierily, and hated herself for it.

'Yes, well,' she said awkwardly. 'He did not deserve it.'

He pulled at the right glove now, gently, the slither of silk a whisper over her skin, and then handed the pair of them back to her.

'Life does not always go to plan,' Radcliffe reminded her. 'And we have both made mistakes where our families are concerned. Archie fell into real danger tonight, and I have been too distracted to notice the signs and was entirely too arrogant to accept your warning. This could have caused irreversible damage to his life and I would never have forgiven myself. I can only apologise to him and try to do better.'

They looked at one another. The room was quiet but for the crackle of the fire, and they both observed it and each other, waiting. Waiting to see what would happen next, as though – whatever it was – was quite inevitable, and they need only wait for its arrival. The silence lingered for one moment, then another. Kitty could feel her heart beating hard in her chest and she squeezed her gloves tightly between her palms. She drew in a sharp breath, unable to bear it a second longer – but then, a loud crash from upstairs interrupted them. They both looked up, listening to the sounds of Cecily stomping about.

Radcliffe picked up his hat. 'I shall leave you to get some rest,' he said. 'And I shall see you Monday night.'

Archie was talking amicably to Lawrence by the curricle when Radcliffe descended, his mood seeming to be very much restored.

'Home?' he asked Radcliffe, a mix of relief and dread in his face.

'Home,' Radcliffe confirmed. 'Let us practise what we are going to say to Mama.'

Archie groaned. 'It's going to be awful, isn't it?'

'The worst,' Radcliffe agreed. 'Apologise profusely – don't give any excuses – and try to hug her as soon as you can. She loves you; she just doesn't want to see you hurt.'

'Perhaps she won't have noticed I was gone,' Archie said, though without much hope. 'I feel such a fool.'

'We must allow ourselves to be fools, every now and then – and especially when we are young,' Radcliffe told him. 'I do not even have the excuse of youth. I should have helped you more, Archie, seen that you needed someone to talk to. Though I wish, too, that you would have come to me.'

'I was going to,' Archie said quietly. 'I even got so far as coming to your lodgings . . . And then I saw Miss Talbot leaving. Thought perhaps – I don't know. With the dancing, and you saying I shouldn't marry her, and then seeing her there – I thought you might have done it all on purpose, for a second.'

Radcliffe sighed: of all the coincidences.

'I danced with Miss Talbot, that first night, because she had asked it of me,' he said slowly. 'She thought they would have an easier time of it in high society, if they were seen to be close to our family. And Miss Talbot called upon me, that morning, to ask if I knew anything of the, ah, the characters of her suitors. And I said you should not marry her, Archie, because I honestly think you would not suit.'

'Oh,' Archie said. 'Oh, well, when you put it like that, it all makes sense. Damned silly of me, really, to suppose your affections were truly fixed. Not our James, eh?'

He jabbed Radcliffe good-naturedly in the ribs – perhaps a

little too hard, he thought in concern, judging from the pain upon his brother's face.

It did not feel worth telling Radcliffe that he had a horrible suspicion that Miss Talbot still intended to become Mrs Archibald de Lacey, after all. No use complicating matters this evening, it had already been such a busy day – and anyway, damned if he knew what he was going to do about that, either. Couldn't bear to let the poor creature down, when she'd gone so far out of her way to help him. But . . . Couldn't help thinking that perhaps Radcliffe had been right and they weren't that well suited after all.

'Should we tell Mama what Miss Talbot did?' Archie asked after some thought. 'Not sure she'd approve, can't say it was at all proper, Hinsley bringing her along.'

Radcliffe shrugged. 'She might surprise you.'

The scene at Grosvenor Square was not a pleasant one. Pattson had reported to Lady Radcliffe the details of Captain Hinsley's visit as soon as she had returned that night, and so by the time her sons entered the drawing room she seemed on the point of calling for the Bow Street Runners to search the Thames.

The narration of Archie's evening only went downhill from there. In the first instance, Lady Radcliffe fell into quasi-hysterics simply from hearing that Archie had been to faro clubs in Soho. This rather irritated Archie, who felt it to be an overreaction.

'If you're going to be like that about *everything*,' he said crossly, 'this is going to take us hours and I'd rather like to go to bed before dawn.'

Radcliffe winced as Archie was taken loudly to task for his

insensitivity towards his mother, whom he had almost killed with his behaviour.

'I am not a well woman!' she reminded him.

The ensuing lecture ended with the lady loudly forbidding him from leaving the house ever again, whether alone or under supervision. After Archie pointed out that they were all expected at Lady Cholmondeley's ball on Monday evening, his mother gave him special dispensation for balls and routs *only*. Radcliffe had been correct, however, in predicting his mother was made of sterner stuff than she seemed – for once the story had begun in earnest, she stayed quiet, hanging on his Archie's every word without interruption. At the end, she turned to Radcliffe and they shared an aghast stare: how close Archie had come to being quite ruined.

'We owe Miss Talbot a great debt,' she said seriously, to them both. 'And we must all do whatever we can to repay her.'

Strangely, this made Archie look more anxious than he had for several hours.

'Must we?' he asked tentatively. '*Whatever* we can?'

'Archie, the girl risked her life for you,' his mother scolded. Archie sighed, looking glum again. Lady Radcliffe dismissed him to bed soon after, and he left gratefully, looking bone tired.

'Goodness,' Lady Radcliffe said into the room. '*Goodness*, what a night.'

'I owe you an apology,' Radcliffe said abruptly. 'You were right to worry – I should have listened.'

'Neither of us could have known the extent of it,' Lady Radcliffe said, waving a hand in forgiveness. 'And I do understand why you were reluctant to get involved. Interference . . . has not always been the right thing, in our family.'

Radcliffe nodded jerkily, looking up at the ornate ceiling. Lady Radcliffe reached up her hands to pat at her hair, still looking shocked.

'And to think,' she said, nervous laughter in her voice. 'To think I was considering letting Amelia come to her first ball. I should rather instead like to lock you all up for *years*.'

'. . . I think it would be a good idea,' Radcliffe said, after a pause. He was still not looking at her. 'To let Amelia try a ball this Season. It is – it is your decision, of course, but that is what I think.'

Lady Radcliffe gave him a tremulous smile.

'Thank you, James,' she said simply.

He bade her goodnight, walking into the hall – but instead of letting himself out of the door and heading home, he walked up the stairs. Without quite knowing how he got there, he pushed his way into the third door on the second floor – into his father's study. It had not been touched since the man's death, though it looked well-tended – someone had clearly been in to dust. Radcliffe traced his fingers over the wood of the great desk, remembering a thousand arguments they had had in this room together. Words of anger thrown at each other like blows, a competition of who could hurt the other the most that both of them had lost. He sat in the chair behind the desk, looking around the room.

'My lord?'

Radcliffe looked up to see Pattson standing in the doorway, observing him with a faint smile. He spread his arms.

'How do I look, Pattson?' he asked.

'Very fine, my lord.'

'I suppose if I am to sit on this side of the desk, and you

that,' Radcliffe said, 'I should probably start letting you know how much you've disappointed me.'

Pattson's lip quirked an infinitesimal amount. 'It would be tradition,' he agreed.

'Worst hours of my life,' Radcliffe reminisced. 'But you know the damnedest thing? As soon as the old man died, I would have given anything to hear one of those blasted lectures again. He did put so much thought into them, you know. Say what you want about the man, he crafted a very impressive telling-off. I should have liked to hear the one he had written for my return from Waterloo. I'm sure it would have been quite powerful.'

Pattson looked at him gravely. 'If I may be so bold, my lord,' he began, 'I have known you all your life. And I knew your father for most of his. I fancy I have a good understanding of both your characters by now. I would ask you to trust me, then, when I say this: he was proud of you. He knew you would be a great man. But you cannot take up residence in his shadow for ever – you are Lord Radcliffe now. And that means as much, or as little, as you choose.'

Radcliffe stared at Pattson with shining eyes. He cleared his throat. 'Thank you, Pattson.'

'You are most welcome, my lord.'

36

Kitty did not tarry long in the parlour, knowing she must go upstairs and face her sister.

Cecily did not turn to look at her, sitting on the bed facing the wall, hands clasped tightly in her lap. Recriminations lay, expectant, upon Kitty's tongue, but she knew that she must do better now.

'I am sorry,' she said at last. 'I am so sorry, Cecily.'

'You are?' Cecily asked, turning with surprise.

'You were right, about everything. I should have listened to you more, and I did not, and I am sorry. I have been so dedicated to securing our family's future, I have not given nearly enough thought to its happiness. I do want you to be happy, Cecily – but this is not the way to go about it.'

'Have you ever thought that maybe I wanted to help?' Cecily said tearfully. 'I thought the whole point was to marry rich. Rupert is rich.'

'Not like this. Scandal does not breed comfort, Mama and Papa taught us that.' She paused. 'Are you truly in love with him?'

'I believe I am,' Cecily said shyly. 'I think of him often and wish to speak to him always. We – we talk about things. Books and art and ideas, you know. Not many people want to talk to me about those things.'

Kitty's heart ached. 'Yes, I suppose we don't. I am sorry for that, too. I suppose I – I suppose I do not want to speak of such things, because I always feel a little foolish whenever you do.'

'You?' said Cecy, disbelieving.

'Oh, yes. In truth, I was always most jealous that you were sent to the Seminary.'

'Really?'

'Yes, indeed. You came back with all these grand ideas, and a love of books, and you seemed so . . . lofty all of a sudden. Whereas I just had to stay, to try to find a husband and look after everyone. It made me feel frightfully slow, in comparison.'

'I never think you slow,' Cecily said urgently. 'You are always so certain about everything, always know what to do and say. I always seem to say the wrong thing, get us into all kinds of messes.'

'And what about us meeting the de Lacys in the first place, hmm? What about Almack's? You did those things, Cecily, not I. I should not have been able to do any of that without you.'

Cecily flushed in pleasure, Kitty's confession giving her the courage to ask the question she had been dying to all evening. 'Do you mean to keep Rupert and me apart from now on?' she whispered.

Kitty exhaled slowly. 'No,' she said reluctantly. 'But this is not without difficulty. If he even whispers a breath of your elopement to anyone—'

'He won't!' Cecily protested vehemently.

'Be that as it may. You need to understand the difficulties of this attachment – if you are to aim this high, Cecily, it is very important to think the whole plan through. To be clever about it.'

Another nod, more eager now.

'Then I shall do my best to help you,' Kitty said. 'Thankfully, if Mr Pemberton does propose – which he may not, after tonight – we shall be much better positioned than we are currently upon the social scene. It might not be so implausible then.'

'Do you want him to?' Cecily asked timidly.

'Want who to what?' Kitty asked.

'Mr Pemberton, to propose.'

'Why of course!' Kitty said, very brightly.

'After tonight, I thought your feelings might be attached elsewhere,' Cecily said simply.

Kitty shook her head. 'They cannot be,' she said, speaking through a tight throat. 'It is quite impossible.'

'Is it? Even after tonight . . .'

But Kitty was shaking her head again.

'I cannot speak of it. Let us go to bed now, Cecy. It has been a long, long day.'

Despite this, after they had blown out the candles, Cecily and Kitty whispered longer still into the night. They talked of home, of their other sisters, exchanged sleepy ideas of how to secure Lady Montagu's approval of Cecily, until – most unusually – it was Kitty who fell asleep first, almost mid-sentence.

Cecily closed her eyes, too. Her heart went out to her older sister. There was such a tragic irony to the whole thing, Cecily thought – almost Greek, really – for Kitty to discover only at this juncture that she was in love with Archie de Lacy after all.

The storm had not broken by dawn. The sisters woke late and – after Kitty had given Sally the day off, and most of their remaining coins as meagre thanks for the great service she had done their family – they spent the day sequestered in the parlour, warming themselves by the fire and watching the rain.

'Is there anything you would like to . . . see, tomorrow?' Kitty asked Cecily, as they sipped on hot chocolate. 'The Marbles again? I know our last visit was brief. Or the museums?'

Cecily smiled, recognising this for the olive branch it was. The next day, the skies were dry and they saw much, Cecily ticking off all the London sights she had most wanted to visit. They started with the Marbles, again, and then walked almost the whole length of the British Museum, gazing at its artefacts. They spent some time browsing the shelves in the library, before finding themselves at Astley's Amphitheatre for the rest of the afternoon. Cecily was a little disappointed to find that the Physic Garden was closed for the day, but was appeased when Kitty promised they could come back tomorrow.

'Really?' she asked.

'We have time, still,' Kitty nodded. She took in a deep breath of the warm summer air. 'Isn't London beautiful, today?'

'"Earth has not any thing to show more fair,"' quoted Cecily.

'Just so,' Kitty agreed.

They returned to Wimpole Street only as the light was fading to ready themselves for the evening. There they found Aunt Dorothy, calmly sipping tea in the parlour.

'Well,' she said, eyeing them critically. 'Sally tells me you had an exciting weekend – though all was resolved, I take it, to satisfaction?'

Kitty was glad that Sally had not been able to keep the news to herself, for it saved her from having to break the whole story to her aunt. Though Aunt Dorothy was not looking nearly so disapproving as Kitty would have expected. On the contrary, a little smile was playing around her mouth and a pleased flush was visible on her cheeks.

'Yes, we were lucky in the end,' Kitty agreed, eyeing Aunt Dorothy carefully. 'How was Kent?'

'Not without excitement, itself,' Aunt Dorothy said. She set down her cup with a clink. 'In fact, my girls, I have a little news of my own. I am now married.'

She held out her hand, where a wedding ring was now glinting on her finger. Cecily let out a gasp and Kitty's brows shot up.

'Married?' Kitty asked incredulously. 'When? And to who?'

'Whom, my dear,' Aunt Dorothy corrected primly. 'To Mr Fletcher, yesterday.'

'Are you meaning to tell me that you eloped?' Kitty said faintly. Was she the only one of them not to try for a clandestine wedding last night?

Aunt Dorothy clicked her tongue in remonstration. 'Foolish child, of course not. An elopement is a young woman's game and quite unnecessary in this instance. Mr Fletcher arranged a special licence, and we married in his mother's church upon Saturday afternoon – all very much above board.'

There was a pause while her nieces stared at her, utterly thrown by the announcement.

'I should have liked you both to attend, of course,' Aunt Dorothy said apologetically. 'But I didn't want to distract Kitty from Pemberton. And, well, neither I nor Mr Fletcher felt much like waiting any longer.'

'Any longer?' Kitty repeated, feeling much like a parrot. 'Aunt, how long has this been going on?'

'Years, I suppose.' Aunt Dorothy was smiling again. 'We were acquainted long ago – it was Mr Fletcher who I spoke about that day in the park, if you remember. He is a widower now and recognised me just as soon as we spoke at the Montagu ball. I did tell you that might happen, my dear, though I cannot be at all cross about it – for we have been courting ever since.'

Kitty digested this with considerable effort, not at all sure how she felt. Foolish, certainly, that both her sister and aunt had been busy with their own love affairs for weeks – without Kitty noticing or suspecting a thing – but that was easily overcome. She'd become so used to Aunt Dorothy being *theirs* these last few months. The idea of Mr Fletcher taking her away from them . . . it made Kitty feel a little odd.

'Congratulations, Aunt,' Cecily said, walking over to kiss her upon the cheek.

'Kitty?' Aunt Dorothy said questioningly.

Kitty shook herself – now was not the time for jealousy. After all their aunt had done for them – for two young ladies who were, in truth, no relation at all – she deserved every ounce of joy the world could offer her. Kitty embraced her, a lump lodged firmly in her throat.

'I am so very happy for you,' she said hoarsely.

Aunt Dorothy whisked a stray tear away from her eye.

'Darling girls,' she said, clasping their hands and squeezing them. Then, with a decisive nod, she stood.

'We must get ready for the evening, now,' she said, clapping her hands. Then, with a roguish wink, added, 'After all, it would not do for mine to be the only wedding of the Season.'

37

There was an air of finality to the silence in which they travelled across London that night – without speaking, all knew that this was likely to be their very last London ball. Whatever happened this evening, Kitty and Cecily would be returning home to their sisters, very soon. The carriage drew up to the entrance. Kitty remembered with a pang how wonderful, how strange, it had all seemed to her that first night. The memory flashed across her mind like fireworks – seeing the candles, the sea of colourful dresses and bright jewels, the taste of champagne, the warmth of Radcliffe's hand in hers.

'We have had quite the time, haven't we?' she said to Cecily, in the quiet.

'The best,' Cecily agreed.

They descended once more into the fray.

Kitty could not see Mr Pemberton inside, and for that she was grateful. Once she encountered the man again, she would have to dedicate her evening to apologising, to assuaging the man's ego, to manipulating out of him the proposal she had expected two nights before. And though it was quite as essential today as it had been any other day, that she leave here – this room, this city – with such an engagement, she could not help but want just a few more moments to herself first.

Aunt Dorothy left their sides almost immediately, in search of her husband – her *husband*, Kitty repeated to herself, still shocked – and Cecily too took her leave.

'I need to find Montagu,' Cecily said.

'Go on, then,' Kitty said gently. 'But stay where we can see you.'

Cecily shot her a cross look over her shoulder – as if it were such a ridiculous thing to say, as if she hadn't tried to elope just yesterday – and then hastened across the room. She passed Mr de Lacy as she walked through the supper room, and they shared a smile of recognition to acknowledge the very strange night they had shared. Cecily stopped him, with a hand upon his arm – she knew Kitty would not want her help, but she had to at least try.

'You should speak to my sister,' Cecily said urgently.

'I should?' Mr de Lacy asked reluctantly.

'Yes. I hope you can forgive her,' Cecily said fervently. 'I know it all seems strange, and that she has behaved most confusingly – but she does love you, Mr de Lacy.'

'She does?' he yelped in a voice suddenly falsetto. 'Oh Lord.'

Cecily saw the silhouette of Montagu in the next room.

'Think on what I have said,' she instructed Mr de Lacy portentously, before leaving him.

'Lord, I will – don't you worry about that,' Archie groaned.

* * *

Kitty could not be sure of her purpose, as she walked through the ballroom. She supposed she could tell herself she was looking for Pemberton – though in truth it was not his figure her eyes were searching for. She spotted Lady Radcliffe across the room, and the Countess waved at her. Kitty returned the gesture – noticing Mr de Lacy standing beside her, though he paled when he met Kitty's eye. Strange. Lady Amelia was there too – her hair up, and her skirts let down. Lady Radcliffe must have felt it a good moment for her daughter to experience something of the Season, before her coming out next year. Lady Amelia looked very fine indeed, standing next to her mother – though the militant sparkle in her eye felt like trouble.

The music struck up, signalling the imminent beginning of the next set – and couples milling about suddenly began to circle one another, ladies picking up skirts, gentlemen holding out their hands. And she saw him, only ten feet away – he must have been waiting for her gaze to fall upon him, for when it did he raised his eyebrows quite mockingly, as if to say, 'You're late.'

She narrowed her eyes back in question. He held out a hand, inviting, and she moved forward without a second thought.

'I shouldn't have thought your rules about dancing would allow this,' she told him, once she was standing in front of him.

'I decided to make an exception,' Radcliffe promised. 'Would you dance with me, Miss Talbot?'

It was their last chance. After tonight, she might never allow herself such a moment again – but at least, at least they would have this. She took his hand as answer. They glided silently onto the middle of the floor. The music started; it was to be a waltz, it seemed. Her first.

His hand moved to her waist, and hers to his shoulder. It was different from when they had first danced – so very different. Then, there had been a veritable ocean of distance between them, whereas now, now they were standing very close to one another. It was much closer than she could have ever imagined it being. Kitty could feel the warmth of Radcliffe's body next to hers, the friction of the smooth fabric of his tail coat against her dress, the press of his hand upon her back – even, though the music should have made it impossible, the sound of his breath in her ear.

She did not – could not – look at him as they began to move in one long circle around the room, spinning every dozen steps in formation. This was not at all what she had expected, and for once in her life, she had not a plan of what to say – of how to turn this to her advantage. This seemed to have occurred to him as unusual, too, for after a few moments he hummed in amusement.

'It is not like you to be silent,' he commented, smiling down at her.

She met his eyes for a moment before skittering them away, afraid of what she might see in them. It was the most nervous she had felt in his presence in weeks.

'I do not know what to say,' she admitted quietly. 'Believe me, it is as strange to me as it is to you.'

He twisted her into a spin, the room flashing around Kitty as his arm guided her smoothly, and then they were back in their embrace once more, hands firmly clasped.

'Perhaps I should speak then,' Radcliffe said. He took a deep breath. 'I have learnt ... much, in these past few months, speaking to you – arguing with you, I should say. You have made me face all my hypocrisies, challenge all my views, made me realise all the ways in which I am still – after all these years – fighting with my father.'

If a few moments before Kitty could not look at him, now she could not look away. His words seemed straight from a dream, but she could almost not bear to hear them – it was too much, too close to everything she had ever wanted but never allowed herself to contemplate. They spun again – she was not paying a single ounce of attention to their steps, all of it fixed upon him, but somehow their feet were moving in quick synchronicity anyway.

'I think I am quite a different person, now,' he continued, eyes not leaving hers for a second, 'for having met you and . . . I like who I am, who I have become, around you.'

Kitty's fingers tightened in his. Every word he uttered was like a strike of lightning straight to the chest, fierce and unrelenting – she was not sure she could bear this, bear hearing him say such things to her, if it did not change anything.

'You asked me once,' Radcliffe went on, gaze fixed intently on hers, his voice hoarse, 'whether your birth would matter if your feelings were true. I didn't answer you then, but Miss Talbot – Kitty. You must know that it does not matter to me any more.'

She sucked in a breath that felt more like a sob. 'It doesn't?' she asked. The music was rising around them, the dance almost at an end. They spun into one final turn, losing sight of one another for one breathless moment, before he pulled her back into the circle of his arms.

'No,' he said.

The music stopped. The dancers curtsied and bowed to one another. Kitty stepped back blinking – Radcliffe's hands lingered upon her as though he did not want to let go, and the room felt colder once he had. She clapped, still feeling stunned – and then she spotted the unwelcome visage of Mr Pemberton behind Radcliffe, approaching rapidly, his face grim.

'Quick,' she said to Radcliffe. 'Let us take a turn in the garden, before—'

'Before what?' he asked, offering his arm nonetheless.

'Nothing,' she said, but she was unable to resist another glance over his shoulder at Pemberton, and Radcliffe caught it. They hastened towards the garden doors, and were lucky enough to find it empty, lit only by the stars and the candlelight streaming from the windows. As soon as the fresh air hit them, Radcliffe stepped back.

'Have you not— Are you still expecting a proposal from Mr Pemberton?' he asked her, his even voice not quite able to hide the hurt within. Her heart ached to see it. Why had Pemberton chosen that moment to appear, *why* . . . She could lie, but she found she did not want to.

'Yes,' she said. 'I am.'

He turned to face the garden for a moment, as if to gather himself. 'Right. I own, I confess I thought you might have called things off, since the other night. But I see that was foolish of me.'

His eyes were colder now, as he turned back to face her. 'May I ask if you are planning to accept his offer of marriage?'

'My lord,' she began, voice shaking. 'Nothing of my situation has changed. I still need to leave London with a rich man as my fiancé, or I will have to sell the only home my sisters have ever known, and find some other way of supporting them, all by myself. I thought . . . I had thought that this no longer mattered to you.' She waved a hand towards the ballroom, as if to encompass all that he had confessed within.

'I did – it doesn't,' he said, running a hand over his face. 'But to find you about to accept another man's proposal is— I do not like it.'

'I don't know what you want from me then,' she cried, casting out her arms. 'For I cannot make my situation any different. I must marry. And so far, I have no promises.'

He would not look at her.

'Ask me then,' she said, voice raw, 'ask me if I should like, if I should *want* to marry Pemberton, were the choice only about me?'

He looked up. 'Would you?'

'No,' she said, voice cracking. 'Now ask me, whether I should still love you, were the choice only mine to make?'

He took a step forward. 'Would you?' he said again.

'Yes,' she confessed. 'I will always choose my sisters. I will choose their need more than my want every day. But I want you just as much as I need money. You see me, in my entirety – the worst and the best of me – as no one else ever has.'

She stared at him, full in the face – without artifice or pretence, her face open and full of emotion. He was closer now. Close enough to reach up and touch her cheek with light, careful fingers.

'Would you – would you like to marry me, Kitty?' Lord Radcliffe – James – asked, voice like gravel.

She gave a helpless little laugh at the absurdity of the question – as if he did not know.

'I would,' she said. 'But first, I feel I must inform you that I come with four sisters, a badly leaking roof, and a veritable ocean of debt.'

He had started to smile now, and once begun it did not seem to stop, overtaking his whole face.

'I thank you for your honesty,' he said cordially, and she laughed. 'May I reassure you that I am desperate to meet your other sisters, the roof sounds charmingly rustic, and the debt does not faze me.' He paused. 'Of course, I understand that you will need to see my accounts before committing yourself,' he went on, and she laughed again, loud and bright.

'I'm sure that won't be necessary,' she said. 'As long as you can promise you're absurdly rich and you'll pay off all my family's debts.'

'I am absurdly rich,' he repeated. 'And I will pay off all your family's debts.'

'Why then by all means,' she said, grinning up at him, 'I would indeed like to marry you.'

His hand caught her jaw now. There was nothing hesitant about the kiss, nothing uncertain. It was as if they'd both read the script beforehand and had – all along – simply been waiting for the cue. Cue given, they both committed themselves whole-heartedly to the scene, and it was some time before conversation was resumed.

'James! James!' They looked up, hurriedly parting, as Archie burst onto the courtyard. 'There you are! Mama is looking for you – she has quite lost Amelia . . . I say, is everything all right?' He eyed them suspiciously.

'Yes, Archie. More than all right, in fact – Miss Talbot has just agreed to marry me,' Radcliffe said, taking Kitty's hand.

'By Jove!' Archie looked quite thunderstruck. 'By Jove, indeed.'

Kitty remembered with a start that this news might not be entirely welcome to him – after all, it was not so long ago that he had thought himself in love with her. By the hesitant look upon James's face, he was worrying about the same.

'Archie?' Kitty said, questioningly. Archie startled out of his reverie and leapt forward to wring his brother's hand.

'Splendid news, congratulations,' he enthused. 'Was just a trifle bamboozled, but quite all right now. Terribly silly of me – bacon-brained, really – but I had quite thought that you meant to marry *me*, Kitty. But must say a relief to know that's absolute stuff – not sure we're all that suited, really, so it is perhaps for the best. You understand, don't you?'

This last was said in kindly tones, an expression upon Archie's face as if he were delivering unwelcome news that she was to take with a stiff upper lip.

Kitty bristled. 'Archie,' she said quite irately, 'are *you* turning *me* down?'

James began to laugh.

38

'You mustn't expect anything grand,' Kitty instructed. 'Netley is a far more modest home than Radcliffe Hall.'

'I shall endeavour to keep my expectations low,' James said agreeably.

Kitty frowned at this. 'Though I should not be surprised if you do find it, in fact, far more characterful than Radcliffe Hall,' she corrected.

'Of course,' he said, apologetically. 'I have no doubt that I will also find it far superior to Radcliffe Hall in every way.'

The Season was over. The wedding was planned. And the Talbot sisters were travelling home at last. Ensconced in the perfectly proportioned and comfortably furnished Radcliffe carriage, their homeward journey was infinitely more pleasant than the outward had been, with the trees and fields and hedgerows passing smoothly by the window. For most of the journey, Radcliffe had ridden beside the carriage, but this afternoon he had opted to keep the ladies company within – perceiving, perhaps, that Kitty's nerves were becoming more ragged as they neared home. She had spent the journey wondering if her sisters would look different when they arrived, wondering what she might have missed in the months they had been parted – worrying too, how they would feel about how she had changed, for she would be returning to them quite different, too. She was finally released from the weight of their crushing debt.

It had seemed almost incomprehensible to Kitty how quickly it had been resolved in the end. The morning after their engagement, Radcliffe had turned up at the doorstep of Wimpole Street quite unannounced, with a promissory note for a draft on his bank. They had sat together in the parlour, she penning the letter to Mr Anstey and Mr Ainsley to inform them that the bill was now paid in full, he adding his note without so much as a blink at the eye-wateringly large sum she had quoted. Within moments, it was done. Such a slim envelope, she had thought, to hold so much weight. With an effort, she had resisted the urge to rip it open to read everything through again – just to be quite, *quite* sure it was done. She looked over to James, intending to confess her disbelief, before all at once realising that they were by themselves again, for the first time since they had stood upon that candlelit terrace. From the look in his eyes, it was a realisation she was not alone in making.

'Your aunt is visiting Mr Fletcher?' he had asked, softly into the quiet of the parlour.

'She is.' The space between them had never felt so small.

'Cecily is still asleep?'

'Yes.'

He gave her a slow smile.

'I should leave,' he said, though making no move to rise from his seat. 'Word is out now; we shall have to start being careful.'

'How terribly boring,' Kitty said glibly, leaning towards him. 'I'm not sure I like the sound of that at *all*.'

He had still been laughing a little as their hands met, and he tugged her towards him gently, from her seat to his. When their mouths met, the air between them was light and conspiratorial. And, despite the warning against impropriety, it was still some time before he had left that morning.

A soft snore brought Kitty out of this pleasant memory, and she looked over to see Cecily had fallen asleep, her head lolling forward on her shoulders. In her hand was clasped a letter from Lord Montagu – penned entirely in very questionable iambic pentameter – and Kitty frowned thoughtfully at it. She really must put some serious thought into how that romance might be promoted.

'You have your scheming face on,' James observed. 'What are you planning?'

'I do not,' Kitty said, with great dignity, 'have a scheming face.'

James eyed her, unconvinced. She arranged her expression into a passable imitation of innocence.

'Do you really think me so conniving?' she asked angelically.

'Yes,' James said promptly, though not without affection. 'I have long known you to be the worst sort of villain.'

It might be a trifle unusual to be so frequently called a villain by one's fiancé, but Kitty had to admit there was some substance to the accusation. And yet, who on earth could argue with her results? It was not, of course, proper to compliment oneself overly, but Kitty could not help feeling that she had handled the past few months marvellously. Returning home not only with their debt cleared, but also with a fiancé she could say, quite truthfully for once, that she loved – why, it could only be considered a Very Good Result.

The carriage started to creak a little, as it began to pass over rougher terrain. Kitty peered out of the window at a landscape that was becoming increasingly familiar.

'We're almost there,' she said breathlessly, reaching for her sister's knee. 'Cecily, wake up.'

The carriage was slowing in truth now, before making a right turn onto a weathered track that Kitty knew better than her own face. Netley Cottage came into view with excruciating slowness, and she stared with greedy eyes at the ivy falling over brickwork, the plume of smoke puffing up from the kitchen chimney, the magnolia partially obscuring the front window. She had missed its bloom, she thought, nonsensically, seeing the petals upon the ground. Kitty and Cecily only barely waited for the carriage to stop before scrambling out in disgracefully unladylike fashion. Kitty could already hear shrieks of delight from inside, and the pounding of running feet as the carriage was spotted. She stood still for a moment, taking in great lungfuls of air that she would have sworn tasted different on the tongue.

There was so much still to do, Kitty knew – much to solve, to discuss, to decide – but after months spent lingering in uncertainty, of constantly doubting whether the risk was worth it, whether the choices were the right ones, whether this plan was cleverer than that one, she allowed herself the indulgence of enjoying the profound relief that was now filling her. They were home, at last. They had done it. And as the front door opened with a bang and her sisters came spilling out towards them, Kitty felt perfectly sure that she was, in this moment, exactly where she needed to be.

Acknowledgements

It might be quicker to name the people who didn't help me write this book, rather than to thank everyone that did – but if you'll bear with me, I'm going to try anyway.

Firstly, thank you to Maddy Milburn and her whole team for taking me on in the first place. Your kindness, passion and – it has to be said – tireless ambition continues to stagger me. Thank you to Maddy, Rachel Yeoh and Georgia McVeigh for your work on those first edits – from the beginning you understood what I was trying to say better than I could – and to Liv Maidment, Rachel again, Giles Milburn and Emma Dawson for answering my incessant questions. Fervent thanks also to Liane-Louise Smith, Valentina Paulmichl and Georgina Simmonds for taking my book out into the world with such energy, for finding such a magnificent international team to work with and for always writing such lovely emails.

Then, huge thanks go to my glorious editors Martha Ashby and Pam Dorman, for your warmth, wit and wisdom. Did you both spring straight from Zeus's head? Perhaps – and regardless, there's no one I would rather discuss the merits of a fine beaver hat with. Thank you for everything you have done to make this book the best it can be. Thank you also to Chere Tricot, my fabulous copyeditor Charlotte Webb, and superb proofreaders Anne O'Brien and Kati Nicholl, for addressing my repetitions, deviations, excessive use of adverbs and keeping a weather eye on historical accuracy.

In the herculean task of publishing a book, my job is definitely the easiest, so thank you to the following people for everything they have done to get *Lady's Guide* published, printed and on the shelves: massive thanks to the incomparable Lynne Drew, to the fabulously talented Fleur Clarke and Emma Pickard for all the stunning and creative marketing, to the outrageously charming Jaime Witcomb and Susanna Peden for the cracking PR campaign, to Caroline Young for the gorgeous jacket, to the brilliant Grace Dent, Dean Russell, Melissa Okusanya and Hannah Stamp for handling everything production and operations with such skill, to Fionnuala Barrett and Charlotte Brown for the sensational audiobook and to Izzy Coburn, Sarah Munro, Gemma Rayner, Ben Hurd and Fliss Porter on the sales team at HarperFiction and HarperCollins. You are unequivocally the best and I'm so very grateful for all your hard work.

Next, thanks must go to Fran Fabriczki, as none of this would have happened without our Sunday writing sessions. Thank you to my house/soulmates Freya Tomley and Juliet Eames, for always making me laugh and for taking my writing as seriously or as frivolously as I needed in any given moment. Thank you also to Fay Watson, Holly Winfield, Lottie

Hayes-Clemens, Martha Burn and Tash Somi for being the best, loudest and funniest hype women in the business – I'm really glad we met.

To Lucy Stewart – who has the dubious privilege of hearing exactly every thought that passes through my head – thank you for the ping pong, the prosecco and God knows what else. To Ore Agbaje-Williams, Catriona Beamish, Becca Bryant, Charlotte Cross, Andrew Davis, Dushi Horti, Jack Renninson, El Slater and Molly Walker-Sharp, thanks for your – occasionally excessive – support and for continuing to act as my own personal thesaurus.

Thank you to my family, the great big sprawling mass of you on both sides of the tree. I'm pretty sure you manifested this publishing deal through sheer force of personality – and I'm so proud to be one of you.

Once again and always, thanks must go to Mum, Dad, Will, Grannie and Amy, for supplying the caffeine, for your patience through incoherent plot discussions, for answering questions like 'do you think this is funny?' with unwavering dishonesty and for believing I could do it even when I definitely didn't. And of course, thank you to Joey and Myla, the best of dogs, for being the most demanding and distracting writing companions the world has ever known. It was just a squirrel, guys – it was always just a squirrel.

Finally, thank you to you for reading it! It still feels extraordinarily strange to be sharing this with readers, and I'm so grateful that you have chosen to spend some of your precious time with this book. I'd love to hear from you, so do get in touch (unless you hated it, in which case I'd rather you didn't).

1

'Come now, Eliza, surely you can manage one tear?' Mrs Balfour whispered to her daughter. 'It is expected from the widow!'

Eliza nodded, though her eyes remained as dry as ever. However many years she had spent playing the part of obedient daughter and dutiful wife, weeping upon command was still beyond her.

'Recollect that we may have a fight on our hands today,' Mrs Balfour hissed, sending a meaningful glance across the library to where the late Earl's relations sat. Nine months after the funeral procession, they had all gathered again at Harefield Hall for the reading of the wills, and from the frosty glances being sent their way, it seemed Mrs Balfour was not the only one preparing for battle.

'Eliza's jointure was agreed in the marriage settlement: five hundred pounds a year,' Mr Balfour reassured his wife in a whisper. 'Somerset has no reason to dispute that; it's the veriest fragment of the estate.'

He spoke with bitterness, for neither he nor Mrs Balfour

had fully reconciled themselves to Eliza's severely changed circumstances. A decade ago, the marriage of timid, seventeen-year-old Miss Eliza Balfour to the austere Earl of Somerset – twenty years her senior – had been the match of the season, and the Balfours had reaped its rewards quite comprehensively. Within a year of the wedding, their first son had married an heiress, their second had been secured a Captaincy in the 10th foot, and Balfour House had been recarpeted entirely in cut-velvet.

Now, however, widowed at seven and twenty years, and without a child to inherit the title, Eliza's position was far less desirable. Five hundred pounds a year . . . Persons could and did live on far less, but on this subject Eliza agreed with her father. Ten years of marriage to a man who had shown more affection to his horses than his wife, ten years of near isolation in the cold, forbidding Harefield Hall, ten years of yearning for the life she might have had, if only circumstances had been a little different . . . Given exactly what – given exactly *who* – Eliza had been forced to give up, five hundred pounds a year felt a pittance.

'Had she only given him a son . . .' Mr Balfour bemoaned, for perhaps the fifth time.

'She *tried*,' Mrs Balfour snapped.

Eliza bit her tongue, hard. Miss Margaret Balfour – Eliza's cousin – pressed her hand under the table, and the clock struck half-past twelve. They had now been waiting half an hour for the new Earl, whose presence would allow the reading to begin. Eliza's stomach clenched in anticipation. Surely – *surely* – he would arrive soon.

'Disgraceful,' Mrs Balfour muttered, her face still fixed in placid, smiling repose. 'Nine months late already, and late today, too. Is it not disgraceful, Eliza?'

'Yes, Mama,' Eliza said automatically. It was always easiest to agree, though the unnatural delay was truthfully the fault of the old Earl, not the new. For it was old Earl who had stipulated his will not be read until all parties named within it were assembled. Since the new Earl of Somerset – Eliza's husband's nephew, previously the heir presumptive Captain Courtenay – had been stationed in the West Indies when the Earl died last April, and since sailing conditions in '18 had been unprecedentedly slow, his delayed return was understandable. Torturous, but understandable.

All assembled in the library had already been waiting many months and the lateness of the hour today was taking its toll: Mrs Courtenay (sister to the old Earl, mother to the new) had her eyes fixed on the door, her daughter Lady Selwyn was tapping her fingers impatiently, while Lord Selwyn sought to soothe his own nerves by regaling the room with various tales of his own superiority.

'And I said to him: Byron, old boy, you simply *must* write the thing!'

Beside him, at the centre of the room, the Somerset attorney Mr Walcot shuffled and reshuffled his papers with a pained smile. Everyone was impatient, but out of all of them, surely none more so than Eliza, who felt – with every tick of the grandfather clock – her nerves reach new, dangerous heights. After ten years – ten long years – today she would see him again. It did not feel real.

He might still not come. A lifetime of disappointments had taught her the virtue of preparing for the worst: perhaps he had mistaken the date, or perhaps his carriage had suffered an awful crash, or perhaps he had decided to return to the West Indies rather than have to see her again. It was unlike him to be late, he had always been so punctual. Or, at least, the gentleman Eliza had once known was punctual. Perhaps he had changed.

Finally, however, as the clock struck quarter to the hour, the door opened.

'The Right Honourable. The Earl of Somerset,' Perkins, their butler, announced.

'My sincere apologies for the lateness of the hour,' the new Lord Somerset said, stepping into the room. 'The rain has made the roads treacherous . . .'

Eliza's reaction was instantaneous. Her heart began to beat faster, her breath became laboured, her stomach clenched, and she stood, not because it was polite, but because the force of recognition reverberating through her meant she simply had to. All the months she had spent imagining this moment, and she still did not feel at all prepared for it.

'Oliver, darling –' Mrs Courtenay hurried over to her son, eyes shining, Lady Selwyn close behind, and Somerset embraced his mother and his sister, in turn. Mrs Balfour clucked her tongue in disapproval of this breach of etiquette – he ought properly to have addressed Eliza first – but Eliza paid her no mind. In many ways, he appeared the same. He was still very tall, his hair was still very fair, his eyes the same cool grey as the rest of his family, and he still carried himself with an air of calm assurance that had always been decidedly his own. Under the effects of a decade long naval career however, there was a greater breadth across the shoulder which had not existed in him as a younger man and his pale skin had darkened under the sun. It suited him. It suited him very well.

Somerset released his sister's hands and turned to Eliza. She was suddenly, horribly aware that the years had not been nearly so kind to her. With a small stature, brown hair and uncommonly large and dark eyes, she had always resembled some sort of startled nocturnal animal, but now she feared – with the all–black ensemble of her widow's weeds, and a figure drawn and tired from the uncertainty of the past months – that she appeared positively rattish.

'Lady Somerset,' he said, bowing before her.

His voice was the same, too.

'My lord,' Eliza said. She could feel her fingers trembling and fisted them in her skirts as she curtseyed shakily, bracing herself to meet his gaze. What would she see in them – anger, perhaps? Recrimination? She did not dare to hope for warmth. She did not deserve it. They rose from their bows as one, and at last, at last, their eyes met. And as she looked into his eyes, she saw . . . nothing.

'My most sincere apologies for your loss,' he said. His words were civil, his tone neutral. His expression could only be described as polite.

'. . . Thank you,' Eliza said. 'I hope your journey was pleasant?'

Thank goodness for pleasantries. They tripped off Eliza's tongue without thinking, which was a good thing indeed, because at this moment she was not capable of thought.

'As much as could be, with such weather as we have had,' he said. There was no evidence, in his manner or deportment or tone, that he was sharing in any of the turmoil churning through Eliza's mind. He appeared, in fact, totally unaffected by seeing her. As if they had never met before.

As if he had not, once, asked her to marry him.

'Yes . . .' Eliza heard herself say, as if from a great distance. 'The rain . . . has been most viscous.'

'Indeed,' he agreed, with a smile – except it was not a smile she had ever seen directed at herself before. Polite. Formal. Insincere.

'Good to see you, old boy, good to see you indeed,' Selwyn had come forward, hand outstretched, and Somerset reciprocated the handshake with a smile that was suddenly warm again. He moved towards the middle of the room, away from the Balfours – leaving Eliza blinking after him.

Was that it? After all their years apart, all the time Eliza had spent wondering over his whereabouts, his happiness, pouring over every memory of theirs together, of all the hours spent regretting every single one of the events that had conspired to keep them apart – and this was to be their reunion? A single, short exchange of commonplaces?

Eliza shivered. The January chill had pervaded the air all morning – her late husband's dictate that fires remain unlit until nightfall had outlived him – but now it seemed to Eliza veritably icy. A whole decade of existing literally oceans apart and yet Oliver – *Somerset* – had never felt more distant to Eliza than in this moment.

'Shall we begin?' Selwyn prompted. Selwyn's friendship with the old Earl had been long-standing, since their lands shared a border, but for the same reason temperamental. Indeed, their last business meeting before the old Earl's death had deteriorated into a quarrel enough to deafen the whole household – and yet from the eagerness in Selwyn's face, he was clearly expectant of a great bequeathment today.

Nodding, Mr Walcot spread out the papers in front of him, and the Balfours, Selwyns and the Courtenays watched from their respective sides of the room, wolfish and hungry. The scene would make for a dramatic tableau. Oils, in high colour, perhaps. Eliza's fingers twitched for a paintbrush.

'This is the last will and testament of Julius Edward Courtenay, tenth Earl of Somerset . . .'

Eliza's attention faded, as Mr Walcot began to list the

many ways in which the new Earl was about to become very, very rich. Mrs Courtenay looked about to cry in delight, Lady Selwyn was biting back a smile, but Somerset was frowning. Was he daunted at the vastness of the hoard now his – perhaps even surprised? He should not be. Even despite the late Earl's austerity, Harefield Hall was still a veritable shrine to the family's affluence: from its walls of horns, hides and hunting trophies to its porcelain tea cups, from its chairs of Indian rosewood to the oil landscapes displaying sugar plantations they had once owned, Harefield wore its loot proudly. And in the work of a few short sentences, this new Somerset owned it all. He was now one of the richest men in England, and one of the most eligible, too. From this moment on, every unattached lady in England would be falling at his feet.

Whereas Eliza ... After today, she could remain at Harefield, to act as the new Earl's hostess until he married, remove to the Dower House on the edge of the estate, or return to her childhood home. None of these options was particularly thrilling. To return to Balfour to live under her parents' watchful eye once more would be ghastly, but to remain here, in such close proximity to a man who clearly felt nothing for her, while she had spent a decade yearning for him ... It would be its own kind of torture.

'To Eliza Eunice Courtenay, the Right Honble. Countess of Somerset ...'

Eliza did not even focus her attention at the sound of her name – but from the way Mr Balfour had leant back in his seat, whiskers relaxing, it was clear that everything Mr Walcot had reported was in line with the marriage settlement. Her future – such as it was – was secured. In her mind's eye, the years stretched out ahead of her, grey and uninteresting.

'In addition, and in respect to her duty and obedience – '

How depressing, to be described in such terms, as one might a faithful hound. Mrs Balfour perked up, eyes brightening with greed, clearly hopeful that the old lord had bequeathed Eliza something additional – an expensive jewel from his collection, perhaps.

'– and conditional upon her bringing no dishonour to the Somerset name –

How like him to attach a morality clause to whatever small bequeathment he had thought appropriate – ungenerous to the very last.

'All my estates at Chepstow, Chawley and Highbridge, for her use absolutely.'

Eliza's mind came to sudden attention. What had Mr Walcot just said?

All at once, a room that had been quiet and still became very loud.

'Repeat that last, would you, Walcot? Must have misheard!' Selwyn boomed, taking a step forward.

'Yes, Mr Walcot, I'm not sure that can have been right –' Mrs Courtenay's voice was high and piercing as she raised herself from her chair. Mr Balfour stood, too, hand reaching out as if about to demand to read the document himself.

'To Eliza Eunice Courtenay,' Mr Walcot repeated obediently, 'in respect to her loyalty and obedience – and conditional upon her bringing no dishonour to the Somerset name – I bequeath all my estates at Chepstow, Chawley and Highbridge for her total use.'

'Preposterous!' Selwyn was having none of it. 'Julius was to bequeath those lands to our son.'

'He told me so, too!' Lady Selwyn insisted. 'He *promised* me.'

'Lady Somerset's jointure was agreed at the marriage

settlement, was it not?' Mrs Courtenay added. 'There was no mention of this, then!'

'Are the Somerset lands not all entailed to the title?' Margaret said, puzzled, only to be loudly shushed by Mrs Balfour.

'If that is the late Earl's bequest, if it is in the will, then you can have no issue with it!' Mr Balfour insisted.

They seemed to have entirely forgotten Eliza was there.

'The estates at Chepstow, Chawley and Highbidge were inherited by the Earl through his mother's line, and therefore were his to do with as he wished,' Mr Walcot said calmly.

'Preposterous!' Selwyn said again. 'That cannot be the correct document!'

'I assure you, it is,' Mr Walcot said.

'And I'm telling you it is the wrong one, man!' Selwyn said heatedly, all pretense of joviality gone. 'I saw it before – and it named Tarquin, I saw it!'

'It used to,' Mr Walcot agreed. 'But the late Earl instructed me to amend this line only a fortnight before his death.'

Selwyn's puce face turned white.

'Your quarrel,' Lady Selwyn whispered.

'We were discussing a loan – it was just business,' Selwyn breathed. 'He cannot have, he would not have –'

Ah, so that was why they had argued: Selwyn had requested a loan. Eliza could have warned him against such foolishness. Incurably frugal and exceedingly proud, the late Earl considered appeals to his purse the very height of impertinence.

'I assure you that on this – and every other matter – the late Earl was quite clear,' Mr Walcot said calmly. 'The lands are to go to Lady Somerset.'

Selwyn rounded upon Eliza.

'What poison did you whisper in his ear?' he snapped.

'How *dare* – ' Mrs Balfour was swelling with indignation.

'Selwyn!' Somerset's voice rang out – cold and remonstrative – and Selwyn took a step back from Eliza.

'My apologies – I did not mean . . . A regrettable lapse in manners . . .'

'What of the morality clause?' Lady Selwyn was not cowed. 'Did my uncle give any other elaboration – any indication of what kind of behavior was meant?'

'I do not see how that is relevant,' Mrs Balfour said. 'Given my daughter's reputation is unimpeachable.'

'Given that my uncle felt it appropriate to include in his will, it feels *very* relevant, Mrs Balfour.'

'We intend no disrespect,' Mrs Courtenay interjected. 'Lady Somerset knows we are very fond of her.'

Eliza very much did *not* know this.

'All the late Earl specified is that the interpretation of the clause is at the discretion of the eleventh Earl of Somerset – and no one else,' Mr Walcot said.

Selwyn, Lady Selwyn and Mrs Courtenay all opened their mouths to argue, but Somerset interrupted.

'If the bequeathment was my uncle's wish, I certainly do not have an issue with it,' Somerset said, voice firm.

'Of course, of course,' Selwyn had clawed back some geniality. 'But, my dear boy, I think it would behoove us to discuss what sort of behaviour would constitute – '

'I disagree,' Somerset said, and speaking in a quietly confident manner and seeming not at all bothered by the glares of his family. 'And unless Lady Somerset has changed a great deal since I was last upon British soil, she is incapable of causing even a raised eyebrow.'

Eliza looked down, her cheeks reddening. In times past,

while she had admired Somerset's conviction, in her he had bemoaned the opposite.

'Exactly,' Mrs Balfour agreed, her voice satisfied.

'But given the . . . unusual nature of such a clause,' Somerset went on. 'I think it ought to remain amongst us, only. None of us would want to cause any gossip, after all.'

There were nods of agreement from around the room – the Balfours enthusiastic, the Selwyns reluctant, while Mrs Courtenay looked about to cry again.

There was a long, long pause.

'How much income do the estates yield yearly?' Selwyn asked.

Mr Walcot made a brief reference to his notes.

'On average,' he said. 'They yield an income of just above nine thousand pounds a year. With her jointure, altogether it is an income of ten thousand annually.'

Ten thousand pounds a year.

Ten *thousand* pounds. Every year.

She was rich.

She was very rich.

A Q&A WITH
SOPHIE IRWIN

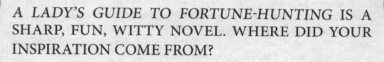

A LADY'S GUIDE TO FORTUNE-HUNTING IS A SHARP, FUN, WITTY NOVEL. WHERE DID YOUR INSPIRATION COME FROM?

It's always been a dream of mine to write historical fiction – it's my very favourite genre to read – but it was a dream that had fallen by the wayside until I was walking to work one morning in 2019, thinking about how in my favourite historical romcoms, the heroines are such beacons of moral superiority. They are heroines because they are kind, thoughtful and above all else unmercenary, while the villains are demarcated as evil for their mercenary natures. Could there ever be a historical romance, I wondered, where it was the heroine and not the villain who was the fortune-hunter – a heroine, in fact, who was resistant to romance, though still utterly capable of falling in love? After that, the character of Kitty strode into my head and demanded (with a certain forcefulness that would become so central to her character) to be written.

ARE THERE ANY REGENCY WRITERS WHO INSPIRED YOUR WRITING? AND DO YOU HAVE ANY PARTICULAR FAVOURITE REGENCY NOVELS YOU THINK READERS MIGHT ENJOY IF THEY LOVED KITTY'S STORY?

Absolutely! My favourite author is Georgette Heyer, who I think of as Austen's daughter in spirit – she's the tragically overlooked mother of the whole Regency genre, and so if you haven't read any of her books, you need to get cracking! The first Heyer novel I read was *Arabella*, which I still have a huge soft spot for – though my favourite is *Frederica*, which features a managing heroine determined to find a rich husband for her sister... Whichever you choose, they are all witty and elegant and deliciously romantic, so you are certainly in for a treat.

KITTY IS WHIP-SMART AND FEARLESS. WAS IT IMPORTANT TO YOU TO WRITE A SUBVERSIVE, OUTSPOKEN HEROINE? AND IF SO, WHY?

Yes absolutely! In fact, the very first scene I wrote was an argument between Radcliffe and Kitty: Kitty calling Radcliffe out for his hypocrisy, outlining all the ways in which Regency society worked against women, and refusing to be shamed for her motivations. Right from the beginning, her outspokenness was a very central part of her character, because without being anachronistic, I did want to bring into the novel some of our modern understandings of feminism and the economics of marriage at this time.

Her fearlessness, too, was there right from the beginning – simply because it was so much fun to write. All my favourite main characters share that particular brand of tenacity and determination, because knowing they are capable of breaking any rule makes them so exciting to read.

THE ROMANCE BETWEEN KITTY AND LORD RADCLIFFE IS THE QUINTESSENTIAL ENEMIES-TO-LOVERS STORY. WHAT ARE YOUR FAVOURITE ROMANCE TROPES, BOTH TO READ AND WRITE, AND DID YOU SET OUT WRITING *A LADY'S GUIDE TO FORTUNE-HUNTING* WITH THIS TROPE IN MIND?

As you can probably tell, enemies-to-lovers is absolutely my favourite trope. I just love the slow transition from insults and arguments to chemistry-filled banter, to understanding, to love… Having said that, I can't remember deciding to make *A Lady's Guide to Fortune-Hunting* an enemies-to-lovers story – it was just so natural, because of who Kitty and Radcliffe both were, that they were going to argue at first!

My other favourite trope is definitely fake relationship – any trope, essentially, where the characters can't admit their feelings for one another until right at the end. All that delicious build up…

WHAT WAS YOUR BIGGEST CHALLENGE IN WRITING THIS BOOK?

Getting through the first draft! As far as I can tell, all first drafts are universally terrible, but that doesn't make it feel any better when it's yours – the biggest challenge for me as a writer, not just for this book, has been powering through to the end of a first draft, even when I think it's the most terrible book anyone has ever written.

MANY REVIEWS COMPARE *A LADY'S GUIDE TO FORTUNE-HUNTING* TO *BRIDGERTON*. DID YOU FEEL ANY PRESSURE WRITING A COMEDIC ROMANTIC REGENCY WHILE *BRIDGERTON* WAS AT ITS PEAK OF POPULARITY?

Luckily for me, I'd already finished my first draft by the time *Bridgerton* exploded onto screens, and so I was insulated a little from the pressure – if anything, I think it gave me confidence, seeing so many new readers flock to the genre, as it proved there was appetite for books like mine.

HOW DO YOU FEEL NOW THAT REGENCY IS HAVING A RESURGENCE IN POPULAR FICTION?

It's so brilliant! *Bridgerton* has done so much to bring attention and praise to a genre that has often been looked down on by literary intellectuals – taking the shame out of escapism and showing many new readers to Regency's doors. My absolute favourite reviews are the ones from readers who hadn't read much Regency romance before – it's such a fantastic genre, so I'm always delighted when my book is the gateway for new readers.

CAN YOU TELL US ANYTHING ABOUT YOUR NEXT BOOK?

My next book, *A Lady's Guide to Scandal*, tells the story of Eliza, the Countess of Somerset. Recently widowed from her marriage of convenience, Eliza is bequeathed a fortune, hers to keep as long as she can stay out of scandal. It should be simple – Eliza has spent a lifetime following the rules – but now that she is rich, titled and independent, misbehaviour is more tempting...

Featuring beautiful Bath as its setting, a wise-cracking best friend, and the most scandalous shape of them all, the love triangle, it has been so much fun to write, and I can't wait to share it with you all.

READING GROUP QUESTIONS

1. Kitty was responsible for her sisters' welfare in an era where women rarely had the opportunity to earn money. What do you think you'd have done in her position?

2. Though Kitty needs to marry for money, she still takes control of her own destiny. What do you think of the themes of feminism in this novel?

3. Aunt Dorothy is a guiding hand and a route into society for Kitty, but she had to hide her past to be welcomed into the ton. What do you think would be the most challenging of societal expectations in that period?

4. Do you think Kitty could have been happy if she'd settled for either Archie or Pemberton?

5. Kitty pulled out all the stops in her schemes to marry Archie. Which stood out most to you?

6. What do you think would have happened to Cecily and Lord Montagu had they managed to elope?

7. What do you think the future holds for Kitty and Lord Radcliffe?

8. There is a distinct cast of characters in this book. Who was your favourite?

9. How do you think *A Lady's Guide to Fortune-Hunting* compares to other Regency novels? Or if you haven't read any, are you inspired to read more?

10. Would you recommend this book to a friend?